Catching Liberty

The present is the past reborn in disguise

Alexa can only hope those words are just a frightening falsehood. She refuses to be a prisoner of her past. There is too much she wants for her future. Bethany's incarceration will soon end and they will finally be together. The demons of their past will continue to pursue them into their would-be hopeful future, but with Bethany by her side, Alexa is confident she can keep them at bay.

But for all that Alexa is trying to outrun, there is one part of her past — one person — whose return she would not fight. The one person those closest to her want to relegate to the depths of her history. Marcus Knight. As she strives to build worthwhile lives for herself and Bethany, Alexa will have to decide if it is wise to let back into her life the one person she loves more than any other, but swore she could never share a future with.

Also available in this series

Marble Road
Waiting for the Silver Lining

Catching Liberty

Naomi Metzl

Published by Midnight Sunrise Publishing

Printed by CreateSpace

ISBN 978 0 9924 3035 1

Midnight Sunrise Publishing

To Ellie, Grace, Mirella, Tom, Santhi and Larissa
For being the first people to give me the courage to slash
and burn, rip and shred.

And to Magdalena
For forcing me to take the next step and make the virtual a
reality.

Without you all, this would have remained a dream.

We've got to hold on to what we've got
It doesn't make a difference if we make it or not
We've got each other and that's a lot for love
We'll give it a shot

Woah, we're half way there
Woah, livin' on a prayer
Take my hand, we'll make it I swear
Woah, livin' on a prayer

Living on a Prayer
Bon Jovi

Chapter One

SUNLIGHT CRACKLED OVER the horizon, setting the fluffy white clouds alight with rays of yellow and orange. Looking out the small plane window through breaks in the clouds, Alexa peered down to the slowly waking land below. Ready or not, she was coming home.

Now just an hour from landing, Alexa felt her stomach churn at the prospect of her return. It was as if the air of her past was leaking into the plane, taking her back to a place she hoped had disappeared with her departure from the country. Perhaps that was naïve. Perhaps that former life had just been lying dormant, waiting for her return. Or maybe it was something she had packed – something she would never be able to leave behind. It made Alexa wonder which would be better – a past she could only escape by running from, knowing running was not an option, or one she could never escape, but could ignore in the hope others would likewise overlook its perpetual presence.

Despite her best efforts to turn her mind in another direction, memories of her past flickered through her brain. They swirled faster, making her recently eaten breakfast twirl sickeningly in her stomach. Rustling through the seat pocket, Alexa found it devoid of a sick bag. The thought of her neighbour's disgust as she vomited all over the floor made her chuckle internally and calmed her enough to glance interestedly at the safety leaflet. Right then the thought of her fiery demise on landing was more enticing than reliving her past, so Alexa concentrated on learning the correct brace position and counted the number of rows between her and every single exit.

The thud of the aeroplane on to the tarmac coincided with the thump of Alexa's heart. She found herself strangely disappointed at not being able to use any of her newly found emergency survival knowledge and was glad she had the monotony of immigration and customs to settle her nerves. The process was always the same, and not just the regulatory ones. At every destination, Alexa had gone through the same pattern of emotions; the near-paralysing fear on disembarking the plane, which softened to anxiety as she made her way through the airport. Excitement then pushed itself into the mix as she told herself everything that was happening was a product of her own decisions. This was not being forced on her. She had a choice. Finally, anxiety transformed into resolve. She had the courage to walk out those doors and see if she liked what she saw. She could run again if she didn't.

The only problem was that this time Alexa knew she could not run. After six months in Europe, constantly moving, she had decided to come home and start living her life. She was not sure she had achieved her initial aim of transforming herself from a child into a woman, but it had been an amazing experience.

On her own, Alexa had felt completely unattached to anything and it had been more liberating than she could have imagined. Staying in hostels, she had been shocked by the sheer number of people travelling the world. She had never met so many people in her life. Their stories and the places they had been made Alexa promise herself this would not be the last time she trekked to foreign lands.

The freedom of being able to leave a place on a whim had been exhilarating. It allowed Alexa to be more adventurous than she thought herself capable. Every day she met someone new, explored with them and discovered things she had never heard of, let alone dreamed of. If she ever became uncomfortable with a person or a place, she simply left. Thankfully, Alexa had rarely fled in fear. The desire to see everything the world had to offer was enough to keep her moving. When she had needed to stop for a while and be truly alone, she had paid for a hotel room, revelling in the seclusion. However, the anxiety of spending too much money had ensured that was a rare luxury.

The only large expense Alexa allowed herself during her trip was a month at a language school in Germany. She had researched it before she left, drawn to the concept by her study of the language throughout high school and the strange enjoyment she found in that class despite doing so poorly in it. It had been tempting to book the course before she left, but she had been unsure if she wanted to spend so much money or if she was ready to go back into a classroom. The decision ended up being made almost without her realising it. The continuous movement of the first couple of months had left Alexa's head spinning. When cheap flights into Germany coincided with the start of a course, Alexa booked everything with barely a moment of hesitation. The female teacher and single accommodation made the experience that much easier. Although Alexa did not leave the course feeling anywhere close to fluent, she found herself spending most of the last months exploring Germanic-speaking countries and delighted in being able to communicate tentatively in the local language.

Those good memories helped to keep at bay Alexa's concerns about the amount of money she had spent. She reminded herself that, in relation to her newfound wealth, it was not much, but she could never be completely at ease with such reasoning. This holiday alone had seen her spend more money than she had in entire her lifetime. That she still had access to amounts many magnitudes more continued to blow her mind.

Eight million dollars. Eight million, two hundred and twenty-four thousand, six hundred and forty-seven dollars to be precise; something Alexa always was.

It was so much money, it was obscene. Occasionally, Alexa found herself just staring at her bank balance, trying to find the glitch – the reality switch – that would take it all away. Then she would remember all the events that surrounded her miraculous windfall and realised reality had already taken its swipe at her. She just struggled to believe it had taken its last swipe. In spite of that, Alexa was thankful for her fortune. Her future was still so uncertain, with the exception of one immovable element.

Bethany.

In many ways, Bethany was Alexa's future, and Alexa knew every single cent of her fortune would be dedicated to Bethany if need be, setting up her life on the outside and keeping her away from heroin. Alexa only feared eight million dollars would not be enough to achieve all that. That fear crept unsolicited into Alexa's mind as she was welcomed home by the friendly immigration official. Waiting for her backpack to appear on the carousel, she tried to recapture some of the enthusiasm and optimism she had felt on boarding the plane home. She would soon see Bethany, and had already enrolled to begin university in a few weeks – just a semester after everyone else.

That she had even been accepted into university continued to surprise Alexa. She could vaguely recall filling in application forms, but when she had received her results she had been sure her plans were all but useless. It was not until she received an offer that she realised just how much Mr Knight had done for her, applying for all manner of special considerations. Part of her wished she had realised at the time so she could have appreciated him when she had the chance. However, appreciating Mr Knight was not something Alexa had struggled with back then.

Perhaps it was better this way. Alexa knew that she and Marcus together was not a good idea. She still loved him, but just eight months ago he had been her teacher. He had been Mr Knight. He would always be ten years older than her, but more than that, he was probably very much over her by now. She was a child, a troubled student, and outside the confines of those two horrific years at Redgrove College he was free to realise how foolish he had been to become so infatuated with her.

There was nothing Alexa could offer Marcus. She possessed no enticements for a man of his calibre. Not even money. That was all for Bethany. Alexa would have even bet her apartment he was back with his ex-fiancée and married by now. Despite all that, Alexa still wanted one chance to see Marcus again. There was so much she needed to thank him for – and forgive. It was not fair to blame him for what happened to her at Redgrove, not when he was probably the only reason she survived it. That one meeting would allow her to finally put that part of her past behind her.

Making it through customs, Alexa's heart began to stammer. She could not help but doubt that Sam and Ben would be there to meet her like they promised. After the events of the last year, Alexa was surprised Sam ever spoke to her again. She had been so terrified of his wrath that she never tried to contact him after leaving school. It was not until he emailed her in late January that they got back in contact. They had kept in touch ever since, but it had been sporadic and somewhat stunted communications. It made it very difficult for Alexa to gauge where their friendship was at, and she worried Sam had arranged this meeting simply to tear her down in public. The only reason she agreed to meet him was because she deserved such censure.

Ben was a different matter. Alexa had no concerns he would yell at her. Yet she was still so unsure about him. He had been nothing but brilliant since she finished school; giving her a place to stay, helping her buy her apartment and taking care of Bethany. It all seemed too much from a man who was somehow connected to her and Bethany's childhood, yet before last year they had not seen for who knew how many years.

Alexa knew all she had to do was ask and Ben would explain their early interactions, but she had never been game enough. Ben had only ever spoken about how guilty he felt over what happened back then. It made Alexa fear she had reasons to distrust Ben, and right now she did not want any. He was too important. He was the only one who had ever wanted them.

"Alexa!"

Alexa's heart leapt at the sound of his voice. He had come and he was not angry. Seconds later Alexa was being lifted off the ground and twirled in a frantic circle, almost beheading a small boy who had walked unwittingly into her path.

"Sam, put me down. Please, you're going to kill someone."

A sheepish smile greeted Alexa. The fear and anxiety that had plagued her trip home vanished. She had forgotten how warm Sam's embrace was, how much she loved his smile and how much he felt like home.

"I've missed you so much," said Sam sincerely, wrapping her in a tender embrace. "Where're the rest of your bags?"

Alexa looked down then back up to her shoulder where a solitary backpack sat. She had shoved her small backpack into it as she went through customs.

"Oh, this is all I have. I didn't take much. And didn't buy much. Anything I really wanted I sent to Ben's while I was away."

"Ha, well Ben's waiting outside with the car. I think he expected you to have a lot more luggage than one backpack."

"Is that the only reason he came?" asked Alexa.

"No," laughed Sam, nudging her with his shoulder to get her moving. "That's just the excuse he gave so he could come. C'mon, let's go. You'll be fine. Everyone's really excited your home."

Taking her hand, Sam led Alexa out into the world. The sky was now steely grey, the colours of the dawn long gone, and Alexa was swamped by its sadness. Her nerves began to twitch in anticipation of seeing Ben. Maybe things had changed. She looked around for his car among the sea of steel. His familiar frame suddenly came into focus. A broad smile broke across Ben's face when they walked into the section he was parked in and Alexa found her legs striding forward, her hand slipping out of Sam's as she stepped into Ben's embrace.

"Long time no see," said Ben in a thick voice as he held her tight.

Alexa pushed in against him, her arms curled up between her chest and his. She wished she could have thrown her arms around his neck and shown him just how much it meant that he was here, but her nerves got the better of her. It was strange, because there was almost no one else in the world she instinctively trusted the way she did Ben.

"Come on, let's get you home," Ben smiled, taking her bag from her shoulder and opening the car door for her.

"How's Bethy doing?" Alexa asked as soon as they pulled onto the road. It was the one question she was scared of being answered honestly.

"She's okay," said Ben softly. "Looking forward to your return."

"But how's she been?" asked Alexa more pointedly, disappointed Ben had not understood the real meaning of her question. "While I was away? I shouldn't have left her alone."

"She hasn't been alone. What am I?" asked Ben melodramatically. Alexa struggled not to roll her eyes, making Ben smirk as he watched her in the rear-view mirror. "Besides, she's had other visitors."

"Really? Who? The Christies?" Alexa queried, wondering if they had loved Bethany the way the Whites had loved her.

"No, there's been no contact from Beth's foster parents," replied Ben with forced calmness.

Alexa tried to swallow her sob. It was not an unexpected answer, but it only reinforced how special the Whites were, and how horrible it was they had the misfortune to have their lives wrapped up in hers.

"I visit her," said Sam softly.

Alexa turned, not quite understanding. Sam kept staring at her, waiting for a response. He appeared fearful of her reaction.

"Really?" replied Alexa, still not entirely convinced until Sam nodded. "Sam, you're so sweet." She moved to hug him, but he pushed her away.

"Actually, Beth asked to see me," said Sam cautiously.

"Bethy asked to see you? Why?" asked Alexa sceptically, pushing away from Sam.

"To talk about you," Sam answered. It was what she feared. "She wanted to know what Ben didn't and what you'd never tell her."

"What did you tell her?" asked Alexa through gritted teeth.

"Anything she wanted to know."

Alexa closed her eyes and turned away. She did not want to be angry, but she was worried about how Bethany would have coped with such revelations. The last thing she wanted was Bethany feeling guilty for her failures.

"You can't protect her from everything," said Ben.

"Knowing everything doesn't always help either," retorted Alexa, and she knew Ben understood the double meaning.

"Beth's different to you," said Sam. "She needs to know. It wasn't easy for her hearing all you went through, but it wasn't exactly fun telling her either."

"See, that's why you shouldn't have —"

"I said it was hard, not that it wasn't right," Sam interrupted. "Watching you almost die. Standing back, never sure if or when I was going to see you again. You think that was easy for me? I'm glad Beth asked me to come. I needed to talk about that stuff."

"Yeah but for six months? How much more is there to tell?" asked Alexa, forcing her voice to remain calm.

"Who said that's all we spoke about?" laughed Sam. "Geez, conceited much."

"But why else would you go see her?" Alexa queried, fearing something else was wrong.

"Because Beth's awesome. And it's not like she's a complete stranger. She ran away to my place almost as much as you. We have more in common than I imagined – more than you, I mean," added Sam. Alexa smiled, thankful for the clarification. "She's a lot like you and I didn't miss you as much when I was with her. She can make you forget you're in a prison when you're just hanging with her."

"Yeah, she can," grinned Alexa.

It was true. Bethany had an amazing gift that way, but Alexa had thought she was the only person to realise it. Most outsiders just saw a heroin addict when they looked at Bethany. That Sam could see the person Alexa saw endeared him to her heart so solidly she wished she could love him as she once had. He deserved so much more than her, but somehow she had been the one he always wanted and she was not even able to give him that.

"So tell me more about how Bethy's doing?" asked Alexa lightly, hoping the less serious tone would be more conducive to answers. "I don't think she tells me everything."

"She's okay. Really," replied Ben, nodding as he glanced back at her. "She's finished her studies up to year ten and they've started her on her carpentry apprenticeship."

"But how about day-to-day?" Alexa asked, trying desperately to get Ben to the point. "How's that going?"

"She's going fine," repeated Ben, as though he believed he already got the point. "It's coming up to a year, so she's over halfway through her non-parole period. I know that's really helped."

"What do you mean helped? What happened?" asked Alexa anxiously. "Why didn't you tell me she was struggling? I would've come back if I knew something was wrong. I shouldn't have gone."

"Yes, you should and you know it. So's Beth. Nothing's wrong," said Ben quickly. "She's in a juvenile detention facility and has over six months before she has any prospect of being allowed out. It's not great, but she's coping as well as can be expected. She hasn't touched heroin in almost a year and is desperate to get out and prove she's changed. She wants to make you proud. That's all."

Tears dripped silently down Alexa's face. It was one thing for Ben to tell her that. It was another to believe it. Sam shuffled closer, pulling her into his body. She was glad he knew not to talk right then.

"You don't think she'll be mad at me for waiting until tomorrow to see her, do you?" asked Alexa. If her body had not been aching from the sleep deprivation of the twenty-four hours of travel she would have demanded they go straight there from the airport.

"No, I don't," replied Ben sincerely. "Beth's working hard. It's a struggle – just like it is for you – but she's okay. Just like you are."

Once more, Ben stared back at Alexa in the rear-view mirror. The part of her that was doing okay agreed with what he said. But the part – the very large part at times – that was still quite happy to close her eyes and never open them again was screaming out for Bethany so they could sleep together forever.

"I'm going to take you home and you're going to rest," continued Ben in a commanding voice. "You'll see Beth tomorrow and she'll be so happy to see you awake and energetic enough to spend your whole day with her."

Alexa nodded. She was too tired to argue anyway.

They drove in silence. Alexa rested her head against Sam's shoulder, her heavy eyelids sliding shut despite her best efforts, but it only took a touch to awaken her. Alexa jerked out of Sam's arms. He apologised softly, pulling his arm into his lap, but it was really not his fault she could not stand being touched in her sleep.

"Where are we?" Alexa asked, stretching off her tiredness as she looked out the window completely disorientated.

"About a block from your apartment. You don't recognise it?" asked Ben with a slight smile.

Looking around to get her bearings, Alexa realised she had no idea where she was. She had never come from this direction. She had only ever seen the apartment twice, and had never stepped foot in it since becoming its official owner. It was not until they pulled into the street that she knew where she was.

The taste of salt was thick in the air when Alexa stepped out of the car and she was sure there was nothing more soothing than a sea breeze. They could not see the ocean from the street, but in the quiet of the day they could hear the soft whisper of the pounding waves. It made Alexa think of Maria and the gratitude she would always hold towards her for making all this possible.

Maria was one of the other miracles of Alexa's life. In the short

time they had known each other, Maria had done so much for her –
befriending her, teaching her to cook, and letting her know about the
beachside apartment her son was selling. The apartment that was
now hers.

Stepping out of the elevator, Alexa's heart began to stammer,
wondering if she would love the apartment the way she had the first
time she had seen it. It was still so surreal that she was opening the
door to a place of her very own – a home no one could ever force her
from, take her away from and make her live somewhere else with
strange people who did not care for her.

Sam gasped softly as Alexa opened the front door. They stepped
into a short corridor. Sam and Ben poked their heads into the small
laundry on the left and again into the bathroom at the next door. The
apartment then opened up into a large kitchen on the right, separated
from the huge living-dining space on the left by a long bench. On the
left side of the lounge room was a large sliding door that led out to
the balcony, which ran along the whole left side of the apartment.
From their position up on the hill, it gave a great view out to the
ocean and was big enough for a table and chairs. Alexa intended to
spend many sunny days out there, basking in the salty warmth.

The corridor started up again on the other side of the lounge,
separating the two bedrooms on either side. The large one on the left
was the one Alexa planned to sleep in. It had taken her a long time to
come to that decision. She had initially intended to take the smaller
room and save the bigger one for Bethany, but had eventually found
the courage to take something she wanted and be okay with it.

"Wow, this place is amazing," said Sam as he wandered from
room to room.

"Thanks," replied Alexa, feeling unsure. She loved the apartment
and was looking forward to living here. It was just that settling down
in one place was the final confirmation she would have to face her life
again, knowing there was no such thing as a truly clean break.

"It's completely empty," said Ben, as though he had actually
expected something else. "Alexa, you can't – I mean, you should –
you're more than welcome to come back to my place – just for a few
days – until you have furniture or something – clothes."

"No, I'm okay. I want to stay here," Alexa replied. "I need to start
facing things and at your place I'll just be hiding away. Besides, I
don't think Penny would be too happy about me turning up on your
doorstep again."

Ben's seemed to have forgotten how uncomfortable things were between her and Penny before she left. It was near confrontational, particularly when Ben had not been home. It was so strained that within weeks of living there Alexa made sure she was rarely home alone with Penny, leaving the house soon after Ben and trying not to return until he had. But then Penny started getting paranoid that they were hanging out behind her back, and that was why they were never home. Though Ben never admitted it, he and Penny fought a lot while Alexa lived with them. Ben had done more for her and Bethany than any past connection could possibly justify, and Alexa was determined she would not be responsible for ruining his marriage.

"Let me worry about Penny," Ben replied, his voice almost a growl, before it softened. "You can't stay here. Where will you sleep? How will you eat?"

"It'll just be for a couple of days until I get to the shops."

"Then why not stay in comfort until then? If it's just a couple of days."

"Because, if I stay with you, I'm scared I'll never leave. You'll be too good to me," Alexa answered truthfully. As bad as Penny had been, that home with Ben had still been one of the best ever. "I need to face up to all this. What's the point of believing in something better?" Alexa saw Ben's mouth open angrily. "I don't mean it like that. Just, what's the point of being taken care of when I'm at the age when I have to grow up and take care of myself?"

"I think you deserve a bit of time where you're taken care of after everything you've been through," replied Ben, his voice returning to its angry growl. "You may think you're all grown up, but you don't realise how young eighteen is. You're practically a child."

"I'm not a child – I never was," replied Alexa, forcing Ben to concede. "Please, just let me do it my way. You'll be the first person I call if I need help. I promise."

"Don't worry, Ben. I'll stay with her," smiled Sam, throwing his arm around Alexa's shoulders.

Ben finally nodded in defeat and made his way to the front door. Alexa followed, wishing she knew how to give Ben what he wanted. The idea of having a father was appealing, but the reality was she knew nothing about being a daughter and could not stand the idea of disappointing him.

"I'll be at work tonight," said Ben, his hand gently upon Alexa's cheek. "Call me on my mobile if you need anything."

"Thank you, but I'll be fine. You don't have to worry about me," replied Alexa, hoping he would anyway – just a little.

"I'm not so sure about that, but for tonight I'll do it from a distance," said Ben gruffly. Alexa smiled awkwardly, knowing she had upset him. "It's okay," he added, before kissing the top of her head and walking to the lifts.

"So it's just you and me then," said Sam with a wry smile when Alexa made her way back into the empty lounge room.

"You really don't have to stay. I'll be fine. I think I'm just going to get some take-out and sleep. I'm fine."

"I know, you keep saying so. The problem is, I know you better," replied Sam with slightly raised eyebrows. "You don't have to tell me how hard this is for you. After all you've been through —"

"Can we not talk about what I've been through?" sighed Alexa. "I'd rather forget."

"I know you would, but you're going to have to face up to it eventually."

"Not if I have my way, I won't." Alexa stomped out to the balcony before Sam could respond. She was out of practice dealing people who knew her past and realised she would have to reacquire that skill quickly.

The drizzle misted the air as she looked out towards the steely grey ocean. Breathing deeply, Alexa reminded herself that it was not Sam she was angry at. When she heard his soft footsteps move towards her, guilt started to overwhelm her anger, especially when Sam just stood silently next to her, his arm gently pressing against hers.

"I'm not sure, Sam," Alexa whispered, turning to him after many silent minutes. "I'm not sure about anything."

"No one can blame you for that," he replied gently. "I feel lost and I haven't been through half of what you have." Alexa glared at him. "I know you don't want to hear it, Lex, but in the last couple of years you've been assaulted, raped, left for dead and had your heart broken by a man who should've never been near it. It's not nothing."

"Sam, it's —"

"Lex, please just listen to me."

"No. Why are you calling me Lex?"

"You're changing the subject," Sam replied, ignoring her question. "You have to start realising you're not superhuman and allowed to feel overwhelmed by everything that's happened."

"Fine," Alexa snapped. "I'm confused and so scared. I feel alone, even though I know I shouldn't."

"Scared of what?"

"That I've been blaming all my problems on a lack of control over my life, but that it's really all my fault," she replied agitatedly. "I don't want to find out that things aren't going to get any better even now I get to make all the decisions."

"That won't happen," smiled Sam, almost dismissively.

"How would you know?" Alexa retorted.

"Because I know you and how amazing you are, and I know what happened to you wasn't your fault," Sam replied seriously. Alexa wanted to believe him, but she could not block out the bad memories. "It's okay, you know. You're allowed to be upset," said Sam softly, as tears flowed down Alexa's cheeks and her body trembled.

Alexa could only shake her head, waiting for the words to form. "I don't want to be sad, Sam," she sobbed, grabbing his top and pulling herself against him. "I want to be happy. I want to be able to move on. Why can't I? Why can't I just forget all about it? Forget all of it ever happened."

"You will move on, but I don't think you'll ever forget everything. How could you? But you'll be okay. I'll make sure of it," he said, wrapping her tightly in his arms.

Sam's embrace was so warm that it took Alexa a while to realise why she was still shaking. "Oh, shit, Sam, you must be freezing," she said. "Why are you only wearing a t-shirt?"

"It's only cold when you're standing in the wind and rain," he chuckled, walking them back inside. "See, all better in here."

It was only just true. Alexa was still chilled and realised she had not thought this plan through. Perhaps she was tired enough to sleep on the hard, carpeted floor with no blankets, pillows or heating. She did not even have a clean towel.

"Any chance you want a housemate for the week?" asked Sam, just as Alexa was about to ask him to help her buy a few essentials.

"Um, what? Why?" Alexa asked.

"Well, you know how Gran and Pop sold the farm so they could move to the city with me? Decided it would be a good chance to keep an eye on me after they won all that money on the pokies," Sam said with a smile. Alexa nodded, feeling her stomach twist. "Well, we can't move into our new place until next week and in a case of very bad timing I had to leave my apartment last week. All my stuff's in storage and I've been crashing with Chad, but I think it's cramping his style a little. We're still friends, but after boarding school and six years together, it's a bit strange sharing a place again."

"But you don't mind shacking up with me?" Alexa asked seriously, but Sam only laughed. "Sam, I don't have any furniture. Or food. Or heating."

"I don't mind," he replied, still smiling. "If you can hack it, I can." Alexa poked out her tongue. "Besides, we can go to the storage place and pick up some stuff. I'll even take you shopping later."

"I don't have a car," Alexa added, hating that there was no way Sam's plan would work.

"But I do," smiled Sam. "It's even here. Downstairs. Ben picked me up on his way to the airport."

"Positive I was going to say yes, then?" smiled Alexa.

"No, scared you might say no."

Alexa laughed as she took Sam's hand and let him pull her weary body out of the apartment. He stayed quiet as they drove, allowing her eyes to slip closed before they had even left the suburb.

"Wake up, sleepyhead."

The words did not register in Alexa's brain before the fear had already coursed through it, causing her to flinch violently away from Sam's touch.

"Sorry," he said. "But we're home. And I don't carry girls across thresholds unless I've married them first," he added with a smirk.

Alexa had to really work to force her tired eyes open. She heard Sam mutter something, but did not understand him. The next time she opened her eyes the smell of food was swirling in the warm air.

"Thai," said Sam, directing Alexa's blurry eyes to the take-away containers on the floor near her.

Alexa pushed herself up into a seated position and realised she was wrapped in blankets, a heater blasting hot air around the room just metres away. "How long have I been out?" she asked, feeling slightly refreshed, but her body still ached with the effort of waking.

"Few hours," replied Sam. "It's about six-thirty."

The darkness outside confirmed Sam's story, but all she could do was nod. Sam chuckled as he walked over and helped her to her feet.

"Where we going?" Alexa asked, horrified that she would have to travel any more today.

"To the bathroom," Sam laughed. "Thought you might need to go." Alexa nodded again, her brain slowly catching up. "Who knew you were so adorable and helpless when jetlagged."

Alexa felt a little more alive after splashing her face with cold water. Eating helped revive her further and after an hour she was close to feeling semi-conscious.

"How you doing?" asked Sam, as she leaned back against the

wall, pushing the empty container away from her.

"Okay," Alexa sighed. "That was nice food. You'll have to tell me what it was."

"Chicken Pad See Eew," Sam replied. "I'll take you out for Thai one day. You'll like it."

Alexa could only nod. She thought she had already told him that she liked it. Looking up, Alexa was about to tell Sam she wanted to go back to sleep when she saw him looking at her strangely.

"Lex, I wanted to ask another favour," he said tentatively.

"Why do you keep calling me Lex?" Alexa asked, pushing herself off the wall as she bit down on less pleasant words.

"Does it matter?" asked Sam with raised eyebrows.

"Well, yeah, it does. No one calls me Lex except —"

"Beth," nodded Sam, shuffling forward and taking her hands. "I guess that's where I picked it up. You want me to stop?"

"I just – I mean … it's stupid, but it's what she named me. When we were kids she wanted to call me Lexus, you know, after the car," scoffed Alexa. "Was her favourite car. Didn't want to be named after a car so finally bargained her down to Lex. It's just special. It's her name for me. Just like how I named her."

"What do you mean you named her and she named you? Beth's two years younger than you. How could she've named you?" asked Sam, looking perplexed.

"What?" Alexa replied, not quite understanding. "No – I, um ..." Alexa's rubbed her head, trying to figure it out. She had always been sure Bethany wanted to name her Lexus, but they settled on Alexa, with Bethany allowed to call her Lex. Alexa had never considered the logistics of it. "No, I guess she just wanted to change my name. Maybe because it's so close to Lexus," she finally concluded, though not completely convinced by her own answer.

"It's okay – A-lex-a. I'll call you by your full name, but I still have something to ask."

Alexa watched Sam shift uncomfortably before he took her hands again and looked straight into her eyes. "What's going on, Sam?" she asked nervously.

"I've had so much time to think lately and no matter how I think about my future, I always come back to you." Alexa's heart started to hammer. She had never wanted to have this conversation. Sam must have sensed her discomfort, because his hands were gripping hers tighter. "We never had a proper chance to find out if we'd work out," continued Sam. "But during all that time – all through high school – I always thought we would."

"Sam, I – we were just fifteen. We've both moved on," said Alexa, trying to stop her body from shaking.

"But that's the problem. I don't think we have. I still love you, and I think you love me too. I feel like we're caught in this strange limbo, like I'm cheating on you when I'm with other people. I feel jealous when you talk about other guys."

"Yeah, I feel like that too," confessed Alexa. "But what can we do about it besides just get over it?"

"We could try getting back together."

Chapter Two

ALEXA'S BREATH STUCK in her chest. It was not like she had never considered the idea before, but she had come home to her future, not her past.

"Not permanently," said Sam, as though reading her mind. "Just for the week – while I'm here. Neither of us wants to get back together properly, but we need the chance to end our relationship on our own terms."

"But what if one of us wants more?" Alexa asked tentatively, not completely convinced it would be Sam.

"Then we'd be ending things more traditionally than I currently planned," Sam answered with a slight chuckle, but Alexa could not be so easily placated. "I just don't think that'll be our problem. I want to move on from you. I'll always love you and be there for you, but I don't want to feel tied to you forever and I know you don't either. If we do this, we get to walk away with a fresh break from our past."

A break from her past was all Alexa wanted. There were still far too many binds holding her to that terrible place. She wished she could sever them all, but knew she would have to settle for loosening a few. When she looked up, she saw the desperate hope in Sam's eyes and realised he probably needed this more than her. With everything she had put him through, he deserved to be free from her. However, like everything in her life, getting back with Sam – even for a week – was not as simple as it sounded.

"This week, if we did this, how would it work? I mean, you and me – like proper girlfriend-boyfriend?" Alexa asked nervously.

"You mean would we have sex?" asked Sam. Alexa nodded slowly, lowering her eyes. "I hadn't been planning on it. It's my heart not my – um – brain that's still tied to you," he said with a smirk, forcing her lips to curl up with his.

"You're an idiot," Alexa said, choking up a sound somewhere between a sob and a laugh.

"Have you been with anyone since …"

Sam's reluctance to say the word raped intrigued Alexa. Perhaps to say raped was to make it sound like it was just once, one guy. But over those five days in captivity Alexa had been raped too many times to count, by so many men, who had beaten her so badly she would never recognise them. Yet the last time she had sex before that was when she had been raped by her teacher, Clinton Marsh. But Alexa was not sure that was why Sam hesitated. The two weeks she worked as a prostitute in a vain attempt to drag Bethany away from heroin defined her in many people's eyes, convincing them she had seduced Clinton Marsh into a relationship rather than believing he had groomed her into it.

That was the view from afar. Alexa never thought of it that way. When she thought about her love life, she thought about Sam and Marcus; her first love and her forbidden love. It was why she found it hard to believe there were no pleasurable sexual encounters after Sam. Marcus had never touched her, yet their bond had been so tender that in her mind it was almost able to cancel out all those other horrible experiences.

Alexa still hoped she would one day find someone who was able to view her past the way she did. She did not want those experiences to define her in other people's eyes, but it was hard to frame anyone else's view that way when her own body was so uncooperative. "I did meet this one guy overseas," she confessed. "Met in Prague. Spent about a week travelling together."

"You like him? What happened? Where's he from? You still in touch?" asked Sam at a slightly slower rate than machine gun fire.

All Alexa could do was shake her head. "It wasn't like that," she sighed when Sam kept staring expectantly. "He was nice. We kissed a couple of times, but as soon as it went any further I freaked out."

"So what happened?"

"Nothing. We went our separate ways."

"You never tried to get back in contact?"

"Sam, it wasn't like that! He was nice, but it was never going anywhere. But when someone else comes along, I want to be able to find out if there could be more without freaking out because he puts his hand on my leg or touches me when I fall asleep."

Tears slowly trickled down Alexa's cheeks. Shuffling closer to her, Sam nudged her forward, away from the wall, and sat behind her, his arms wrapping around her. "We don't have to do this," he said sincerely.

Resting her head against Sam's chest, Alexa thought about what this week would be like if they stayed just friends. She imagined it would be a lot like this – curling up in each other's arms, being close, maybe kissing if the moment felt right, but never confronting their past. Then, at the end of it, they would walk away, assuming they were still just friends, but Alexa imagined seeing Sam with another girl and her heart stabbed with jealousy.

"No, you're right. We need to do it, but I need all of it. I don't want Leo to be the last man I've been with. I don't want to think every guy I meet's going to rape me or hit me and hurt me. You're the only one who can change that for me. You're the only guy I've ever made love to. I need you to teach me how to love again."

Sam rested his chin on Alexa's head, but said nothing. Perhaps he did not want to have sex with her again. The idea of Sam rejecting her had Alexa on the verge of running off when his finger moved under chin, turning her to face him. There was desire in his eyes and it made her stomach twist in a way it hadn't for a very long time. His lips moved towards hers. Alexa's body quaked fearfully. "You're going to have to trust me," he whispered softly.

"Just not tonight, I —"

"Alexa, you know I'd never hurt you. You have to trust me," Sam said again, gently lying them down on the blankets.

Alexa did not want to agree. She would trust him if he just promised, but maybe he thought she needed to trust him first. Countering the urge to be sick, she nodded slowly, hating having to give that away and give Sam control. Sam smiled softly and pulled her hand up to his face. She had forgotten how soft his skin was. He leaned down and kissed her. Tingles rushed through her body. It really was hard to believe he would ever hurt her.

Cupping Sam's face with one hand, Alexa held his shoulder with the other as they kissed tenderly. When Sam pulled her close, Alexa was glad he kept his body alongside hers and did not move on top of her. Perhaps she could trust him, but still wished he would promise things would not go that far tonight. Thankfully, just as she finished that thought Sam pulled back and sat up against the wall. He pulled her up into his arms, tucking her head into the crook of his neck.

It was warm in his arms. The way he held her was so encasing and protective. It allowed Alexa's eyes to slip closed, the jetlag no longer able to be kept at bay. She felt Sam chuckle as he shuffled her body back down to the floor. His hands started to undress her, slipping off her shoes and pulling off her jacket. She tried to protest and push him away, but he only shushed her. Forcing open her eyes, Alexa saw Sam stripping off his own clothes. He moved closer and pulled off the rest of her clothes, even slipping off her bra. He left her underpants on, along with his own, but she doubted that would be for very long when he pulled her body in against his.

"Shh," said Sam, stroking her hair. "Go to sleep."

"But I don't want to," Alexa murmured, not talking about sleeping.

"You're already halfway there," Sam chuckled. "I promise I'm going to let you sleep. I just want to hold you close, okay, like we did back on the farm."

Alexa closed her eyes, content now Sam had promised. She snuggled in closer, loving the feel of his skin on hers and the warmth of his embrace as she fell into a deep slumber.

It was wonderfully warm when Alexa woke the next morning. She stretched, expecting to feel Sam next to her and jerked fully awake when she found herself alone.

"Hey, sleepyhead. How you feeling?" asked Sam, walking out from the shower with a towel around his waist. "Closer to conscious this morning?"

"So it was a dream?"

"What?"

"Getting back together. Me and you. Last night."

Alexa looked down at her mostly naked state under the blankets more confused than ever.

"It wasn't a dream and nothing happened. You seriously think I'd get it on with you when you're half asleep. I told you, you need to trust me."

"I do. Of course I do, Sam. I was just really out of it yesterday."

"So much so that you don't want to do what we agreed to?"

"No. I still think that's a good idea," Alexa smiled as she took in Sam's semi-naked state.

"What?" asked Sam. "Why are you looking at me like that?"

"It's just been a long time since I've seen you like this," Alexa replied, blushing. "You're much more man-like than I remembered."

"I'll take that as a compliment," smiled Sam, sliding to sit down next to her and gathering her in his arms. "Now go have a shower and wash off the last of your jetlag."

As soon as Alexa was dressed – in her last set of clean clothes – Sam switched off the heater, grabbed her jacket and headed for the door.

"Um, where are we going?" Alexa asked hesitantly.

"To Beth. You wanted to see her, right?" Sam replied as though she was daft.

"Yeah, of course. I just didn't realise you remembered," Alexa smiled, before hesitating. "We can grab coffee on the way, right?"

"Anything you want," smiled Sam.

Alexa could not help it. She rushed into Sam's arms and pressed her lips to his. He reciprocated, running one hand down her back as the other opened the front door. It was so carefree as they walked hand in hand to the car. Alexa could already see their future. If they were married that day, she was not sure they would spend an unhappy day together.

"Sam, can we talk about something," Alexa said hesitantly.

"Alexa, I really don't think we need to talk about that."

"About what?"

"It's comfort and safety you're feeling, not love," said Sam, turning to face her briefly before returning his eyes to the road. "I feel the same way. It's so easy being with you, but it's not love." Alexa was not convinced. Sam turned back to her. When he returned his gaze to the road, there were hard lines on his face that had not been there before. "You know if Mr Knight walked by now, you'd have no thought of staying with me," he said firmly, as if determinedly making the point.

"I don't know about that," replied Alexa, forcing herself not to consider the possibility.

"I do," retorted Sam bitterly. "You'd be scared and a little wary, but he's not our teacher any more, so it's no longer illegal. He's old, but in a few years a ten-year age gap won't even raise an eyebrow. And you still love him, even if you no longer talk about him. You forget how well I know you."

"What about you?" Alexa asked, changing the subject as Sam's voice became more agitated. The idea that dating Marcus would one day be socially permissible obviously did not sit well with him. "You fallen in love with anyone?"

"I've had a glimpse of love," replied Sam cryptically, though his voice softened and the hard lines fell from his face. "But it's far too complex to even consider right now and definitely not until me and you are sorted. Give me time and I'll figure something out."

Alexa could tell Sam did not want her to probe further, but his secrecy revealed one thing; he was serious about this girl, whoever she was. Instead, Sam told her about university and how their high school friends were. Sam, Ezra, Lizzie and Bianca were all studying at the same university Alexa was enrolled in. Alexa was thrilled by her choice of uni, not because of her friends, but because it was so close to her home.

The sight of the razor wire as they approached the detention centre tore at Alexa's heart. Most would argue Bethany deserved to be locked up for what she had done, but they had not deserved their childhood. No one ever seemed to take that injustice into account.

Walking into the meeting room after clearing security, Alexa could not stop herself from examining the faces of those who joined her in this dreary place. There was very little joy or hope in their eyes. There were few reasons for either, but Alexa refused to greet Bethany with a heavy heart. This was the start, not the end, of their lives and Alexa was determined they would face that future with hope.

"Lex!" squealed Bethany, as she rushed into the room.

Alexa dashed forward and pulled Bethany into a tight embrace that was only separated by the guards.

"Oh, my Angel! I missed you so much and you've grown again. I can't believe it."

Bethany beamed as they sat down, obviously proud of the way she now towered over Alexa. It was an achievement that defied Alexa's understanding. Despite the heroin Bethany had poisoned her body with, every time she was clean, she continued to grow. Alexa could not remember the last time she had grown.

"I've missed you too," said Bethany, grasping Alexa's hand tight despite the glare of the guards. Alexa had made Ben tell her what the punishment was for prisoners who disregarded the no contact rules, so tried to disentangle her hand, but Bethany only held it tighter. "I don't give a shit," said Bethany. "How was the flight home?"

It was pretty much the only part of the trip Bethany did not know about. No matter where Alexa was, she sent Bethany letters. The only chance Alexa had to hear how Bethany was doing was during scheduled call times. So regardless of the time or the cost, Alexa made those calls. The separation would have been unbearable otherwise.

"Not too bad. Didn't get much sleep, so I was a bit of a zombie yesterday. Sam can tell you all about it, I'm sure," Alexa added with a hint of bitter sarcasm.

"Um, yeah, sorry about that," grimaced Bethany, trying to hold back her grin. "But you know you would've got all stressed and come home if I'd told you he was coming."

"If you told me why, yeah, probably," confessed Alexa with a short laugh. "But I'm actually super-stoked you're friends. And I'm sure you've said all you need to about me and my past."

"Of course, Lex. I promise no more talking about your past. We'll just talk about your present instead. I mean, you know, if Sam still wants to come."

The fear in Bethany's eyes as she looked down broke Alexa's heart and she hoped Sam had not been lying when he said he thought Bethany was awesome.

"The next couple of weeks'll be hectic moving, but I'm going to keep coming," replied Sam earnestly. "Just might not be when Alexa comes. If Alexa trusts me."

"Of course, I trust you," spluttered Alexa, trying hard to contain her tears as she hugged Sam.

"So's that mean you let Sam shack up with you this week while he's homeless?" asked Bethany, smiling broadly. Alexa nodded, wiping her eyes. "Got plans?"

"I might let you guys catch up in private," said Sam suddenly.

"What? No, it's fine. You don't have to go," said Alexa quickly, but he was insistent and with a smile, wave and a promise he would visit Bethany again soon, he was gone.

"What's that about?" asked Bethany.

"I'm guessing the fact that we're getting back together," answered Alexa. "Probably embarrassed about what I might say."

"I don't get it. You only just got back. Were you planning this before?" asked Bethany in a concerned voice.

"Whoa, no!" Alexa laughed in response. "He sprung it on me last night. And it's not permanent. Just for the week. We got back together so we could break up properly, apparently."

Alexa laughed, thinking how ridiculous her life sounded when spoken out loud. Bethany laughed with her, drawing surprised looks from around the room. Laughter was not a commonly heard sound within these walls.

"So you're building up to a big fight?" asked Bethany. "I reckon I know a few things that would tick him off."

"Ha, we can't start fighting too soon. He's promised to help me have sex again."

"Help you? What does that mean?"

"What do you think?" laughed Alexa. "Stand there and give me pointers as I screw some guy? Me and him, you know – I mean, we're getting back together."

Bethany nodded and smiled, but Alexa could see tears in her eyes. Alexa thought they had been joking. When she tried to comfort her, Bethany only pulled away.

"I'm so sorry, Lex," cried Bethany softly.

"For what?" Alexa asked, truly not understanding.

"For everything I've put you through!" replied Bethany in an anguished voice. "You're scared of a guy touching you and it's all my fault. I've made your life so horrible and yet I sit in here wanting you to come see me all the time. I want everything from you and I'm the one who's taken it all away."

"Hardly, Angel. The things you want are the things I want to give. I want to see you all the time too." Bethany glared at her. "You'll get mad if we start talking about blame. I hate that I failed you so bad you ended up here. I don't care about the rest. I would've gone through it a thousand times over if it meant sparing you – if it meant you'd never known the taste of heroin. Bethy, I hate our pasts. Hate that we had to live so many years apart, but I don't and will never, ever hate you. I refuse to. I don't even know how."

"But you should. You could've been happy with a great family. Instead, you're scared and alone and only think about me."

"What are you talking about," cried Alexa. She had never felt so selfish in her life. "I went on holidays. I bought an apartment. I'm making things right with Sam. I'm starting uni in a few weeks —"

"Yeah and how much is really for you, and how much for me?"

"The holiday wasn't for you," smiled Alexa, but Bethany only scowled. "I want to be able to look after you. It's not a crime."

"But I don't want to be why you're unhappy," said Bethany softly.

"That's not possible. You're the reason I live," replied Alexa.

"What's your apartment like?" asked Bethany, with the obvious air of changing the subject.

Alexa did not like that Bethany did not see it as their apartment and was tempted to force the issue, before reconsidering. It was probably hard for Bethany to consider anything on the outside hers.

"Ah, it's great, just empty," smiled Alexa. "We have a couple of blankets and a heater courtesy of Sam, but that's it. I'll have to shop soon, but while there's hot water and electricity it's good enough."

"You don't have anything? Furniture? Nothing?" asked Bethany, as if unconvinced by the bareness of her apartment.

"I wanted to start afresh. It's stupid, but I wanted to be able to choose what went in my house – even down to the last teaspoon."

"That's not stupid," said Bethany, smiling understandingly before her face suddenly turned hard, as if she just remembered something terrible. "But what are you doing here? You need to go shopping. You can't live on the floor."

"I've been away for six months, I had to come and see you. If I wasn't going to fall asleep in front of you I would've come straight from the airport yesterday."

"Well you've seen me now, so go furnish your apartment," said Bethany in a wavering voice. Alexa was about to retort when Bethany spoke again. "And I don't want to see you until you have."

"It's not that important," replied Alexa, smiling dismissively as she stroked Bethany's face affectionately.

"Lex, you're killing me. I want you happy. Have your own life."

"I do, but you're the biggest part of it. I can't live without you. You know I'd move in here if it meant we could finally be together."

"Don't say that," replied Bethany in a tortured whisper.

Alexa wondered if Bethany found that idea as enticing as she did. The truth was that anywhere without Bethany felt like a prison, so she could not fear any place where she and Bethany could be together.

"Lex, please, I need you to have a life outside of here. I need something to look forward to and dream of, or I won't survive. And I can't do that knowing you're sleeping on the floor."

"Okay, I'll try," nodded Alexa, willing to do anything for Bethany. "For you, I'll go buy a bed to sleep in," she added with a sighing smile, but Bethany only scowled. "Fine. For me. All for me. Nothing for you. I'll pick colours and styles you hate just to prove I wasn't thinking about you."

"You'd have to think about me to do that," retorted Bethany with a smiling sob.

"Yeah, well, see, I suck. But I'll do it. And just because you can't stop me, I'm going to think of you the entire time. So make sure you think about the kinds of furniture you want. I'll be channelling you."

"I will, I promise," nodded Bethany, tears slipping down her face as she did. "Now go shopping and next time when you come, you can tell me all about it and your week with Sam. Go."

It was easier said than done. There was nothing Alexa found harder than walking away from Bethany. They stepped slowly in opposite directions until their hands finally pulled apart.

Alexa struggled to remain composed as she left, and by the time she stepped out into the cold winter air tears were slipping down her cheeks as tortured sobs pushed against her lungs.

"What happened?" asked Sam frantically, pushing off the bonnet of his car and pulling her into a warm embrace. "This isn't because of you and me, is it?"

"What? No," Alexa cried, wondering why Sam would ever think that. "I just miss her and she wouldn't let me stay."

"Why not?" asked Sam with genuine concern.

"Cos I don't have any furniture."

Sam started laughing, but stopped when she pushed out of his arms and glared at him. "Sorry, but she has a point. And you know you would've done the same thing," he added before she could reply. "You both care so much about each other."

"What's wrong with that?" asked Alexa with a sense of annoyed petulance, sick of being told how much she should care about Bethany.

"Because you love each other to the point where it's almost crippling," answered Sam gently. "You both have to start living your own lives, not each other's. Don't you see? When you're happy, she's happy – and the other way round. So find a way to be happy. That's what will help her."

"Getting her out of prison is what will help her," Alexa retorted.

"Yes, but there's still six more months until that's a possibility. You going to wait until then to get furniture? You want Bethany to get out to your life in chaos because you refused to get it sorted without her? She needs you to sort out your life, not hers."

The sigh was internal, but Sam's smile was knowing. It was unfair the way he fought her at her weakest points.

"Can you take me shopping, then?" Alexa asked tentatively.

"You know I can. Just tell me what you need to get."

"Everything."

It was not a quick shopping expedition. If not for Sam reiterating, many times, that there were always going to be trade-offs between price, time and quality, it could have taken much longer. For the most part, Alexa chose price. She needed her furniture to be functional more than fashionable, but if she was going to make that sacrifice, she wanted to be sure she was getting the lowest price available. The only real sticking point came trying to furnish the bedrooms. The second bedroom was not as big an issue. Alexa was willing to make some compromises there, but not when it came to the bed she would have to sleep in.

In front of Sam, she said nothing of the real reason for her finicky state. He knew it was not money, as she passed by many cheaper beds, but there were not the words to explain why she could not buy a bed with any kind of posts at the corners. If possible, she did not even want one with legs. Thankfully, after an hour of searching, she found exactly what she was looking for. The bed had a padded headboard and the other end was a single wooden panel that did not extend above the height of the frame. With a tight-fitting mattress, there would be nowhere anything could be tied to it.

With that minor victory, they trekked to Ikea to buy all the smaller household items, resulting in Alexa purchasing much more than she had ever conceived possible. Getting everything into the car, and then from the car to the lift was an exercise in strength and coordination neither she nor Sam hoped to repeat, and when they finally got to the apartment, Alexa practically fell through the front door under the weight of her wares.

"Remind me to never go shopping with you again," said Sam, as he dragged their bags into the lounge room.

"Let's just leave the stuff here and go out for dinner," replied Alexa, feeling her legs weaken beneath her. She refused to look at her watch, determined to deny how many hours she had expended continuously spending money.

"Oh no, you're not going anywhere," replied Sam with a boyish smile. He cupped her face gently, kissing her once before pulling back. "We both need to just chill and relax for a bit."

Sam took Alexa's hand and led her to the blankets on the floor, putting the heater on as he went. Alexa's heart was pounding, but she was thankful that it was not completely out of fear. Desire and arousal were also starting to flow through her veins, allowing her to pull Sam's lips to hers and kiss him passionately. Alexa ran her fingers through Sam's hair as he held her close. As the room warmed, Sam delicately undressed her. It was good that she had the cold to disguise her shivers. She did not want Sam to think she was scared of him and was grateful when he simply rubbed his hands over her limbs, warming them with friction.

It surprised Alexa how quickly they were naked, and how many of their clothes she had been responsible for discarding, but she liked that she was enjoying this. She liked that she had the choice to continue or stop. Sam never pushed the pace, always waiting for some silent signal that she was okay to continue. Even when he rolled his body on top of hers, he did not push straight into her. He kissed her lips and neck, holding her tight until her desire built and it was her pushing against him, wanting more.

"You sure?" Sam whispered in her ear.

Alexa nodded against his cheek, before turning and letting his lips capture hers as he pushed in closer. She gasped as he entered, suddenly terrified by the slight pain. Sam continued, pushing slowly, before holding still. Kissing passionately, Alexa was again surprised that it was her body moving to his. The pain had gone and there was only pleasure as they moved together in their most intimate embrace.

"I love you," said Sam, tenderly brushing the hair from Alexa's forehead, before rolling on to his side and pulling her into him.

Alexa snuggled closer, resting her head in the crook of his neck as she traced circles on his muscular chest. "I love you too," she replied. She meant it with all her heart, but somehow this moment had not changed the depth or nature of her feelings for him. "And thank you. I know this can't be easy for you."

"It wasn't exactly difficult," laughed Sam. "Do you realise how long I've thought about being with you like that again?"

"Was it okay? I mean, as good as you imagined?" asked Alexa.

"Better," Sam whispered into her ear. "You're perfect. Well, in bed – in the sack, perhaps," Sam added with a laugh as he looked around their pile of blankets. "In the shops, now that's another matter."

"I'm sorry," smiled Alexa, remembering just how frustrated Sam had been getting with her. "But you know, really deep down, you were having fun. Just like you know you're going to have lots of fun helping me assemble all my furniture." Sam grimaced and groaned into her hair, making her laugh. "Not what you thought you were going to be doing this week, huh?" Alexa chuckled.

"No, I guessed we'd be doing something like this," replied Sam with a supressed sigh. "I just never expected you'd be so finicky. You were just shopping to satisfy Beth. I thought you'd just buy the first nice thing you saw, but you just kept going back, checking prices, comparing them, then checking them again."

"You check the price of stuff before you buy it," replied Alexa, not really understanding Sam's point. She was still surprised he watched her spend so much without batting an eyelid. Perhaps it was normal for people to be able to spend that amount of money in one afternoon.

"Yeah, but I'm not a millionaire," laughed Sam.

Alexa froze.

It felt like even her heart had stopped. The concerns of a moment ago seemed trivial compared to this revelation, and she did not know how to react. She wanted to run, but nothing was functioning, not her body or her brain.

"It was kind of obvious that you, Ezra and Bianca were the ones who won that lottery," Sam continued softly, sitting them up. "There was such huge coverage. I remember reading that story about the dream and I thought of you – even before you started spending all this money you never had."

"I sued the school," said Alexa weakly, still unsure whether to lie or not. "That payout was big enough to let me do all this."

"Yeah, I know," Sam replied, squeezing her hand. "Our lawyers told us they settled your case pretty quick. We were stoked, hoped maybe they'd settle our too, but they're fighting it."

"I'm sorry about that. I should've really been in with you guys. I didn't even know I was suing them. I mean I did, but that time was such a blur. Peter was so insistent. He was so angry about everything that happened."

"Any normal person would be. So how much did you get out of the bastards?"

"More than I thought possible. But that wasn't the best part. They could've given me nothing, but just to hear someone say that wasn't normal, that it wasn't my fault and no one else goes to school and cops that shit. That was what I wanted."

"Well the rest of us already knew it wasn't right. Chad's parents tore strips off him for not telling them everything that happened. Same as Chris and Stacey. I think Nick's parents thought that after Con and the pipe bombs they couldn't complain about anything."

Alexa nodded, but said nothing else. She was hoping they had spoken enough to make Sam forget how the conversation had started, but the way he suddenly lowered his gaze to meet hers was not promising.

"But you did win that lottery money as well, didn't you?" Sam asked. Alexa bit her lip, refusing to meet his eyes. "Alexa, relax. It's okay. You scared I'm going to ask for money or something? I already know you're the one who gave Gran and Pop all that money they said they won on the pokies." She looked up. He was not smiling. "What you've done for us – I could never ask for more. I'm not sure I can even thank you enough."

"You didn't tell Bethy, did you?" breathed Alexa, not worried by Sam's thanks. She was the one who still owed them.

"No," he replied sincerely. "I guessed you had your reasons for keeping it from her."

"I'm not going to let her get out of gaol just to sit around, bored with a whole lot of money in her wallet. She'll find out in time, but she's still a heroin addict. You can't ever forget that. Just because she's not using doesn't mean she doesn't want to. Her body craves it in a way you'll never understand. I have to make sure she sets up her life, has a job and is settled before she finds out. This money's security, not to live off. We'll both have to work."

Alexa felt Sam's hands stroking her as if to pacify her. She could not understand why until she realised her body was shaking.

"I'm sorry," he said, pulling her into his arms and kissing the side of her head. "I just thought you realised everyone knew."

"It's okay," Alexa whispered, hoping it was. "I just don't like to think of it that way."

"What way?"

"Like it's real. Like today. Who can spend money like that? I reckon I've stolen more than I've ever owned and now I have more than anyone can conceive. And I can't even back pay those people I hurt."

"Those people are okay. You don't owe anyone anything. You don't owe Gran and Pop. I love what you did for them. It was sweet and kind and beautiful, but you didn't owe them. They weren't some of the people you hurt."

"I would've given them more if I wasn't so scared I wouldn't have enough to care for Bethy. I'm just so scared no amount of money will be enough to protect her – keep her away from drugs. All I've ever wanted is to live a normal life, but so far that costs so much more than I expected. But that's okay. I'll spend all of it if we can just be happy and normal. Just like everyone else."

"Normal sounds good," replied Sam delicately, as if choosing his words with care. "I think you're doing the right thing. What else have you spent the money on?"

"The trip, this place. Gave some to the Whites – a million. I thought it might ease my conscience, but it didn't really help."

"Probably because it's what none of you really wanted. I'm sure they would've preferred to see you than take the money. I'm sure you would've wanted that too if you'd dared to wish for it."

"No, Sam, no," replied Alexa desperately. "The last thing I can want is to see them again. They were the only foster family to care and include me and I led Leo to them. It was her eleventh birthday. How can I ever make that up to them? Money will never be enough, but it's all I have. I was the punishment they never deserved and I'll never be that again. I don't care how much I want to be with them, I'll always love them too much."

"Alexa, will you stop that," said Sam angrily. "You're forgetting nothing happened to them." She was about to argue, but he spoke over the top of her. "Sure, it would've been a shock having those brutes burst into their home, but you're the one who copped it. You're the one that was raped and beaten for five days before being dumped, barely alive, off a bridge. You saved Hayley."

"Never would've needed to if I'd never been there," muttered Alexa. Sam stared at her. "Doesn't matter," she said dismissively.

"It does matter," cried Sam, jumping to his feet. "When are you going to stop thinking everything's your fault? When are you going to stop thinking you don't deserve anyone's love?"

Alexa did not answer. Trying to make her feel better about what she had done was not what she needed. Unless she remained realistic about the threat she posed, there was too great a chance she would risk the Whites' safety for her own selfish desires. When she made the mistake of trying to explain that to Sam, he only yelled at her more. Frustrated by Sam's inability to see past his visions for her future, Alexa dressed hurriedly and stormed out of the apartment.

Walking down to the beach, Alexa could not hold her memories at bay. For the past twelve months she had done her best never to think about the Whites. Losing them had nearly destroyed her, because living with them had been the closest to happy she had ever been. The only flaw had been Bethany's absence.

Alexa knew the reason she could not bear to think about the Whites was because she had never fully forgiven Bethany for what happened that night. When it had come to down to choosing between Bethany and the Whites, Alexa had not hesitated, but in choosing Bethany she had chosen to love her through everything and that would never be possible if she continued to think about the Whites.

"I was starting to worry," said Sam, as soon as Alexa walked in the front door.

"Sorry," she replied petulantly, annoyed at his frustrated tone.

"Um, yeah. You know what, maybe I should go and come back in a couple of days."

Sam's suggestion pierced Alexa deeply. After all he had done, she knew it was unfair to treat him so badly, but she was speaking before she even knew what she was saying. "Yeah, fine, you know what, Sam. I'll tell you where you can go." And she did.

Sam's eyes widened at the coldness of her words. Alexa could not blame him for his disappointed look as he grabbed his belongings and walked out the door. It would have been so simple to pull him back, apologise and beg for forgiveness. Instead, she just spat more angry goodbyes. When the door clicked shut behind him, Alexa fell to the floor in a daze that took far too many minutes to lift. The clarity of thought that returned was not particularly welcome. Grabbing her keys, she dashed downstairs, her heart rising when she saw Sam's car still in her parking space. A soft creak caught her ear. There he sat, swaying sadly on the swing in the park next to her apartment block.

"I'm sorry," said Alexa, standing in front of Sam's swing, holding the chains to prevent his departure. "You've been so good to me and I go and say all those horrible things to you."

"It's just not the way I imagined this week," murmured Sam. "I thought we'd be happy and smiling, having fun. We made love, but within an hour we're fighting. It wasn't supposed to be this way."

"Not yet anyway," said Alexa softly. "We were always going to have to break-up. Bethy even offered to help come up with things to piss you off, but apparently I can do that all by myself." Sam turned away, looking down towards the ocean, though it was not visible from where they were. "I'm sorry," Alexa continued sincerely when Sam stayed silent. "I really wasn't angry with you – okay, I was, but not in that way. There're just a lot of things I try not to think about."

"But you make things harder for yourself. You keep blaming yourself for everything and never let anyone help you," cried Sam, finally turning back to face her.

"I've accepted your help, haven't I?" Alexa retorted.

"To an extent, sure, but you won't let anyone try and convince you of your worth. What'll it take to convince you you're a wonderful person, an amazing person I wouldn't want to live without? What will it take to convince you so many other people feel that way?"

"I have my reasons," Alexa replied, refusing to answer Sam's questions.

"No you have excuses," cried Sam, finally losing his composure. "I know you've been hurt before, more than hurt and more than just a few times, but that's in the past. You have control of your life now. Let us help you, because, damn it, Alexa, you need help."

Alexa slumped into the swing next to Sam. Everything he said was true, but she felt like it skipped over all the things she had achieved. It was as if because she still had problems she had not done enough. "It's not that easy," she sighed in defeat.

"I know, but I'm not going to let you throw the rest of your life away," said Sam, his voice a touch softer. "You deserve more than that and I'm going to make sure you get it, but you have to try too."

"I wouldn't have the first clue where to start," confessed Alexa, knowing already that she would fail. If everything she had done so far was not good enough then she could not foresee anything she could achieve in the future meeting Sam's high standards.

"You can start by inviting me back in." It took a moment for Alexa to realise Sam was no longer yelling at her. "C'mon, it's freezing," he said, his hand gently cupping her cheek. "Let me back in and help warm me up."

Chapter Three

"SAM, WAKE UP. Come on, you have to get up."

Alexa shook Sam forcefully, wondering how he could possibly sleep through her physical assault.

"What?" mumbled Sam as his arm moved over his eyes and ears.

"We're going out for breakfast."

"We do that every morning. Why the sudden emergency?" Sam asked grumpily, though Alexa could hear he was waking up, so started pulling at him insistently.

"This is with Maria. I organised it before I came home – before you hijacked my plans. It's why I had to organise for the furniture to be delivered in the afternoon. Come on. It'll be really rude if we're late. She'll think I don't want to see her and that I just used her to buy this apartment."

Sam huffed, but pushed himself out of the blankets. He tried to encourage Alexa into the shower with him, but she was dressed and ready to go. "Where's the fun in showering alone?" he sighed, closing the bathroom door behind him.

"There is none," Alexa called. "But the rewards will come later. Trust me. Maria's cooking will be worth it." Alexa was not sure that Sam heard her, but doubted he would have believed her if he did. She was not sure she would have believed someone like Maria was real without meeting her either. In her world, there had never been any good female role models. Pam White was the only one who had come close to fulfilling that role, but Pam's desire to be her mother had always caused complications that had never been overcome. Maria was different. She was too old for Alexa to consider her in a motherly light, but Alexa also had no recollection of her own grandmothers, so did not know if Maria was taking on that role or not.

Throughout Alexa's months away, Maria had been her second-most frequent correspondent after Bethany. Maria had rarely taken more than a day to reply to any of Alexa's emails. Ben and Sam had been content to reply within the week. That she and Maria found enough things to talk about always surprised Alexa. Maria had been born in Croatia and had travelled Europe extensively in her younger years, so frequently suggested places for her to visit. The greatest disappointment Alexa had was that she never made it to Croatia. Her plan was to take Maria there when she finished her degree.

"So you said she had kids, right?" asked Sam as they got in the car. "Will they be there? Are they our age? Is that how you got to know her?"

"No, I met her because I accidently stepped all over her groceries when I was going to check out an apartment for sale in her block," replied Alexa, cringing at the memory.

"And how exactly did you get to know each other after doing that?" Sam asked through his amused laughter.

"I think she was lonely, and I was around," answered Alexa. Sam turned to her in horror. "I'm not that much of a trouble magnet. Maria's different. Her husband divorced her and left her with three kids in a foreign country to fend for herself. Her family was well off, so she never struggled financially. Gave her kids everything. Now they're really successful and busy and never around. She's proud of them, but she's lonely."

"I'm not sure I'm convinced, Alexa," Sam replied hesitantly.

"Yeah, well, just keep that to yourself. Don't make Maria feel bad just cos she made friends with some screwed up kid."

"I never meant it like that."

Alexa could not answer. She could accept that Sam would second-guess her decisions, but the thought of anyone distrusting Maria was more than she could take.

The rest of the drive was spent in silence. Sam took Alexa's hand as they got out of the car, but she was still nervous about how he would act. Perhaps she should have left him to sleep in and made her own way to Maria's. It would have left her mind free to think about the last time she had been here. If not for the chill in the air, Alexa could have almost imagined it was the same day.

Scanning the benches in the park that looked out onto the harbour, Alexa found herself almost surprised not to see Marcus waiting there for her; as though he would always be there waiting for her. With a sigh, Alexa turned away and walked across the road to Maria's apartment block, but it was hard to have a heavy heart when Maria's excited voice crackled over the intercom.

"Oh it's so good to see you again, Alexa," cried Maria, as soon as she opened the door. "It's been so quiet since you left. No one to impart my wisdom on. How are you?"

"I'm okay. Getting there," replied Alexa. "Though not fast enough according to Sam," she added with a hint of petulance.

"Ah, so this is the famous Sam?" smiled Maria, turning to greet at him as he stood awkwardly behind them.

"Yeah, sorry. Maria, Sam. Sam, this is Maria," said Alexa, quickly introducing them.

"It's wonderful to meet you, Sam," said Maria warmly, walking them inside. "I've heard so much about you. I'm really glad you ended up getting in touch with Alexa. I wish I'd been able to convince her you'd still want to be her friend at the end of last year. I've never seen someone so down about losing a friend."

Sam turned to Alexa with wide eyes, but she quickly looked away. She did not want to remember those terrible months at the end of last year and was thankful when Sam asked for the bathroom.

"Maria, promise you won't say anything about Marcus," said Alexa hurriedly, dragging Maria to the kitchen.

"Of course."

"Thank you. Sam cares, but he's too protective. I need that to stay between you and me. Please."

"Oh, Alexa, you worry too much," smiled Maria dismissively, but Alexa got the feeling Maria liked being her secret-keeper.

"Um, Maria, is this all for us?" asked Alexa, noticing all the food. "But I never even told you Sam was coming. How are we going to eat it all?"

"If you coming home isn't an excuse for an extravagant breakfast, nothing is," smiled Maria.

With no breeze and the morning sun flooding the balcony, they set up there for breakfast overlooking the harbour. It was stunning, and Alexa found her faith in better things ahead being renewed.

"Now, what's Alexa apparently doing to herself?" asked Maria with a slight scowl when they all had food in front of them.

"Shutting the world out in the hope she'll never feel pain again," answered Sam, seeming pleased by the prospect of an ally.

"Oh, Alexa, you can't do that," sighed Maria. "Pain will always find you. The trick is to have fun between its visits."

Sam smiled smugly, but Alexa was just as pleased by Maria's comments. It may have been the same sentiment he had been trying to convey, but Maria managed to say it in a way that did not make her feel completely useless.

Sam did not worry much for conversation, trying to prove that none of the food would go to waste, while Alexa and Maria discussed things they had mentioned in their emails, but never had the time to detail, and Alexa's move into her apartment.

"You'll have to come and see it when I have somewhere for you to sit," smiled Alexa, though her heart thumped erratically at the idea.

"I look forward to it," beamed Maria.

Alexa was about to respond when she saw Sam going back for his third serving. "What? I'm a growing boy."

Alexa thought it bordered on rude how much he was eating and wondered if she had been underfeeding him. "You might need to define which way you're growing if you keep eating like that," Alexa replied, deciding to keep it light in front of Maria. Maria would never complain anyway.

"You would've been a worthy opponent once."

"Seeing that, I'm glad I'm not," replied Alexa. "Besides, I don't mind me at this weight."

"You were just as beautiful before," responded Sam angrily.

Alexa believed that if Sam stopped being so defensive about her weight he might realise that she was not underweight and hardly starving herself. Her relationship with food had changed. It was no longer a source of comfort or distraction, and with money in her pocket, it was no longer an insecure resource.

"And you gave this boy up?" asked Maria with a look of amused shock. "I'd have him myself, if I was a bit younger."

"Well, I do have him – for the week, anyway," replied Alexa with a cheeky smile, keen to move the conversation away from her weight.

Maria held up her finger indicating Alexa should stop talking as she packed away the plates and uneaten food. Alexa jumped up to help, but Maria only shushed her away. When Maria returned, her little trolley was adorned with cups, tea and coffee.

"Okay, now just explain that last comment," said Maria, sitting down with her tea.

"We decided to get back together for the week," said Alexa simply, before taking a sip of her coffee.

"And what happens at the end of the week?"

"Big bust up, I suppose," smiled Alexa. "Something to make sure we're rid of all our tender feelings for each other."

"We're not going to have a big bust up," sighed Sam. "We didn't get together to break up. We just need to sort through a few things."

"Going well so far?"

"Brilliantly," replied Alexa. "If you exclude my moods."

"Then why would it just be for the week? If you both get along so well and like each other as much as you say, why constrain yourself? Perhaps there's something more that's worth fighting for."

Alexa regretted starting this conversation. "Me and Sam broke up a long time ago. We were just kids. It was never going to work. We've both moved on, been with other people," she muttered quickly.

Maria turned to Sam. It was annoying that Maria had worked out that she was always very sparing with her answers.

"The problem was it was never our choice to break up," explained Sam. "We were forced apart. But I think the rest is true."

"What do you mean by forced apart? Your parents didn't approve?" asked Maria hesitantly.

"It's hard to explain," continued Sam. "What we knew at the time and what came out afterwards was so different. But mostly it was a teacher at our school. Mr Marsh. He targeted Alexa, set things up so she'd have such a bad time that she'd turn to him. Without his protection, she risked being hurt. In exchange, she had to give him what he wanted."

Alexa could see Maria silently questioning her and could only shake her head. The only teacher she had ever told Maria about was Marcus, and she did not want her ever thinking he was anything like Clinton Marsh.

"I won't ask any questions if you don't want me to," said Maria.

"I won't answer any questions anyway. Anything you want to know, Sam can tell you. I have to go to the bathroom."

"Alexa?" said Sam anxiously, reaching for her hand as she rose from the table.

"You can tell her everything. I just can't. I trust her to know."

Sam nodded and let her go. Alexa immediately rushed from the balcony. She wondered how long such a conversation would take, because reliving those memories as she sat in the bathroom was harder than she thought. This was the room she had always been in with her razor, expelling her pain by cutting her skin. Now, with her promise to her lawyer, Peter Lam, that she would never do such a thing again, it was more enticing than ever. Fearing what she would do if she was left alone with her own mind, Alexa headed out to the kitchen and started cleaning. She could hear Sam and Maria talking, but was glad their voices were soft enough that she could not make out the words. Putting on the radio, she was able to drown them out completely.

"You know it's going to be a good day when the kitchen fairy pays you a visit," said Maria, walking in with their mugs. "Sam said you'd have to leave soon to be there when your furniture arrives. You need any help?"

"No," replied Alexa, shaking her head. "But thank you. I think me and Sam need this time to ourselves."

"When does Sam leave?"

"Saturday."

"Why don't you come over then and we'll amuse ourselves."

"I have to see Bethy. Is it okay if I come after that? Is it still okay to visit you?" Alexa asked, feeling her voice break.

"Absolutely," smiled Maria. "I'd be very sad if you didn't."

Alexa nodded, but was still not game enough to meet Maria's eyes, even after Maria pulled her into a consoling hug. It was a relief when Sam took her by the hand and led her back to the car. They drove in silence. Alexa was tempted to ask what he and Maria spoke about, but it was easier not to. Maria was prepared to allow her back into her house, so either she was one of the most remarkable people in the world or Sam did not tell her very much. For now, Alexa was happy to believe the former.

The first delivery truck turned up soon after they arrived home, surprising Alexa with their efficiency. When they had given her a four-hour window, Sam told her to expect them towards the end of that time; no one ever got deliveries on time.

"Beginner's luck," Alexa smiled happily.

"Yeah, maybe," Sam smiled back, hugging her tight.

The whitegoods were installed immediately, as was some of the furniture, but most of it had to be assembled by them. It was a more daunting prospect than Alexa envisaged.

"I warned you," laughed Sam. "We're going to be spending our entire week building furniture."

"I don't remember you saying that," Alexa replied seriously.

"Well I definitely remember thinking it – a lot. But it's okay, because you're going to remember this moment and you're going to owe me big time whenever I move."

"But you're moving next week."

"Yeah, but we're getting removalists. I'm going to hold you to this forever. Even if I can only use it for my kids. You will repay me."

"Any day," Alexa replied with a laugh. She could imagine Sam bringing this up in thirty years.

"Okay, well let's start in your bedroom. I want somewhere comfy to sleep tonight," said Sam seriously.

It was a good plan, especially as her bed had very few pieces to assemble. It gave them a quick sense of achievement to help spur them on. The lounge and dining rooms took a bit longer, but nowhere near as long as Alexa had feared. It was worth the effort.

"Wow," gasped Alexa looking around each of the rooms.

Now she was excited about living here. It was like a real place and it was hers. It did not matter that the furniture was not top of the range. It was the best-looking place she had ever stayed in.

"I'm stuffed," sighed Sam, collapsing on the lounge.

"Hey, no shoes," Alexa cried before she could stop herself. For what Sam had done, she guessed he had the right to put his feet anywhere, but Sam only smiled as he swung his feet off the lounge.

"You sound just like my mum," he said. "It's okay," he smiled, walking over to her and stroking her cheek, obviously seeing the concern in her eyes. "That's not a bad thing."

"Do you like thinking about her?" Alexa asked. Sam rarely spoke about his parents to her without tears. "Doesn't it make you sad?"

"Sometimes. But sometimes it makes them feel closer, like they're not gone completely."

"Do you want to talk about them now?"

"Not right before I kiss you," Sam smiled. "Come on, let's go test out your new bed."

***

"Hey, Sam," said Alexa cautiously as she put away the last of the groceries the next morning. "If I cook you a really nice dinner tonight, will you take me to see Bethy now?" she asked tentatively.

"When does visiting start?" asked Sam.

"Should be opening when we get there," Alexa replied, biting her lip.

"Big dinner?" Sam asked in mock seriousness. Alexa nodded her assurance. "Well, yeah, okay then. I can probably manage that."

Alexa rushed at him, wrapping her arms around him as he playfully scolded her for being an idiot. However, Alexa could never be so easily reassured. So far this week all they had done was what she wanted. Perhaps that was how Sam was convincing himself he was better off without her. She was not sure she would want to stay with anyone as selfish and demanding as her either.

Bethany had clearly not been expecting them back so soon and practically danced into the room. Alexa loved the way Bethany's excitement overcame all her concerns.

"I told you not to come back so soon," said Bethany, squeezing Alexa's hand and frowning as much as her grin would allow. "You have to look after yourself."

"You tell me you're honestly not happy I'm here and I won't visit so often," replied Alexa.

"I can't, but —"

"Good, because I wanted to see you," cried Alexa, trying hard to hide her desperation. "I hate that there're days and times where I'm already not allowed to see you. I can't handle anyone else adding to that, not even you. Part of me being happy is seeing you. Anyway, you only said that I had to get the house furnished and I did."

"Already?" questioned Bethany, looking between Alexa and Sam.

"We spent all yesterday assembling furniture," said Sam, holding up his calloused hands. "But it looks really good."

"So I did what you asked and now I'm here to see you."

Bethany smiled broadly and held Alexa's hands tight as she asked her to describe every room.

"See, I told you that you should've bought that digital camera," laughed Sam when Alexa continued to try and explain the exact layout of the apartment.

"It was over five-hundred dollars. I can't justify that," replied Alexa.

"Of course you can," laughed Sam.

"What are you talking about?" cried Bethany. "The only reason Lex has a single cent is because she was tortured in that stupid school. She's spending it on stuff she really needs, not stupid things like a camera to show me stuff she can tell me about – stuff I'm going to see for myself soon anyway."

"I didn't mean it like that," said Sam softly.

"Lex is smart. She knows how to make sure she has enough to see us through. It's not like we can go get brilliant jobs. This might be all the money we ever have."

Bethany turned away from Sam, and Alexa could see the tears in her eyes. Alexa took her hand and squeezed tight. "Oh, my Angel, it's okay. You know what I'm like. I stress about things. I promise we've got enough til I get a job. You'll have your apprenticeship when you get out. It won't be a lot, but we don't have to pay rent, because we got the apartment cheap. Peter keeps doing all the legal stuff for free, even when I tell him he doesn't have to. And Ben didn't charge me board while I stayed with him. I know I wasted a lot overseas, but now the apartment's furnished, I don't need to spend much. I can even walk to uni – save the bus money. I'm not going to let us go without again. I promise."

Bethany smiled slightly, nodding as tears escaped her eyes. Sam's hands joined theirs as they all held each other tight, but he did not speak much after that. It did not matter. Midweek visiting times were short and they had to leave soon after.

"You weren't serious about everything you said in there, were you? About the money," asked Sam as they walked back to the car. "You know you don't have to be that strict. You can afford to do the things you want, and you deserve to."

"I get what you're saying, Sam, but I'm not going to waste money just because I can. We aren't going to go without, but I don't get a kick out of buying things and I'm glad. Let me do this my way. I think I've proven I can spend money, and I don't think being diligent with the rest is a bad thing."

"No, it's not. But I get why Gran and Pop love you so much. You're just like them. My parents would've really liked you too. They would've thought you could've straightened me out."

"I'll give it a go," laughed Alexa, wondering how someone as crooked as her could possibly straighten anyone out. "Me and Bethy, we'll make a man out of you."

"Sounds good," smiled Sam softly.

The weather turned sour as they drove home. Alexa was thankful her apartment was now fully functional and that she promised Sam a big home-cooked meal rather than a nice bought dinner. She let him rest while she cooked, and was surprised by the way he was able to lounge in front of the television for hours. She joined him when she had nothing to do in the kitchen, but television had never enticed her. The only reason she bought it was because Sam told her it would be really odd if she did not have one.

When dinner was finished, they snuggled on the lounge as the rain continued to pour down outside. Sam turned on the television, but Alexa did not care to watch it, so found herself stroking his body and kissing the parts she could reach. He would reciprocate in the ad breaks, but as soon as the show came back on he turned away from her. It quickly became a challenge to see what it would take for her to be more enticing than the television. Thankfully for her self-esteem, Sam quickly chose her.

Sam stroked Alexa's face as they kissed. Alexa let her fingers trace lines up and down his back. With the heater on and the room warm, they soon shed their jumpers. Alexa made sure Sam did not stop there, pulling off his top as well. She loved the feel of his solid chest and quickly shed her own top so she could feel his skin against hers. Sam's kisses moved down her neck and back up to her mouth as his hand stroked her still-clothed leg and pulled it around his body. Her hands reciprocated, moving through his hair and over his muscular shoulders. When his lips moved back down her neck, his hand followed, pulling her closer, his thumb caressing the base of her neck.

The response was instantaneous. Alexa's unexpectedly violent reaction caught Sam off-guard and he tumbled from the lounge. Looking around desperately, Alexa grabbed her jumper and threw it on to cover her body as she tried to figure out which was the best direction to run. Away from Sam was her only answer, forcing her through the closest door and out on to the balcony. It was not the best escape route, but she did not need long to process what had really happened and realise she had nothing to fear from Sam. However, that only made her more ashamed, causing her body shake with sobs.

When Alexa heard the balcony door open, she threw herself into Sam's arms, hoping it would be a great enough sign of remorse. He held her tight to his chest as he walked them back inside and onto the lounge. She immediately shuffled into his lap and pushed her body into his.

"I'm sorry," said Sam solemnly, holding her tight.

"No, please don't say that," Alexa cried. "You didn't do anything. You didn't. I don't know what's wrong with me. I thought I was over it, but it just hit so quick. You touched my neck and next thing I was terrified you were going to strangle me. I swear I don't think of you like that. You know I'd never think that about you, right?"

"Of course. I just should've been more careful. I should never've put my hand near your throat."

"But that's my point. You touched my throat. You didn't strangle me. How do I explain that to some guy who has no idea of my past?"

"With the truth, I guess," Sam replied softly.

"And who'd stay with me after they heard all that? Any of it. Tell them all of it and they'll run screaming."

"No. Not someone who loves you," replied Sam. "Not someone who's worthy of loving you."

"You live in a fantasy land. It's not possible. There're no people in the world who could love me knowing all that," Alexa replied, though she knew it was a lie. There was one person.

"I love you knowing all that," replied Sam sincerely, nominating the wrong person.

***

"Good morning, sleepyhead," smiled Sam from the kitchen, as Alexa dragged herself to the bathroom. Sleeping in a proper bed for the first time in many days meant that she slept much longer than intended. She wished it meant she felt better for it, but the trauma of the night before still clung to her, tinting her mood in a shade of grey that was matched by the morning skyline. "I hope you're ready for big day. Thought we should have a look around the uni – check out where all your classes will be and make sure you know your way around, know where to find me," said Sam with a grin. Alexa was about to respond happily when he continued over the top of her. "And then I've organised for us to meet up with Chad, Bianca, Ezra and Lizzie."

If Alexa had been able to speak, she would have protested, but Sam just pulled her to the bathroom and turned on the shower before walking out with a promise of breakfast to follow. She did as he asked, but only so she had the time to refine her argument.

"I'm not ready to see them," Alexa said seriously as she sat at the kitchen bench to eat.

"Are you ever going to be?" replied Sam, leaning against the kitchen sink, seemingly unprepared to be too near.

"This is different. You don't understand. That day … Sam, I was looking forward to the future for the first time in ages. I had a plan. I had hopes and they all got taken away from me. I know it's not all Ezra and Bianca's fault, but if we'd waited – done it some other way, I would've left Redgrove with everything. Instead, I left with nothing."

"I know," Sam replied tenderly. "But you still have to face this – even just to find out you can't be their friends. Besides, Chad's been your friend for as long as me. He and Lizzie, they deserve this. You might even find it's not as bad as you expect."

Alexa knew nothing was going to dissuade Sam from his plan. And if she could face them, then she would have her friends back. It was not exactly the clean break she intended on returning home, but if they were all going to university together then they would hardly be able to avoid each other.

The university was huge, and the way Sam criss-crossed it left Alexa completely disorientated. Sam openly wondered how she had navigated her way around Europe by herself, but she had rarely been by herself and she had a natural affinity with city streets. Perhaps it was the school-like environment that was screwing with her normal sense of direction, because she should not have found it so daunting.

"At least there are no fences," Alexa said, taking Sam's hand.

"No one will even notice if you don't turn up to class," he replied. "As long as you make an appearance at your tutorials and pass your assessments, you'll get through. You don't even have to speak to your lecturers. I've barely spoken to any of mine."

"And that's okay? They don't ask questions? Call you to their office?" asked Alexa fearfully.

"No. You can be as small and anonymous as you want here. Trust me. It's the best part of going to such a big university."

Alexa nodded just as her stomach rumbled, turning her mind to other things. Glancing at her watch, she became uncomfortably aware of the fact that their lunchtime reunion was now less than half an hour away.

"Still nervous?" asked Sam, walking them towards the café.

"I haven't spoken to Ezra or Bianca for like eight months," Alexa replied agitatedly.

"Seriously? Not even Bianca? After all that happened, you just walked away and never said a word to anyone?"

"Finally starting to get why I'm so nervous about this? I couldn't do it. I couldn't face anything associated with that place – especially not them." Alexa hesitated, waiting for Sam's response, but he just stared straight ahead. "I told them I wanted to go back to school," she continued, deciding he needed to understand. "I never wanted to sneak out in the first place, but they promised we'd be back before dinner. Instead, they drank and Bianca drank more and more until I had to carry her back. We got caught and I got beaten up by a crazed teacher while the man I loved stood aside and let it happen."

"I didn't think Mr Knight knew about Ms Carter," snapped Sam, his voice full of anger.

"He didn't," sighed Alexa. "But he would've stood up for me and he certainly would've come the next morning if I hadn't hurt him by betraying his trust. It just wasn't how it was supposed to turn out."

Sam squeezed Alexa's hand, sighing heavily, but he stayed silent until the café was in sight. Alexa could even see Chad and Lizzie sitting inside by the window. "It's only a couple of hours of your life," said Sam. "Then it'll be over – and I'll let you take your revenge on me tonight if it's as bad as you imagined."

Alexa smiled, loving that Sam knew just the right words to make things bearable. It gave her the strength to be the one who walked in first to greet Chad and Lizzie.

"Oh my God, Alexa!" cried Lizzie. "How've you been? How was Europe? When did you get back?"

Lizzie's embrace was so warm and welcoming that it made Alexa question her decision to hide away from everyone. When Lizzie released her, Chad took her place and hugged her just as warmly.

"How's it going?" Chad asked.

"Yeah, okay, I guess. Strange being back. Bizarre that I'm starting uni in a week. I'm a little freaked out after walking around there. Reminds me too much of school – even without the high fences."

"Don't worry about that," said Lizzie. "It's nothing like school. It's so much better. So much more freedom. I love it."

"Yeah, you'll be fine," said Chad with a reassuring smile. "So you spent your millions yet?"

"Oh my God, I can't believe you guys won all that money," gasped Lizzie. "Bianca went crazy. You should've been at some of the parties she threw last semester. I couldn't believe it."

"What about Ezra?" asked Alexa, suddenly realising there was no way she could have kept her secret as she had planned.

"She's still living with her parents, but I know she went on holidays and bought a car and heaps of new clothes. I think they were both pretty upset you never contacted them."

"I just ran from that place and never looked back," Alexa replied, hoping Chad and Lizzie would understand. "I wanted to forget everything about that day."

"You're not alone there," muttered Sam in a soft voice Alexa was not sure the others heard, revealing the reason behind his sudden mood change. Alexa could not believe she had not considered how hard it would be for him to relive that horrible day. It had torn his family apart, finding out his sister was in love with Clinton Marsh.

"So what did you do with all your money?" asked Lizzie chirpily, though her eyes darted warily between Alexa and Sam.

"All of it?" laughed Alexa. "I still have most of it. You think I could've spent eight million dollars in six months?"

"Bianca's spent a lot of hers. She bought this huge penthouse in the city and a few places overseas."

"Well, I bought my apartment and furnished it and I went to Europe. I think that's enough extravagant spending for a while."

"You got a payout from the school for what happened with Mr Marsh and Ms Carter, didn't you?" asked Chad, smirking slightly.

"Yeah, they were pretty keen to settle, and Peter – my lawyer – he drove a hard bargain. It was good. I hadn't been looking forward to testifying."

"I heard that even with the new administration the school lost half its students, especially the boarders," said Chad. "Hopefully, once our lawsuit is finished they'll have to close down."

"Here's hoping," smiled Alexa, turning to Sam, but he was

glaring at Chad.

"What happened to Mel? Did she stay for this year?" asked Lizzie, watching Sam cautiously as he shook his head minutely.

Alexa did not understand. This was not something Sam had to protect her from. She was glad the rest of the G7 were bringing a suit against the school. She would face those things if it meant everyone knew how much they had all suffered at Redgrove, and that it had not just been her.

"No," answered Sam sadly. "The cops got involved after all she admitted about Mr Marsh and Ms Carter, but she ended up retracting most of it. She reported Ms Carter. She never hit her, like Alexa, but it was pretty horrible."

"What about Mr Marsh? She admit they were together?" asked Lizzie.

"No," replied Sam grimly. "Mel said Mr Marsh had been really good to her, supportive, whatever, but that nothing ever happened. I don't know whether to believe her. A couple of former students apparently come forward and said Ms Carter had made their life hell and Mr Marsh helped them out. It's a sick pattern."

"So Mel realised Mr Marsh had been using her?" asked Lizzie, sounding hopeful.

"I wish. No, she thinks the others back her up – that Mr Marsh's a great guy and Ms Carter's the evil one. Doesn't believe Mr Marsh raped Alexa. Thinks Alexa made it all up. I don't feel like know her any more."

No one spoke. It was a difficult topic to come back from. Chad's solution was to order food, but Lizzie wanted to wait until Ezra and Bianca arrived.

"Then we will order entrées," replied Chad, obviously thinking he had solutions to every problem. "You can't object to entrées."

"I know I don't," smiled Alexa, as her stomach rumbled again, making Chad smile more broadly.

The drinks and nibbles managed to slowly revive the mood of the table, but when Ezra and Bianca turned up it became awkward once more. Alexa took Sam's hand under the table, squeezing it anxiously. Sitting across the table from Ezra and Bianca had her heart stammering, wishing this was already over with.

"So, this is awkward," said Lizzie, as the silence dragged on.

"Why don't we order?" said Sam, sitting forward. "I'm starving."

"Then you should've ordered an entrée," replied Chad sarcastically. "It would've helped tide you over – get rid of some of that hungry-angry mood you've been modelling so beautifully for us all today."

The whole table laughed and picked up their menus. Alexa could have kissed Chad for how wonderful he was being. His joviality lightened the mood so much that Alexa found herself talking to Ezra without even thinking about it. "So how have you been?" she asked after they had ordered. "Lizzie said you went overseas."

"Yeah, that was awesome. I went over to America and Canada for most of the summer – well winter. It was freezing, but so beautiful. I took my parents. They've always wanted to go."

"How about uni? You liking it?"

"About a thousand times more than school," laughed Ezra. "Bit stressful at exam time, but I really like my course."

"What are you doing?" asked Alexa, realising she should know.

"Environmental science. It's good."

Alexa was glad the food started to arrive then. Everyone had started talking about their courses, and what they were doing was so impressive. Alexa had been able to get into a fairly generic course and would choose the majors she was interested in. It was a good option and she was happy with it. It just did not sound impressive next to engineering, science, industrial relations and marketing degrees.

"So what've you been doing since school?" asked Ezra tentatively.

"Not much," Alexa replied with a laugh. "I went to Europe at the start of the year and I just got back. So that's all I've been doing."

"Oh yeah, that's all I've been doing, just trotting all over Europe. No agenda. Not a care in the world. Pfft. You're like the master of understatement," laughed Chad. "You visit how many gazillion places and you're just like – oh, yeah, been travelling a bit."

Alexa stuck out her tongue in response. This was turning out to be a really awesome lunch. Then she looked Bianca's way and realised she had not yet spoken directly to her.

"So how've you been, Bianca?" Alexa asked. "You're doing marketing, right? How's that?"

"Oh, yeah, okay. It's all I've been doing," Bianca replied.

If it had been Chad who had said that, they would have been laughing, but the bitterness and sarcasm in Bianca's voice left Alexa cold. "Are you enjoying it?" she stammered, unsure what else to say.

"I'd rather be living your life of leisure," replied Bianca blithely. "My parents are making me do it. So, no, not really."

"What the hell's your problem?" cried Chad before Alexa could reply. "You reckon this is easy for Alexa? Would it be too hard to make a bit of an effort?"

"Oh right, yeah, I forgot. Nothing's easy for Alexa. What's the sob story now? She has all the money she can ever need – no need to earn her keep – why are we feeling sorry for her now?"

"I haven't seen anyone feeling sorry for her. We've been having a conversation, which you've chosen not to join, at least not civilly. You want us to feel sorry for you?" asked Chad aggressively. "Because you have to buy your friends? Because no guy will stay with you when they realise you can't be faithful? Because you're barely capable of walking past a guy without screwing him, but want to go around calling Alexa a slut? You want us to tell you who the rest of us think the real slut is?"

"Chad, that's not fair," cried Alexa.

"I know what she's said behind your back," replied Chad in a softer voice, turning to Alexa with apologetic eyes. "She doesn't dare associate herself with us or Redgrove. Doesn't want anyone to know who she really is, but's happy to denigrate you. You think that's fair?"

Alexa looked at Chad unsure what to say. She and Bianca had never been good friends and doubted what Bianca said behind her back was any more pleasant than what she had said to her face, but still did not think it was right for Chad to publicly attack Bianca. The only reason she did not say anything else was because she felt that much of Chad's anger had to do with the way Bianca had treated him while they had been dating.

"I wasn't asking for sympathy," said Bianca in a shaky voice. "Don't you think I felt bad about what happened? Don't you think I would've changed things if I could? But she left without a word. None of you would tell me where she was so I could contact her and make it up to her. Now we're just supposed to forget everything and be friends again like nothing happened. I'm sorry, but no. I'm sick of just hanging around waiting for you to tell me when to jump. You're ready for an apology so now I'm supposed to drop to my knees and beg, pretend it's all okay."

Alexa could only stare, unsure what she was supposed to say.

"Fine, I'm sorry," sighed Bianca. "Is that what you want to hear? I've said it. Is all forgiven? Are we all friends now?"

"Seriously?" stammered Alexa, unsure which part of Bianca's little speech she was even referring to.

"We are sorry," said Ezra quickly, and much more sincerely. "You have no idea how bad we felt when we heard what happened. I just wish you'd told us why you wanted to get back so urgently."

"I did tell you," cried Alexa, before controlling her anger. "You think I knew that'd happen? I thought it was all over with. Ms Carter hadn't touched me in a year. Maybe she would've tried something before I left, but I wouldn't have been served up to her on a platter."

Silence fell across the table and Alexa could see Bianca trying to speak, but was unable to find the words. Exchanging glances with Ezra, who just shrugged awkwardly, Bianca pushed back from the table. "I have to get going," Bianca said without looking at anyone. "I'll see you guys later."

"I doubt it," muttered Chad under his breath, as Bianca left.

"She doesn't know how to deal with all this," said Ezra softly. "She thought she'd be happy with all the money, but with everything that happened she feels real guilty. I think that's why she spent so much of it, hoping that if it goes away so will her unhappiness."

"She could get rid of her attitude. That might help her," said Chad bitterly.

"We both feel really guilty," continued Ezra, ignoring Chad's comment. "You don't understand how upset Bianca was when she found out. We just thought we'd see you – be able to sort things out, even if was just for you to tell us how much you hated us."

"I don't hate you. Either of you. I just didn't know how to deal with it. I was scared about seeing you guys – scared of how angry I'd be."

"Yeah, we were scared of that too," smiled Ezra. "But we want to be friends again. I hope we can."

"Of course," nodded Alexa. "I'd really like that."

Ezra smiled, and Alexa paid no attention to the looks of surprise Sam and Chad exchanged. They would never understand how much she needed to put these things behind her, and friends was much better than enemies.

Chapter Four

ALEXA WOKE WITH a sense of sadness. This would be her and Sam's last full day together. It was not as though she was dreading being alone; she was almost craving time with just her own thoughts. Nor was she fearing the loss of their relationship. The more time they spent together, the more obvious it was that they no longer wanted to a romantic relationship. Despite that, this day represented the end of something – something Alexa had loved for such a large part of her life – that it was difficult to let go.

"Wakey, wakey. Rise and shine," called Sam happily, waltzing into the room. "It's a big day, so you need to start getting ready."

It took all of Alexa's self-control not to groan. The one thing she had not wanted was a big day, cramming more and more things into fewer and fewer hours. However, she would never let Sam believe she was ungrateful for everything he had done for her, so rolled out of bed and trudged sleepily under the shower.

"I don't want to pester, but you need to hurry," said Sam as soon as she emerged from the bathroom.

"Sam, I love you, but if you try and make me do anything without a coffee, I can promise you it won't be a happy day."

"I don't know when you started drinking coffee, but for the sake of your future happiness, you might want to reduce your reliance on it," he retorted. Alexa glared at him, making him smile broadly. "But for today, you can have whatever you want."

Alexa was granted coffee and toast, but not exactly in a leisurely manner. As soon as she was finished Sam dragged her down to the car and started driving.

"Sam?" she asked tentatively.

"I know how very restrained you're being right now," he said, his lips pulling into a tight smile as though he was trying not to laugh. "But just this once, can you trust me? I want it to be a surprise."

"You're lucky I love you," Alexa replied, her voice almost a moan, making Sam chuckle as he squeezed her hand.

They did not talk much as they drove. Sam seemed content to concentrate on driving, a slight smile on his face, which morphed into an amused grin every time Alexa glanced curiously his way. All she could do was turn her eyes out the window and try to figure out where they were going. It was a fruitless exercise. She had very little experience with days out. When they turned off the main road and started following the signs towards a national park, Alexa figured that had to be their destination. Biting back her concerns, she began to wonder if Sam knew her at all. Hiking had never been her thing.

Her worst fears were realised when Sam parked the car near the start of a track and smilingly told her that they had to walk for a bit. But that was nothing compared to the concern she felt when she saw how much he had packed and now expected them to carry.

"Would you relax," Sam sighed. "I'm not asking you to run a marathon."

"Um, where did all this even come from?" asked Alexa, realising Sam had not prepared this with her and they had barely been apart all week.

"There's not much that can get me up early, but our last day is one thing I was going to make an effort for. I was really worried you were going to wake up and freak out. I rang Maria last night while you were cooking dinner."

"While you were having your nap?"

"Yeah. I can't believe you fell for it," Sam laughed. "Maria said I could come over this morning because she had a picnic blanket and basket. I was going to shop, but I think she may have spent the whole night cooking and filled it herself. She's really amazing. I told her she'd have to meet Gran and Pop when they moved down. She was so excited, I promised to invite her over once we're settled. And you know she was really excited about doing something nice for you."

"Oh, Sam, you're so great. That's such a nice thing to do for Maria. She'll love Gran and Pop."

"Come on, let's get where we're going," said Sam.

Alexa thought she heard him mutter something about not having done all this for Maria, but when he slammed the boot shut with his elbow, he just smiled and nudged her towards the track. They did not walk for very long before Sam stopped and turned towards her, directing her attention to the end of the path. It opened out to the most amazing beach Alexa had ever seen. The sand was bright white and the water was an amazingly clear blue. And there was no one else in sight.

"This is where we're going?" Alexa asked almost disbelievingly.

"You forget how well I know you," replied Sam, rubbing her chin and kissing her gently.

It took less than fifteen minutes for them to set up their little picnic. Maria had also lent them a small pop-up dome tent. Alexa set it up and threw the picnic blanket over its floor, lying their towels out in front of it. When Sam pulled her swimmers out of another bag, Alexa scurried back into the tent to change, annoyed that Sam was not ready when she was. He tried to suggest that she could swim without him, but she was not having that.

Alexa dived straight into the calm, flat water, while Sam waded in more tentatively. "Hurry up," she called back at him.

"Alexa, there aren't enough expletives in the world to describe how cold this water is," Sam replied, taking another hesitant step. Alexa could not resist the temptation. She rushed at him and, despite his shouted warnings, pushed him into the shallow water. "Oh, you are so dead," he cried, running through the water after her.

Laughing and giggling, they splashed around for almost ten minutes before Sam claimed that the movement could no longer stave off the cold. He went back to the tent to lay out lunch as Alexa continued to swim. It was cold, but the swirl of the water over her body and the freedom of the moment was blissful.

"Lunch!"

Alexa looked up to see Sam waving her to the shore. As if on cue, her stomach gave an angry grumble. From the way he smiled, she was sure he heard it too.

The wind picked up as they ate, forcing them to retreat into the tent. "You're freezing, Alexa," said Sam, watching her shiver. "Get out of your swimmers. You'll get sick if you swim again."

Sam did not wait for her to act, stripping her wet clothes off her body. He wrapped a blanket around her, before pulling her close and rubbing her limbs to try and warm her.

"Thank you," said Alexa when she had finally stopped shivering. "This is one of the best days of my life."

"Haha, I'm glad, but you have to admit I don't really have a lot of competition in that area," Sam replied with a smile. "I could've done a lot less and still qualified."

"I guess so," Alexa sighed, rolling on to her back and staring at the roof of the tent.

"Sorry."

"No, it's all right. You're right," she shrugged. "But maybe that's not a bad thing. I don't want to say things can't get worse, but you've helped me realise that they'll probably get better."

"I really think that true," smiled Sam, tucking her hair behind her ear. "It's not going to be all plain sailing – and you'll still face some tough times – just like the rest of us – but I don't think it's going to be anything like what you've been through these last few years."

"And I'll still have you and Ben and Maria to lean on."

"Absolutely – and don't forget Gran and Pop. They'll want to see you too. I'm sure they'll take you on as their surrogate grand-daughter. They practically think of you that way already. It might even help them mend the pain of losing Mel."

Sam turned away. He rarely mentioned his sister – not around her – but Alexa wanted him to be able to talk to her about anything, no matter how hard it was for her to hear.

"What happened? I didn't think she'd stop talking to you guys," Alexa asked tentatively as she sat up next to him.

"She didn't, well not exactly," replied Sam softly, his voice quivering. "Gran and Pop wanted her to promise she'd never see Mr Marsh again. You wouldn't think it was too much to ask, but she refused. When they threatened to throw her out, she left."

"But where'd she go?"

"His apartment. Can you believe it? She's living in that bastard's apartment – where he raped you. Urgh. But I think he used to take her there too. She won't say so, because she was so young, but I think he slept with her. I just can't believe we've lost her to him."

"He wants her there? I can't see that," said Alexa stuck on that thought. "I can't see Clinton actually wanting to settle down. It would make it harder to do what he does."

"Yeah, but you forget how blindly loyal Mel is. She won't see anything she doesn't want to – won't believe anything that doesn't fit with her view of things. She's the perfect girl for him. He could do anything and as long as he says the right things – which he always seems to – she'll stick to him. I lost her, Alexa. I've lost my sister."

Sam started shaking as sobs tore through his body. Alexa shuffled closer and wrapped her arms around his heaving body, wishing she could make this situation better. All she could do was console him – until the blanket fell from her body. Rushing to cover herself, Alexa noticed Sam pulling the zipper to close the tent. He turned to her with desire burning in his eyes, stroking her body tenderly as he laid her down. It was passionate, but there was a sense of finality about the way their hands moved over each other's body, as if they were memorising every inch.

"You're shivering," said Sam as he held her.

The wind was blowing more forcefully now, pushing at the sides of the tent. Just the sound gave Alexa goosebumps. Sam insisted she get dressed, telling her they would have to get going soon anyway.

Sam held her hand as they drove, urging her to close her eyes. She needed little encouragement and was soon asleep, not waking until Sam touched her cheek once they pulled up in front of her apartment.

"Geez, I wish you'd wake up a little more subtly," said Sam, grabbing her as she jerked awake.

"Sorry I slept," Alexa replied groggily, rubbing her eyes.

"I really don't mind that part. It's nice listening to you mumble my name as you sleep."

"I was talking?" she asked, mortified by the revelation, though considered it was better than having a nightmare.

"Only a couple of times. Nothing bad," Sam smiled. "Now hurry up. We need to get dressed up for dinner."

"I don't have any dressed up clothes," Alexa replied, biting her lip.

"I know. Maria brought something over. I hope it fits."

Alexa was intrigued. There, laid out on the bed, was a long blue dress. Sam left her to get dressed and moved into the spare room. It was odd. He never got dressed in there, but she could not worry about it as she slipped the dress over her body. It fit perfectly. Turning in front of the mirror, she was even prepared to say it looked good.

"Wow," said Sam. "You look beautiful."

"I'll be cold," Alexa murmured, hating that it was true.

"Then you should wear a coat."

"But it'll look crap."

"It'll look fine. Trust me. Now, stop worrying and hurry up. The car's here."

"Car?" Sam did not respond, only taking Alexa's hand and leading her downstairs – where a limousine waited for them. "Sam, you didn't have to do all this. It must've cost you a fortune."

"Can you please not worry about that sort of thing for just a few hours. We missed out on our year twelve celebrations and you know I would've taken you and made a big fuss. So this is our celebration."

The limousine drove them to a restaurant in the city. It looked more expensive than the car and Alexa felt very out of place. Despite the slight chill in the air, she slipped off her jacket. Their table looked right out over the harbour.

"Sam, this place is amazing."

"I saw it on TV once and thought it'd be nice to come here. You know, do something grown up and sophisticated."

Alexa laughed with Sam at the idea of them being sophisticated.

The glare of the other patrons only made them laugh more. She was glad she was not the only one who felt ridiculously out of place.

"Would you like some wine?" asked the waiter, who was looking at them as if they were on crack.

"No, thank you," replied Alexa. "Can I just have a coke, please?" Sam smiled as he ordered the same. "What? You know I don't drink."

"I heard a rumour you used to. What happened? You're eighteen now. An adult. Responsible. You could drink if you wanted to."

Alexa shook her head. "I drank a lot after my mother died," she said, pulling her hands out of Sam's grasp. This was one part of her history she was truly ashamed of. "Bethy was in hospital. I remember being so scared I'd lose her – so much it physically hurt. I was only eleven, but it was pretty easy to find grog in most of the foster homes I went to. Don't remember much of that time. Wanted to block it all out and wait for the day Bethy would come home to me."

"So what happened? You had to stop drinking because they sent you to boarding school? There sure wasn't any alcohol there – unless you were holding out on me."

"Haha, no. I stopped before that," Alexa replied, shaking her head sadly. "I kept drinking after Bethy got out of hospital. Even let her drink too. Better than heroin. To me, anyway. So anyway, me, Bethy and one of my foster brothers got real drunk one night. Went out. He decided to steal a car. I didn't object. I wasn't ever looking to stay out of trouble.

"We crashed. Weren't hurt bad – okay enough to run away. But Bethy had a sore leg for about a year after that. It was like a constant reminder of the danger I put her in. Never drank after that. Didn't matter how bad I wanted it. I thought about Bethy being hurt because of me and that was enough to stop me."

"What do you mean her leg was sore for a year?" asked Sam with a horrified expression. "Wasn't she checked out? Taken to a doctor?"

"You're mixing up our childhood with someone else's."

Sam pursed his lips, looking up with concerned eyes. Thankfully the waiter soon returned with their drinks and took their food order.

"To us," said Sam, holding up his coke.

Alexa charged her glass against his, repeating his toast. This was a much better way to end their relationship than with a big fight, but after all Sam had done for her this week, she had to do something in return. "I hope you realise I'm paying for dinner," she said in a tone she hoped he would not argue with.

"I may have actually been counting on you saying that," smiled

Sam guiltily. "Chad and I had a big week last week."

"I thought you said you were getting in each other's way," Alexa replied in a scandalised voice.

"So I was a little liberal with the truth," replied Sam with a guilty grin. "Chad was always going to let me stay if you knocked me back. But you probably saved me a lot of money and hangovers. See, and you think you don't do enough good things for me."

They talked all through their meal, and well after it. When they realised they had been at the table for an hour after finishing their dinner, they felt guilty enough that they ordered more drinks and dessert. An hour after that, Sam looked down at his watch.

"We have to get going?" asked Alexa.

"Soon," Sam smiled. "Didn't think we'd stay this long. I'd planned for us to walk along the harbour after dinner, but this has been perfect."

That was the word for this day. Perfect. It did not change as they slid back into the limousine, or as they slipped out of their clothes and into their pyjamas. It had not even been a conscious decision.

They hopped into the bed and snuggled together under the cold sheets, waiting for warmth to come. When they kissed, it was the kiss of a friend. Sam held Alexa against him, his lips pressing into her hair as he urged her to sleep. It made Alexa glad they had taken this chance. They could finally walk away from their relationship never, having to wonder about what could have been.

***

"You look so happy," smiled Bethany as she and Alexa sat down at a sun-soaked table.

"I'm always happy to see you. It's what makes all the other days liveable," replied Alexa sincerely.

"You shouldn't say things like that."

"Says who, Angel?" retorted Alexa angrily, knowing someone else had put that thought in Bethany's head. "You're the other half of me and I won't let anyone tell me that's not okay. I haven't been whole since the day we were torn apart and I won't be whole again until you're back with me – until there's nothing and no one stopping us from seeing and talking to each other whenever we want."

"I feel that way too," replied Bethany softly, as if ashamed.

"Good," said Alexa firmly, before smirking. "It'd suck if it was just me who was that crazy about you."

Bethany truly smiled this time.

They did not get to spend very long together. It was a busy day, which meant they were timing the visits. When Alexa saw the guards look their way, she knew their time was up, but refused to let them be the ones to tell her she had to go. They would keep hold of even the tiniest fraction of control they could, so they stood and started saying their goodbyes. Holding hands, they walked in opposite directions, only letting go when distance pulled their fingers apart.

Knowing it had been their choice was the only thing that kept the tears at bay as Alexa caught the bus towards Maria's place. The sight of her sorrowful face must have worried Maria, because she bundled her into the apartment and held her on the lounge as she mastered the urge to cry.

"This better not be because the dress I got you didn't fit," said Maria in a semi-serious tone.

Alexa choked on the sob that had been pressing in her throat as a laugh tried to escape her chest, leaving her coughing, laughing and crying in equal measure. "Aww, that hurt," Alexa coughed, holding her throat. "No, the dress was perfect," she smiled. "I'll have to find an occasion to wear it again in the summer. It was such a shame to have to wear a jacket over the top of it, but it was so cold last night."

"How was yesterday?"

Alexa recounted the day, leaving out the more intimate details. She could see Maria was waiting for the part that would leave her upset enough to almost cry in front of her, but when there was nothing, she immediately asked about her visit to Bethany.

"It's a shame they can't take into account the change in her external circumstances and release her early," mused Maria, pulling Alexa into the kitchen. "But I suppose you speak to the girl who was shot and she'd say she never wanted Bethany released."

"I'm the one who should've been punished," muttered Alexa.

"I really hope you don't believe that. You're barely more than a child yourself. It's just that there are always two sides – sometimes more – to every story and it's funny how biased being on one side makes you. I feel as if I know Bethany, you talk about her so much, and I find it very hard to believe she doesn't deserve a second chance sooner rather than later."

"It's hard being away from her," confessed Alexa.

"Of course it is. And it's okay that you miss her," replied Maria soothingly. "I know everyone's telling you to get on with your life, but of course part of you is holding back, waiting for your sister to be released. That's fine too, as long as it's not too big a part. Now, what should we cook today?"

Maria pointed to a couple of different recipes on the kitchen bench. They were cakes. Chocolate ones. It was the best thing about Maria. There was not a single emotion Alexa displayed that Maria said was inappropriate or wrong. She had always let her be angry or sad or frustrated or hopeful or joyous – whatever it was she felt in that moment – though she always guided her towards contentment, stating that it was more sustainable and peaceful than happy.

"Can we start with the simple one?" Alexa asked. "I like cooking with you, but on my own I always go for quick and simple over tasty and gourmet."

"And you think you're not normal," laughed Maria.

They were about to start when Alexa's mobile rang. It was Ben.

"Is it Bethy? Is she okay?" Alexa asked frantically.

"Whoa. I thought you were going to see her today. What's going on?" asked Ben anxiously. "Has something happened?"

"I don't know," Alexa replied, just as mystified by his response. "You called my mobile. I assumed something must be wrong."

"How else am I supposed to contact you?"

"The way you always do – email."

"That was really only while you were overseas," countered Ben in a lighter voice. "I was thinking that now you were back instantaneous communication would be more practical."

"Oh, right. Okay. Um, so you wanted to actually talk to me?" Alexa asked, not really sure what to say.

"I can go one better. I was hoping to see you. I have tonight off. Did you want to come over for dinner?"

"No, I can't. I'm at Maria's."

Alexa bit her lip, not sure what else to say. It seemed Ben did not know either and with a muttered response he quickly said goodbye.

"Alexa, can you tell me why you didn't either invite Ben over here for dinner with us or suggest another night to have dinner with him?"

"I just think he was being polite. He's not going to really want to see me," Alexa answered.

"I've only met Ben twice, but in that very short time I could tell how much he loves you, how much you mean to him and how much he wants to be a very big part of your life," said Maria firmly. "I know you've never had that sort of thing before, but please don't let that destroy this chance to build the family you've always wanted. Call him back, invite him here for dinner and if he can't make it, ask him when he's free because you would love to see him too. And don't even try to tell me that would be a lie. I can see in your eyes how much you want to see him."

Maria smiled, then nodded again. Alexa liked that Maria was so good at giving the easy-to-follow instructions she needed without sounding patronising.

"Hi, Ben," Alexa said as soon as he picked up.

"Hi, Alexa," replied Ben in a cheerful voice.

"Um, yeah, I just wanted to see if maybe you wanted to come to Maria's place for dinner instead, you know, since I can't come to your place. Or, um, we can do something another night if that works better. I don't have much on this week so I can be free when you are. Just whatever works for you," said Alexa, her anxiety making her words to run into each other.

"I might let you and Maria have your own time tonight," replied Ben in a light voice. "But if you're free tomorrow, Penny and I would love to have you over for dinner."

"Yeah, okay," Alexa replied nervously, wondering how much Penny really did love the idea.

"Would you like me to pick you up on my way home from work?"

"No, no. It'll be out of your way. I can get there myself. I'll come from seeing Bethy. It'll work out well."

Logistically, it did work well. It was the one thing Alexa had liked about living with Ben; his house was very conveniently located and had great public transport linkages. Unfortunately, the one thing that had made living with Ben so uncomfortable had not changed either.

The prospect of seeing Penny again made Alexa's stomach churn. Even Bethany was nervous about the encounter. Bethany had still never met Penny, and Alexa had tried to make sure she never said anything negative about her, but the absence of praise was probably telling enough.

"It'll be great," said Bethany encouragingly when it was time for Alexa to leave. "Break it down for me in your next letter."

"Every minute," replied Alexa with a relieved smile.

That was Bethany's signal that she wanted the full story. Perhaps it was getting close enough to her release that she realised she needed to know the truth about how Penny felt about them. Ben had stated aloud that he wanted to be their father. Alexa may have had her doubts about the claim, but he had made it and been a part of their lives. Penny had never once visited Bethany or even asked Alexa how she was doing. Alexa knew Penny's future role in her and Bethany's life might well be determined by the events of this night. If Penny showed an interest in being a part of their lives, Alexa would soften her review of their previous interactions in her letter to Bethany. If not, Alexa believed it might be time for Bethany to find out just how little Ben's wife wanted them in her life, and for them to start preparing for a future without Ben.

"Oh, good, you came," said Penny stiffly as she opened the door. It was not a promising greeting. "Ben's not here at the moment."

"Oh, um, okay," replied Alexa, shuffling awkwardly. Penny did not invite her in and Alexa was not sure she wanted to be alone with her anyway. "I'll, um, come back later."

Walking back towards the train station, Alexa was tempted to call Ben and make up an excuse for not being able to make dinner, but could not be sure Penny would keep quiet about her early arrival. Checking her watch, Alexa wondered if Ben would have arrived by now. He should have, but if he was running late she would be stuck in the same unpleasant situation. On the other hand, if she was late, she could easily claim to have missed a train, so kept trekking in that direction. She made it a block before a car suddenly turned the corner in front of her. Alexa automatically stepped back from the curb.

"You're walking the wrong way," called Ben through the open window. "You change your mind? Don't want to come to dinner?"

The disappointment in Ben's voice pierced Alexa's heart. Worse was the look in his eyes that suspected something closer to the truth, and the anger that burned behind that suspicion.

"No, I – I was halfway there, but realised I didn't bring anything. I didn't want to look rude. I was just going back to the shops near the station – you know, buy some chocolates or something for you and Penny."

"Get in," laughed Ben, reaching over and opening the door. "You're beautiful, you know that," he smiled as she slid into the car. "You don't have to bring anything. I want you to think of my place as a second home. You've still got that key I cut for you last year, so you can come as go as you wish – stay whenever you like."

Alexa could only nod. She could not explain how uncomfortable she felt at his house. If it was just them, it would have been fine, but she had no right to demand that, and since Ben always organised things with Penny, it seemed he did not want that either.

"Look who I found wandering the streets," said Ben cheerfully as they walked into the house, before recounting Alexa's story. Penny smiled cruelly as Ben spoke, but did not contradict him.

When Ben started asking Alexa about her first week in her apartment over dinner, Alexa took the opportunity to let Penny know just how independent she was. As she spoke, Ben's eyes flicked between her and Penny, and she could see the words building in his mouth, just waiting to explode out once she stopped talking. It kept her talking longer than she otherwise would have.

"I'm glad you're settling in," said Ben in a tightly controlled voice. "But I want you to understand that no matter how independent you are – now or in the future – I still want to be a big part of your life and will be there for you whenever you need it. Big or small. Any time. Anywhere. Do you understand that?" The only response Alexa could give was a weak nod. She did not dare to look Penny's way. "Alexa," said Ben softly, drawing her eyes up to his. "You and Bethany are like daughters to me. I didn't get to be there for you both when you needed me most, but I'll be there for you now. I promise."

It was hard not to smile. Alexa was not sure such a promise could be kept, but liked that Ben had made it. However, it did not escape her attention how that promise had subtly changed. Before she went overseas, Ben had always said that he and Penny saw them as their daughters. Apparently now it was only him who felt that way. It made the rest of the meal a very quiet affair.

When Penny gathered the plates in determined silence, not even acknowledging Alexa's thanks, and strode out to the kitchen, Ben stormed after her. Their angry hisses were soft enough that Alexa could not make out the words, but the bitterness could not be disguised. Quickly gathering her things, Alexa popped her head into the kitchen to say goodbye and thanks before scampering to the door.

"You don't have to rush off," said Ben, catching her at the door. He looked bitterly disappointed, but not particularly surprised.

"Yes, I do," Alexa replied softly. She contemplated telling him the truth, before choosing to spare his feelings. "I remembered on the way over that I need to go shopping for textbooks and stuff. Can you believe I didn't even think about needing pens and paper? So I need to get up early tomorrow."

Ben smiled softly and she guessed he saw through her lie, but liked that he did not call her out on it.

"Let me grab my keys. I'll drive you home," said Ben quickly, holding up his finger to keep her still.

"You don't have to," Alexa replied. Just the offer was kind enough.

"I know, but the connections will be terrible on a Sunday night. It'll only take me a minute."

They drove in silence. Alexa would have talked, but Ben seemed to be in his own world. It did not look like a happy place.

"Would you like to come up? Check it out now it has furniture?" Alexa asked when Ben pulled up in front of her apartment block. He had not pulled into a parking space.

"No, I need to get back home."

"Ben, can you not be mad at Penny because of me. Please," begged Alexa, hoping she could undo a little of the damage she had caused. "She doesn't have to like us. I don't want things to be bad between you guys because of me."

"Are you free on Wednesday night?" Ben asked, looking up at her apartment. "I finish work at four. Maybe we can have dinner and I can check your place out then."

"Can we eat down at the beach? I haven't been down there yet – not to eat."

"Anything you want," Ben smiled. "Absolutely anything."

Alexa hoped that meant he agreed with her about Penny. Perhaps it did, because the next day he asked if she wanted to go over for dinner on Tuesday night. Alexa declined, lying that she had arranged to have dinner with Maria. Then she called Maria, hoping she would be free. Maria made her explain the situation before agreeing. It was a deal Alexa did not like to make. She was not used to justifying herself to anyone, but supposed that when she was the one asking for all the favours, she could not refuse to give anything in return. Maria wanted Alexa to tell Ben the truth, but Alexa was sure that would be more damaging. When Ben agreed at the last minute to join her at Maria's place for dinner, it did not take Maria long to come around to Alexa's way of thinking on the issue.

It was clear Ben suspected Alexa had concocted this evening with the sole purpose of avoiding dinner at his house. However, he was determined to try and force her and Penny into a state of mutual acceptance, though he stopped pretending it was not an issue. "Penny's just going to have to accept that you and Bethany are a part of my life," Ben replied curtly when Alexa had dared to express her concern about Penny's reception of her.

"Alexa, I didn't bring any sauce out for dinner. Can you please go to the kitchen and find some," said Maria pointedly.

Ben huffed and crossed his arms as Alexa looked quizzically at Maria, but Maria just flicked her eyes to the kitchen. Alexa left, but stopped by the door out of sight, wanting to hear what was said.

"I appreciate everything you've done for Alexa these past few months, but this has nothing to do with you," said Ben in a voice that did not even come close to being polite. It was so rude Alexa almost stormed back into the room with the intention of asking him to leave.

"There might be others who'd say the same to you," Maria responded, before Alexa could more. "Alexa's not a possession and she's certainly not a pawn in your marriage. What are you doing putting her in the middle of arguments with your wife? Don't you think she's been through enough already?"

"I want to give her and Beth the life I promised them," replied Ben, his voice tightly controlled, though Alexa could not be sure if it was anger or sorrow he was trying to hold at bay.

"But that's clearly not possible. For whatever reason, your wife isn't interested in being a part of their lives," replied Maria in a softer voice, though there was still a commanding tone to it.

"But I want her to be. She's my wife. I want us to be a family."

"Exactly. Right now, it's all about what you want – not Alexa or Bethany. They want you. I don't think they care if your wife wants them or not. You can give them exactly what they want. You risk losing them, especially Alexa, if you continue trying to give them what you want."

The room went silent. Alexa waited a moment to see if anything more would be said before dashing to the kitchen. Rummaging through the cupboards, she pulled out every bottle of sauce she could find to cover the length of her absence. Placing all the sauces in the middle of the table, Alexa smiled innocently at Maria and Ben. Maria appeared at ease, but it took a while for Ben re-join the conversation with any sort of enthusiasm. Even on the drive home Ben remained quieter than usual. It made Alexa worry about how dinner would go the following night. It played on her mind so badly that she called Maria first thing in the morning and begged her to talk her through cooking something really nice.

Alexa was not sure if it was the food or the fact that they were alone that had Ben in a chattier mood as they sat down to eat. "So did you get all the pens you needed?" Ben asked.

"Ha, yeah. Got a computer. Laptop. I can't say I've really enjoyed spending so much money though," Alexa added with a grimace.

"That's the problem with starting anything. The outlay is always the largest at the beginning," replied Ben in an understanding voice. "But now you have it all, most of it should last you right through your degree. Then you'll be working and it won't seem as bad."

"I thought you might tell me not to worry – you know, that I shouldn't care now I have so much."

"I think some of the people we respect the least are those who are changed by money. And to waste money – waste this amazing gift you've been given – would be disgraceful. I'd much rather you be ruthlessly prudent than wasteful."

Alexa smiled happily. She was not sure if Ben was telling the truth or just what he knew she wanted to hear, but if it was the latter, she was glad he knew what it was she wanted to hear.

"However, I'm concerned that you're not doing as well at that as you could be," Ben continued, making Alexa's heart stop. "I thought we were going out tonight. I was planning on buying you dinner. I know you're an independently wealthy woman, but I'd still like to take you out every so often."

"That'd be nice," nodded Alexa, battling the urge to reject Ben's paternal smothering. Taking her to dinner was hardly the worst thing he could want to do. It was just something she could not relate to and feared she did not know how to be the daughter he wanted her to be.

It was a concern that played heavily on Alexa's mind. She wanted friends and a family, and if she had to create her own because her biological family was in tatters, then she would do it. At least then her family would only include people who liked her. However, when Ben again asked her to dinner at his place, Alexa realised that might not be possible. If she wanted Ben in her family then Penny would always be around somewhere, even if only on the periphery.

Chapter Five

ALEXA WAS SURPRISED by how swiftly her first day of university arrived. Her stomach churned horribly all morning. The day was clear, so she decided she would test out the walk, giving herself twice as much time as she needed. Nearing the university, Alexa became terrified she would not be able to find her way to class. Even trying to arrange a place to meet Ezra had her on the verge of a panic attack.

"You know, I honestly forgot how worked up you get about new things," said Ezra as she approached from within the university. "For someone who knows how to survive on the streets, I really wouldn't think going uni would be a struggle."

Alexa smiled meekly. Ezra was right. Even while she had been waiting, she had started to get her bearings, but it did not stop her fears getting the better of her as they walked towards her first class.

"I'm going to have to leave you here," said Ezra, looking at her watch. "I have a lecture on the other side of campus. All you have to do is wait for everyone to come pouring out of the lecture theatre and follow everyone else as they stream in. If it gets to the hour and no one's come out, then the room's probably empty and you can go in." Alexa nodded, but she was sure her face was bone white. "You'll be fine," smiled Ezra. "You're just freaking yourself out. If you survived school, you can survive this. But text me any time."

Unable to physically speak, Alexa simply nodded, grateful Ezra was prepared to put up with her idiosyncrasies with a patient smile.

Doing as Ezra instructed, Alexa jostled into her lecture theatre. There were so many students that Alexa wondered if hers was the most popular course in the university. Taking a seat in the back corner, she made sure she sat away from everyone, fearful of their comments when they realised she was new.

It took about half the lecture, but Alexa eventually realised no one was taking any notice of her. Most people were in groups, but there were others like her who sat by themselves. The lecturer did not ask for any of their names. She did not seem to care in the least where they had come from. Her entire focus was on the structure of the course for the semester and what was expected of them. Even when the lecturer did ask questions, she seemed content to accept responses from those who wanted to answer.

It left Alexa feeling a little more relaxed – until she had to head to her next lecture. The sight of many students from her first lecture making the same trek was reassuring. She even heard a student ask if this was the correct lecture theatre. It made Alexa smile just slightly. If not for her natural shyness of strangers, she might have introduced herself, but there was always something niggling in the back of her mind that kept her from doing such things. When she sat dared to sit near people, Alexa's nerves went into overdrive, but this lecture was just like the last. It might be all right after all. Alexa was just not prepared to believe that until she had sat through every class at least once.

Every day was like the first. Though her heart pounded mercilessly before each lecture, none of Alexa's fears were founded. If anything, Alexa was surprised by how easy university seemed. Enrolled in four subjects, she had just twelve hours of classes a week; although they were spread out over all five weekdays. There were plenty of readings for each class, but moulded by years of routine at Redgrove, Alexa found they were easy to complete and was even a little bit ahead by the end of the first week.

The only thing Alexa had not achieved was conversation. Too much of the chatter she overheard revolved around people's personal lives, background and schooling. The best she managed was a slight smile to a couple of girls who were in most of her lectures and often arrived outside class at the same time as her.

Alexa considered whether she should get a job, hating spending her winnings, but she had purposely selected tutorials that did not clash with visiting hours at the detention centre. When Alexa mapped out class and study time, visiting hours and travel, it was surprising how few hours were left. If she factored in seeing Ben and Maria, there was almost nothing. Forgoing visits to Bethany would have left her with plenty of time for a casual job, but that was one thing Alexa would not compromise on.

The trill of the home phone made Alexa's heart stutter, wondering who it was and if it was bad news. "Hello?" she answered tentatively.

"Um, hi, is that Alexa?"

"Yeah, hey, Bianca. How you doing?" asked Alexa, relief flooding her body at the sound of the familiar voice.

"Okay. I hope you don't mind that Ezra gave me your number."

"No, no, that's fine," replied Alexa, guessing Bianca would not call just to start a fight.

"How was your first week?"

"Not bad. Nothing like school, so that was good," Alexa replied, hoping the answer would not irritate Bianca.

"Yeah, I know what you mean. Anyway, um, look the, um, reason I called – I – last week – I just wanted to say sorry. It —"

"Listen, we've both made mistakes. Why don't we call it even? I know you never meant for me to get hurt. I want to be friends again." Alexa frowned, but was fairly certain friends meant the same thing to Bianca as it did to her – not enemies.

"Well, I'm having a back to uni party tomorrow night. Do you want to come?" asked Bianca hesitantly.

"Yeah, that sounds great. I told Ben I might see him tomorrow, but, no, I'll come."

"Good. I'll send you the email with all the details. Lizzie and Ezra are coming as well. I have a bit to organise so I'll see you tomorrow."

That call topped off Alexa's week. It gave her the courage to hope that her university career presented an opportunity to achieve where she had only ever scrapped through.

Feeling light-hearted, Alexa went out onto the balcony. Ben had stopped asking her to come over to his house and said he would drop by after work. Sitting on the tiled floor, Alexa peered through the salt-crusted glass to try and see his car approaching. It was dusk and the cars were hard to distinguish, but she liked to wait; she liked that she had someone to wait for.

Ever since she found out Ben wanted to foster her and Bethany when she was just five, Alexa had not been able to stop wondering what her life would have been like if he had taken on the role of their father. Sometimes that idea scared her so much she became irrationally hateful of him. Had he been around all those years, he was sure to have hurt them. It made Alexa wonder what Ben would do now he was trying to be their father, and what would ultimately banish him from their lives. Shaking her head, Alexa forced herself to stop thinking about such things. She did not want to hate Ben for wrongs he had never committed.

As Alexa scanned the landscape below, a young girl on the swings in the park next door caught her eye. She could not have been more than fifteen and looked so very sad as she swayed in the wind. Alexa wondered if she had looked that sad to the world and if there was anybody who cared for this girl. If someone had cared for her at an earlier age so many bad things might not have happened. However, as she contemplated going down to the girl, Ben's car pulled up.

"Hey, how're you going?" asked Ben brightly as soon as Alexa opened the door, pulling her into a tight hug before she could reply. Alexa let him hold her until fear overwhelmed the comfort of his embrace, but from the way he smiled, he did not seem to notice.

"I'm good," Alexa replied, walking towards the kitchen. "Bianca called today. Invited me to a party tomorrow night."

"So I dinner's out then?"

"Maybe, depends on what time it starts. Sorry, but I have to try and make things better." Ben scowled, so she quickly changed that subject. "How was work?"

"Ah, you know," he sighed, as if deciding what to say. "It's tough work catching all the crims."

"Would you like something to eat? I have left-over dinner," Alexa said, pointing to the fridge. Knowing Ben might be over, she had plated his up, but also had leftovers from other meals, finding it much easier to cook a large amount and eat the leftovers for lunch or dinner. It also saved money, something she liked very much.

"That'd be great. I think Penny was going out tonight."

"How's Penny?" asked Alexa, trying to sound friendly, determined she and Bethany would not be the reason Ben's marriage failed.

"Oh, um … all right, I guess," replied Ben evasively.

"You guess? What's that mean?" Alexa asked, her heart sinking.

"It means that every marriage has its ups and downs and right now we're a little down."

"Because of me?"

Ben smiled as he joined Alexa in the kitchen. He put his arms around her and held her tight, but it did not escape Alexa's notice that he would not look at her as he replied. "Not every bad thing that happens is because of you. Every marriage has rough patches. We'll be fine. We just need time to get some perspective," he sighed, and Alexa was not sure even he believed what he was saying.

***

Wind swept through Alexa's cold, salty hair as she walked home from her morning swim. She loved living so close to the beach and even in winter was determined to make the most of her location. It was bound to make her sick at some point, allowing her body to get so cold, but right now she just felt alive.

As she neared her apartment block, Alexa noticed a girl sitting sullenly on the swings in the park next door. She wondered if it was the same sad-looking girl she had seen the night before and detoured via the park. Alexa smiled at the girl. She did not smile back, which made Alexa grin broadly. She would not have smiled at a stranger either. Alexa was about to continue up to her apartment when she caught a glimpse of the girl's left arm. Just visible below her jumper was a cut Alexa instantly recognised.

"How you doing?" asked Alexa, backtracking to the vacant swing. She had not spoken to anyone at university, but felt compelled beyond all reason to get to know this girl, as though she was someone she already cared deeply for.

"Okay," the girl replied hesitantly. She was small and slim with long, silky blond hair and a very young face. She did not look up, but Alexa could see the girl watching her from the corner of her eyes. It was as if Alexa was looking into a mirror of her past, so tried to think of how she would have reached out to her younger self.

"I just moved in next door a few weeks ago, unit nine. My name's Alexa. What's yours?"

"Charlotte."

Alexa smiled. She would not have answered that question. "Hey, Charlotte. You lived here long?"

"I don't," snarled Charlotte.

"Oh, how come you play on the equipment? You live nearby?" stuttered Alexa.

"Why? You think it belongs to the rich kids in there?" Charlotte asked bitterly, jabbing her thumb at Alexa's apartment block.

"Hell no. I just thought it'd be good to know a neighbour. Barely seen any kids in this apartment block. It's the most redundant play equipment ever."

"I don't come to play. I just come to sit on the swings," muttered Charlotte, clearly unimpressed by the conversation.

"Yeah, swings have that therapeutic air about them, don't they?"

"S'pose."

Charlotte was clearly uncomfortable, but Alexa believed it was little more than a front. She had never been pleasant to inquisitive strangers either, but had always hoped they would see through the façade and give a damn.

"I should go," said Charlotte, hopping off the swing.

"You have somewhere to be? I mean, if you don't have anything else to do, you could always come up to my place. Hang out," offered Alexa, her heart thrumming with the fear of rejection.

"Why would I want to do that?" asked Charlotte harshly.

"I don't know – something to do besides slicing your arm."

Charlotte's face turned white. Alexa kept hers blank, not ready to admit her own history in that area. Looking down at her arm, Charlotte's face became fierce. "What the hell do you care what I do to my arm?" cried Charlotte, her voice shaking.

"I don't, to be perfectly honest," Alexa lied. She cared much more than was reasonable. "I don't know you, but I know you wouldn't do it if you were happy, so I thought I'd offer you help – or a place to go when you don't want to be wherever it is you hate. If you don't want it, I don't give a shit. I have my own life to contend with."

"If you don't care then why'd you say anything?" spat Charlotte.

It was hard for Alexa not to smile. She had never had such a sense of arguing with herself before, and had to remind herself Charlotte would think she had escaped from an asylum if she told her the truth.

"Look, my offer stands," replied Alexa as casually as possible. "If you want to come up, maybe get away from whatever's troubling you for an hour or so, that's fine with me. You can talk about it or you can keep your mouth shut, doesn't worry me. Unit nine."

As Charlotte sat back down on the swing in a state of confused shock, Alexa walked upstairs to her apartment and straight under a hot shower. She thought Charlotte was trusting and curious enough to take up her offer at some stage, but was sure it would take a few more chance encounters. The buzz of the intercom as she stepped out of the bathroom was more trusting than she believed possible.

"Um, hey," smiled Alexa as she opened the front door and finished dressing at the same time. "Sorry, just got out of the shower. Come in."

The nonchalant scowl on Charlotte's face was a look Alexa knew well. She had always tried to make the world believe everything she did was on her terms, even when she was being forced into it. It made her wonder if Charlotte had felt as compelled to come up here as she had been to speak to her.

"Wow," said Charlotte, walking into the lounge room. "You must be mega rich. Do you live here by yourself?"

"Yeah, I went to boarding school and shared a room with four other girls for six years. Thought time by myself was sorely needed."

"So did your parents buy this apartment for you?"

Alexa could hear contempt in Charlotte's voice at the thought of someone having so much money and such an easy life. It stung more than it should have. "Actually, my parents are dead. I went to boarding school on a scholarship and spent the holidays in foster homes," replied Alexa shortly, mixing truth with fiction. "I bought this place with the inheritance I got when I turned eighteen."

"Oh, but they still must've been rich before they died," muttered Charlotte, as though trying to backtrack while maintaining her stance.

"I don't remember," replied Alexa flatly. Charlotte walked silently around the apartment while Alexa fixed them something to eat. "You live nearby?" asked Alexa, setting the food on the dining room table.

"Yeah, couple of blocks away. Nothing like this, though. We live in housing commission."

"It's the first time I've lived in anything like this. Foster homes, remember," said Alexa. She might not be up to telling Charlotte her life story during their first meeting, but she needed her to know she understood that world – her world – better than this one. "You don't like rich people, do you?"

"They think they're better. I hate going to school around here. All the other kids get whatever they want and look down on you because you're not rich. And that's the little bit poor kids, not even the mega rich kids."

"So you wish you were rich?" asked Alexa, fishing for clues.

"I don't give a shit. Shouldn't matter how much money you have. Should be nice anyway."

Alexa could tell money was a touchy subject, but was not sure it was the reason Charlotte took to her arms in frustration. It was too simplistic – and Alexa knew the simple explanations were the ones offered up to avoid explaining the truth most people did not want to hear anyway.

"Do you have any brothers and sisters?" asked Alexa, changing the subject away from money. It was a touchy subject for her too.

"Both, well, half-brother and half-sister. My dad and step-mother refer to me as their half-sister, so I guess that's all I am. What about you?" asked Charlotte quickly.

"I have a little sister. Bethany."

"Where is she? Why doesn't she live with you?"

Alexa felt she had lied enough. If they were going to get to know each other, she would have to give something of herself, and Bethany was not someone she could lie about. If anyone could not accept Bethany, they could not be in her life – even her younger self.

"She's in gaol," answered Alexa in a soft, steady voice, not quite meeting Charlotte's eyes.

"Why?"

"She was a heroin addict and did some bad things while she was on drugs."

Silence fell between them as Charlotte picked warily at the food.

Alexa watched her carefully, trying to glean what she could from her body language.

"So what year are you in at school?" asked Alexa, reinitiating the conversation as she cleared away their dishes.

"Year eight."

"So you're fourteen?"

"Just turned thirteen this month. I'm one of the youngest in the grade," answered Charlotte, shifting uncomfortably.

"You look it," nodded Alexa, with a casual shrug of her shoulders.

"So do you. Surprised you owned this. Didn't think you were much older than me."

"I'm not. Still only eighteen. I was one of the oldest in the grade," added Alexa with a smile.

"I guess. Anyway, I should go," said Charlotte, suddenly pushing away from the table. "Um, thanks for the food."

"No worries," nodded Alexa, in a nonchalant voice. Charlotte had stayed longer than she expected and making her stay against her will was not part of the plan. "But don't forget you can come back anytime."

"Yeah, maybe," replied Charlotte tentatively. "Bye."

Alexa wondered if she would see Charlotte again. Charlotte seemed to distrust people almost as much as she did, so guessed she would not be back anytime soon.

With Charlotte's departure, Alexa rushed to see Bethany. She was not late enough that she would miss visiting, but still hated not being one of the first through the doors. They talked about her first week at university, although Bethany already knew most of it. Between visits, they always wrote to each other, including their more personal thoughts and feeling they rarely mentioned in their face-to-face visits. There was just no point starting those kinds of conversations only to be pulled apart halfway through.

However, over the last few months, Alexa felt as though there had been a change in the nature of their correspondence. Bethany's letters were that bit too rosy to pass off as true and Alexa suspected Bethany was confiding in Ben; something she was not completely at ease with. As much as Alexa liked Ben, she thought it unwise to rely on him. He had no real ties to them and could leave whenever he wanted. Given the troubles in his marriage, Alexa thought that day was rapidly closing in, but it was not something she could convince Bethany of. After detailing the truth of the situation regarding Penny, Alexa had been sure Bethany would agree they had to start pulling back from Ben's life and give him the chance to save his marriage. Bethany suggested the exact opposite and even went as far as hinting that Ben would choose them over his wife, something Alexa refused to believe.

Sensing this topic was something that could ruin the mood of the visit, Alexa decided to tell Bethany about Charlotte. There was not much to tell, but she thought Bethany would be happy with the effort she was making, not only to be social, but to help someone other than her. However, Bethany just listened with passive interest, until Alexa realised how hard it would be for her to hear to such a story while stuck in gaol.

"I thought you might be here," said Ben, appearing at their table before Alexa could reassure Bethany that no young girl in need would ever be more important than her. "How's it going?"

"Okay," said Bethany, her face brightening. "Lex's found herself a new pet project."

"She's not a pet project," protested Alexa, wondering if this was Bethany's way of dispersing her pain.

"I don't think you could convince anyone else of that," sneered Bethany playfully.

"Yeah, well, you've been getting into fights," Alexa retaliated, annoyed at the impression Bethany was going to give Ben.

"What? How do you know that?"

"I can tell when you have bruises and you try to cover them up," replied Alexa simply.

"Okay, okay," said Ben, smiling slightly as Bethany stuck out her tongue and Alexa returned the gesture. "Do you have to get going soon?" he asked Alexa.

"Yeah," replied Alexa, smiling distractedly. They had moved to finger gestures. "It takes me forever by public transport."

"Okay, well, I won't be long. Why don't you wait in the car for me. I just want to chat to Beth alone for a minute."

Alexa looked over at Bethany for her consent. Glad they had at least ended the visit on a friendly note, Alexa moved around the table to hug Bethany.

"See you soon, Lex," said Bethany softly.

"Before you know it, Angel," Alexa replied, stepping away, but she had gone less than a step before Bethany's hand grasped hers.

"Hey, wait a minute," said Bethany, pulling her back into a seat. "I just remembered Sam told me you were having issues about him calling you Lex and that you remembered that I wanted to call you Lexus. I thought you'd forgotten that."

"You remember Beth naming you?" asked Ben in a shocked voice.

Alexa was thrown by their phrasing. Naming. It was what she had thought, but surely they meant re-naming. "I remember I helped name Bethany when she was born," said Alexa, measuring every word so as not to confuse herself again. "I wanted to call her Angel, but I don't know, I keep thinking Becky, but maybe that's what Mum wanted and we settled on Bethany."

"And what about Lexus?" asked Ben cautiously.

Alexa noticed the wary looks he and Bethany were sharing, as if they feared her reaction, and she could not understand why. "Bethy's favourite car was a Lexus," Alexa replied carefully. One reckless word and they would think she was losing her mind. "I guess because my name was Alexa she wanted to change it to Lexus. I could've killed her when she wanted to name me after a car. At least she did a better job with Tracey as my middle name."

Ben and Bethany exchanged curious looks. Alexa waited for some explanation, but they just continued to stare at her. Bethany turned to Ben, her eyes imploring, but Ben shook his head. That look, Alexa understood.

Ever since Ben had told Bethany about how he had come into their lives, Bethany had been on his back to tell her as well. Alexa was not convinced. What she remembered of her childhood was more than enough. To add to it with several more years that, as far as she was concerned, she had forgotten for a reason, was not on the top of her to do list. If it was a happy story, Bethany would have just told her.

"Listen, Alexa, I just want to chat to Beth for a bit," Ben said warily.

Annoyed at the way they were both acting, Alexa was happy for the excuse to leave. She could confront Ben on the drive home.

It took half an hour for Ben to emerge. He had a stern, worried look on his face, but tried to wipe it clean as he approached the car.

"All right, now let's move on to you. Who's this pet project and why?" he asked as he started the car.

Alexa felt like Ben had been given orders to interrogate her by Bethany, but she was not going to give any answers without getting some first. "You tell me about Bethy. Is she in trouble?" she replied combatively, but Ben looked as though he had expected this response.

"She's a tough kid and isn't afraid to stand her ground," he replied. "It's caused her a few problems, but I've told her to pull her head in. She'll be up for parole in under six months so she needs to concentrate on behaving."

"She tells you all the bad stuff, doesn't she? She won't tell me what it's really like."

"Did you ever tell her how bad it really was for you at all your foster homes or at school?" countered Ben. "It's a tough life and she's making the most of it, but we all know it's not a nice place to be." Alexa nodded solemnly. "Now, about your project."

Alexa told Ben about Charlotte as they drove. He, like Bethany apparently, thought she was trying to avoid her own problems by focusing on those of this strange girl, but when Alexa confessed in frustration that Charlotte was unlikely to even return Ben dropped the topic. Alexa knew they were just trying to help, but hated that everything she did seemed to be wrong in everyone else's eyes.

"You want to stay for dinner?" asked Alexa, as they pulled up in front of her apartment block.

"I thought you had a party to go to," replied Ben apprehensively.

"Doesn't start til ten. Not sure I'm going to stay awake til then. Part of me would prefer to just go to sleep, but I need to make things right with Bianca. Was only going to make something simple, so if you don't need gourmet I'm happy for you to stay."

"Sounds good. I'll just give Penny a call and tell her where I am."

"If you need to go home that's okay. I don't want to cause trouble," said Alexa quickly, wishing she could take back her invitation.

"It's fine. Just give me a minute. I'll meet you up there."

Watching from the balcony, Alexa could see Ben and Penny were arguing. If Ben had wanted to go home he would have, but Alexa still felt guilty. Ben's marriage had been strained before she and Bethany came back into his life, but their presence had made the situation much worse. Between Ben's work and the time he devoted to them, Alexa could not blame Penny for feeling neglected. More than once, Alexa had suggested he should spend less time with them, but he always dismissed her with a wave. This time, he dismissed her with an angry growl and stormed into the bathroom. When he emerged, he was rubbing his face with wet hands.

"Sorry," said Alexa meekly. "Everything okay?"

"I'm thinking about moving out," Ben huffed as he plopped down at the kitchen bench. "It's really not working. All we ever do is fight."

"I have a spare room," said Alexa, feeling recklessly hopeful.

Ben smiled weakly before shaking his head. "I saw a place to rent nearby. Thought it was close, without being too close. I get the feeling you wouldn't do too well with a parental figure around all the time."

Alexa's heart deflated. She was independent because she had to be, but often craved the idea of having parents. Life with the Whites had been so peaceful and enjoyable, because it was the only time she got to pretend to be a carefree child. Burying those desires, Alexa told herself that life with Ben would be nothing that. She had the feeling Ben was a man who was used to being taken care of by a woman, and she did not have the strength to maintain that dynamic.

"I know this probably seems really selfish," said Alexa, deciding to change the subject. "But I was hoping you'd teach me to drive and help me buy a car. It's killing me spending so much time getting to the detention centre. Miss one bus and it takes twice as long."

Ben smiled genuinely, moving into the kitchen and patting Alexa's shoulder. "I'll definitely help you buy a car. We'll see about the lessons. A professional may be better. Teaching people you know to drive is one of the best ways to never speak to them again," he laughed.

"I'm not that bad," Alexa replied softly, offended by his comment, though from his laughing manner she was sure she should not be.

"Oh, you can be, but we'll give it a go."

Hiding her sigh, Alexa started dinner. Ben offered his assistance, but she refused. She could not figure out which parts of her life he wanted to be around for. Living and driving, definitely not; cooking, perhaps. Maybe just the good parts – nothing too hard. The problem was, Alexa knew she was more bad parts than good. It only reinforced her fears that Ben would not hang around. Once Bethany was released he might think his job was done.

"Sure you've got it all under control?" asked Ben again.

Alexa nodded, not trusting her voice right then. Ben smiled and walked out onto the balcony. He leaned against the railing and started smoking. It was not a habit Alexa liked, but Ben had always been very conscious of not smoking near her. Walking to the fridge, Alexa pulled out a beer. She always had some around for him, but never enjoyed watching him drink it. If she gave it to him now, he would drink it on the balcony. Ben gratefully accepted the beer, downing it in a few minutes. When dinner was still not ready, he grabbed another and walked back out to the balcony to smoke. Alexa turned her back, not daring to watch. She had not told anyone – not even Bethany – how uncomfortable Ben's habits made her. She might have doubted Ben would be around for long, but she wanted him to stay for as long as possible.

As they sat down to eat, Alexa could smell the beer and tobacco on Ben's breath. She had to control the shiver in her body, but he did not appear to notice her discomfort. They chatted about the week. Ben seemed happy about her progress at university, though he laughingly dismissed the notion that she had any reason to be nervous. It made her apprehensive to tell him more. Whatever emotions she felt were never quite right.

"How you getting into the city?" asked Ben as she cleaned up.

"Bus, I guess. Suppose I should get ready."

"If you really don't want to go …" said Ben tentatively.

"It's fine," replied Alexa, stalking to her room. She knew Ben did not understand her determination to go. He thought Bianca was the one who needed to make the effort. Alexa just wanted a settled life where everything was not a constant battle.

Walking to her closet to find something suitable, Alexa could not stop the wave of despair that flooded her body. It was useless. No matter how many things went right, there were still too many things that continued to go stupidly wrong. Now this.

"Alexa?" called Ben tentatively from the other side of the door. Alexa did not respond. The sound of Ben's voice only reinforced how ridiculous this situation was, and forced tears to well in her eyes. Ben knocked again before walking slowly into the room to see her curled up in a ball on her bed. "Alexa? You okay?"

"I don't have anything to wear," she replied softly, trying to keep herself from sobbing.

"Ah, the eternal female problem – a cupboard full of clothes and nothing to wear," Ben laughed, walking to her wardrobe. "This it?"

Alexa nodded and buried her head back into the ball of her body as Ben continued to open drawers and doors. There was silence for a long time. She felt a light touch on her shoulder right before he spoke. "Why don't you go have a shower and I'll find you something," he said, gently pushing her off the bed.

Alexa complied, but mainly to escape the lecture she knew was coming. Perhaps Ben would use this as a reason why she should not go to Bianca's party, or maybe yell at her for not being capable of living independently. Standing under the shower with her head against the wall, Alexa felt like crying, but only water fell down her cheeks. She was so empty, not even tears remained.

Trudging unhappily out of the bathroom, Alexa was not cheered by the sight of Ben sitting calmly on the lounge, and scurried quickly to her bedroom. This day was too long already. Maybe she would just go to bed. However, the sight of two outfits laid out on her bed made her heart instantly swell. It was just jeans and t-shirt combinations, but it was more than she would have been able to assemble.

Mixing the two outfits, Alexa stood in front of the mirror in a pair of blue jeans, black boots and a simple, black top. For a jacket, she wore one of her only two jackets that were also laid out on the bed.

"Looking good," smiled Ben when she emerged nervously from her room. "You want a lift?"

Alexa nodded, grateful that was all he said. She even let him wrap his arm around her shoulders as they walked down to the car.

"We're early," groaned Alexa, when Ben pulled up in front of the club.

"Only just," said Ben, pointing at the clock. It was nine-fifty. "You'll be right. Just mingle a bit. I thought you were enjoying uni."

"Can't we drive around the block a few times?"

"Look, Alexa, if you don't want to go —"

"No, I do, I just don't want to be the first one there. Please."

Ben sighed and pulled out into the traffic, searching for a legitimate parking spot. It took more than ten minutes, but Alexa was no less nervous and no more prepared to head to the party. "Let's just go somewhere for a drink first."

"Alexa," sighed Ben.

"Just one drink. You did make the effort of finding a parking spot, after all."

Ben smiled and rolled his eyes. He directed Alexa towards a café he said he used to frequent when he worked in the area. She was tempted to ask about those days and see if they coincided with the years Bethany had inhabited these streets, but she did not need to know about more near misses.

"I got you a tea. Didn't think coffee would be all that beneficial in calming your nerves," said Ben, sitting down with their drinks.

"I'm sorry. I just didn't want to feel awkward," replied Alexa, needlessly stirring her tea.

"That's one feeling you're going to have to get used to. There's barely a person in this world who doesn't get nervous walking into a room full of strangers. Hell, I do."

"Really?" asked Alexa brightly.

"Yes, really," smiled Ben. "You're not that odd. I know you feel different, but I think you'll start to find there are many people who didn't have a conventional upbringing."

"I just find having to tell people that I'm an orphan can be a real conversation stopper or leads to questions I don't want to answer."

"You don't have to tell people your life story and, if they don't really matter, just lie if it makes you feel better. Tell them I'm your father and your mother is – I don't know – Cindy Crawford."

"Who's Cindy Crawford?" asked Alexa perplexed.

"Supermodel," replied Ben with a slight smile.

"I don't think anyone will believe that," chuckled Alexa.

"No, but it means I got to sleep with Cindy Crawford and I'm fine with a lie like that."

"I think I'm finding out way more than I ever needed to know about you."

Ben laughed and took a sip of his coffee. Alexa watched him, trying to work out their relationship. Just hours before the sight of him drinking and smoking had scared her almost to the point of irrationality. He often frustrated her when they talked, so much so she found it hard to believe they really liked each other, and yet he was here, smiling and trying to make her feel better. It made Alexa wish there was some kind of handbook that explained how to be a daughter and what it was parents did.

"Come on, let's get you to this party."

If Ben had left Alexa to make her own way, she was sure she would have been tempted to just catch a bus back home, but Ben walked her right to the door of the club.

"Go in there and have a great time. The music'll be so loud you won't be having conversations anyway."

"I don't know anyone."

"Then get to know them. You don't know anyone before you've met them."

Ben leaned down and hugged Alexa, kissing the side of the head. Alexa heard sniggers from those close by. There may have been a lot she did not know about the world, but she knew most eighteen-year-olds were not being escorted to clubs by their fathers.

"Go on," said Ben, pushing her towards the entrance, looking embarrassed.

Alexa walked in and stopped. Knowing Bianca hired out the club for her personal use, Alexa assumed it would be half-full – an intimate gathering of friends – but the place was packed and Alexa did not recognise a single person. She tried to calm herself with the idea that everyone was as overwhelmed and nervous as herself, but they sure did not look it.

"Alexa," cried a familiar voice. Alexa turned, but was grabbed from the other side and spun into the arms of Lizzie. "I'm so glad you came. Ezra's over there."

"Great," Alexa yelled back, trying to be heard over the music as they passed under a speaker.

When they slid into seats with Ezra, Alexa started to relax a little. It was nice to be with people she knew, but she was still not sure this was a way she would happily choose to pass her time.

"How's it going?" asked Ezra.

"Okay. Does Bianca really know all these people?" Alexa asked.

"Surprisingly, yes," nodded Ezra. "I think she's dated half of them as well," she added with a sly smile. "Though she's settled on this one guy for the last four weeks. That's a record for her at the moment. She's not very big on commitment."

"So what happens at these parties?" asked Alexa, desperate not to feel more ignorant than she already did.

"We eat, drink and be merry," smiled Lizzie, holding up a glass and pointing to the platters of food on the table.

Having already eaten, Alexa did not touch the food. She grabbed a soft drink, but was not inclined to drink copious amounts of sugar. Perhaps if she was drinking alcohol like everyone else she would not have been so concerned about what she was consuming.

"Come on, let's dance," said Lizzie when she noticed Alexa looking down at her watch. She had been at the club less than an hour.

Dancing was fun, the music pulsing through Alexa's body. A few guys moved closer until they were dancing next to them, but Lizzie and Alexa ignored them. When thirst and hunger drew them back to the table, Alexa saw Bianca for the first time. She was seated in the booth near theirs. Lizzie slid into the seat at their table. Alexa moved over to Bianca's table and stood at the end, flashing what she hoped was her friendliest smile.

"Hi," she waved, not sure what else to say. "Great party."

"Yeah, thanks. Looks like you were having fun tearing up the dance floor," replied Bianca light-heartedly. Alexa nodded and smiled, again lost for words. "Certainly getting all the guys' attention."

"I didn't notice," Alexa replied truthfully.

"Still oblivious to guys who're hung up on you, huh?" smiled Bianca mockingly.

"No one's hung up on me. Besides, I'm quite happy being single," added Alexa quickly to hide her annoyance.

"Well, sometimes having a guy around can be fun as well. Oh, I should introduce you to Mathew, my boyfriend."

"Hi," muttered Mathew in a disinterested voice, turning from his conversation at Bianca's poke.

"Hey," replied Alexa, unsure what else she should say, but was spared the trouble when he went straight back to his conversation. "I think I'm going to dance a bit more. You want to come?"

"Nah, I'm right. Thanks," smiled Bianca.

Alexa turned back to her table, only to see that Ezra and Lizzie had both gone. Walking to the bar to grab a drink, Alexa looked out on the dance floor for them, but did not see them anywhere. Swaying slightly so she did not look like a lost idiot, Alexa was surprised when a girl dancing in a group near her turned to open up their circle. She looked vaguely familiar and Alexa wondered if she was in some of her classes. She was about to talk to her when a guy suddenly moved in front of her, shunting her away from the other girls.

"My name's Damien," he said with alcoholic breath, wrapping his arm around her shoulder. Alexa pulled back quickly. "What's wrong?"

"Nothing. I'm just not easily taken by drunken men."

"I'm not drunk," Damien slurred. "Been trying to talk to you all night. I think you're real pretty."

"I'm not sure that's a compliment," replied Alexa. "You're so drunk you'd find any man attractive."

"Man? You're not a man," replied Damien, staring intently at her chest.

"I'm glad you can still be that observant," retorted Alexa, unconsciously folding her arms.

"Hey – I seen you when I was sober. You were pretty then, too."

"Yeah, but now you're drunk so you've missed your chance."

"So I have a chance if I'm sober."

"I didn't say that."

Alexa could not help but smile. Damien was attractive and it made her feel good that he had paid her so much attention, even if she did think he was too drunk to remember her once he sobered up.

"Well, wait," said Damien, putting down his full glass of beer. "I'm not that drunk. Give me an hour and I'll be sober."

"Who said you had that long?" laughed Alexa, fully expecting Damien to lose interest within the next five minutes.

"Come on. You won't regret it, I promise. One hour."

"Fine, but we keep dancing until then and you keep your hands to yourself."

Damien pulled Alexa to the dance floor and, disregarding her request, tried to pull their bodies tight. When he left for the bathroom, Alexa decided it was too much. She ducked back to the table to collect her belongings and headed for the door, but Damien must have seen her. He was at the door waiting for her.

Chapter Six

"SO WHERE TO now?" asked Damien, following Alexa out of the club.

Alexa looked at her watch. It was two-twenty. All she wanted was to go home to bed, but she was not going to say that to Damien. "Somewhere where there're plenty of people," she replied firmly.

"Wow, you really don't trust me, do you?"

"I don't know you. You could be any sort of unsavoury character."

"That's something I haven't been called before," said Damien, appearing taken aback. "What exactly do you think I want from you?"

"What does every guy want from a girl?" replied Alexa.

"Well, yeah, I can't say it hasn't crossed my mind, but for tonight I'm quite happy just to talk to you."

"Good. Then you won't mind doing it where other people can bear witness."

Damien smiled and shook his head. "You're a strange girl."

Fifteen minutes later they stumbled across a McDonalds. Alexa ordered a coffee, while Damien set himself up with a meal.

"So you regretting coming with me yet?" asked Damien.

"I'm reserving my judgement," smiled Alexa.

"You're a tough nut to crack, you know that?"

"Who said I wanted to be cracked?"

Alexa was enjoying their banter and had to admit Damien was cute, perhaps even nice, but she did not want a relationship. Friendly conversation was one thing. Opening up and trusting someone was something else entirely, and it was clear Damien wanted more than friendship.

"So how do you know Bianca?" asked Alexa, making small-talk.

"Oh, you don't really have to know Bianca to go to her parties. She has lectures with one of my mates, who she dated for a total of three days, but that's how we got invited. And you don't pass up an invite. There aren't many parties where you get everything paid for."

"Yeah, it must cost her a fortune. I'm surprised she does it."

"Well, she can certainly afford it. I heard she won like ten million dollars or something with a couple of people from school. I wouldn't mind meeting the others. How do you know her?"

Alexa felt sick. She could not believe how reckless she had been with such simple conversation. She did not want to be one of the 'other winners' and she certainly did not want Damien finding out about her past through rumours and news reports. Too many of the events of the past three years had been reported in the media. Though her name had been suppressed, Redgrove, Clinton, Ms Carter and Leo, had all been named and Alexa did not want anyone piecing her life together based on that information alone.

Remembering what Ben had said, Alexa quickly formulated a lie she hoped would be simple enough to remember.

"So you going to uni? You don't really look old enough, but I had to assume you were over eighteen to be in the club," asked Damien, hardly allowing for a pause in the conversation.

"Yeah, I'm studying commerce. What about you?"

"Marketing, first year."

"I thought you were older than that."

"Took a gap year. Worked, travelled," said Damien.

"Yeah, I didn't start til this semester. I was over in Europe for the first half of the year."

"Why not go for the whole year?"

"I wasn't working."

"Yeah, it can get expensive."

Alexa was surprised Damien did not question her more and ask how she had been able to do so much when she had come from so little. Watching him, she became convinced it was not an act. He truly saw her as one of them – a normal person. It was amazing. For no other reason, she was now glad she had gone to Bianca's party. However, with that little triumph, all she wanted was to go home.

"Can I have your number? I'd like to see you again," said Damien when she rose to leave.

"I don't think that's a good idea," Alexa replied, stepping back, starting to panic.

"Then let me give you mine. That way if you change your mind you can call me."

"Look, I had a good time. I'm just not looking for anything else," she said as she continued to retreat.

"Do you have a boyfriend?" asked Damien, a hard edge entering his voice.

"You think I would've spent the whole night with you if I did?"

"Well, we can just keep talking, I mean next time, not now."

"You won't even remember my name when you wake up," said Alexa seriously.

"I'll remember everything about you."

Alexa smiled before waving and walking away. She had made it down the street before Damien caught up to her and handed her a piece of paper. It had his phone number on it. Wanting to escape, Alexa put it in her pocket and waved goodbye again. Damien was still drunk and she had no illusions about what he really wanted. Arriving home, Alexa put her hand in her pocket, looked at his number and threw it straight in the bin.

Feeling more confident about her second week of university, Alexa could not stop smiling as she walked home on Monday afternoon. The weather was very slowly warming up as the days lengthened, encouraging her to change straight into her swimmers and jog down to the beach. The water was cold, but refreshing as she dove under the waves again and again before pulling her clothes over her swimmers and jogging back up to her apartment. Puffing slightly as she reached the driveway, Alexa was surprised to see Charlotte walking away from the intercom, turning in hesitant circles.

"Hey!" cried Alexa, as Charlotte turned away. "Charlotte! You want to come up?" Charlotte hesitated, but Alexa had reached her now and with a reassuring smile waved her inside. "Um, you're going to have to excuse me for a sec," said Alexa as they walked into her apartment. "If I don't have a shower I'm going to freeze to death. Make yourself at home. I'll be a couple of minutes tops, I promise."

Alexa half expected Charlotte to have left by the time she emerged from the bathroom. The sight of her milling hesitantly near the front door made Alexa smile and speculate if it was possible to be reincarnated without dying first.

"You want food?" Alexa asked, rushing out of her room as she threw on a jumper. "I'm starving. Won't be able to study if I'm only thinking about food." Charlotte nodded hesitantly and Alexa smiled. Although in many ways Charlotte was as untrusting as she was, in others she was more trusting than Alexa ever could have been. "Um, I don't really have snack foods," said Alexa, suddenly concerned. "I was just going to have toast and tea. That okay?"

"You have Vegemite?" asked Charlotte casually.

Alexa shook her head. "I have strawberry jam," she offered, hoping that was okay.

"Next best thing," replied Charlotte, smiling tentatively.

They ate at the table. Neither spoke very much. Alexa decided against asking Charlotte why she had come by and what made her look so sad. She knew how she would have reacted to such questions. However, when she pulled out her uni work, Charlotte decided it was time for her to go.

"You don't have to leave," said Alexa, though she realised she probably did not sound very convincing. She did not want Charlotte to stay anywhere she was not comfortable – not even with her.

"No, you need to study," replied Charlotte, continuing towards the door.

"Well, you can come back any time. I'm home by five nearly every day. Thursday I'm later. But if the weather's good I might go down to the beach."

"Okay."

The response did not leave Alexa with the impression Charlotte would be back again soon, but the next afternoon she saw Charlotte sitting on the swings. When she walked towards her, Charlotte held up a jar of Vegemite.

Charlotte watched Alexa meekly as she opened the jar. It was half-empty; clearly something she had swiped from her own pantry.

"You need to take this back home?" Alexa asked, holding up the jar. "Or do I get to hold it as ransom so you come back and visit?"

"Nah, there was another jar in the cupboard," smiled Charlotte.

"Oh, yum, thank you," replied Alexa after taking a bite of her toast. "I forgot how great Vegemite tastes."

"How could you forget?" asked Charlotte incredulously.

"I've been overseas most of the year. Just got back. No Vegemite in Europe."

Charlotte raised her eyebrows and took a sip of her tea. Alexa wished she could explain, but understood Charlotte's response. She just did not know how to make Charlotte see what her life was really like without talking about things she was trying hard to forget.

Once again, as soon as Alexa pulled out her books, Charlotte rose to leave. If Alexa was not so determined to do well, she might have forgone her study to get to know Charlotte better, but there was only so much she was going to sacrifice for anyone besides Bethany.

"Hey, Alexa," said Charlotte at the door.

"Yeah?" Alexa replied, looking up.

"You said before this isn't really your life – when you were my age – you said your life was more like mine."

"I guess. Some parts, maybe," Alexa replied, hesitant to agree.

"No, but I mean you didn't have everything – money and stuff."

"No. Definitely didn't have money. Didn't have lots of things."

"But you do now," stated Charlotte.

"I have money," clarified Alexa.

"I just mean – you seem normal. You think I could have a life like you? Be successful – go to uni and stuff."

Alexa struggled to comprehend that there was someone in the world who looked at her and saw success, but if anyone was going to say such a thing, she was glad it was her younger self.

"I couldn't promise you the money. It's only luck I have that," Alexa answered honestly. "But the rest, yeah, I think you could do that," she added, speaking just as truthfully. Charlotte did not seem anywhere near as screwed as she had been at that age. It was true Alexa had other people to thank for her current position, but if she could be that person for Charlotte, she would.

Alexa was not surprised to hear Charlotte's voice on the intercom the next afternoon. What did surprise her was the smile on her face when she opened the door. Perhaps Charlotte was not a younger her. The only reason Alexa was so comfortable with Charlotte was because she felt she already knew her so well. However, Alexa was strangely reassured when Charlotte flinched badly after she accidently brushed her hand in the kitchen.

"Did your parents like you?" asked Charlotte as she took her tea.

"No," replied Alexa, shaking her head. "My mother hated me – and I hate her."

"What about your dad?"

"I don't know my father. I know I told you I was an orphan, but I actually have no idea who my father is and if he's dead or alive, so I'd put that down as a big no," explained Alexa. Charlotte said nothing. "My sister loves me though," Alexa smiled. "She's my whole world. Helps makes the other shit bearable. Same for you?"

"I don't remember my mum. Walked out on me. Left me with my dad," replied Charlotte with an unaffected shrug.

"What about your dad?"

"He used to like me, but my step-mum hates me. She's never liked me. Then they had the twins. They had their perfect little family and I'm just the reject kid of the reject first wife."

"I'm sure your dad still loves you. You're his kid. If he stuck around, he must like you," reasoned Alexa.

"Well you go live with him and find out," snapped Charlotte. Alexa smiled internally at the fiery response. "They don't care. Nothing I do's good enough. Used to do good at school, but Dylan and Mia were always better, even in kindergarten. Then I started to do real bad and getting in trouble. Still took no notice. Dad just locked me in my room.

"They talk all the time about what Mia and Dylan will be when they grow up. Talk about them going to uni and being successful. When they look at me they talk about getting a job and paying my way. Tell me I'll have to move out when I get a job, but I know they'll let the twins stay as long as they want."

"Is that when you started cutting?" asked Alexa tentatively, unsure she should broach the subject.

"Yeah," Charlotte nodded, looking up briefly. "Didn't used to hide it. Tried it – where anyone could see. Thought someone would notice, ask what was wrong. Thought someone would care. That's when I knew I was on my own and stopped wanting anyone to ask me about it. But no one's seen it. No one's ever cared."

Charlotte looked up at that statement and it made Alexa wonder what category she was putting her in. The defiance in Charlotte's voice made it clear this admission was a test. The problem was Alexa did not know Charlotte's rules for passing and failing. It made her think of Marcus. He had been the first person to ever care about her self-harm, but she also remembered how futile his attempts at stopping them had been.

"Well, as a child of the foster care system, I'd say that as crap as your home is, you'd still probably prefer it to most of them."

"I doubt that," scowled Charlotte.

"Don't," Alexa replied seriously. She was not sure if it was the people who became foster carers, the horrible existence she and every other foster child was escaping, or the bitterness and distrust that typified every foster sibling she had ever had, but foster care was rarely the salvation outsiders thought it was. "I think you can trust me on that one. I've been in almost thirty of them over the years."

"Why?" asked Charlotte, her voice displaying a hint of distrust.

"My mother was a heroin addict. There were a few times while she was alive we were taken from her, but they always made us go back. When she died, there was nowhere for us to go. Never stayed anywhere very long. No one wanted both of us and I caused too much trouble if we were split up. In the end they found us one place, but they loved Bethany and hated me. That's why I got shipped off to boarding school."

"You didn't have any good foster families? Not even one?" asked Charlotte.

"Yeah, there was one."

"What happened to them? How come you didn't get to stay with them?" questioned Charlotte, a strange urgency in her voice.

Alexa bit her lip, but she could feel it quivering. Turning away, she tried hard to keep her mind from those thoughts. It did not matter how open and honest she and Charlotte were starting to be. This was one conversation she was not going to have.

"You know, I think we're going to get sick of toast pretty soon," said Charlotte in a nonchalant voice. "We should think of something else to eat. You know how to cook pancakes? They're pretty easy. Flour, milk, eggs."

"Been learning to cook new stuff," replied Alexa, loving the way Charlotte had shifted the conversation. "But with just me, I've never seen the point in making cakes. Way too much for one person."

"Brownies are better," nodded Charlotte thoughtfully.

Charlotte moved to the lounge and stared into her tea. Alexa drained the last of hers and moved to the table.

"You got homework? Cos I do," Alexa said, pulling out her books.

"You want me to come by and do homework?" asked Charlotte with disgust.

"I don't mind what you do," laughed Alexa. "Just pointing out that's what I do in the afternoon – in case you haven't noticed. I spent all of school being crap. I plan to do well this year."

Charlotte shrugged and shook her head, grabbing the remote and turning on the television. She kept the sound down, but the noise did not bother Alexa. She was used to the rumble of people nearby, but Charlotte clearly felt in the way and soon left.

The next day, Charlotte brought her school bag.

Having Charlotte around was peaceful. She was company without being overbearing, and within a week had become a regular part of Alexa's life. Alexa found herself being very honest with Charlotte. Although Alexa rarely went into details, she never lied, preferring instead to stay silent when the truth was too much to be spoken aloud. Charlotte never pressed those issues and even started using the same technique.

"Do you mind me being here so often?" asked Charlotte meekly, as the sun faded from the sky the following week.

"You don't think I'd tell you to go home if I did?" asked Alexa.

"I don't know. I thought maybe you just felt sorry for me and – well, you were tired of me now?"

"What makes you say that?"

"I don't know. I just don't know why you care," said Charlotte, almost accusingly. "You know I cut my arms, but you never tell me not to do it. You let me stay, but don't tell anyone my parents suck."

"I know you're unhappy at home, but your parents aren't violent or abusive, so I guess I don't feel the need to tell anyone," justified Alexa, though it was not the whole truth. "I let you come over to have a break from them, maybe give you the chance to work things out."

"Like that'll ever happen," muttered Charlotte.

"And as for your arms, the reason I don't pressure you is because I know how you feel," Alexa confessed, her heart stuttering erratically.

"How?" questioned Charlotte sceptically.

"I used to do the same thing," replied Alexa, her insides trembling.

"Why?" asked Charlotte, her eyes wide, as though she could not quite believe it.

"Because I couldn't handle my life and the things I had to face. I didn't like emotion – still don't – so I used to turn my pain into something I could handle and I did that by cutting myself."

"Do you still do it?"

"No. I stopped a bit over a year ago."

"Why?" asked Charlotte tentatively, as though she sensed she was reaching a boundary between them.

"Because someone did something very important for me and in exchange they told me I had to stop."

Alexa's insides continued to quiver, thinking about that promise. She wished she could take it back or defy Peter, but he had not once checked up on her, always believing she would keep her promise.

"I wouldn't've thought you'd like someone telling you what to do?"

"I didn't," smiled Alexa, before her face turned serious again. "But what he did for me was so important I couldn't refuse."

"Who was it? What'd he do?"

"It was my lawyer and he helped make a deal so I wouldn't have to testify in court and the person went to gaol anyway."

"Is that what you're going to do with me? Do something nice and expect me to stop in return?"

"No, I was just going to be your friend and hope it helped enough for you to stop on your own," explained Alexa. Charlotte just nodded absentmindedly. "If I told you to stop, you think you would?" Alexa asked seriously. Charlotte smiled as she shook her head. "Then don't get mad at me for not doing it," replied Alexa solemnly. "I don't know how to help you. Don't expect me to have answers or solutions or anything like that. I can only be a friend."

With Charlotte over so often, the opportunities Alexa had to see with Maria decreased dramatically; at the mention of anyone else coming by, Charlotte would rush off, and Alexa did not know how to balance the situation. She tried to make up for it on the weekend, but with travel to the detention centre, there was so little time left, leaving her feeling horribly guilty. To her credit, Maria seemed to understand, but Alexa never guessed that the knowing smile that crossed Maria's face had been something more cunning.

When Maria turned up unexpectedly at the apartment on Tuesday afternoon, Charlotte had no choice but to meet her.

"If the mountain won't come to you, you go to the mountain," smiled Maria, waltzing into the apartment with the sweet-smelling promise of banana bread. "You must be Charlotte," said Maria, turning to her. "And I hear you're a little frightened of meeting me. I don't know what Alexa's said, but no need to be afraid. Tea?"

Maria did not wait for them to answer. She started the kettle and organised the table for afternoon tea. There would not have been an opportunity to stop her if they had wanted to.

"I'm not sure you've put her at ease," whispered Alexa when Charlotte ducked off to the bathroom.

"Oh, hush, she'll be fine. I'm no different to when I first met you," replied Maria happily.

"Yeah, and you scared me too," replied Alexa. "Had no idea why you'd want to talk to someone like me. Reckon Charlotte's braver. I nearly jumped in the harbour the first time you approached me."

Charlotte emerged at that point, sitting confidently at the table, making Alexa wonder if she heard them. Maria did not require Charlotte to show further signs of acceptance, and led much of the conversation. Sam had come good on his promise to introduce Maria to Gran and Pop, and she had just come from their second outing.

"They're such lovely people," smiled Maria. "And they think the world of you, Alexa. It's been interesting hearing stories about you when you were younger."

"Like what?" asked Charlotte as Alexa groaned.

"Hmm, well, like Sam teaching Alexa to ride a trail bike, and no matter how many times she fell off, she got back on it until she could do it. Stubborn and determined. I think they were the words they used."

"Yeah, they're usually the words people use to describe me, but rarely in a complimentary way."

"That's because they're not the best traits for all occasions. Either's being continually happy," added Maria. "I'm not talking about always wearing you heart on your sleeve. I'm talking about moderating your display of emotions to what's appropriate. Someone can be irritating the hell out of you and you can still smile politely."

"I could try," laughed Alexa, not sure she would ever be able to achieve such a feat. When she saw Charlotte looking bewildered, she knew Charlotte would struggle just as much.

It was a good afternoon. They laughed and chatted, and Charlotte opened up about things of little consequence – her favourite subjects at school and what she might want to do with her life. Her dismissive curiosity in a legal career led Alexa to believe it was a genuine interest and she was glad when Maria embraced it as a possibility.

"Any type of lawyer in particular?"

"I've thought about criminal law, but that's the one you hear about. Guess I'd wait til later – but you have to be real smart to get into law. Probably never happen."

"Not with that attitude, it won't," sighed Maria. "Talking yourself out of it before you've even had a chance to try. You want it, you go for it. You're worried people won't think you're good enough, then don't tell them. Keep it to yourself and fight for it until you don't want it any more."

"Yeah, and seriously, heaps of people don't get the marks to get straight into law," said Alexa, waving her hand casually. "Just get into something and you can transfer later or post-grad."

"When did you know what you wanted to do?" asked Charlotte.

"About ten seconds before I had to apply," Alexa replied with a grin. "And there was more necessity than interest. I'm giving myself a year to figure out if it's what I actually like."

"What else would you do?" asked Charlotte curiously.

"I have no idea," laughed Alexa. "So I'd better like it, eh."

Charlotte smiled as she looked tentatively over at Maria. It was clear she was still a little apprehensive, but when she rose to leave, Maria gave her a warm hug and expressed her genuine happiness at having met her.

"Is she for real?" whispered Charlotte at the door.

"I haven't managed to catch her in the act yet," replied Alexa.

"So you get why I don't – get her, right?"

"Absolutely. We're nobodies. But I really think she's okay. And I think she likes you."

With Charlotte accepting that, it was not too difficult to convince her to stay for dinner on Thursday to meet Ben. However, Alexa had to soften the deal with the promise Maria would be there too. It was a difficult introduction. Ben was much less inclined to openly accept Charlotte. He was still convinced Alexa was avoiding her problems by focusing on Charlotte's. Alexa did not care what Ben thought. She just wanted him to make Charlotte feel welcome.

"How you doing, Char?" Alexa asked quietly as they cleaned up in the kitchen after dinner and started preparing dessert.

"Okay," Charlotte replied hesitantly. She looked over at Ben for a moment before turning away. "What's with Ben's cop act, though?"

"What do you mean?"

"The way he talks. You know, the way he leans forward to ask questions, and the way he phrases shit – like it's an interrogation."

Alexa could not help but laugh. The way Charlotte imitated Ben was superb. She could not fathom how she had not noticed it before.

"Um, Char. He is a cop."

"Oh," she replied, her face reddening.

"Didn't I ever tell you that?" asked Alexa, genuinely surprised.

"Um, no. I think I would have remembered that. How do you put up with it?"

"I guess I always knew he was a cop so I never paid any attention."

"How do you know him?" smirked Charlotte. "I mean, he's not exactly Mr Personality. He one of your foster dads?" Alexa bit her lip. "Shit, sorry. Forget about me."

"No, it's fine. Don't ask me to explain why I'm okay with you or why I feel like I can trust you. It's just a long story."

Charlotte nodded, but said nothing else. She did not stay for dessert, claiming the need to get home. When Alexa walked into the lounge room, she could see Ben whispering conspiratorially to Maria.

"Just say it to my face," Alexa huffed.

"Okay, I don't think Charlotte's a very good friend for you," said Ben directly.

"Why not?" Alexa replied, just managing to keep calm.

"I have to agree with Alexa," said Maria before Ben could answer. "Charlotte seems like a lovely girl, and Alexa – I think she's better with Charlotte around."

"She always seems better when she's ignoring her own life and focusing on someone else's," retorted Ben. "Bethany's not around so she's taken on Charlotte."

"That's not fair," replied Alexa, her voice breaking.

"Have you made any friends at uni yet?" asked Ben pointedly. "Spoken to anyone?" Alexa could not answer. "And that's my point. That's how I know you're hiding from your life."

"It's not as easy as you make out. There're hundreds of people in my classes. They all have their groups cos they met at the start of the year. And I'm shy. I've never liked talking to people I don't know."

"I'm not even sure how to believe such a claim, Alexa. You never had any problem talking to all manner of drug dealers on the street."

"That was different. That was to find Bethy," muttered Alexa.

"Ben, you've asked her to make friends. Why's it a problem that her first friend is Charlotte?" asked Maria.

"If Charlotte was eighteen, I wouldn't have a problem, but Alexa needs friends her own age."

"I have friends my own age! I have all my high school friends," cried Alexa.

"Who you don't talk to," countered Ben.

"I do! We have different timetables, but we're in touch. We email. I don't gossip on the phone, but I never did. Hell, I went to Bianca's party – danced half the night with them. What more do you want?"

"I had to practically drag you to that party, if you remember," Ben argued.

"What I remember is you telling me it was okay to be nervous, but I guess what's okay for me to feel depends on what mood you're in," Alexa spat, rising from the lounge. "But you know what? I don't need your permission. I don't need you to say it's okay. I'm going to be friends with Charlotte whether you agree or not. If you have an issue with that then you don't have to come visit."

Alexa grabbed the plates and cups on the coffee table and stormed to the kitchen, dumping them noisily in the sink. She could hear Maria and Ben muttering in the lounge room. It made her nervous. She did not want Ben saying anything mean to Maria, but when Maria arrived in the kitchen she was smiling softly.

"You sure know how to entertain," said Maria, squeezing her hand. "Now, I'm going to give you some very good advice, which I hope you'll take on board in the next five minutes." Alexa turned and waited, knowing she was not going to want to hear it. "Never let the sun go down on an argument."

"Sun's already down," Alexa replied.

"Don't be smart," said Maria firmly.

"You're lucky I like you."

"And you're lucky I know how much you love Ben," continued Maria in softer voice. It was nice the way she never stayed angry. "Now go do the right thing and patch things up. His methods mightn't be the best, but he loves you."

92

Alexa rolled her eyes. She was not sure what it was about Maria that made her comply with so many of her requests. Maria had a way of cutting through her crap and pulling out the better parts. Perhaps it was the fact that Maria continued to believe there were better parts hidden below.

"I'm sorry if I was rude," said Alexa.

From the corner of her eye she could see Maria shaking her head, but thankfully Ben seemed somewhat more appeased by her apology.

"I'm sorry too. You're right. I don't have the right to tell you who you can be friends with. I just want so much for you."

"But I'm capable of getting those things myself," said Alexa. "Why can't you believe that? Why can't you just be there for me?"

"I can. I will be, I promise," nodded Ben.

It was a promise Alexa decided not to test, especially after her next visit to Bethany.

"So, how's the pet project going?" asked Bethany with a smirk.

"Can you please not call her that," sighed Alexa.

Bethany only grinned more broadly. Then Ben turned up, and Bethany suddenly had an ally. It was clear they had been discussing this issue when Alexa was not around.

The visit did not last long after that, and Alexa was glad Ben had to go to work, saving her a trip home with him. On the way, Alexa started writing Bethany a letter. It was harder than she thought, trying to explain why Charlotte was so important to her and why she needed Bethany to accept her. Dropping the letter in the post box, Alexa hoped she would finally have Bethany on her side. It pained her that she even had to explain these things, but supposed it would be hard for her to judge from a distance. Once Bethany met Charlotte, she would understand.

Charlotte was sitting on the swings when Alexa arrived home. Her eyes were puffy, but clear of the tears that had recently stained them. Alexa took her hand and led her upstairs. They had not been physical up until that point, but when Charlotte suddenly burst into tears, Alexa could not stop herself from hugging her. Charlotte reciprocated, holding tight on to her arms as they held her. It made Alexa doubt Charlotte was hugged very often.

"Want to talk about it?" Alexa asked when Charlotte's tears ran dry. Charlotte shook her head just as the phone rang. "Good thing, really," Alexa smiled as she jumped up to answer it. "Hello?"

"Hey, Lex – a!"

"Hi, Sam," Alexa smiled, slumping into the lounge. "What's up?"

"Gran and Pop want to see your new place – and I want to show off my handiwork. Want to cook us a big Sunday breakfast tomorrow?"

"Sam!" Alexa heard Gran scold, making Sam laugh.

"You know you owe me."

"Yeah, yeah, lifetime of Sunday breakfasts. I remember," replied Alexa casually.

"Awesome. We'll be there about ten. Oh, and Gran and Pop want to know if Maria's free to come too."

If Maria was going to come, Alexa knew she would have to invite Ben, which meant she hoped Charlotte would agree to be there too. It was the kind of gathering that needed more support on her side. Charlotte agreed, but Alexa was not convinced by her conviction. When Maria arrived early on Sunday morning to help with the cooking and there was no sign of Charlotte, Alexa was not sure she should expect to see her.

"She's been over a lot. Maybe she needs a break," said Maria gently. "I know you just want her to be a part of things and feel welcome, but maybe it's all a bit overwhelming."

"I think it could be something else, although you're probably right," sighed Alexa. "Charlotte asked who Sam was and I ended up telling her about him."

"Just him?" asked Maria. Alexa shook her head. "About the teacher as well?"

"Yeah," Alexa nodded. "I didn't go into detail, but I think it sounds worse then." Maria scowled. "Charlotte got upset – started saying she understood why I didn't think she had any problems and all that. It's not true. I just worry that if I start making a big deal of her situation, it'd make things worse. I can't fix her problems. I wish I could."

"I guess we just wait and see then."

"Maria," Alexa said hesitantly, nodding her agreement. Maria turned and waited for her to continue. "I'm not ignoring my life – with Charlotte – I'm not ignoring the things that are important to me. I just don't want to focus on the past or the bad stuff. I'm ignoring that. Maybe I can't forever, but do I always have to think about it? It's depressing."

"You said that to Ben?" asked Maria tenderly.

"He won't listen to me," sighed Alexa.

"Then you need to find a way to make him," replied Maria firmly. "You're doing fine. I don't know what the fuss is, but don't let it come between you and Ben. He loves you and you forget that he doesn't have the advantage of having been there your whole life. It's hard to be a parent at the best of times. Give him a chance and you might find he does the same for you."

Ben arrived first. He looked harried as he sat down at the kitchen bench. Alexa made him a coffee, which he accepted with a smile, but it did not reach his eyes.

"You didn't have to come if it's a pain," Alexa said softly, feeling guilty.

"No, I just didn't sleep much last night," murmured Ben. "I left Penny yesterday. I'm renting a place a couple of suburbs away."

"Yesterday? But I saw you yesterday – with Bethy. You didn't say anything."

"I didn't want to worry you."

"So Bethy doesn't know?" asked Alexa.

"No, I told her after you left," replied Ben.

Jealously pierced Alexa's stomach. It took all her restraint to hold back the bitter retorts and concentrate on the fact that it was Ben who was having a bad day. She just did not understand why she was being deliberately left out. Ignoring her hurt was made easier by the arrival of Sam and his grandparents. Ben roused himself dramatically to greet them, showing nothing of his earlier sour mood.

Alexa had not seen Sam since their week together and was surprised by the flatness of her body's response to him. In years gone by her heart had always lurched just a little when she saw him. Now it was little different to greeting Chad.

"Hey, party time," smiled Sam, looking around the room. "And by that smell I believe I may be duly compensated for my previous toils in this apartment."

"You've done a good job with the place," said Pop.

"Thanks, but Sam's right. I couldn't have done it without him. I think the memory of that day's what's kept him away so long."

"It would've kept me away as well," joked Pop.

"I'm very proud of you," said Gran, rubbing her shoulder. "And thank you for what you did for us. It's wonderful being here with Sam. We missed them a lot when they were at school."

"Have you spoken to Mel?" asked Alexa tentatively.

"She writes occasionally, just birthdays and the like. It wasn't easy letting go, but we had to. She wouldn't contact us if we said anything against Clinton."

"I'm sorry about all that," said Alexa guiltily.

"Don't you be sorry about a thing," growled Pop. "That monster took her from us. He's the one who needs to be sorry."

Alexa was thankful the buzz of the intercom let her escape the conversation. The memories of Clinton and Mel were already making her insides quiver. "Hey, Char, you made it," Alexa smiled happily as she opened the door. Charlotte was not smiling. "You okay?"

Charlotte shook her head and pulled down her sleeves. Alexa hugged her briefly before leading her into the lounge room. Looking around, Alexa realised this was overwhelming and decided to stop trying to immerse Charlotte in her world.

"Everyone, this is Charlotte. Charlotte, this is Sam, Gran and Pop."

Sam smiled broadly before shaking Charlotte's hand, as Gran and Pop greeted her with a wave from the lounge where they were seated with Maria.

"So that's the pet project, hey?" whispered Sam in Alexa's ear.

Alexa glared at him, and noticed Charlotte's eyes flick his way before she scurried to the bathroom.

"Don't you ever say shit like that near her again," Alexa hissed. "I don't care what Bethy's told you. You don't know anything about it."

"You can't run away from your life forever," replied Sam flatly.

"I'm not running from anything."

"I'm not so sure about that," Sam replied, this time with a grin.

Alexa rolled her eyes and walked to the kitchen to finish cooking. She laid out the food on the dining table with Charlotte's assistance, and made sure Charlotte sat between her and Maria. The conversation was jovial, even with Sam throwing Alexa bemused glances. Charlotte stayed quiet. Maria did her best to bring her into the conversation, talking proudly about her to Gran and Pop. Alexa could hear her stuttering in response to the nice things Maria was saying, and smiled encouragingly.

"You okay?" asked Charlotte, when Alexa again shook her head warningly at Sam.

"Yeah, Sam just thinks I'm messing up my life. Just promise that no matter what they say about me concentrating on everyone but me, you know I really like having you around. They just don't get it."

Charlotte paled, but nodded in agreement when Alexa made her promise again. Alexa was about to smile when she heard Sam clear his throat, silencing the table. "One of my friends has been banging on this past fortnight about a girl he met at Bianca's party," Sam said to the table. "You were there, Alexa, maybe you can help me."

"I didn't really talk to many people," Alexa replied, unsure where Sam was headed with this.

"We'll give it a go anyway," Sam replied dismissively. "My mate watched this girl all night, basically, and tried to make a move, but she didn't seem interested. When he finally caught her alone, she whinged that he was drunk and made him sober up before she'd talk to him. Do you have any idea who the girl might be?"

Alexa blushed as everyone turned to her.

"Did you hook up, Alexa?" asked Maria.

"No, I did not hook up," replied Alexa in a scandalised voice. "We just went to McDonalds and talked –"

"– for the rest of the morning," added Sam. "He didn't put her in a cab until dawn."

"Bus," clarified Alexa. "I don't see how this is any of your concern."

"You said you weren't running away from your life."

"I'm not."

"She's just running away from this boy, it seems," said Gran.

"Do we really have to discuss my life in a committee?" Alexa asked, trying to keep her voice light.

Everyone smiled as they looked around the table.

"Yes," replied Sam.

The discussion about Alexa's night with Damien continued, with everyone questioning her about how they met, what they talked about, why she did not give him her number and why she had not called him. It was mostly in good fun and Alexa assumed the topic would be dropped once she had sated everyone's curiosity, but Sam was not letting it go.

"I'm not ready. Is that okay with everyone? I thought I was doing well just talking to the guy," replied Alexa with an exasperated sigh.

"You did, but you don't get how much Damien likes you," said Sam. "You're all he talks about and he doesn't even know I know you. He'd never shut up if he did."

"Yeah, well, I'd preferred it stayed that way. He knows too many stories already about Bianca and the girls she went to school with. I want him to go on believing the story I told him."

"Which was?" asked Sam.

"That I moved from interstate and know Bianca through people at uni – just like him."

"I can stick to that if you just call him and get him off my back."

"I'm not interested, Sam. I'm sorry," replied Alexa firmly, hoping that would be the end of it.

"Might be nice to go out with him," said Charlotte softly. "I mean, I'd like it if someone liked me that much. How bad could he be if he talks about you all the time?"

"Yeah, Alexa, how bad could he really be?" teased Sam.

"I'm more than aware of how bad he could be!" Alexa snapped, sick of not being allowed to make uncontested decisions.

Sam slumped back in his chair as Charlotte slunk into hers. Alexa wished she and Charlotte were alone so she could explain why she was not upset with her, but all she could do was start gathering plates and escape to the kitchen.

"He was only joking," said Ben quietly, following Alexa into the kitchen with the crockery she could not carry.

"I know," she sighed. "But it just tweaked something in me."

"I can see that. So why don't I see if I can tell you the real reason why you didn't call Damien.

"Marcus Knight."

Chapter Seven

ALEXA'S STOMACH ROLLED over. There was more truth in Ben's statement than Sam's, yet it was not the whole truth. If she had felt even a fraction of what she had for Marcus, then she would have called Damien as soon as she got home.

"Ah, see, now I thought that might be it," replied Ben when she turned away. "I know you loved him and that you even still might, but he's gone. It was never going to work. There were too many obstacles. It's time to move on. I'm not saying Damien will be the one or that it'll last more than two weeks, but it's time to start looking at the other fish in the sea."

Although Ben was not right on the mark with his advice, combined with Sam's comments and everyone else's determination that she was reacting the wrong way to this situation, Alexa decided to accept they may be correct. It was not as though she had a good record with men. She should never have liked Marcus, so if she was going to have a socially acceptable relationship, perhaps it did have to start like this.

When everyone bar Charlotte had left, Alexa sat down with the piece of paper Sam left with Damien's number on it.

"Maybe if you go on one date with him they'll get off you back," said Charlotte, slouching down next to her looking very apologetic.

"Yeah, maybe, but I already kinda did that and didn't care to see him again," sighed Alexa. "Yeah, screw it. One date. You can help me think of reasons they'll accept for not going on a second."

Charlotte smiled and rested her head on Alexa's shoulder as Alexa picked up the phone and dialled. Alexa was surprised that she did not have to explain who she was. When Damien suggested they meet up that night, she hesitated for only a moment before agreeing. His excitement at seeing her made her stomach squirm. He did seem very nice. Maybe she could give dating a go.

Hanging up the phone, Alexa could not help but regret making the call. Away from Damien's enthusiasm, she seemed to have lost her own. In the back of her mind, she had hoped she would simply run into Marcus somewhere when she arrived home. She was not sure if it would have led to anything, but she would have known if her lingering feelings for him were real or simply memories. What was more, she had determined that when she did move on from Marcus, it would be with a man she loved as much or more. That man was not Damien.

However, since everyone else was so convinced that seeing Damien was a good thing, Alexa decided she would do it their way. Then, if it crashed and burned, they could not blame her.

Alexa refused to dress up for the date, determined that Damien would have to accept her dressed the way she normally did; though it did not escape Alexa's attention as she caught the bus that she was almost hoping he would be put off by her dress sense.

"Hi," Alexa said nervously, shuffling awkwardly at the table where Damien was waiting.

Damien jumped up with a relieved smile. She had stood outside the café for over ten minutes, watching him anxiously check his watch, before she plucked up the courage to enter. What she had really wanted to do was turn around and go home.

"Hey," Damien breathed, pulling out a chair for her before quickly resuming his seat.

"Sorry I'm late. Bus took forever," Alexa lied.

"That's okay. I'm glad you called. Was starting to think you never would."

"My life's a little complex at the moment. I wasn't sure I was ready for a relationship or anything like that."

"But you're sure now?"

"No, not really," Alexa answered with a smile. "My friends just seem to think I need to move on and take a chance."

"So you decided to take a chance on me?" asked Damien, and Alexa sensed a hint of smugness in his question.

"I had a good time the other night. I didn't just choose you because you were there," Alexa replied, but realised that was probably a lie.

Damien did not seem concerned, quickly moving the conversation on. They talked about university and traveling. Alexa was surprised they had so much in common. It was nice, but she found it hard to consider herself attracted to Damien. After dinner they wandered around the city until they reached the harbour.

"It's a nice night," said Alexa, peering over the sandstone harbour wall into the dark water. It reminded her of her last night with Sam.

"Yeah. You look cold though," said Damien moving next to her.

"I am a bit."

"Why don't I warm you up a little?"

Damien gently turned her to face him and leant forward, pressing his lips to hers. It was a strange sensation. It reminded Alexa of the first time she kissed Clinton, but she quickly blocked that thought, hoping this relationship could not end the same way that one had.

Realising this was the point where her body was bound to freak out, Alexa simply stood there and let Damien kiss her. He did not seem entirely aware that she was not kissing him back. When the panic attack failed to materialise, Alexa felt her body relax slightly. Damien's hands were placed firmly on her waist and back, and Alexa found herself unexpectedly aroused. She began to kiss Damien with greater intensity. Damien's hand moved up and down the sides of her body, tingles accompanying his touch. His hands moved to her head, stroking her hair as their lips remained locked.

"Are you cold?" asked Damien, breaking away as Alexa shook. When he released her hair, she had the courage to nod.

Alexa' heart was thrumming erratically and she had to force her breaths to slow and muscles to release. Damien smiled as he took his jacket off and wrapped it around her shoulders, before leaning in to kiss her again. Alexa did not feel the same desires she had just moments ago. All her concentration was on where Damien's hands were and their intentions. When his hand moved down her neck, Alexa reacted automatically.

"Alexa, wait. What happened?" called Damien, frantically trying to catch up with her, but her strides did not slow.

Alexa did not want to face him. She felt stupid and defective. All she wanted was an escape – from Damien and the fear that was torturing her. The door of the taxi was almost closed when he finally reached her. He grabbed the door, forcing her to look up at him.

"What's wrong? What did I do?" Damien asked, his face a strange contortion of concern and anger.

"I have to go. Please, just let me go," replied Alexa, turning away.

"Just tell me what I did?" Damien's voice did not harbour any of the anger she had seen on his face, but was full of hurt and confusion and made Alexa feel horribly guilty.

"Here," she said, grabbing his hand. "Just give me a couple of days."

The moment the cab moved off, Alexa regretted giving Damien her number, but conceded it was probably just her. Everyone would tell her it was the right thing to do. It just did not feel like it.

Alexa was ashamed knowing her deficiencies ruined the date. Her one chance to prove she was fine, and she failed. The only person she could talk to was Bethany, but even then it could only be done in letters. Charlotte, around so often, knew something was wrong, but it was a few days before she came straight out and asked.

"You don't want to talk about school and why you're having problems," countered Alexa.

"Yeah, well if you're supposedly ignoring all your problems by focusing on mine, why can't I do the same?" replied Charlotte jovially.

Charlotte had started to open up to Alexa, if not with her words at least with her personality, when they were alone. It was nice. Charlotte was like an incredibly unjaded version of herself, and it was interesting to see what she could have been like if she had been vaguely trusting. So even though she did not want to talk about it, Alexa told Charlotte what happened on her date with Damien.

"Why didn't you just tell him you were scared because someone once tried to strangle you?" queried Charlotte.

"How do you know about that?" asked Alexa.

"Heard them talking. They must think I'm deaf or just don't see me. I'm invisible to everyone."

"You're not invisible to me," said Alexa, leaning into Charlotte's shoulder. "How much do you know about my past?"

"Only bits and pieces. I thought I'd ask you about it in time."

"Well, I don't want *him* to know about my past," replied Alexa firmly, hoping Charlotte would understand the emphasis and not be put off, but Charlotte did not ask any more questions. "We'd better start on dinner. You're staying, aren't you?"

"Considering I got suspended today, I'm in no rush to go home."

Alexa swung around to see Charlotte shrug indifferently.

"What do you mean suspended? What'd you do?" Alexa asked. She had done so many things at school and never been suspended.

"I hit another kid," answered Charlotte casually. Alexa had never done that. "She just said something that pissed me off."

"You can't hit people just because they piss you off. You can't hurt people like that," Alexa said softly, feeling the sting of all the slaps she had received just because she had pissed people off.

"Why not?" spat Charlotte "It doesn't matter if people hurt me. Say whatever they want and I'm s'posed to cop it. I think it's better to hit someone than hurt them with words."

"Haven't you ever heard about sticks and stones?"

"Yeah, well, the person who wrote that doesn't know shit."

Alexa could not believe the casualness with which Charlotte was speaking. It shocked her that Charlotte was able to hurt anyone in such a manner. She would never have predicted it and it made her question how similar they really were.

"Charlotte, it doesn't work like that," said Alexa, almost pleading, because she could not have someone in her life who hit people. "And in the end it's you who's disadvantaged. She gets away with it because what you did was worse. You have to show the world how bad they are by being better, not worse. You just – you can't hit."

"I don't care," muttered Charlotte, turning away.

"It'd be much easier if that was true, wouldn't it?"

"It is true. I don't care about anything. Why should I? No one cares about me."

"If that were true you wouldn't be afraid of going home to face your father," said Alexa. "You know he'll be angry and upset."

"No. I know he won't be," retorted Charlotte angrily.

Alexa continued to try and make Charlotte see her point of view, but it was difficult. The more they discussed the issue, the more she came around to Charlotte's way of thinking. She could not condone Charlotte's actions, but when it came to the rest of it, she found herself silently agreeing – even when she knew she shouldn't. The situation was so ridiculous Alexa could not help but laugh.

"What?" asked Charlotte angrily when Alexa continued to shake with mirth.

"I feel like I'm arguing with myself. Everything you say, I remember thinking and I'm trying to figure out how I was convinced of what I'm saying or if I'm a giant hypocrite, cos I'm on your side half the time." Charlotte smiled, letting a small laugh escape her lips. "I guess my point is, I understand," said Alexa. "You just should never hit," she added firmly. "You been hit before?" Charlotte shook her head. "I have – and not just by adults. Once by a girl at my school – my friend. If you were on her side, you could probably argue it was justified, but it sucked. Just – I can't be okay with that. Understand?"

Charlotte nodded and they did not talk about it again. It was more of a lecture than Alexa would have withstood.

Alexa wanted to know how Charlotte's parents reacted when she next visited, but when Charlotte did not volunteer the information, Alexa did not ask for it. Slumping on the lounge after Charlotte left, Alexa was almost asleep when the trill of the phone startled her awake.

"Damien? How'd you get my number?" Alexa asked, unable to keep the surprise from her voice.

"You gave it to me. Said I could call you in a couple of days," answered Damien uncertainly.

"Oh, yeah, right," Alexa replied, remembering why she regretted giving him her number. "How you been?"

"Okay, I guess. How are you going?" he asked pointedly.

"I've been better. I'm – I'm a little worried about Charlotte at the moment," Alexa answered honestly.

"Is that what made you run off the other night?" asked Damien's unable to conceal his agitation.

"No, look I'm sorry about that," said Alexa, suddenly realising the true meaning of his question. She had tried to forget about her hasty departure and hoped that he had too. "I just … it was nothing to do with you – I mean, it wasn't personal. I just —"

"You just what?" asked Damien a little more forcefully.

"I freaked out a bit. It has nothing to do with you. It's just – it's been a long time and …"

Alexa knew she could not give a satisfactory explanation without divulging her past and resigned herself to never seeing Damien again, though could not find the energy to be too upset about it. The whole thing had been tiring enough already.

The strained silence continued for almost a minute. Every so often Alexa opened her mouth to talk, but the words were not forthcoming. She did not know how to tell him that she was not worth it.

"So does this mean you don't want to see me any more?" asked Damien in a low, hurt voice.

"I liked being with you, but I can't promise I'm going to be any more functional than the other night," Alexa answered, hoping to let him down easy.

"I like you. I'd like to see you again. Are you free on Friday?"

"Really?" queried Alexa. He had to be insane.

"Yeah, really," Damien laughed.

"Um, yeah, okay. Friday sounds good," Alexa replied, buoyed by the idea that Damien had not been completely put off by her panic attack. Perhaps he was one of the few men who would accept her for who she was. And she could learn to love him in time, if he could look past all her dysfunctionalities and love her.

With that object in mind, Alexa was pleasantly surprised by their second date. She thought it might not even be too difficult for her to learn to like Damien. She enjoyed his company and there was rarely any shortage of conversation. They talked through dinner and walked hand in hand around the city streets afterwards. Damien even bought her an ice cream.

It was surreal. Alexa felt like she was walking along in an alternate universe. Plain, normal activities like this were just not part of her world. What was more normal was the fear that pierced her body when Damien touched her. Every time he leaned in to kiss her, she shivered uncontrollably. It was frustrating. It was hard remaining open to the idea of liking Damien as more than a friend, but the whole process would have been easier if she could let him touch her.

The fear of her fear meant Alexa could barely tolerate holding hands. Damien's every touch turned her insides to ice. The thought of seeing him again only became more odious as she contemplated how she would prevent his hands from moving over her body.

"What the fuck's your problem?" cried Damien when Alexa again casually moved his hand off her leg. "How can you say you like me when you won't let me touch you? You act as though I'm contaminated – like the very thought of me makes your skin crawl!"

"I don't have to justify myself to you," Alexa cried defensively, scared of Damien's anger. "Just because I won't jump into bed with you doesn't mean I don't like you."

"Jump into bed? Who's talking about sex? You're such a cock-tease!" spat Damien, holding his hands up as if in surrender. "You barely let me hug you or give you more than a peck on the check. Lead me on, then cut me down. Shit, I liked you, but this's been a fucking game to you. Well, you know what? You can shove your game where the sun don't shine. I'm over it. I'm over you. You're not that hot that you can be such a slut, you know."

And that was it. Damien stormed off without a backwards glance. Alexa was confused by the tears that slipped down her cheeks as she sat alone on the beach. She knew she deserved Damien's wrath, but still thought his words had been meaner than necessary. Yet she had had worse things said to her and not felt this way. It made her think that perhaps she had started to like Damien, but that conclusion did not seem quite right either.

The confusion was perhaps the worst part of the breakup. Alexa spoke about it to no one but Bethany, detailing the event in her letter, though she left out Damien's parting words. She did not want to be told she deserved such censure. When the news spread, Alexa was glad Bethany kept the details to herself. Alexa would have confided in Ben or Sam if she was not so worried they would take any lingering doubts about her feelings to suggest she was still hung up on Marcus. But in the end, Alexa did not need to tell Sam anything. Damien told him everything. Then Sam told him some secrets of his own.

"What did you tell him, Sam?" stormed Alexa. "I hope you realise I kept my life away from him for a reason. Hell, he doesn't even know we're friends."

"Well he does now," retorted Sam. "Look, I just mentioned a few things about your past."

Alexa felt as though her skin was the only thing keeping her from exploding. "My past? My past! Don't you think there's an important word there? My! My past, not yours! When do you get to suddenly decide what people know about me?" cried Alexa.

"I didn't go into detail," replied Sam meekly.

"Well that makes it okay then. Just gave him the basic overview?"

"All I told him was that you'd been raped and that this was your first real relationship since."

"And who'd you say raped me? Cos you sure have a choice."

"I didn't," replied Sam defensively, before continuing in a calmer voice. "He needed to know he wasn't the reason you didn't want to be touched. You should've been the one to tell him, not me."

"But it's my choice," cried Alexa, wondering why her opinion did not count. "Maybe I didn't want him to know."

"I'm sure you didn't, but I told you I'd be there for you and that includes saving you from yourself. You can't keep hiding from your past and Mr Knight isn't waiting around the corner for you. He's gone. It's time you gave the future a go."

Alexa could not argue any more, defeated by Sam's comments and the idea that if she considered her own feelings she was only going to get herself in more trouble. She also hated that Sam insisted on calling Marcus Mr Knight, like he was reminding her that he had been their teacher. She was not a school girl any more, but knew that was a conversation to be avoided if she did not want another lecture.

Looking down at the piece of paper Sam left behind, stating a time and place to meet Damien, Alexa knew this was one thing she would have to do their way. And perhaps she did owe Damien a meeting – even if it was to end it all. Again.

"Sorry I'm late," said Alexa, as she joined Damien at the table. It had taken her a long time to force herself out of the apartment.

Damien looked strangely hopeful, which confused Alexa. She wanted to get this over with and tell him there was no point even ordering, but the words would not come out.

"I know you're unlikely to be very happy with what Sam told me, but I'm glad he did. I just wish you'd trusted me enough to tell me yourself."

"It's not something I think about let alone talk about," replied Alexa, her voice flat.

"Perhaps you should."

"If you're here to tell me I need help then you're wasting your breath and I should go."

"That wasn't what I wanted. I want to go out with you," Damien said firmly. "I want to be your boyfriend and I want you to trust me." Alexa eyes flicked up. This had to be a sick joke, but he seemed to be telling the truth. Her heart warmed slightly, even as her breath stuck in her throat and her stomach rolled over. Trust was not something she had a lot of. She opened her mouth, but the words would not come out. "Seriously. I don't want to hurt you. I like you."

"I like being with you too, but it's not that simple for me," Alexa conceded, finally finding her voice.

"I know, but we can work through it. Just give it a go. If you don't like it or don't trust me you can leave now, no questions asked."

"What do you mean give it a go?"

When Damien moved his chair next to hers, Alexa was sorry she asked. She held her stomach tight. Damien would not want to be her boyfriend if she vomited on him.

"I won't hurt you, I promise," said Damien, as he brushed a wispy bit of hair from her face.

"Don't make promises you can't keep," replied Alexa, her voice barely above a whisper.

"I can keep my promises."

Damien leaned forward and cupped her chin, bringing it gently towards him. Tingles rushed through Alexa's body as their lips met. Damien held her for a moment before releasing her and looking into her eyes. "Now, like I said, if you didn't like that you can go now and I won't bother you again."

Alexa did not move and, with a smile, Damien leant forward and kissed her again.

With every date, Alexa found herself settling into her relationship with Damien. They had enough in common to fill their conversations and Alexa learned to tolerate Damien's touch. After two weeks she even apologised to Sam for her outburst.

"See. Knew you liked him. You just had to accept that," said Sam.

Alexa was trying to accept that. Never before had she worked so hard on a relationship – and it was work – but with every date she could see her efforts paying off. Each day Alexa could say she liked

Damien that little bit more, or could let him push the physical boundaries that bit further. Damien was very supportive and always pulled back when he overstepped her limits. He was doing everything right and Alexa told herself time and time again he was right for her.

So everyone knew how seriously she was taking the relationship and how much she was improving, Alexa vocalised how wonderful Damien was, often hoping the more enthusiastically she pronounced those emotions, the more likely she was to feel them. It never crossed her mind to tell anyone, not even Bethany, that she still did not like Damien the way she expected to; nowhere close to how she felt about Sam and Marcus. They would simply tell her she was wrong and she wanted so desperately to be right.

However, the effort of sustaining her relationship with Damien and the time he demanded of her left Alexa with little time for anything else. Charlotte's visits became shorter and much less frequent. The nature of them even changed and Alexa found Charlotte a lot less open. Alexa tried to spend time with Charlotte and Damien together, but it never worked. Damien did not want to get to know Charlotte, and Charlotte seemed uncomfortable around Damien. When Charlotte stopped coming over all together, Alexa felt her heart ache strangely. The only time she saw Charlotte was when she was sitting on the swings, but every time she went down to see her, Charlotte was gone. Alexa tried to talk to Damien about it, but he did not care.

"She's not your problem, you know," said Damien, frustration evident in his voice. "Even Sam doesn't get your obsession. She has a family and friends, is years younger than you. Why do you even care about her? What's she to you?"

"She's just like I was at her age," replied Alexa cautiously, realising this was another aspect of her life where the consensus was she was in the wrong.

"Then she'll grow out of her problems just like you did," said Damien dismissively. "If she wanted your help she'd still come over."

"She used to. You made her feel unwelcome," retorted Alexa.

"Well I mean call up and find out a good time. She was just turning up whenever she felt like it. We have the right to time alone."

Alexa did not argue further, but was determined to let Charlotte know she would make time for her, but since Charlotte always came to her, Alexa had no idea where to find her. It was the first thing that had gone wrong in this new life and Alexa felt the failure more acutely than she supposed was reasonable. She had not known

Charlotte very long, but the connection they shared – that connection to her younger self and the chance to do something right – had been one of the strongest she had ever formed with a stranger. To turn her back now felt like a betrayal. However, almost everyone else was of the same opinion as Damien and thought she should just forget about Charlotte. Move on.

"Yeah, cos it always works out for the best when you walk away from kids in need," said Alexa angrily, storming out from her visit with Bethany, unable to withhold her frustration any longer.

Bethany called for her to come back, but Ben told her to let her go. Striding forcefully, Alexa half expected Ben to chase after her, but no one came. Ben had offered to drive her home, but she went straight to the bus stop. The bus arrived almost as soon as she reached the stop and she boarded gratefully.

The sight of Ben's car outside her apartment block was not a surprise, but Alexa had to breathe deeply to control her temper. Ben was waiting at the front entrance. He was not smiling.

"Can I come up?" he asked when she reached him.

Alexa nodded, not yet trusting herself to speak. They remained silent as they entered the apartment and Alexa boiled the kettle.

"Do you feel as though I abandoned you?" asked Ben as he stared into his coffee.

"I don't remember you. How could I possibly feel abandoned when I don't even know what happened?" asked Alexa petulantly.

"Well that comment today was for my benefit, wasn't it?"

Alexa closed her eyes and sighed. Perhaps she had meant it to sting, but now that she knew it had hurt Ben, she felt horrible. "You've always told us how guilty you felt for not keeping track of us and how you wished you'd done things differently," she said in a controlled voice, her eyes still closed. "I was just pointing out that I feel guilty for not being a better friend to Charlotte. I offered her my friendship and I expected I'd keep that promise. No, I don't think I've done anything wrong per se – just like you didn't – but that doesn't stop me from feeling guilty."

"Fair enough," nodded Ben. "We're just worried about you – worried that you're focusing your energies in the wrong direction."

"Yeah, I know," replied Alexa tersely, not in the mood for another lecture. "I just thought Bethy understood."

"I think she does, but she worries more than the rest of us – not about the same things," Ben added quickly. "I think she worries about what you're not telling her and our accounts of your activities probably clash with yours."

Alexa went to the kitchen under the guise of clearing up. She did not want to be angry with Ben, but it was more difficult than she expected to let go of her failure with Charlotte. The only solace Alexa found was with Damien. He may not have understood her friendship with Charlotte, but at least he did not read anything more into it. The sanctuary Alexa found with Damien strengthened their relationship, progressing it faster than she expected. Damien started to push her physical limits. For the most part, she was able to handle it, but every so often she was overcome with fear. To his credit, Damien continued to be understanding and tolerant.

"You don't think I'm pressuring you, do you?" asked Damien as Alexa collected her things. They had made it to half-naked before she freaked out and had to push him off her. "I just want to show you that I won't hurt you and that you can trust me."

"No, I know, but I do have to go," Alexa replied, trying to keep her voice even.

"As long as you know I'd never hurt you."

Alexa smiled and leant over to kiss Damien as he sat on his bed. He was very sweet and she knew he was a good guy. She kept telling herself he was everything she could ask for in a boyfriend. It was like a mantra that ran constantly through her head, so that by the time she arrived home, she was smiling at the realisation that he was hers.

As Alexa strolled through the parking lot to her apartment block, she noticed a police car parked outside the front door and hoped they were not there about Bethany. An officer soon appeared from behind the building with a young girl in tow.

"Charlotte, what happened?" puffed Alexa, racing up to them.

"Do you know this girl?" asked the young officer.

"Yeah, I live here. Charlotte comes over to my place occasionally."

"Hello, Alexa," said a pleasant voice, as a second officer emerged from the other side of the building.

"Hi, Parker. What are you doing here?"

"Ben's off sick today. Got myself a new partner for the day. You know Charlotte?" asked Detective Shane Parker. Alexa nodded. "Ben know her?" Alexa nodded again. "Hmm, trust him to be off for this. He would've had a better idea of where to find her."

"What do you mean?" asked Alexa.

"We've been playing cat and mouse with Charlotte for over an hour today."

"What'd she do?"

"Shoplifting," answered Parker. "Right in front of us too. Almost like she wanted to be seen – or just plain stupid."

"Oh, Charlotte, why didn't you come to me?" cried Alexa.

"Like I even rate a mention in your life," Charlotte spat, sliding into the police car with a hateful glare.

Alexa stared at the empty driveway long after the police car disappeared, feeling worse than guilty. She rushed upstairs to call Ben, but he was reluctant to promise her information. "She's a juvenile," said Ben, coughing as he spoke. "I can't go giving out the kind of information you're asking for."

"I just want to help her."

"I'll find out what I can, but I'm not ruining my career for this. She has a family and she's their responsibility. I can't tell you where she lives. I can't tell you what we're planning on charging her with – not when we haven't even discussed it with her parents."

Alexa hung up feeling disappointed, but knew deep down that Ben was being reasonable. Needing to get out of the apartment that all of a sudden felt very encasing, Alexa went down to the swings to contemplate her failure. In the darkness, she noticed someone walking towards her. As they stepped into the light, they stopped, shuffling their feet before turning and walking away.

"Hey, wait. Where're you going?" cried Alexa.

"Go to hell," snapped Charlotte, striding faster.

"Been there. Where're you going?" asked Alexa again, grabbing Charlotte to turn her around before immediately releasing her.

"Away. They kicked me out."

"What? Your parents?"

"They've had enough. Don't want me being a negative influence on their wonderfully perfect children any more."

"You have anywhere to go?" asked Alexa, her voice quivering.

"I'll figure something out."

"You don't want to live on the streets."

"Like you would know."

"Yeah, I do, so you're coming with me."

Chapter Eight

ALEXA WAS NOT sure if Charlotte slept that night. The spare bed was made up when she woke, looking completely unused. Charlotte was on the balcony, gazing out at the ocean. She did not acknowledge Alexa when she came out and did not touch the food Alexa brought her.

"I have to go see my sister," said Alexa quietly, walking out on to the balcony after her shower. "You can stay here if you like or come with me. There's a spare key on the kitchen table, but like I said before, if you betray my trust, you'll be out of here in an instant."

Charlotte stared back and said nothing until Alexa turned to go inside. "Have you really lived on the streets?"

"Not for extended periods," replied Alexa, sitting down next to Charlotte. "Bethy did. I often went looking for her. That would take a few days, so I was on the streets then. It wasn't fun. There aren't many ways of supporting yourself. Your options are fairly limited and, well, they're not decisions you want to make."

"Why'd you make them?" asked Charlotte, her voice somewhere between curious and sceptical.

"Because I didn't have any other options. I'm giving you a choice. You should think long and hard about taking it."

"You turned out okay."

"I was lucky," laughed Alexa mirthlessly at the irony of such a statement. "You don't know how lucky. I almost died a couple of times. My sister's in gaol. Believe me, it could've gone either way. I don't think it's worth you taking that chance. Why don't you trust me on this one?"

Charlotte remained silent, looking out to sea. Alexa was about to leave when Charlotte spoke again. "But I don't get it. You live here," she cried. "How can you talk about understanding me and going through all those things when you live here?"

"I lied," sighed Alexa. "I didn't know you. I didn't want to explain … can I tell you now?"

Charlotte nodded slowly and Alexa took a deep breath. It was a very abbreviated version of the truth and her explanation of the money only included the settlement from Redgrove, but it was enough for

Charlotte to start to see that this life was the aberration.

Leaving Charlotte on the balcony, Alexa was not sure what to expect when she arrived back. Bethany said little about the situation, so Alexa stopped talking about it after a few minutes. When Ben joined them, Alexa slipped out of the conversation entirely. Alexa loved that Bethany got along so well with Ben, but just wished she did not feel so left out when the three of them were together.

"You want me to give you a lift home on the way to work?" asked Ben when Alexa rose to leave.

Her home was not on the way to Ben's work from the detention centre, but pointing that out had never made any difference. When she nodded her agreement, Ben smiled broadly. It made her wonder why such a thing would make him so happy when they could barely have a conversation.

"Just so you know," said Ben as he pulled up in front of her apartment block. "Charlotte's parents sorted things out with the shop owner. She's not being charged. But you didn't hear that from me."

"Thank you," nodded Alexa.

"She's their problem. Don't get your life caught up in that world again because of some messed up kid. You need to focus on your life."

"Anyone ever say that to you?" retorted Alexa. "Focus on your life instead of getting caught up in the lives of some messed up kids?"

Ben bit his lip, but did not reply, and Alexa stalked away. She tried breathing deeply, not wanting to face Charlotte in an agitated mood. However, the smell of food helped to dispel her frustrations as she walked into the apartment to see Charlotte cooking dinner.

"I thought about what you said," said Charlotte meekly, noticing Alexa watching her. "If I try, I mean, make an effort and not get into so much trouble, can I stay with you?"

"That all depends on your parents. You aren't sixteen yet. You can't just leave home."

"I don't want to go back there," said Charlotte firmly.

"Why don't we give it time? But you can stay as long as you're allowed, okay?"

"I guess."

Alexa knew it was not the response Charlotte wanted, but she did not want to make the situation more complicated than it had to be. Until she was sure Charlotte's parents really did not want her, she did not want to be responsible for taking Charlotte away from them. After all, they had cared enough to sort out the situation with the police.

The next day, Alexa walked down to Charlotte's house to talk to her parents. She tried to get Charlotte to come with her, but she was adamant she was not returning home. The welcome Alexa received was not entirely warm and she realised she must have looked like one of Charlotte's school friends. When Alexa did manage to get Charlotte's parents talking, she found them nice enough, but there was a definite edge in their voices when they spoke about Charlotte that was not there when they spoke about her younger siblings.

"We're tired of her antics," said her step-mother in an irritated voice. "We don't know what else to do. She's disrespectful and can't keep herself out of trouble. We're trying our best to bring up our children and it doesn't help when she's causing so many problems."

"She's one of your children too," cried Alexa before calming herself. "I know you're doing your best. All I know is Charlotte believes she comes last in the family and by a long way," she continued, trying very hard to remain diplomatic.

"If she showed her step-mother and I a bit of respect, perhaps we wouldn't be in this situation," said Mr Jammel sternly. "We're can't drop everything every time she wants attention."

"But she needs —"

"We have more important – she's thirteen. She can get the attention she needs from her friends."

"She's your daughter. It's your responsibility. God, she cuts her arms to get you to realise how upset she is," implored Alexa.

"Then perhaps she needs a psychiatrist more than a father."

It was clear Charlotte had not been exaggerating about her parents' attitude, but Alexa was not sure it was quite as bad as it seemed. By the end of her visit, Charlotte's father left her with the impression that he was struggling to cope with a troubled child and loved Charlotte more than Charlotte realised. However, Alexa still did not have the news she knew deep down Charlotte wanted to hear.

"So I can stay?" asked Charlotte hesitantly.

"Yes," Alexa nodded solemnly. "Your parents weren't too sure, but I told them you needed time out and you'd go and visit occasionally to try work through your differences."

"Yeah, right. Like they gave a shit where I was," spat Charlotte bitterly, and Alexa guessed her proficiency at lying had not improved.

"They do, actually," Alexa continued. "Ask them if you don't believe me. They're not be the best parents, but doesn't make them heartless. We don't become infallible once we become adults." Charlotte crossed her arms and threw herself on the lounge. "But since you're staying, I have a few conditions."

"What conditions?" asked Charlotte with bitter scepticism.

"Well, like keeping out of trouble at school," replied Alexa, trying to figure out what would make their lives harmonious. "And letting me know where you are when you're not here. I don't need trouble."

"You're not my mother," muttered Charlotte.

"No, but it's my place. Oh, and you have to visit your family at least once a week," Alexa added quickly as the idea flashed across her mind.

"What? But —"

"I don't care if it's for one hour or one minute. You will go and see them – every week, at least once, no excuses."

Despite her initial protests, Charlotte did everything Alexa asked. They went shopping for personal items and other essentials. Alexa found Charlotte both wise and considerate of the money she was spending. They were a similar size, so she also gave Charlotte free reign over her wardrobe. Although that was not a huge contribution to her clothing situation, Charlotte did not mind. In fact, Charlotte did not seem to mind much at all. It took less than a week for them to settle into living with each other. Charlotte cooked and cleaned without prompting and took many of the household burdens off Alexa's hands. Of an afternoon, they would do their homework before cooking dinner. Alexa was rarely able to convince Charlotte to run down to the beach for an early morning swim with her; it was still much too cold for Charlotte. But on warm afternoons, they would delay their study and throw themselves into the cold ocean.

The new living arrangement was so agreeable that Alexa had to remind herself that it really was not her preferred outcome. What she wanted was for Charlotte's parents to turn up and ask Charlotte to come home, but it never happened, and Charlotte's brief visits were clearly not convincing them they were worse off without her. Though she did not say so, Alexa assumed from this point onwards Charlotte would be a permanent member of her household.

Given how badly Charlotte and Damien got along before, Alexa reassured Charlotte it would not be a problem this time around. She did not want Damien over very often, and never let him stay the night. Charlotte moving in was actually a lucky break. She had been running low on excuses to keep him out of the apartment. That did not mean they rarely saw each other. They were often together at uni and went on dates two or three times a week, usually ending up back at Damien's place. Damien wanted her to stay over. It was something Alexa had so far avoided, but realised she would have to submit if she was going to maintain a hard line about her apartment.

It quickly resulted in every date starting or ending in Damien's bedroom. Alexa could now tolerate his hands running over her naked body without her trembling, though that meant Damien stopped being so secret about his desire to take things further. Her ability to satisfy him in other ways was losing its charm.

For Alexa, the next step was more a logical progression than something she truly desired. She again found herself drawing parallels between her relationships with Damien and Clinton. She had never been physically attracted to Clinton, not in the way she had been to Sam or Marcus, but their relationship had started well and the sex had been enjoyable until the jealousy set in. So when Alexa's next date with Damien inevitably led to his bedroom, she did not resist his probing suggestions. But when he moved on top of her and held her hand loosely above her head, her heart pounded fearfully. Determined not to let fear get the better of her, Alexa rolled on top of him. Damien made no objections as she kissed his chest and moved her hips to his.

"You know today's our three-month anniversary," said Damien, holding her to his chest. Alexa wondered which date he was counting from. "It's the longest I've ever waited for a girl."

"Are you disappointed?" asked Alexa.

"No! I didn't mean it like that. It's just different. I think it actually meant more after waiting so long. I'm proud of you."

"Because I slept with you?"

"Because you trusted me. Because you finally realised I wasn't going to hurt you and let me close."

Alexa hated to break his delusion so kept quiet. She had slept with Damien, but could not see it as anything more than sex. It was just something couples did.

"I think I love you," said Damien, disrupting her thoughts.

"What? Umm, well, thanks," Alexa murmured awkwardly, unsure how to reply to such a statement. "Why don't you get back to me when you know for sure."

"Okay, I love you," replied Damien immediately. "Is that better?"

It wasn't. Alexa had never even considered love. She had battled to get herself to like. As much as she was sure about anything, she knew she did not love Damien, but did not know how to say that. Feeling the seconds pass by, Alexa knew Damien was waiting for a response, his arms twitching around her body. Hastily weighing up her options as she lay naked and vulnerable in his bed, Alexa realised the truth was not one of them. Even a close version of the truth seemed too risky. Thinking quickly, Alexa decided on the desired truth. Damien loved her. He was gentle and kind, if a little too possessive. What more could she hope for? Good men were never going to be interested in a girl like her. She did not love Damien yet, but if she committed herself to it, then perhaps one day she would. There was just no point expecting she was worthy of any more than this.

"I love you too," she replied softly.

Damien smiled broadly, turning her in his arms as he kissed her passionately.

***

"You don't love him, Lex," cried Bethany. "Why would you say that?"

"What? How do you don't know I don't love him," replied Alexa, shocked by Bethany's claim. She expected Bethany to be happy for her. It was the only reason she shared such intimate details in person and not in their frequent letters.

"Because I know you better than I know myself."

"All I ever get told is how I'm holding myself back and I can't wait around for something better. But when I push myself forward, you're not happy either. I can't win."

"I never told you to jump into this relationship," replied Bethany pointedly. "Pretending to be in love isn't going to make things better."

"I'm happy with him. I like being around him. We slept together for God's sake."

"Sex doesn't equal love."

"I'm well aware of that," snapped Alexa, trying not to think of all the sex she had had where love had not been involved.

"Yes, but you want it to," replied Bethany quickly, squeezing her hand. "You need it to. I'm just not sure you've found it with Damien."

"I've made my choice. I chose to move on, so I'll just have to make the most of it."

"Wow, now that's a profession of love."

Alexa left the detention centre with an angry fire in her heart. After everything everyone had said to her, she finally thought she was getting things right, but Bethany was not the only one who seemed surprised by her feelings. Ben, Maria and Charlotte had the respect to say very little, but there was one person whose objections were fiercer than Bethany's.

"Damn it, Sam, not you too!" cried Alexa when he accused her of lying about the depth of her feelings for Damien. "How the hell would you know how I feel?"

"Because I know you," Sam countered. "I know what you were like with me and when you fell in love with Mr Knight. You're not in love with Damien."

"You've been talking to Bethy. She's the one who's put this in your head. I love him, okay. Done deal, case closed."

"I'm so sorry. I can't believe I pushed you into this situation," said Sam, as she walked faster along the beach in an attempt to out-stride him. "I shouldn't have forced you. I feel terrible."

"I haven't been pushed into anything," muttered Alexa. "I just took your advice. Damien's a nice guy. He's sweet, kind, gentle and I'm giving him a go."

"Yeah, but love?" questioned Sam, with a distorted grimace.

"Are you sure this isn't jealousy?" asked Alexa.

"I'm not jealous. I just don't want to see you get into something you don't want."

"But you were the one pushing me into this in the first place."

"And that's what I'm saying. You don't love him."

"Fine, it might not be love," Alexa conceded, hoping that would satisfy Sam. "It's nothing like what I felt for you or Marcus, but then the two of you felt completely different. I'm just taking everyone's advice and giving this a go. At least then if it doesn't work no one can say it was because I didn't try. And damn it, why can't I love him?"

The more everyone told Alexa she was not in love with Damien, the more convinced she became that she was. It was the only logical way of looking at the situation, and if she could no longer trust her feelings then logic was all she had left to rely on. Yet it was not quite the relationship she had dreamed of. Every date now involved her and Damien in bed. Alexa complied with every one of his requests, feeling like they were part of her girlfriend duties, but never again did she let Damien on top of her. As long as she did not feel like she was pinned down, she would do whatever Damien wanted. It was an unspoken compromise Damien appeared completely at ease with.

The other major compromise in their relationship was something Damien was much less tolerant of. Alexa still refused to let him stay over at her place. Charlotte was her excuse. It was a plan she and Charlotte had come up with together, but as there was neither truth
118

nor necessity to back it up, relations between Damien and Charlotte quickly became very strained. Alexa reassured Charlotte her presence was not an issue, but with Damien's spiteful mutterings, Alexa was not always sure Charlotte believed her. Charlotte began spending the weekends at her parents' house and even talked about moving back permanently.

"You know I want you here, right," said Alexa, standing at the door of Charlotte's bedroom as she packed her bag for the weekend.

"I thought you wanted me to go back home to live," said Charlotte with a smirk.

"I do," relied Alexa with an awkward smile. "You should. I really want you to get along with your family and think you should live with them, but I miss you. I've gotten used to you living here."

"You were right about us needing space, and I love my dad. I'd like to be able to live with him and you don't need me cramping your style."

"Well, exams are soon, so there'll be no one here to worry about cramping. Just know that I'm not kicking you out, okay."

Charlotte smiled as she swung her bag over her shoulder. Alexa walked her to the door then headed to the dining room table. It was covered with textbooks, notes and study guides. From morning to night, she sat at that table and diligently tried to learn every word. Never before had Alexa applied herself so industriously. The results so far had not been spectacular, but they were better than anything she had achieved at school. With so much riding on these final exams, she wanted to make sure she had no excuses for not doing well.

Dates with Damien became shorter and less frequent, the date part all but eliminated. Alexa simply packed a textbook and caught the bus to his place, studying along the way. After they had spent a couple of hours in his bedroom, she headed home.

The only other person Alexa made the effort to see was Bethany. Having told Ben it was better if he stayed away from the apartment while she studied, he tried to make sure he was at the detention centre when she was, but Alexa often wished he wasn't. Her visits were never as free and open when Ben was around, but she did not dare say so. The only person Alexa could tell was Charlotte. Every night, Charlotte cooked dinner for her, and in return Alexa set aside an hour to talk to her. It was good to hear about the small advances she was making with her family and how much better she was getting on with her siblings.

"Well, they've never really been the problem. Mia and Dylan are actually pretty nice," shrugged Charlotte, collecting their plates. "Real problem is we don't really know each other. They think I'm rebellious and cool, but hate that I cause fights. So they're usually too scared to hang with me."

Alexa struggled to smile. The similarity between Charlotte's situation and her life when she had first been placed with the Whites was extraordinary. It made Alexa wonder what Hayley now thought of her and if any of her former admiration survived that brutal night.

"The Whites?" asked Charlotte as Alexa stared blankly into space. Alexa nodded. "Sorry."

"Not your fault," shrugged Alexa.

"At least let me be the solution. Here." Charlotte handed Alexa one of her textbooks. "I'll get the tea."

Alexa looked at her watch. "Better make it coffee," she sighed.

Charlotte smilingly complied.

Over the next three weeks, Charlotte practically waited on Alexa. She cooked, cleaned, shopped and supplied Alexa with everything she needed. If Alexa had not been so stressed out after her first exam, convinced she had failed, she might have made Charlotte stop, but the truth was she needed someone around to help her out. She just wished it was not a thirteen-year-old child.

Walking out of her final exam, Alexa felt like a thousand tonnes suddenly dropped from her body. She had survived her first semester of university. Hanging around for a while, Alexa chatted to some of the other people in her class. She was not sure she would go as far as calling any of them friends, but through Jessica, with whom she shared most classes, and Damien, she had developed a small network of acquaintances. If it had been enough to convince Ben and Sam that she was making an effort, she would have been happy. All they ever wanted to know was why none of them were over at her place as often as Charlotte was.

After a quick celebratory lunch, Alexa headed home. She was tempted to go down to the beach, but was determined this day be dedicated to Charlotte. There was no way she would have done half as well if Charlotte had not been around. Alexa met Charlotte down the road from her school and dragged her to the beach. The weather was warm and they swam happily, diving in and out of the waves. Dinner was back down the beach. Alexa wanted to make it a grander affair, but Charlotte insisted what she really wanted was to try out the local pizzeria. They ordered take away and sat on the stairs leading down to the sand, watching the waves crash rhythmically on to the shore.

"So, um, this might not be the best time to tell you," said Charlotte hesitantly as they finished the pizza. "But I'm going to move back home now you've finished your exams." Alexa could only stare. Charlotte smiled. "I wanted make sure you got through them okay."

"You shouldn't have stayed just for me if your family wanted you back," cried Alexa, feeling sick with guilt.

"Well, it's not like they've actually invited me back," said Charlotte, making Alexa scowl. "Yeah, maybe my dad has. He was impressed that I wanted to stay until you'd finished. Said he thought I'd grown up. Don't think Carla cares if I come back or not, but it's nice that me and my dad are getting on better. We talked a bit. I'm not going to get as upset about Carla and he's going to try and get her to like me."

Charlotte seemed content with that compromise. Alexa wished she could be. It was selfish, but she wanted Charlotte to stay and certainly did not want her returning home when things appeared so combative. Charlotte only laughed at her concerns.

"You have to come visit," reiterated Alexa as they packed the next morning. Charlotte laughed. It must have been the thousandth time she had said that since finding out Charlotte was leaving. "And stay sometimes. You have to. We're friends now."

Charlotte swore this would not be the last time they saw each other as she swung her bag over her shoulder. As if to prove the point, she nodded towards the dressing table, where some of her belongings still sat. Alexa smiled, but still felt strangely empty when the door clicked closed. It made the start of her long summer holidays much bleaker than it otherwise would have been. However, with three months of freedom ahead, Alexa could not stay forlorn. Just the warm weather made her feel more alive. Then there was the time. There was suddenly so much more of it. All that made her first week of holidays busier than most of the year combined. Alexa was rarely at home to do more than sleep. When she was not visiting Bethany, she was with Maria. If she was not with Maria, she was with Damien. Ben sometimes slipped in, occasionally by himself, but mostly during visits to Bethany or Maria. Then there was the beach, which was everywhere in between.

The only person Alexa rarely saw was Charlotte. With Charlotte trying to make things work at home and studying for her own exams, she had little time for visits. However, when Alexa received her results, she made sure she was free when Charlotte was. She had received two credits and two distinctions. In one subject she had even been a single mark off a high distinction. It was the first time she had ever received such marks in her life and knew Charlotte had been a major factor in her achievement. It deserved a celebration.

Alexa made sure there was not a strict dress code before she booked the restaurant, because she did not want to tip Charlotte off that she was taking her somewhere nice. Just the mention of going to the city had Charlotte anxious about the fuss Alexa was making, but by the time Charlotte cottoned on to where they were going, they were already in the lift to the city's revolving tower restaurant.

"This isn't for you," Alexa lied when Charlotte tried to complain. "It's for me to celebrate. You just got invited cos you live close."

Charlotte shook her head disbelievingly, smiling as she did. Even though Charlotte did not believe her lie, Alexa could understand why she needed to hear it, and it allowed them both to thoroughly enjoy the night. The array of food at the buffet was incredible, and they ate much more than usual, just to try it all. Watching the revolving skyline, they tried to spy Alexa's apartment in the cluster of buildings, as they marvelled at how vast the city was – until Alexa pulled out a small blue box.

"For you," she said, holding it out. "For everything you've done."

Charlotte shuffled indecisively, before finally taking the box. She held it for a long moment without opening it. When Charlotte did lift the lid, her eyes widened expressively as they took in the diamond pendant hanging on the thin gold chain.

"Too much," Charlotte whispered, just staring at the necklace.

Ignoring Charlotte's slowly shaking of her head, Alexa took the chain out of the box and hung it around Charlotte's neck.

"You've been my saviour this year," Alexa said sincerely, pulling Charlotte into an embrace.

Charlotte's hug was brief but tight, and as she pulled away she managed to surreptitiously wipe her eyes on Alexa's shoulder. Alexa went to smile reassuringly when she noticed Charlotte tucking the necklace under her top and out of sight. "Just between us, okay," said Charlotte softly.

***

The increase in the number of trips Alexa was making to the detention centre directly correlated with the increase in the number of driving lessons she was trying to fit in. While she was at uni, the long trips had been put to good use, but now there was nothing to fill the time and Alexa became acutely aware of how much she was wasting.

The large number of hours she was required to complete before sitting for her driving test made Alexa anxious not to have to pay an instructor for all of them. Ben had finally agreed to teach her how to drive, but insisted a driving instructors was the best person to teach her how to pass the driving test. Alexa was just starting to appreciate the difference. If it helped her appreciate Ben's other advice more, things might have been better. After just one lesson in his car, Ben insisted Alexa buy her own car to learn in. His official reason was that it was important for her to be comfortable with the car she would be driving, but she suspected it had more to do with her accidently accelerating while she had been in reverse and thought she was in drive. She had mounted the gutter, but thankfully not hit anything. Ben had yelled a lot after that, but from Alexa's point of view, he had been shouting a lot before then. That was what had made her so flustered she made the mistake. If not for the break from their lessons and the acquisition of her car, Alexa might never have driven with Ben again.

Ben had said he would take her out for a drive when he came over today, but Alexa was worried about how it would go. This would be their first drive alone together since the disastrous lesson that had almost fractured their relationship, but thankfully when Ben arrived, it was with his partner, Shane Parker.

"Hey, Alexa," smiled Shane from the front passenger seat of Ben's car. "Sorry to ruin your plans. Duty calls. Ben thought you might like to take a drive to visit your sister."

"You calling shotgun?" Alexa asked tentatively, turning slightly to Ben, though she refused to meet his eyes.

"Hell yeah," Shane smiled, waving her towards the car.

Alexa genuinely liked Shane. He was very nice, but never tried to be anything more than Ben's colleague who was helping Ben more than her. Perhaps he really was. She and Ben might not be talking if not for him. Shane had been in the car the day she had driven them to lunch. From the very start Ben had been yelling. Whatever she did – whatever other drivers did – he yelled. It put her on edge and she consequently made many more mistakes than she ever did when she was with her driving instructor. When Alexa had finally parked, she was almost in tears. Ben slammed the car door on his exit, lamenting her attitude and temper.

Lunch had been a tense and somewhat silent affair, with Alexa determined not to drive back. However, when Shane pushed Ben into the back seat and insisted she drive with him, she had just enough courage to agree. It had been a remarkable turning point, and Shane had taken her for nearly every one of her private lessons since. Even though Ben was always in the back seat with them, he stayed quiet and let Shane take control. Shane explained what she needed to do, rather than expecting her to just know, and kept her calm enough to actually learn rather than just do.

"Thanks, Parker," said Alexa as she pulled into the detention centre parking lot.

"No worries," he smiled. "We can't stay though. You right to make your own way home?"

"Of course!" Alexa replied, jumping out of the car, feeling guiltily glad they could not stay. She wanted time alone with Bethany.

It would not have been so bad if her relationship with Ben was not so volatile. They seemed to have the ability to rub each other the wrong way, but in their quieter moments there were few whose company she enjoyed more. Alexa just wished she could be the daughter Bethany somehow managed to be.

"Should we have dinner tomorrow night?" asked Ben, walking around to the driver's seat.

"Sounds good," Alexa replied happily, loving the way Ben smiled when he asked those kinds of questions. "Come over and I can cook something."

"We can even go for a drive, if you like – now Parker seems to've tamed your temper," added Ben with a chuckle.

Alexa scowled and turned away. If she had not seen Shane drop his shaking head into his hand, she might have explained how wrong Ben was, but hoped Shane might do that for her.

"You have to cut him some slack," smiled Bethany ten minutes later, after Alexa confessed her annoyance; she rarely discussed these things with Bethany. "You do have a temper. You need to stop using up all your patience on me. Spread it round a bit."

"Yeah, I forgot, everything's always my fault," muttered Alexa.

"You're not perfect, Lex."

"Either's Ben," she retorted, hating that Bethany thought he was.

"No, but you guys are pretty close," Bethany smiled.

Alexa could only roll her eyes, a smile breaking across her face. It was impossible to stay mad at Bethany. "Where do I get a pair of those rose-coloured glasses you're always wearing?"

"Come on, Lex. You think I'm pretty perfect," smiled Bethany.

"No, I don't. I know you're not. I'm far too aware of my failures and where they've left you."

Bethany did not reply. She just took Alexa's hand. They laid their heads on the table and spent the rest of the visit in silence.

The next visit was nowhere near as silent. Alexa made the effort to appear cheery as she recounted her dinner with Ben. It was not a lie. She and Ben had a good night together. Bethany smiled happily as they spoke. Alexa sometimes felt Bethany spent much of her life brokering her and Ben's relationship.

"How's Damien going?" asked Bethany.

"Things are going well," replied Alexa, answering the question Bethany was really asking.

It was a question that was getting easier to answer as time went on. The longer she and Damien were together, the more things tallied in his favour. Even his immovable disapproval of Charlotte was not enough to outweigh the fact that he loved her. That he was even capable of such a feat would outweigh almost every other negative trait. Thankfully, everyone else seemed to have caught on to that fact and had stopped commenting on their relationship. Except Bethany. "You don't love him," she cried. "You may've been able to convince him and everyone else and possibly you, but I know you."

"And even if that was true, which it isn't, what's it matter?" asked Alexa. "It's not like we're getting married. We're hanging out, having fun."

"But I think you're actually looking for more. You don't like fooling around. You want your relationships meaningful and long-lasting."

"But I'm not deluded enough to think they all will be."

"You've been with him for what, four months? I think you're trying to convince yourself you can do this long-term. I'm not saying you can't, but while you're lying to him and yourself, it'll only end in tears."

"I love him," replied Alexa firmly.

Bethany shrugged, which Alexa knew meant that she had given up for this visit, but Alexa was determined to prove to her wrong. If she could not be trusted to be guided by her feelings, she had to rely on logic. And Alexa was no longer convinced her feelings for Damien remained all that neutral. She had to feel something for him. That too was only logical. So when she met up with him that night, she paid a lot more attention to their interactions.

"Hey, sweetie," said Damien, as he kissed her hello. He took her hand and led her towards the beach. "How you going?"

"All right," replied Alexa slowly, concentrating too hard on whether she had been appropriately excited by the sight of Damien and aroused by his kiss to give a better answer.

"I didn't think I'd see you today. How was your sister?"

"Okay, I guess. She gets a bit sadder leading up to Christmas. So do I, for that matter."

"Talking about Christmas, I want you to celebrate it with me," said Damien expectantly.

"Thanks, but I spend the day with Bethy," Alexa replied quickly, never considering any idea that took her away from Bethany.

"You can just come in the evening – after dinner if that's all you can make. I'd really like you to come."

Alexa felt her body flush. Damien was sweet, kind and genuine. She did not know how the feelings she had for him could possibly be anything but love. Perhaps she simply did not feel intensely any more and this was all that remained of her emotional depth. The more she considered it, the more strongly she concluded she was in love with Damien and the feelings she had were what love now felt like.

"Umm, I'll have to think about it, okay," Alexa replied. "I'm really not that great at Christmas. I don't know that it'd be the best day for me to be introduced to your family."

"You don't have to wait until Christmas to meet my family. They're dying to meet you. I talk about you all the time."

"Really?" asked Alexa sceptically. "What do they know about me?"

"As much as I know, which I don't think's very much sometimes," laughed Damien, though not fully in jest. "We've been going out nearly five months and you've told me almost nothing about your past. Most of what I know I've guessed or heard from other people. I know you don't have parents and that you have people you've met along the way and kinda formed into your family. I know you went to school with Sam, and I think he's got a massive crush on you." Alexa could not help but laugh. "What? You don't think he likes you?"

"What me and Sam have goes way beyond like. He's my best friend. I love him, but he doesn't want to date me and I don't want to date him," smiled Alexa.

"You love him, hey?" asked Damien.

"Of course I do," replied Alexa automatically, before realising that might not be the response Damien wanted to hear.

"It's good to have friends like that," said Damien, after an awkward pause. "It's good."

Alexa did not know whether to explain the situation more clearly. She was sure Damien was a little jealous and knew there was a good chance he would get the wrong idea if she tried to explain the past, particularly the more recent past. Instead, they spoke of more general things and organised the rest of their week. The conversation was light and unrestrained and Alexa went to bed that night more convinced than ever she had made the right choice. Damien was not Sam and he was certainly not Marcus, but he did not have to be. He made her laugh and had never made her cry. That was good enough for her.

But now that Damien had broached the issue of Christmas, Alexa knew she would have to face its existence sooner rather than later. Bethany had asked her not to buy her a present. Alexa understood, but was caught between her long-held desire to learn to love Christmas and her terror of the disasters the day always brought. After deducing that her life this year had been something between brilliant and the usual crap, Alexa decided her Christmas could be something in between as well. She would celebrate, see everyone and buy presents, but in a subdued manner. However, if she was going to shop for everyone, she could not in good conscience buy nothing for Bethany. She decided to get Bethany a pack of essentials she could use while in the detention centre and kept an eye out for presents she could keep for when Bethany was released.

Damien became more pressing about whether she would come to his family Christmas, but his was not the only offer Alexa received. Ben and Maria both asked her around to their places for breakfast, lunch or dinner, while Sam and his grandparents invited her over for lunch or dinner. To appease all and please none, Alexa refused everyone and made a counter-offer of hosting Boxing Day lunch. Bethany would be the only person Alexa would see on Christmas Day.

"I'd still like to see you on Christmas Day," said Maria, the week before Christmas. "You feel like family now. It wouldn't feel right not seeing you."

"I thought if I avoided everyone then no one could get angry at me," explained Alexa. She had wanted to see Maria too.

"What are you going to do?" asked Maria with a tender smile.

"Spend the day with Bethy. They put on a big lunch. You can arrive from ten and don't have to leave until five. So I'll be there when the gates open and go when they kick us out. What about you?"

"I'll be here alone most of the day," replied Maria in a voice that tried hard not to betray her sadness. It made Alexa's heart ache. "My kids have their own families and they do alternate years with each side of the family. This is not my year."

"But surely they'll come and see you?" queried Alexa, horrified that Maria's children would abandon her on Christmas Day.

"Oh, yes, Viktor said he'd drop by with the kids on Christmas Eve. Jovana said she could pop in for a quick hello on Christmas morning, and I haven't heard from Vesna. I'm not actually sure she'll even be in the country."

"You can – I mean, it's not a great day, but if you want – it's just an idea, but you can come with me to see Bethy."

"Oh, um, I'm not sure. You don't want me intruding on your day," said Maria with hesitant dismissiveness.

"I've told her all about you and I know she'd love to meet you. I mean, I can understand if you don't want to come," adding Alexa quickly, realising there could be another reason for Maria's tentative answer. "Gaol's not the greatest place to spend Christmas."

"Would Bethany mind me coming?" asked Maria.

"Not at all, but I can check if it'll make you feel better."

"Perhaps you should," nodded Maria, but Alexa could see the inclination in Maria's eyes and believed she was desperate for any form of company on Christmas Day.

Alexa left Maria's to finalise her Christmas shopping. She wanted to finish it today before she headed off to see Bethany, but doubted she would. The shops were full of sales and Alexa hoped it would help her actually purchase something. Present buying had never been one of her skills, and practice was not making her more proficient.

Walking along, Alexa kept looking alternately down at the list of people she still needed something for and around at the shops, seeking inspiration. It made her a hazard. She had already walked into a bin. When she looked up again, she noticed a very solid body in front of her, and that he was as distracted as herself. Alexa stepped to the side, but it was not enough and the man slammed heavily into her shoulder, spinning her slightly. He did not say anything, so Alexa quickly muttered an apology, keeping her eyes to the ground in case she had just enraged a psychopath.

"Alexa?" gasped a breathless voice as she turned to rush away.

Alexa's heart started pounding. It was impossible. Her feet slowly turned her around, her eyes travelling up the man's body until she reached his face. It still felt so surreal, but there he was. She was looking straight into the chocolate brown eyes of Marcus Knight.

Chapter Nine

THERE WAS SILENCE for many long seconds as they stared at each other in mute shock. Marcus tried to speak, but he could not move. Even breathing seemed difficult.

"Hey," said Alexa casually.

"Hi," replied Marcus, just managing to squeeze out the breathless words.

Marcus could not get his brain into gear. All he could do was stare and take in Alexa's beautiful face. He had been left with memories of a fragile schoolgirl and it made him sick, but the woman before him was not a schoolgirl. Her face still looked barely a day over sixteen, but he could see in her eyes that she had grown up. There was a sense of confidence and self-assuredness he had rarely seen in her before. It made his heart ache in a way he could not comprehend. It was not just longing, it was —

"Christmas shopping?" asked Alexa, breaking his thoughts.

"No, um – ah …"

"Do you know why you're here?"

Marcus could see the concern in Alexa's eyes and wondered if she regretted bumping into him or was just worried about his lack of coherent sentences. "Yes," he replied, regaining control over his brain. "I have an appointment with the real estate. Me and my – my, um – I'm moving into a new place with – um – my girlfriend."

Marcus closed his eyes as he finished the sentence. The idea of being with someone else seemed like a betrayal now he was standing in front of Alexa. He knew they should never be together, but he had promised her so much that he felt he owed it to her to stand by those promises until she outright rejected them. Opening his eyes, Marcus half expected to see Alexa stalking off, but she took the news with the same passive expression she always used to hide her emotions.

"Are you here with your girlfriend?" asked Alexa, looking around cautiously.

"No, she couldn't make it," Marcus replied, thankful for that, despite being livid moments before. "So I guess it's my choice where we live."

"What time's your appointment?"

"Not for two hours, actually. We were supposed to have lunch first, but something came up at the last minute and she couldn't make it."

"Well, I'm sick of people and shops, so if you want we can have something to eat to help pass the time."

"Really?" Marcus asked, sure he had to be hearing things.

"I did offer."

Marcus smiled and nodded, but as he did so he noticed a glimmer of gold around Alexa's neck. His hand automatically reached out for it, but he caught himself and pulled back. Alexa immediately pulled the gold chain out from under her top.

"I took it off for a while, but not for long," she murmured.

Happiness spilled through Marcus's body at the sight of the pendant he had given her, but it was quickly mopped up by the anguish over what he had put Alexa through and the reason they had been strangers this past year.

"I wasn't sure if you were trying to ignore me or if you really didn't see me," Marcus said with a half-smile as they sat down in a nearby restaurant.

"I didn't see you," replied Alexa firmly.

"How have you been?" Marcus asked quickly, desperate to know she was okay.

"All right. Just finished my first semester of uni. Went to Europe for the first six months of the year."

"Are you seeing anyone?" Marcus knew the answer, but still had to ask. Alexa simply nodded. "Yeah, Sam mentioned that."

"Sam? You've seen Sam? When?" asked Alexa, her voice a mixture of curiosity and anger.

"Only briefly a couple of times. Meetings with the lawyers – about the case they're filing against the school. You know about that, right?"

"Yeah, I knew about it, but Sam never mentioned seeing you."

"I don't think he's my biggest fan. He warned me off you the first moment I saw him. Told me you wanted nothing to do with me. Can hardly blame you for feeling that way."

"He never told me he saw you," repeated Alexa softly, as if to herself, buoying Marcus with the idea she may one day forgive him.

"I'm sure he thought he was doing the right thing. He's protective. I'd probably have done the same thing if I was your boyfriend"

"Boyfriend? What?" asked Alexa, looking up with confused eyes.

"Sam – you – your boyfriend."

"I'm not going out with Sam," replied Alexa, looking thoroughly perplexed.

"Oh, I just assumed – you guys always had a special bond and after everything that happened last year – it was obvious he still liked you and given what you found out – I just presumed the two of you might've given it another go."

"We had a lot to work through, but we both realised we'd moved on and there was no point trying to recapture the past," said Alexa, looking down at her hands, giving Marcus the impression there was more to that story.

Thoughtful silence sat with them until their food arrived. Marcus watched Alexa eat, curious as to the extent of her recovery. She looked fine, she looked amazing, but still thin and he hoped there were no lingering problems from last year.

"I'm really sure why my eating habits entertain so many people," said Alexa with a smile as he continuing to stare at her plate.

"Sorry," Marcus murmured, embarrassed he had been so obvious.

"It's okay. So how long have you and your girlfriend been going out?"

"A bit over six months."

"And you're already moving in together?"

"Yeah, it's a bit of a hair-brain relationship," replied Marcus with a slight smile. "She makes me smile and, well, she's an old friend and really helped me through this last year. How about you?"

"Almost five months," nodded Alexa thoughtfully. "Though I have no plans to move in with him. Don't even let him stay over."

"I'm sure that'll change soon enough," replied Marcus, knowing it was true and the thought made him slightly ill. Alexa had the right to be happy, but he still hated the idea of her in the arms of another man.

Alexa smiled and started praising the food. Marcus was surprised how easily their conversation flowed. He had always imagined that the dynamics of their relationship would have changed, but it was just like old times – better, because the life Alexa now spoke of was so different she truly could have been another person.

"What?" Alexa asked when he started chuckling softly.

"It's just that there was this part of me that was so worried about how you'd cope this year. I'd been fretting that you were in trouble and needed help – guidance – my guidance – and you're doing brilliantly. It's great. I underestimated you. No, maybe not, I think I underestimated how much of your troubles were caused by external factors."

"You think I'm doing okay?" Alexa asked, as though she genuinely doubted that. It made Marcus wonder what everyone else was telling her.

"No," Marcus replied firmly. "I said you were doing brilliantly. What else are you supposed to have pulled off this year?"

"Some people think I'm focusing too much on Charlotte – so I can ignore my problems. Probably do sometimes, but she's like me and I don't want her to go through everything I did."

"You find her a lot like you?" asked Marcus curiously. Alexa nodded. "And you're trying to keep her on track? How's that going?" he asked with a slight smirk.

"What? You think I'm an idiot too?" retorted Alexa in a fiery voice.

"No, I'm wondering if karma works the way everyone says it does," Marcus replied with a purposely light voice.

"Oh. Yeah, that," said Alexa, scowling lightly. "It's harder than I thought, especially cos I don't think I always agree with the sensible stuff that's been somehow drilled into me. She's given me a bit more appreciation of what you guys all went through dealing with me."

The maturity Alexa displayed was amazing. It was hard to fathom the growth that had occurred in the past twelve months. Marcus took some comfort in the fact that Alexa was only more attractive to him now than she had been when she was younger, though a much larger part wished there was no attraction at all.

They continued to chat easily, Alexa smiling whenever he caught her eye, which he did often. It was almost as if the horrors of the year before had not happened. Almost.

"So how's Redgrove going? Did they give you another year to advise?" queried Alexa bitterly, after Sam's lawsuit had been briefly raised again.

"No, I didn't stay there. I couldn't," said Marcus, shaking his head. "I guess Sam really didn't tell you anything."

"No."

"After what happened – all of it, not just you – I couldn't stay there. I wasn't even sure I wanted to keep teaching. I couldn't believe I'd been part of a system that allowed all those things to happened to you and the rest of the G7. That's why I backed them up with this lawsuit. Redgrove's fighting it, but there're a lot of teachers who've come forward in support of them and plenty of students too."

"So what are you doing now?"

"Still teaching. I'm at an inner city high school. No boarders. I seriously considered quitting teaching all together, but I was offered the position and I needed the money, so I took it." Alexa nodded, but she had turned away and Marcus knew he had to make this right. "Listen," he said nervously. "I want to apologise for what happened at the end of last year. You have to know that I —"

"Please don't. I know I brought up the subject of school, but please, can we talk about something else. I don't want to think about it. Please," begged Alexa in a small voice.

Marcus nodded, hating that Alexa would never be able to fully forgive him, though he despised himself more for expecting her to. That she even spoke to him was generous enough and he deserved to feel the shame of his actions. Just the way she shrunk into herself when she was forced to confront those events was a horrible reminder that although she could move on, there was nothing that could erase those events and his actions from her life.

"So where do you live now?" Marcus asked. He was not sure it was an appropriate question, but it was the first thing that came to mind. "You still living with Ben and his family?"

"No," Alexa replied hesitantly. "I live in an apartment in the east. It has a nice view of the ocean. I like it."

"That sounds good," Marcus smiled. "You live by yourself?"

"Yeah, after years of sharing a room with four other girls it makes a nice break."

Marcus smiled more broadly, though tried to hide it. He knew Alexa had received a substantial settlement from Redgrove and was glad she was now financially secure, but wondered if she realised just how expensive the east was compared to the rest of the city. Perhaps it was better she was naïve. She deserved that luxury, but he had to wonder if the same images were conjured in her mind as his every time she looked out at the ocean.

"What about you?" Alexa continued, staring at him as his thoughts drifted. "Why are you moving so close to Christmas?"

"Just worked out that way. Lucy's roommate was leaving and I thought it might be nice for us to see each other more often, so I suggested we get a place together. Will hopefully have everything finalised this week and can move between Christmas and New Year."

Alexa again nodded and turned away and Marcus guessed that it was as uncomfortable for her to hear about Lucy as if was for him to talk about her. When Alexa looked surreptitiously at her watch, he knew their time was up. He tried to insist on paying, but Alexa was just as determined to pay her share and he could not be sure if it was because she did not trust him or she believed it was the right thing to do. Either way, Marcus had the feeling this would be the last time he saw Alexa and was glad he could say goodbye on pleasant terms.

"Um, why don't I give you my number," said Alexa suddenly as they stood awkwardly outside the restaurant. "I mean, it was nice catching up and I thought – maybe – it might be nice to do it again." Marcus searched Alexa's face quickly, sure she must be joking. "I mean – I guess – if you don't want to –"

"No, no, I was just a little surprised. I didn't think – I'd love to see you again."

Alexa nodded, smiling just slightly, and Marcus quickly pulled out his phone. He immediately rang Alexa's number and watched her face colour as she rejected his call. His stomach turned over when she saved his number under the name of Marcus and not Mr Knight.

They walked together in silence to the real estate agent, where they said their goodbyes. Marcus had never had a greater urge to hug someone in his life, but perhaps it was just the idea of letting Alexa go that really troubled him.

"Hey, Alexa," he called when she had gone a few metres. "You end up learning how to change a car tyre?"

"No," she smiled broadly. "Haven't needed that one yet."

"If you ever need to – I can do that – call me – I can teach you."

"Sounds good," she nodded, making his heart swell. "And you can call me if you ever need to learn how to scale downpipes."

"Downpipes," Marcus mouthed slowly, as Alexa chuckled, finally confessing how she had escaped the confines of Redgrove.

She was more amazing than he had believed, and he could do nothing more than stare as she walked down the street and out of sight.

Looking down at her watch, Alexa panicked and ran. Her bus was at the stop as she rounded the corner. She sprinted for it, thankful for the passenger who had taken their time buying their ticket. Slumping into a seat, Alexa tried to comprehend what just happened.

She had met Marcus. In that moment, she felt as though she had finally returned to some form of sanity. He had not been a figment of her imagination. Her feelings for him had not been a lie. She had loved him, but could not as easily determine if she still did.

After spending five months convincing herself what she felt for Damien was love, Alexa could not begin to fathom what it was she felt for Marcus, even more so because entwined within the passion was still undeniable pain.

The rapid beating of her heart had barely settled by the time she reached the detention centre – with just fifteen minutes of visiting time left. After clearing security, there was only five minutes remaining and Bethany rushed into the room as if she had been caged all day.

"I was starting to think you weren't coming," said Bethany, as she sat down next to her in the rapidly emptying meeting room.

"I'm sorry. Something came up. I …"

"What happened, Lex? What's wrong?" asked Bethany anxiously.

"I saw him," breathed Alexa.

"Who?"

"Marcus."

A broad smile spread across Bethany's face. "Where? How?"

"At a shopping centre. I walked straight into him."

"Romantic reunion."

"It wasn't a reunion," replied Alexa flatly. "He's about to move in with his girlfriend."

"And you're with another man you say you love. People who've lost their true love will do stupid things like that."

"He may not've been my true love. I was seventeen – eighteen."

"Yeah and now you're nineteen you know it all?"

"Time's up," said a burly guard, standing Bethany up.

"You'd better come back tomorrow," called Bethany, as she was pushed towards the door. "I want details!"

Alexa did not disappoint and was back as soon as the doors opened the next morning, detailing every moment of her meeting with Marcus.

"So you gave him your number?" asked Bethany with a slight furrow in her brow.

"Okay, I admit that was a bit off the cuff. I was putting my number in his phone before I even knew what I was doing."

"But do you still like him?"

"I wanted to kiss him when we left – just on the cheek, but I really wanted to," Alexa confessed.

"Did you?"

"Are you kidding? We didn't get any closer than two feet and even then …"

A vague, distant look came across Alexa's face as words failed her. All she could think about were those moments they had shared back at Redgrove, never touching, but feeling as close as any two people could. But those memories were never relived without the more painful ones – Marcus walking away from her, leaving her to the brutality of Ms Carter; Martha telling her he would not come to see her despite knowing she was ill; and the tortured, desperate look on his face as he begged for her forgiveness.

The silence continued for many minutes. Alexa felt the occasional tear slip down her cheek and a heaving breath leave her chest, but Bethany stayed quiet, allowing her to recover in her own time.

"Oh, I almost forgot. I asked Maria if she wanted to come here for Christmas," said Alexa in a controlled voice, squeezing Bethany's hand. "She wouldn't say yes until I found out it was okay with you."

"She doesn't really know me," replied Bethany warily.

"She knows everything about you. I tell her everything about you and me and all that. She always asks how you are."

"I know. I'm just not sure that this would be the best place for her to spend Christmas. Who's going to want to come here for Christmas?"

"Me, of course," smiled Alexa genuinely. "Wouldn't be anywhere but where you are. And I agree, but she'll be alone all day otherwise."

"Sure she can come if she wants. Just let her know we still both hate Christmas. And no presents. Let's not have her expecting too much. Phff, prison Christmas, the place to be."

"Don't worry, I'll make sure she understands. I think Ben was going to come for a little bit as well."

"Yeah, but he didn't know when. He was still trying to smooth things over with his wife in the hope of having a family Christmas," explained Bethany, which was more than Ben had told Alexa. "I told him he didn't have to come, but he insisted he would."

"Christmas with the two of you, I wouldn't miss it for the world."

Bethany smiled brightly at Ben's appearance. Alexa smiled, but not as warmly. She loved that Ben was always around, enjoyed his company and the interest he took in them, but for reasons she could not explain she could not feel as close to him as Bethany appeared to be.

"I thought you might be here," said Ben, planting a kiss on Alexa's head. "So what've my girls been up to?" Alexa shot Bethany a look and shook her head minutely. "What? What's happened?"

"Nothing," said Alexa innocently.

"I may not be able to tell what you're thinking, but I've gotten pretty good at knowing when you two are keeping secrets."

"Come on, Ben, we don't keep secrets," said Bethany in a light voice. "We always keep you in the loop."

"Yeah, when it benefits you, you do. Fine, I'll find out eventually. Which one of you is it about?"

Ben looked between them, but Alexa and Bethany continued to

smile mischievously. Alexa knew there was nothing and no one that could make them break their code of silence.

Alexa did not stay long after Ben arrived. She always gave the excuse of wanting to let Ben and Bethany catch up privately, but the truth was she found it difficult to interact with them while they were together. Ben and Bethany's relationship seemed to be so free and easy, and Alexa could not emulate it no matter how hard she tried.

"I suppose you want a lift home," said Ben, walking out from the detention centre to where she was seated.

"As long as you let me drive," smiled Alexa.

"I have to get back to work."

"Come on, I drive almost like a normal person now. You still don't trust me with your car, do you? I'm heaps better than I was then."

"All right, you can drive," sighed Ben. "You should be almost ready to take the test, shouldn't you?"

"Yeah, so you shouldn't be scared of driving with me any more. I booked it for the first week of the New Year. Scary, huh? I could be behind the wheel all by myself. On the road, right next to you."

"Let's not talk like that before you get behind the wheel of my car, all right," said Ben, trying to be joking, but Alexa was not sure he was.

Alexa smiled as she took the keys from Ben. This was one route she knew well and was probably the only reason Ben let her drive. He was even complimentary when she pulled up in front of her apartment.

"Got time to come in?" she asked, smiling at her small triumph.

"No, running late, actually."

"You should've told me," said Alexa, quickly jumping out of the car. "I could've just caught the bus. I'm sorry, Ben."

Ben walked at a normal pace around to where she was waiting at the open driver's door. He pulled her into a tight embrace and kissed the top of her head. Alexa did not reciprocate, knowing he was just trying to placate her.

"You should go," she nodded, pushing him into the car.

"You got dinner plans tomorrow?" Ben asked out the window. Alexa shook her head. "Want company?" Alexa nodded and Ben smiled. "Good. See you then."

Walking into her apartment, Alexa was almost glad Ben had been too busy to stay. With her mind focussed almost entirely on Marcus, she was worried she may have let something slip and tried hard to push Marcus to the back of her mind. It did not work very well. As she sat on the lounge, all she could think about was Marcus, her fingers running constantly through the necklace he had bought her. It was a relief when Charlotte buzzed on the intercom.

"Charlotte, what's wrong," cried Alexa upon seeing her distraught face. Charlotte could not answer, simply shaking her head as she made her way to the floor of the lounge room. "You have to talk to me. What happened?" Charlotte continued to shake her head as tears streamed down her face. Alexa carefully pulled Charlotte's cardigan from her body to reveal fresh cuts along her arm. The sight made Alexa's heart drop. "Just tell me what happened."

"Nothing," sobbed Charlotte angrily. "I'm just fucked. Everything makes me sad and angry, but nothing really happens. At least you had a reason to hate life, but they don't hit me or take drugs. Must be right. Just me who's screwed up and worthless."

"You're not screwed up and worthless," said Alexa. Charlotte shot her an angry and disbelieving look before returning her gaze to the carpet. "Okay, you're a little screwed up, but definitely not worthless. You've been a great friend to me this year. I love having you around."

"You're the only one."

"I don't think you have no right to be sad. People don't have to hit you to hurt you. Why else would you cut your arm? Physical pain's just not as hard to cope with as emotional pain. Your parents treat you like you don't matter. That's unforgivable. Just because you have a home, clothes and food to eat doesn't mean you can't be unhappy when people hurt you."

"I just wish I could deal with it better, you know, not feel any of the pain and not worry about them," said Charlotte, expressing one of Alexa's long-held desires.

"Yeah, it seems like a good plan, but to shut out one person you have to shut out everyone," replied Alexa, trying hard to be something more than the shattered little girl she felt like on the inside. "Believe me, it may seem worth it for a while, but there'll come a time when you'll want to let certain people in and you won't be able to, because you just don't know how to any more."

Seeing Charlotte in pain and thinking the same way she used to – and sometimes still did – made Alexa realise everyone's concerns about their friendship were unfounded. She could not push her life aside when she was with Charlotte. It confronted her in everything Charlotte said and did.

Charlotte ended up staying the night and Alexa was glad. They made popcorn, hired a movie and pretended everything was great, laughing and joking about all the things that did not matter. When Charlotte left the next morning, Alexa looked at her phone wondering if it would be wrong to call Marcus. Right then, he was the one person who would understand. When the phone rang, Alexa found herself disappointed by the sound Damien's voice.

"Hey, sweetie, where've you been? I've been trying to call you for a couple of days now. I was starting to worry," he said in her tired ear.

Alexa had noticed the missed calls, but had never thought too hard about calling him back. "Oh, sorry. I've been frantic with Christmas shopping and visiting Bethy. Then Charlotte was really upset last night so I turned the phone off," she explained dismissively.

"I don't want to sound wrong or anything, but do you ever get the feeling that I'm at the bottom of your priority list?"

"You're definitely not right at the bottom," joked Alexa, but the silence that pressed in against her ear told her Damien was not amused. "Look, Bethy's my sister. She's in gaol and it's a week before Christmas. I'm not sure if you realise it or not, but gaol's a really shitty place to be this time of the year – any time of year. And Charlotte gets upset and I'm one of the few people she trusts enough to turn to. Maria, Ben and Sam are like family and I treat them as if they were. So if you expect me to push you up above my family on my priority list then you should find yourself another girlfriend."

Alexa was not sure where this anger and frustration had come from. It had been a simple enough question that had not even been asked in full seriousness.

"Maybe I should talk to you later," said Damien in a low voice.

"Are you still coming on Boxing Day?"

"Do you want me there?" asked Damien petulantly.

"Of course I want you here," Alexa replied with a frustrated sigh.

"I'll see you then. Enjoy your Christmas."

Alexa threw her phone into the lounge and stormed out on to the balcony. She could not understand what was going on or why Damien still failed to grasp the complexities of her life. It was not as though they had not discussed them. She may not indulge in conversations about her past, but he knew almost everything about her present.

Damien did not call back, only increasing Alexa's irritation. Bethany offered what she believed to be the most obvious explanation for the situation. Marcus. That did not comfort Alexa either. She did not want to ruin her relationship with Damien for a man who had not only moved on from her, but had already broken her heart. If she could not have Marcus, she saw no point in being alone without him and, until a few days ago, she had her heart firmly set on Damien. In order to put an end to her confusion, and prove Bethany continued to see the situation through irrationally romantic eyes, Alexa caved in and called Damien.

"I was wondering what you were doing tonight?" Alexa asked, her voice light, hoping Damien would not bring up their last conversation.

"Not much. Some mates are going out for a drink so I might join them. Why?" asked Damien in a slightly combative voice.

"I just hoped we could spend some time together."

"Would've thought there'd be more important people to spend your time with on Christmas Eve than me," he sneered.

"Look, I shouldn't have said what I did," conceded Alexa, trying to contain her growing annoyance.

"That's not exactly the same as you didn't mean what you said." Alexa threw her hand up in the air and collapsed into the lounge. "I'm guessing you need me to pick you up?" asked Damien in a tone of annoyed compliance, just as Alexa was about to hang up.

"That would be good," she replied in a soft voice.

Alexa immediately focused on shedding her anger and frustration. She owed Damien more than that. It was not easy, but he did not rush over, so by the time he arrived she had managed to turn her mood around, with her attention solely on making him happy. When she opened the door, she greeted Damien with a warm and loving hug and felt his anger fade away in an instant.

"I've missed you," he said, taking her hand and leading her out the door. "Where do you want to go?"

"We don't have to go anywhere if you don't want," Alexa replied.

It had not been her plan and she regretted it the instant the words left her mouth, but it was too late. A smile spread across Damien's face as he wrapped his arm around her waist and walked them back inside. Alexa sat down on the lounge and Damien was immediately on top of her, kissing her wildly. She did not care. She simply rolled on top of him and began undressing them. It was easier to give him what he wanted right from the start.

Sex with Damien was highly mechanical. It was as if he was a client she had to please rather than a boyfriend she wanted to love, but Alexa rarely noticed the transition, it was so easy.

"You sure you're going to be okay?" asked Damien, as he prepared to leave the next morning. "I can stay a bit longer if you like."

"No, I'm going to be a horrible person to be around today, so it's best you avoid it, especially since I only just got you back onside."

"I was never offside. I just wished I ranked a bit higher in your life. I know you've got more to deal with than me, but I love you and will wait for things to settle down. Maybe then you won't find it so hard to juggle everyone."

"I don't mean to hurt you."

"I know," smiled Damien, sweeping the hair from her face before enveloping her in a soft embrace. "You're too sweet to intentionally hurt anyone. That's why I love you so much."

Alexa felt sick as she waved goodbye to Damien. She really did not deserve anyone as good as him.

Ben arrived half an hour after Damien left. He was a welcome sight and Alexa rushed into his arms as tears burned her eyes.

"It'll be all right," Ben said soothingly. "Just remember, this is the last year you'll have to do this. Next year she'll be out and you'll have a wonderful Christmas." Alexa knew Ben was right, but could not stop the liquid sadness flowing down her cheeks and into his freshly ironed shirt. "Come on. It won't be that bad and Beth'll be even more upset if she sees you upset."

"Why's Bethy upset?" heaved Alexa, trying desperately to control her tears.

"The very same reason you are," replied Ben, holding her tighter. "It'll be all right. Maria's waiting in the car, so we'd better go. I'll even let you drive if it'll make you feel better."

"I don't think I should drive today. Even if I'm not crying I'm not going to very observant."

"I know. It's okay. I'll drive."

Maria greeted Alexa with a hug and a kiss, and did not comment on her red eyes. She was sure Ben warned her that she and Bethany were unlikely to be in very good moods, though Bethany managed to put on a much better act that she did. Bethany smiled brightly as she walked into the visitor's room. The smile did not penetrate her eyes, but it was still more than Alexa had achieved that day.

Despite the restrictions on physical contact, Alexa hugged Bethany until the guards pulled them apart. Christmas had never been a particularly happy day at any stage of their lives and Alexa could not help but wonder if next year really would be that much better.

Bethany sat down, looking awkwardly across the table at Maria. Maria was scanning the room, looking at all the faces of the inmates and families with a strangely contented expression. "Are you okay, Maria?" asked Bethany softly.

"Oh, yes I'm fine," smiled Maria happily. "Just taking it all in. It's not as bad as everyone painted made out. My children were aghast I was coming here." Bethany looked down guiltily. "Oh don't worry about that. I think it's wonderful I get to meet you on Christmas Day. Alexa never stops talking about you."

"All good, I assume," said Bethany with a hint of bitterness, her eyes looking away from Alexa.

Alexa was concerned by such a response. They had always loved the blind loyalty they had for each other. It was part of who they were.

"All honest. No story about a sister can be all good. That just wouldn't be all true then," replied Maria with a small chuckle.

Bethany smiled and Alexa nodded reassuringly. She had tried to explain how nice Maria was and how she never looked down on them because of their situations. Bethany had never been able to believe a rich person could be like that. Even the average person struggled to not see them as low-level trash. Bethany reached out and squeezed Maria's hand affectionately, holding Alexa's tight in her other.

Sam and his grandparents arrived an hour before lunch. Greeting the crowded table, he took a seat next to Bethany while Gran and Pop sat down next to Maria. It was as nice a gathering as Alexa and Bethany could have hoped for, and they smiled, joked and pretended the day was great, but it was not true and they both knew it.

"I have to go," said Ben, as they finished their lunches. "Penny agreed to let me come over for dinner and I think I should make a bit of an effort. Were you going to stay?" he asked Alexa.

"Yeah, I can catch a bus home later."

"I might go as well," said Maria.

"You don't have to," said Bethany.

"No, you two should have some time together and I've had a really good time already."

When Alexa and Bethany were alone, the topic of conversation quickly turned to Marcus. "So have you heard from him yet?" asked Bethany with a grin.

"No, and I don't know if I even expect to."

"Have you told Damien about him?"

"There's nothing to tell," said Alexa. "Marcus is an old friend. That's all I'll say if he asks."

"But that's not all he is," countered Bethany.

"That's not true. Besides, me and Damien sorted through things last night. Things are better now."

"Sorted through or slept on it? You let him stay over, didn't you?"

"So?" asked Alexa defensively, not sure how Bethany knew that.

"You've never wanted to before. Why the sudden change of heart?" asked Bethany pointedly.

"Because I thought I needed to. After I snapped at him I had to give him something. I did regret it, but it has nothing to do with him."

"I know. It has to do with you being in love with another man."

"I'm not still in love with Marcus," sighed Alexa. She did not need that complication in her life.

Alexa could see Bethany did not believe her, but she let the conversation drop. Instead, they spent the afternoon discussing more trivial issues, neither bringing up Bethany's impending parole hearing. They were both so desperate for her to be released – to the point where they felt their worlds would collapse if she wasn't. It made leaving each other much harder than usual and it was not achieved without tears.

It was still hot and bright when Alexa trudged home, but it could have the depths of the darkest winter with the mood she was in. The emptiness of her apartment was so potent it seeped mercilessly through her body, dragging her to the corner of her closet. It was a spot she rarely ventured to. Grabbing the hidden photo album, she flicked slowly through the pages. It had been given to her the Christmas before last by the Whites. That day Brett and Hayley had given her a bracelet that was yet to leave her wrist. It and the photo album were some of her most treasured possessions.

Tears trickled down Alexa's face as her fingers traced the faces of her lost family. She had come so close to belonging to them and at times she wished she did, but knew their safety was more important than her happiness. Bethany was not clear of her former life and, until that day, it was too dangerous to contact them. Alexa just hoped that one day she might be able to see the Whites again and they would not hate her for all she put them through.

The phone rang several times, but Alexa ignored it, too consumed in her grief to answer. She rarely looked at the photo album, all too aware of the affect it had on her, but at Christmas she could not help it.

The room faded into darkness, but Alexa remained in the corner, drained of tears and energy. There was no motivation to move. She just sat there until the buzz of the intercom brought her out of her daze. Thinking it must be Charlotte, Alexa put the photo album away and buzzed her up.

"I've been trying to call you," said Ben anxiously as Alexa opened the door. He took one look at her red eyes and pulled her into a tight embrace.

"I'm all right," Alexa said, suddenly very tired as she pushed out of his arms. "Do you want to come in?"

"Yeah, thanks," replied Ben, as if unsure whether or not to say more.

"I'll make tea. How was your dinner?"

"Could've been better," replied Ben, his voice cracking before turning hard. "Turns out Penny didn't ask me over to sort things out. She's seeing another man."

"Oh, I'm sorry."

"It's okay. Probably for the best. I was the one who moved out. I'd just never considered myself with another woman. I think it's been going on longer than she admits. They're already moving in together."

Alexa did not know what to say. She had always found herself rather pathetic at trying to cheer other people up. She had rarely had to. There had been very few times where she had not been the saddest person in the room.

"I'm all right," said Ben with a slight smile, looking at her worried face. "Anyway, that's my excuse. Why've you been crying?"

"Everything," Alexa sighed. "It's Christmas night and I have no one around."

"What am I?"

"You know what I mean. No family – I mean, you're great, but—"

"You and Bethany mean the world to me. You know that, right?" asked Ben with a sense of urgency. "You two really are like —"

"Please don't say it," said Alexa quickly, holding up her hand as Ben approached. "I can handle losing a friend or someone like that. I don't want to lose more people that are closer. I'd just prefer to pretend you don't mean that much to me."

"Oh, Alexa, things'll get better," said Ben genuinely, ignoring her retreating steps and pulling her to his chest. "You're not going to lose me. I promise."

"Don't make promises you can't keep," she whispered.

Ben did not contradict or reassure her. He just pulled her closer and kissed the top of her head.

***

Light glittered through the open curtains of the lounge room, rousing Alexa from her sleep. She looked around the room, but it was empty, and wondered if Ben went home after she fell asleep. Checking the apartment, Alexa found Ben fast asleep in the spare room. Closing the door, Alexa showered and dressed, before preparing for lunch. She was almost regretting the whole idea and wondered why she thought waiting one day would make Christmas any better.

"Why didn't you wake me?" yawned Ben, as he stretched his way into the kitchen a little after ten-thirty.

"I thought you might need to sleep," replied Alexa as Ben rubbed his face in his hands.

"What time did you wake up?"

"A bit after six," said Alexa, trying to stifle a yawn. "The curtains aren't very heavy in the lounge room. I like it. Makes the room nice and bright, but does nothing for sleeping in. Guess it's why I never sleep in there," she added with a smile, trying to force herself into the chirpy mood she wanted to be in.

"Do you need any help?"

"Yeah, I actually don't have any drinks," Alexa replied gratefully. It was a major oversight in her preparations. "Would you be able to pick some up for me?"

"Sure," Ben replied dutifully, grabbing his keys and heading towards the door.

"Um, Ben," Alexa called after him. "I actually meant after you showered – maybe had some breakfast. You don't look so crash hot, so I'd at least have the shower."

The reflection that greeted Ben in the bathroom mirror horrified him. He looked old and unhappy. He felt old and unhappy. Staring at his reflection, he tried to work out where it had all gone so wrong. His marriage was over and he was convinced Penny had been having an affair well before he left. Bethany and Alexa remained the only shining lights in his life, though they were also a constant source of guilt. Their ordeals since he backed out of fostering them so long ago still gnawed at his conscience, and for the past year and a half he had been working hard to rectify the wrong he committed by turning his back on them.

That guilt had certainly played a part in his marriage breakdown and it had disintegrated further during his attempts at redemption. He had poured so much energy into Alexa and Bethany, Bethany in particular, that there was little left for anything else.

It was a situation Penny did not want to understand. She was one of the people who had protested hard against his commitment to the girls and, with others, convinced him not to fight their return to their mother. If he had known about their mother's death at the time, he would have taken them in a heartbeat, but by the time he found out, Alexa was at boarding school and Bethany was taking heroin. His attempts to convince Penny they needed a second chance were futile and he had tried his hardest to simply forget them.

It was not until the trial of Clinton Marsh that Ben was called back into their lives. Peter Lam held grave concerns for Alexa's mental stability if she was forced to testify. Peter had tried to organise a plea bargain, but to no avail. It was then that Peter called him, asking for his help to pressure the prosecutors to offer a plea. Ben's involvement had not been well received, but he had made enough connections over the years to prevent his exclusion from the investigation. That was when the true extent of the debacle had been revealed.

Detective Matthews had been seduced by Clinton's charms, resulting in an investigation that focused heavily on blaming and discrediting the victims. The bias Detective Matthews brought to the investigation had been so subversive that the extent of Clinton's crimes would probably never be tried.

Victims had started coming forward the day after Clinton was arrested, but so had supporters. Clinton appeared to have taken great pleasure in seducing young, vulnerable girls, but it was clear he did not treat all of them as badly as he did Alexa. By far, the majority of the girls who came forward professed their disbelief that Clinton was capable of such violence. They had a terrible time at Redgrove, and he had supported them through some of the worst years of their lives. However, it had not been difficult for Ben to find a distinct and disturbing pattern in Clinton's behaviour.

The most vulnerable – those with the most to lose and fewest people to turn to – were the ones most likely to be tortured by Clinton. Those brave enough to come forward were so traumatised by what they suffered they struggled to articulate what he had done to them. Against the poised praise of his supporters, they appeared less than credible in the eyes of Detective Matthews, and their statements had been treated with the same contempt Alexa's had. The welfare of these girls had never once been considered.

It should have been the trial of the century, but instead the best Ben managed was a pitiful plea bargain that would see Clinton released back into society in the next year. Most of the other girls had been so traumatised by Detective Matthew's callous investigation they refused to lodge official statements. Although another team had been assembled to take over the investigation, Ben knew they were struggling to regain the victims' cooperation. All the while Clinton's supporters continued to cry over the injustice of his incarceration.

Alexa had never cared for the details and not once had she asked about the other victims. In many ways, she had closed off that part of her past. Ben wished he could, but he could never stop himself ruminating over what could have been. It had taken all of his restraint not to march into Redgrove and snatch Alexa after the plea bargain was settled, but Peter convinced him such actions would do more harm than good. Looking back at what followed, Ben was not so sure.

It was true Alexa did not remember their interactions from her childhood, but she did recognise him; a fact that had never changed Peter's stance, and Ben still found him rather too protective of Alexa for his liking. They got along much more harmoniously while dealing with Bethany. Ben often got the feeling Peter did not trust him and dealt with him only because he had to. It was not helped by the fact that he had not told Peter about Alexa going missing from the Whites. It turned out to have been a near-fatal mistake. Ben never realised Peter had remained so involved in Alexa and Bethany's lives. It was only after Peter came to them that they were able to start to piecing together all the clues and arrest Leo.

"It's almost eleven. Are you going to keep running up my water bill or go and get me some drinks?" cried Alexa in a light-hearted voice, knocking on the bathroom door.

Ben quickly turned off the water and jumped out of the shower. He needed to be in a good mood for Alexa today to show her he was not leaving, and that Christmas could be a wonderful time.

Damien arrived as Ben was leaving and went straight to work tidying the apartment. Alexa watched him move, concentrating on his body and imagining his hands on her. They were pleasant thoughts and Alexa knew she was making the right decision by choosing him over Marcus. Ignoring the feelings she knew she could not trust, she put her faith in the logic that told her Damien was her only option.

"Hey, how's my master chef going?" asked Damien, as he wrapped his arms around her waist.

"I'm good," smiled Alexa, loving that it was possible for Damien to continue to want her.

"Well the place is officially clean. What time's everyone coming?"

"Between twelve-thirty and one."

"Good, well that gives us a bit of time."

Damien led Alexa out of the kitchen and into the lounge room, lying her on the lounge. He climbed on top and kissed her gently. The kissing and caressing became more passionate. Damien moved his lips from Alexa's and made his way down her neck. Alexa turned her head and saw with a fright a shadowy figure standing before her. Her body tensed and her heart pounded, but Damien did not notice. He kept kissing her, his hands groping, pulling her body to his.

"Get off her," growled the shadowy figure.

Alexa panicked. She did not know how he had found her, but hoped Damien would protect her. Yet Damien did not turn. He could not see the threat. Alexa tried to alert him, pushing him away and get him to see the danger that was now hovering over them.

The shadowy figure reached out for them. Alexa gasped, knowing she could not escape. It picked Damien up and threw him off her.

Then it came for her.

Chapter Ten

"ALEXA," CALLED BEN, shaking her shoulder. "Alexa, turn around. It's all right. Turn around."

Fear continued to paralyse Alexa, but Ben's voice slowly penetrated her mind, calming her enough to turn around.

"What happened?" asked Ben, pulling her into a quick hug before releasing her shaking body.

"You pulled me off her and scared the crap out of her. That's what happened," cried Damien from behind Ben. "What the hell were you doing?"

Alexa saw Ben's face contort with rage, but then smoothed out again as he locked his eyes on hers.

"What happened?" Ben asked again gently.

"Is he gone?" asked Alexa fearfully.

"No, he's still here. I pulled him off you."

"No, not Damien. The other man," whispered Alexa, as though the shadowy man was hiding somewhere in the room, just waiting for Ben to move away.

"What other man?" asked Ben, scanning the apartment.

"There was a man. He was standing over us – coming for me."

"What did he look like?" asked Ben in a very police-like manner.

"I don't know. Dark, like a heavy shadow – like the man from my dreams."

"I didn't know you were still having nightmares," said Ben with a hint of anger in his voice.

"I'm not, only occasionally," Alexa replied defensively, unsure why people were so agitated by her continuing to have the dreams that had plagued most of her existence.

"What about like this? When you're awake? How often does this happen?" asked Ben urgently.

"It's the first time," Alexa answered, thankful it was the truth.

Alexa could see Damien looking at her with mingled fear and fury as she continued her whispered conversation with Ben. She could only imagine what it had been like for him having Ben throw him off her, but was more concerned about how she was going to explain this to him. What other conclusion could he draw except that she was crazy? Needing to compose herself, Alexa rushed to her room, but even from there she could hear Ben's growling voice.

"How much attention can you be paying to your girlfriend when you don't even notice she's having a panic attack beneath you?"

Alexa did not hear Damien's response and wondered if he would have protected her when he did finally notice. Scared of the answer, Alexa took a deep breath and returned to the kitchen to finish lunch.

"You want me to leave?" asked Damien in a shaky voice, creeping into the kitchen behind her.

"No," said Alexa, turning. "I'm sorry. That hasn't happened before. I just … I – I don't know what happened, but I want you to stay."

"Ben doesn't."

"Don't worry about Ben. He just worries."

"So do I, you know," replied Damien defensively.

"And that's why I'm asking you to stay."

Before Damien could reply, Sam arrived. Alexa was relieved. She wanted to forget what happened and pretend she was not losing control of her own mind.

"Hey, how's it going?" asked Sam with a wide grin.

"Could be better," replied Alexa in his ear, as she hugged him.

"What's wrong?" he asked, holding her tighter.

"Nothing, I'll be okay," replied Alexa, quickly pushing out of his arms. "How was the rest of your Christmas?"

"Oh yeah, all right, I guess."

Alexa could tell there was something he was not telling her, but decided she could wait to find out. She was not in the mood to guess.

Maria arrived shortly after Sam and his grandparents, and when Charlotte arrived the feast began. Damien was still upset as he took his seat. Alexa held his hand under the table, but it did not help. He ate much less than usual, sapping Alexa of her appetite. Thankfully, everyone else was hungry enough to make up the difference.

Maria made a traditional Christmas pudding and Alexa served it up with lashings of cream and ice cream. Despite everyone's claims of being full before dessert, no one refused the pudding, resulting in everyone sitting on the lounges with a slight stomach ache.

"Oh, I think I'd need to walk for an hour just to sit properly," said Ben, as he shifted awkwardly on the lounge.

"That was a damn good feast," said Pop.

"Think of it as repayment for all the meals you cooked me when you let me stay after running away," said Alexa with a grateful smile.

"I thought you deserved to stay," smiled Gran. "After all, you'd made it over five hours out to the property. If you were that desperate to run away you at least deserved a hot meal and a bed, though I think you were coming for Sam more than the meal or the bed."

"Oh, I don't know. I think Sam and the bed went pretty much hand in hand," chuckled Pop, winking at Sam.

Laughter exploded around the room. Alexa and Sam exchanged embarrassed grins as their faces burned. They had always thought their activities had gone unnoticed, but suddenly realised how naïve they had been. As the laughter died down, Alexa noticed there was one person who had missed the joke.

"Come outside for a minute?" said Alexa, taking Damien's hand.

Damien followed reluctantly. "So when was I going to find out about you and Sam?" he spat, throwing off her hand.

"Well, I kinda thought you knew. Besides, I don't think it's a big deal."

"You used to fuck him. I think that's a big deal," snarled Damien.

"Did you notice the words 'used to' there? We dated when we were fourteen. Why should I justify that to you?" asked Alexa, trying to temper her indignation.

"Maybe because the guy's still in love with you and you've told me you love him," Damien retorted angrily.

"I do. I always will. Nothing you or anyone else says will ever change that, but he's not *in love* with me and I'm not *in love* with him."

"How the hell do I know that?"

"Because I'm telling you," cried Alexa. "Look, I'm sorry I never told you. I'm sorry you found out like this, but I'm with you now. Me and Sam are ancient history. You have to trust me."

Alexa turned away, expecting Damien to leave, but he remained on the balcony and she wondered how long he would stay.

"I'm sorry," Damien said after a minute. "You're right. If I don't trust you then there's no point in us being together. I guess, after this morning, I was just taken aback. I wished you'd told me beforehand. I wouldn't have been mad. I just would've liked to've been in on the joke."

"I never really thought to tell you. Sam was always your friend and everyone's always just known about us."

"Listen, I'd better go," said Damien in a lighter voice. "Me and the guys are going away this afternoon and I haven't packed yet. I'm not sure if our phones work down there so —"

"It's okay. I can survive a week without hearing from you."

"I'll call you the minute I get back," Damien promised.

"Okay, well, have fun."

"I will. I love you."

Alexa struggled to reciprocate the sentiment as Damien pulled her into tight embrace and kissed her, and could not stop a slight sadness seeping through her heart. Damien had the right to be upset at everything that had happened and all she had not and would not tell him, but she wanted the situation to be simpler. Every time he found out something, he reacted angrily, and he had only yet found out the least worst parts. It made her wonder how he would react if he ever found out about the worst of the worst.

"Hey," smiled Sam, joining Alexa on the balcony. "Why'd Damien rush off?"

"He's going away and had to pack," replied Alexa simply.

"Why didn't you tell him you and I used to date?"

"I don't know. Why didn't you?" she retorted. Sam smiled and shrugged. "He told me once he thought you had a huge crush on me. I told him it was nothing. We loved each other as friends. He didn't seem very comfortable with that, so I wasn't going to go into more detail."

"What are you going to do?" asked Sam tenderly.

"Nothing. He knows now and says it's okay."

"What about this year? You tell him about that?"

"He just freaked finding out we dated when we were fourteen," Alexa reminded him. "Can you think of a way to explain our week together that he'd understand?"

"No," replied Sam, shaking his head with a concerned look on his face. "So the two of you are okay?"

"Yeah, we're fine."

"It's just that Beth thought you guys were having a few problems and that they may have gotten worse. It kinda looks like she's right."

Alexa smiled. Bethany and her theories. Of course she would tell Sam, and Alexa knew Sam would report back. No wonder Bethany seemed to know everything.

"We're fine, okay. Why don't you tell me about the rest of your Christmas? Why'd you seem so evasive before?"

"I wasn't being evasive," replied Sam defensively. "I just – it was fine – normal – just the family."

Sam would not look at Alexa and she remained confused until she finally understood what Sam's definition of family must be. "So how is Mel?" she asked, trying to hide her bitterness.

"I'm sorry. She asked if she could come. She's my sister. I wanted to see her," cried Sam desperately, turning to Alexa with apologetic eyes.

"You don't have to apologise," said Alexa sincerely.

"I just felt so guilty, like I had to choose between you and I can't."

"I'll never make you choose, Sam," Alexa said softly, wrapping her arms around his shoulders as he leant against the balcony railing. "I know how hard your situation is. Don't you think part of me wanted to leave Bethy to rot? But she's my sister and I'll always love her. I don't begrudge you for wanting to see Mel."

Sam quickly wiped away the tears welling in his eyes and smiled nervously. "I just don't want you to think this means I've forgiven her for what she did to you," he said in a stronger voice.

"Or you?"

It took Sam a few minutes to answer as he held her hands. "No, I guess not," he shrugged. "We never broached the issue. In fact, we didn't talk about any of it. We just acted as if none of it ever happened."

"Did it work?" asked Alexa curiously.

"For a while," Sam nodded. "It was nice and there's a side of Mel that's so great – so easy to love – the part that's the sister I knew – but she's still committed to Clinton. She's living in his apartment and visits him whenever she can. I just don't understand that part." Neither could Alexa, but did not say so. Just hearing Clinton's name made her insides turn to ice. "I'm sorry. I shouldn't be talking to you about all this."

"You know you needed to. You needed to hear me tell you that you haven't done anything wrong and you haven't. Family's family. You deal with it the best way you can and maybe the more you see her, the better chance you have of prying her away from Clinton. It's him, you know, not her. I know I blamed her, but she was a kid. It had to be him behind it all. He had to be grooming her."

"Yeah, that's what we think too," replied Sam sombrely. "But it's impossible to convince her. We tried, but she just clams up. Believes everything Clinton tells her. All I want is to get her away from that bastard and get my sister back."

"I'd never begrudge anyone for trying to get anybody away from Clinton."

Sam smiled and hugged Alexa enthusiastically. "You're the best, you know," he whispered in her ear as he dragged her inside.

The approach of the New Year started to fill Alexa with fresh hope. This was the year Bethany would be released from gaol and that, above all else, was what had Alexa counting down the days with enthusiasm. However, she was determined to see through the rest of Bethany's incarceration before claiming the coming year would be better than the departing. Her hope could not extend beyond that. Once Bethany was with her for good, she would dare to dream. It made Alexa want to pass the last few days of the year as quietly as possible, determined not to let the year take one last swipe at her when she was sure she was through with it. It meant quiet days close to home, which were more relaxing than Alexa imagined and she told herself she should do nothing for a day more often.

"Hello?" answered Alexa casually, as she picked the phone while sitting lazily on the lounge eating breakfast.

"Alexa?" croaked a slurred, male voice.

"Marcus, is that you?" asked Alexa, sitting up so quickly she almost spilt her cereal.

"I'm sorry I called, I —"

"What's wrong? What's happened?" Alexa asked anxiously.

"I'm sorry. I shouldn't have called you like this."

"No, it's okay. You're drunk, aren't you?" queried Alexa, her heart fluttering erratically. She was not sure she wanted to know what kind of drunk Marcus was.

"I stopped drinking a few hours ago."

Alexa looked at her watch. It was only eight-thirty in the morning. "Where are you?"

"At my new place."

"Okay, I'll be over in a minute. Just tell me where you live."

It took almost fifteen minutes for Alexa to get the address out of Marcus as he apologised profusely for calling her. When she reached her car, she took her L-plates off and shoved them in the glove box. This was not a good time of the year to be breaking the road rules and she hoped she would not see any police. Ben would be less than impressed if he ever found out. Entering the traffic alone for the first time, Alexa felt as though her pounding heart would bruise her chest. She double-checked her blind spots and drove so cautiously it bordered on dangerous. With a huge sigh of relief, she parked the car and rushed towards Marcus's apartment.

"Hi," Marcus answered with an embarrassed grimace. He did not look nearly as bad as he had sounded on the phone.

"This is better than I expected," said Alexa, walking behind him into the apartment.

"I've been ploughing my body full of coffee and water since I got off the phone. I didn't want you to see me like that. I can't believe I even called you. I'm so sorry."

"What's going on? Where's your girlfriend?" asked Alexa cautiously as she looked around the apartment. It was huge, but bare. There was nothing but a few blankets and several boxes, all full of Marcus's belongings by the looks of them.

"She's at her new place," Marcus replied with a savage grin.

"Huh? I thought the two of you were moving in together."

"So did I." Marcus slid down the wall into the blankets below, his head in his hands. It was a pitiful sight and Alexa was sorry to see it.

"Did you two break up?"

"No, she just decided she wasn't ready to move in with me and moved in with another friend of hers. So now I have this place, which I can't afford by myself, but I have no choice. Real estate doesn't even open for another week."

"Okay, let's go then."

Alexa took Marcus by the hand and pulled him to his feet. She pushed him in the direction of the bathroom and ordered him into the shower. Closing the door, she took the opportunity to look around the apartment. It had one-bedroom plus a study, was near new and looked expensive. It made Alexa wonder how much teachers earned or if Lucy was in a high-paying role.

Moving to the kitchen, Alexa found coffee-making facilities, but nothing to replace her half-eaten breakfast. She made herself a strong coffee and Marcus an even stronger one and waited for his return.

"Now do your best not to look drunk," Alexa said, as she put the L-plates back on the car. She had insisted that Marcus would not be able to fully assess his situation until he sobered up, and she was starving. "I had to drive here illegally and you're supposed to be sober, but hopefully luck will shine on me a little longer."

"I really am sorry I called you," said Marcus. Alexa turned with a slightly bemused look and waited for him to elaborate. "No, I mean, I'm glad you're here. I'm just sorry I called you when I was drunk and forced you to come over here. It wasn't very fair."

"You were upset and I'm your friend. What else do you expect me to do?" Alexa asked, suddenly worried her reaction had been wrong.

"So we are friends?"

"I'd like to be," she replied softly. "I've missed talking to you. I thought maybe friends would be good."

"Friends is great," smiled Marcus, sighing as he settled into his seat. "Ah, do you need me to actually instruct you?" he asked, sitting up.

"Not really," Alexa chuckled. "But might be wise to keep an eye out. You know, tell me if you think I'm going to crash. Don't just assume I know what I'm doing."

Marcus never asked where they were going. He just let her drive towards the beach near her apartment. He did not even give her any instructions until it came time to park. The spot was tighter than those Alexa usually attempted to park in, but he assured her the car would fit. Keeping a very light hand on the wheel so she could concentrate on reversing at the right speed, he guided her into the spot first time.

"So apparently you can teach me to reverse park too," Alexa smiled as she pulled on the hand brake.

"You're a good driver. That was only mildly horrifying," Marcus said with a laugh. If it had not hit so close to home with what Ben had said over the months, she might have been able to laugh with him. "Alexa, I'm joking. That was good driving. Come on, let's eat."

The cool sea breeze eased the sting of the burning sun as they sat on the beach with their fish and chip lunch. It had been Marcus's choice, though from the nauseated look on his face, he was starting to regret it. Alexa could only look out to sea to hide her grin.

"I'm glad my pain amuses you," said Marcus with a grimace.

"Hey, don't expect any sympathy from me. You chose to drown your sorrows with alcohol, so you pay the consequences. I always told you it was no way to cope." Alexa smiled, but it faded as Marcus stared involuntarily at her bare left arm. "I told you my cuts would heal better than your liver," she added in a more serious tone.

"I should've listened. You were right about nearly everything else."

"I wouldn't say that. You had your moments," Alexa replied, before turning the conversation from her past. "Have you thought about what you're going to do now you've sobered up a bit?"

"I'm not sure what I can do," Marcus replied in agitated defeat. "I signed a lease. I have nowhere else to go and it's a one-bedroom apartment. I can't even get a flatmate. It was at the limit of our budget with the two of us. There's no way I can afford it by myself. Even if I get out of the lease, it won't be for a couple of weeks and I'm sure they'll make me pay extra, in which case I won't have money to move again."

"You sure are in a pickle."

Marcus could not help but laugh. It was the most fickle thing Alexa could have said. He was in more than a pickle. He was close to financial ruin. He had been reckless with his finances this last year, spending nearly everything he earned – just to keep himself busy and away from his memories of her. Now he had nothing to fall back on and expenses that literally meant he could pay his for rent or food, but not both.

It had been stupid to even consider such an expensive apartment. There had been cheaper around, but Lucy had always loved the area and, after finding out where Alexa lived, Marcus wanted to be closer to her in the hope they would bump into each other.

"Okay, so perhaps not the best description," said Alexa, while he recomposed himself. "Maybe there's something I can do about that. I know someone around here with a spare room. They don't need the rent, so I'm sure you could come to some agreement about the money."

"I don't know anybody with a spare room who doesn't need money," Marcus replied sceptically. "Especially around here."

"You might know more than you think," Alexa grinned, refusing to tell him who this person was.

It was true, her friends from Redgrove mostly came from well-off families, but Marcus was not keen to live with a former student – and he was not sure they would want to live with him. The only reason he continued the conversation was because Alexa appeared so keen to help, so much so that he could see the fear of rejection in her eyes when he hesitated. "Well, sure, that'd be great, but I don't want to put anyone out," he said non-committedly.

"Why don't we go check out the place and then you can decide."

Alexa jumped up with speed that took Marcus by surprise. She grabbed his hand and pulled him to his feet, not allowing for non-compliance. It was nice the way she was able to casually touch him without anyone watching, waiting to misconstrue the interaction. It was nice to think that if they could be friends he would know the touch of her skin and the warmth of her embrace.

The drive took only a few minutes and when Marcus saw the place Alexa was suggesting, he knew this was never going to happen. The apartments looked huge and most had views out to the ocean.

"I don't think I'll be able to afford this either," Marcus said hesitantly, as they walked towards the entrance.

"I told you, they don't need the money," shrugged Alexa.

"That much is obvious. So who's this friend? They home?"

"No, not right now," replied Alexa tentatively, as though she was deliberating the answer.

"Then how are we going to look at the place?"

"With these," answered Alexa with a mischievous smile, holding up a pair of straightened paperclips.

"Alexa, you can't break in – I don't – you can't –"

"Coming?" she asked, as the door clicked open.

Heart pumping, Marcus followed Alexa into the lift, and scanned the hallway nervously as she picked the lock to the apartment. This was way beyond anything he was prepared for and was not sure why he continued to follow her. Perhaps he really was incapable of walking away from Alexa.

"You can't go breaking into people's places. No one's going to –"

"Anyway, this is the bathroom and the laundry," said Alexa.

"Alexa, you're not listening to me."

"And this is the kitchen and the lounge-dining."

Marcus followed Alexa unwillingly into the apartment, determined to drag her out of it if he had to. However, even as he stormed after her, he was able to take in what a great place it was and could not possibly believe he would be able to afford to live here, no matter how discounted the rent was. Alexa continued her appraisal, but Marcus's eyes were arrested by the clothes hanging on a rack on the balcony.

"Whose apartment is this?" he asked warily. Alexa turned to him with the same mischievous smile she had given him downstairs. "Is that my shirt?"

"Yeah," she replied softly. "I kept it from that day you took me to the beach. Use it as a night shirt. You want it back?"

"No, you keep it," replied Marcus. "So there is no friend?"

"I guess that depends on what you classify me as."

"You have a spare room?"

Alexa nodded and walked through a door to her right. Marcus followed and looked around the room in awe. He was still not sure he understood. Despite everything he knew about Alexa's situation, he would never have assumed she would make an offer like this.

"It doesn't look all that spare," said Marcus, picking up a hair brush from the dressing table.

"Charlotte stays over occasionally," replied Alexa with a shrug of her shoulders. "If you want the room, it's yours. Like I said, I don't need the money, so you can move in and get your finances sorted before you have to start paying rent here."

"How much would the rent be?"

"I don't know. How much can you afford?" asked Alexa with a smile. Marcus smiled back, still confused by the proposal. "I haven't really thought about it. I reckon a hundred a week would cover it."

"It'd have to be more than that. The rent here would be as bad as what I'm stuck with and that's over seven hundred a week."

"I don't pay rent. I don't pay a mortgage. I own this place. I bought it with the money from the settlement with the school. I don't need to charge you a cent and I want it in cash. I'm not paying tax on your rent. You get a place to stay, I get some company and a bit of extra money – enough to cover the strata, which is great, because I hate paying it. It's a good situation for everyone."

"Are you sure?" asked Marcus, even though they were not the words he knew he should be speaking.

"I did offer. No one forced me to. Are you sure?" Alexa asked back.

"No, not really," he answered honestly.

"Well, why don't you think about it. I'm going to call you a cab. I've done enough illegal driving for one day."

Alexa left Marcus standing in the doorway of the spare room contemplating her offer. He knew what he should do – turn and walk away and never see Alexa again – it just was not what he wanted to do. He wanted to stay. Besides Alexa, there was no reason not to. It was a great apartment, and perfectly located. His school was only a twenty-minute drive away, the beach was just down the road, it was not far from the city and all other essential amenities – and the price was fantastic. If he did not have to live with Alexa, he would have accepted in a heartbeat. That was not say he did not want to live with her. He just knew he should not. Alexa was beautiful in every sense of the word and Marcus loved her more than he could describe. It was not just a physical attraction. Thankfully, he found that the least of his concerns. But then, he reasoned, it was the physical relationship everyone cared about, and they knew how to deny those feelings. They could be friends.

Friendship was not everything Marcus dreamt of, but it was all he had ever truly desired. Though he could imagine kissing Alexa, he could rarely construe an acceptable situation in which it occurred. Most of the time, it involved him comforting her, but he knew he would never take advantage of her that way. Fortunately, Alexa did not seem to need any comforting. Outside of the intense environment

Redgrove had forced them into, Marcus became surer he could live with Alexa and pose no threat to her. He did not care how much it tore at his heart to live so close and never be with her, or to watch her with another man. He would suffer all that and more to be a part of Alexa's life.

"Your cab's here," said Alexa, breaking his thoughts. He had not even heard her walk into the room.

"Oh, thanks," Marcus replied slowly, feeling like the moment he walked away Alexa would disappear.

"So have you decided yet?" she asked flatly.

"You know I would love to stay, but —"

"Great, so when're you moving in?" Alexa was so matter of fact it made Marcus wonder if he was blowing this out of proportion.

"After the New Year, I guess – if that's okay."

A slight smile touched Alexa's lips, making his heart swell. It made him wonder why he did not move in that minute, but Alexa deserved a cooling-off period and the chance to change her mind.

"Of course. Just let me know so I can get you a key cut," she said casually. "And if you need help covering your other rent til you get out of the lease let me know. You can pay me back with extra rent."

"That'd be great," Marcus nodded, wishing he did not need the assistance.

"No worries. I guess I'll talk to you soon then."

"Hey, thanks. You really didn't have to do this."

"You saved my life twice. I don't think this is such a big deal," Alexa replied dismissively.

"You're saving my life now, so I think we can wipe the slate clean," Marcus smiled with a grateful sigh. He did not want Alexa to ever feel indebted to him. She was owed more than the world could repay her for the life she had endured in her short nineteen years. He was only glad he could see in her eyes that she was not doing this out of guilt or obligation. He only wished he did not look quite so incapable in front of her as she placed fifty dollars in his hand.

"For the taxi," she explained as he tried to hand it back.

"Oh, yeah, shit. Thank you. I'll pay it all back," he said earnestly.

"I know," Alexa smiled. "Besides, I know where you live."

Marcus's heart swelled, knowing that very soon it would be with her. Lucy's betrayal now seemed like the best thing that had ever happened to him.

***

"Oh, ho, ho, this is too good. You have to let me be the one to tell Ben," laughed Bethany when Alexa recounted the story the next day.

"No, I'll tell Ben. I'm just not sure how – or when," replied Alexa nervously.

"You're going to have to tell him soon. You don't want to wait til Marcus moves in. He's going to have a fit. I hope you realise that."

"That's why I don't think I will tell him beforehand," said Alexa, making up her mind. "I'm nineteen. I can make my own decisions. Everyone needs to stop thinking I need their protection, especially from my own life. I have to be able to do some things right."

Alexa was not looking forward to hearing what Ben and Sam had to say about Marcus's reappearance in her life, because she did not care if it was the wrong decision. It was one she wanted to make.

"Hey, I'm all for it," smiled Bethany. "Might give you the chance to finally realise you're made for each other."

"He has a girlfriend," Alexa pointed out.

"Who ditched him," Bethany retorted. "He would've been screwed if you didn't help him out."

"And I have a boyfriend," continued Alexa.

"Who you don't trust enough to tell him about your past."

"Well, that's going to change, isn't it?"

"And suddenly because Marcus is around you're just going to trust Damien and reveal everything?" asked Bethany sceptically. "Wake up! Why do you two insist on denying how you feel?"

"Because things've changed," cried Alexa. "Marcus is with another woman. He was going to move in with her, goddamn it. He doesn't want me any more."

"You don't think he'd give her up in a second if he thought he could have you?"

"I don't want him to. I want him to want me so much that he doesn't want to be with another woman."

"Then what are you doing with Damien?" asked Bethany seriously.

"I – I ..."

"You what? You're no different."

"Yes I am. I can't face being hurt again. Damien's never hurt me,"

"That's just because you've never loved him."

Ben's arrival brought the discussion to an abrupt end. He was still aware they were hiding something, but obviously thought it nothing of consequence because he did not press them about it.

"Would you like to drive home?" Ben asked Alexa, as they walked across the car park.

"Seriously? Can I?" Alexa asked a little sceptically.

"You're a much better driver now. And you do have your test next week, so you should get in as much practice as possible."

Now that Alexa did not need instruction so much as supervision, Ben had become a lot more amenable to letting her drive his car. Or at least that was what he said to her face. Alexa still suspected Parker may be responsible for the change of heart.

"Can you stay for dinner? Charlotte's coming over," said Alexa when they arrived at her apartment.

"Sounds good," smiled Ben, his arm around her shoulders.

"Are you okay?" Alexa asked, looking up at him.

"Why wouldn't I be?"

"You just seem a little down. Is there anything I can do for you?"

Ben chuckled softly, squeezing her tighter as he pulled her closer. "Do you ever think about yourself?" he asked.

"All the time, actually," Alexa replied with the frustration that had been plaguing her lately, pulling away from his embrace. "Anyone would think you want me to become the world's most selfish person. I only have a few people that really mean anything to me, who've stuck by me through everything, and I care about them. I don't think I should stop caring about you all just because my life's no picnic. There's only so much I can do, only so much progress I can make in one day."

"Alexa, I —"

"No, I'm tired of being told not to care about my own sister. Or Charlotte, or Sam, or you, or anyone but myself. I didn't think I was doing that bad."

"You're not. I'm sorry," said Ben sincerely. "It's just ..." Ben sighed heavily. "I was married for over twenty years. I know I wasn't the best husband – hell, cops have the worst divorce rates – but I loved her."

"What happened?" asked Alexa quietly, feeling bad about her rant when Ben's mood had nothing to do with her.

"Penny's engaged. Gave me the divorce papers today. Asked that I don't contest it. Everything'll be split fifty-fifty. She wants to get married as soon as it comes through."

"I'm sorry, Ben."

"Yeah, well," he sighed with a dismissive wave of his hand. "I still have you and Beth."

"I don't think that's much of a consolation," Alexa replied, horrified Ben was pinning his life's happiness on them. There was no way she could live up to his expectations of a daughter – though Bethany appeared to be doing well so far.

"Trust me, it is," Ben smiled warmly.

It was not reassuring, and only gave Alexa more reasons to believe Ben could never be a permanent part of their lives.

Dinner was a sombre affair. Ben's mood did not improve, so he excused himself as soon as he finished eating. Alexa knew he was going to the pub. Always one to drink a little with the occasional cigarette, he was now a regular at the bar and up to a pack a day. They were habits Alexa hated, but Ben had stopped drinking and smoking around her after she confessed to Bethany how much it bothered her. It annoyed Alexa that Bethany told Ben how she felt. She had made that confession in confidence, but Bethany only countered that she would have done the same thing if the situation had been reversed. It was true, but Bethany had never played that role in her life before and she missed the loss of the confidence more than she hated Ben's habits.

Ben always claimed Bethany had nothing to do with the situation, and that he was just trying to cut back. If Alexa had been braver, she might have called his bluff, but she did not want to give Ben any more reasons to leave them. That made her think about Marcus, and Ben's inevitable reaction, but there were other people who needed to know – and who might be just as put out.

"I need to talk to you about something," said Alexa nervously, as she and Charlotte sat down with a bowl of popcorn to watch a movie.

"What?" asked Charlotte, clearly concerned by Alexa's tone.

"You know how you stay over in the spare room? Well, I've kind of offered the room to someone else – to stay in – permanently."

"Oh, yeah, that's cool. I'll just stay at home from now on," replied Charlotte, curling her legs into her chest.

"No, you don't have to – not unless you want to," said Alexa quickly, trying to turn Charlotte to face her. "I've bought a trundle bed that goes under mine, so you could either stay in my room, or we can set it up out here. I still want you to stay. I just have one favour. Don't tell anyone, not until they all know anyway."

"Why?" asked Charlotte with a slight smile. "Who's moving in?"

"Just an old friend."

"Otherwise known as?"

"Otherwise known as Marcus," answered Alexa, her heart beating in her throat.

"Seriously? Well you can count on me to keep my mouth shut.

I'm way too scared of Ben to tell him," said Charlotte, shaking her head.

"How much do you know about Marcus?" asked Alexa, curious of her reaction.

"Most stuff, I think. They talk about him when you're not around – when they discuss your life in their committee."

"Well then, you'll understand why I need time to tell everyone," replied Alexa, trying hard to contain her annoyance at that revelation.

"Are you two getting back together?" asked Charlotte.

Alexa realised Charlotte sounded hopeful and wondered if it was because of what she had heard about Marcus or experienced with Damien.

"No, he's just my friend," answered Alexa, playing down the situation. "He needed a place to stay. I'm just helping him out, but I don't want you to feel like you're not welcome. I know that's why you moved back home, because you felt like you were imposing on me and Damien. I want you to come over and stay whenever."

"You won't have time for me when Damien comes back. I can't share a room with the two of you," muttered Charlotte.

"Then how about this – Friday is our night," Alexa suggested. "Unless there's something super spectacular happening, we have the night together to do what we want. Go out, stay home, whatever."

"It doesn't have to be Friday night. That's a going out night. You don't want to spend it with me."

"Actually, I do," replied Alexa truthfully. "I hate clubs. I don't drink and bars are noisy and smelly. I'd much rather spend my Friday nights with you."

"Okay," smiled Charlotte, clearly buoyed by the idea that her company was preferable to anything. "But I don't think Damien'll be happy – about me or Marcus. You don't even let him stay over and now you're letting your ex-boyfriend move in."

"Marcus isn't my ex. We were never together."

"Maybe not, but you loved Marcus more than you loved Sam – and that's saying something."

Chapter Eleven

ALEXA WOKE WITH a sigh of relief. One more year behind her. It had not been an exciting end, trying to keep it as low key as possible. Ben had wanted her to celebrate so badly he even suggested she go to Bianca's party, but combining one of her least favourite activities with one of her least liked days was never going to happen. When Charlotte turned up and voted for no celebrations, Ben was outnumbered. He stayed with them until late, when he was called into work, after which Alexa and Charlotte immediately proceeded to bed, allowing the year to quietly disappear.

Not needing to be anywhere else, Charlotte accompanied Alexa to Maria's apartment. Maria was still a little upset Alexa had not chosen to spend New Year's Eve at her apartment to watch the fireworks, but Alexa could not have faced it.

"This isn't about Marcus, is it?" Maria asked. "You're not worried he'd turn up, are you? Well, I've looked and he's not out there."

Alexa's stomach rolled as she stated that she truly had not expected Marcus to be there. However, it was Charlotte's panic-stricken look that caught Maria's attention.

"What? What's going on?" asked Maria, looking between them.

"I wasn't worried about seeing Marcus here because I've already seen him," confessed Alexa warily.

"And?"

"And he's moving in tomorrow."

"Moving in? Tomorrow? What? Have you and Damien split up?" asked Maria frantically.

Alexa sighed and shook her head before proceeding to explain Marcus's situation. Maria listened in silence, her shock slowly etching itself on her face. "And what did Ben say?" asked Maria, refraining from any other comments.

"I haven't told him," replied Alexa firmly.

"Oh, Alexa, you should. You really should," said Maria in a pleading voice. "Ben's like a father to you. You know how he feels about Marcus. Don't you think he deserves to know?"

"He'll try and talk me out of it," replied Alexa desperately. "Ben and Sam, they're just going to have to accept it and I think that'll be more likely if they find out afterwards. Please, Maria, please don't tell them."

Maria agreed, but would not let Alexa leave without again letting her know that she believed Ben needed to find out before Marcus moved in. However, that was one thing Alexa would not be swayed on. She was not going to be convinced not to do this.

When Alexa woke the next morning, she was surprised by the nerves that fluttered in her stomach as she realised that by the end of the day Marcus would be living with her. Alexa went to the detention centre early, wanting to spend as much of the day with Bethany as possible, hoping that would make it go faster. They chatted about everything but Marcus – until it was time for Alexa to leave.

"Good luck," smiled Bethany. "Tell me everything."

Alexa nodded and hugged Bethany tight.

Marcus was waiting patiently outside her apartment block when Alexa arrived home. "Hi," he said shyly as she approached.

"Hey. Sorry, you been waiting long? I thought I'd make it back in time," replied Alexa, feeling guilty about making Marcus wait.

"No, I was early. Didn't take long to pack and I was pretty keen to get out of there. Not exactly full of happy memories, that place."

"Is that all you have?" asked Alexa looking at the single duffle bag at Marcus's feet.

"No, I have a few boxes in the boot, but not many. I let Jackie take everything when we broke up and stayed in furnished flats since."

It took less than ten minutes for Marcus and Alexa to bring his belongings up from the car and an hour after Marcus arrived he was unpacked and settled into his new home.

"How's it feel?" asked Alexa, as Marcus sat down on the lounge with his coffee.

"Amazing, thank you. You saved my life. I don't know how I would've gotten myself out of that situation without you."

"Well, you could've always rented out that second room," Alexa shrugged. "It was small, but at the right price I reckon you would've got someone in."

"You never mentioned that before," said Marcus. "You don't regret this, do you? I don't want to stay unless you're comfortable with it."

"I was just pointing out that there're always other options – perhaps not great ones, but they're there."

Marcus started laughing. Alexa looked at him quizzically, but that only made him laugh harder. "Sorry," he coughed. "I just find it very amusing that you're saying that to me."

"I don't mind you being here," replied Alexa with a smile, liking the reversal of fortunes. "It's a little strange. I thought maybe I'd run into you one day, but I'd kinda given up hope."

"I'm not sure I had. I just never expected to be moving in with you – ever. It's certainly not what I'd planned a week ago."

"What's going on there? Have you guys broken up?" asked Alexa apprehensively.

"We haven't really done anything. I've been avoiding her and that question, but I guess I'll have to figure that out," answered Marcus.

"I don't want to sound rude, but I'd rather she didn't stay over – her or any other girlfriend. I mean, I know I can't really stop you from having people over, but at least not very often," Alexa clarified, trying not to sound like a tyrant. "I rarely have Damien over. I want to keep this place as my own. She's welcome, of course, just not all the time. I only invited one person to live with me, not two."

"It's your place. I won't do anything to make you uncomfortable. I'll keep guests to a minimum – all guests," Marcus emphasised. Alexa knew she was being unreasonable, but was glad he was kind enough not to argue. "That's absolutely fine with me. And, hey, I'm not even sure I'll have a girlfriend much longer after what she did."

"Yeah, you will," replied Alexa.

"You sound so sure."

"You forget how well I know you."

***

Marcus woke with a start. It took him a few seconds to recall where he was as he stared around the foreign room. Then reality rushed back and he closed his eyes and smiled. He was with Alexa. They had somehow found each other and, in the year that passed, Alexa had found a way to forgive him. It seemed too good to be true.

Then Marcus recalled the rest of his reality and sat up in his bed wondering what he was going to do. He had not told anyone about moving in with Alexa. His family and close friends found out about her at the end of the previous year. The breaking off of his engagement and distress over the events surrounding Alexa's departure concerned those close to him. Needing support in a way he never had before, he finally confessed, but the support he craved never materialised.

Everyone had been horrified by his feelings for Alexa. They had stopped short of calling him a paedophile, but only just. Marcus had never been able make them understand how different Alexa was, how special she was, and how his love for her was not purely physical. He wanted to help and guide her, not possess or control her. But that was not what he was going to say to his family and friends this time. Even with the extreme financial situation Lucy had put him in, their reactions would be unpleasant at best. Marcus now understood why Alexa was so sure he would stay with Lucy. He would have to do everything to make that relationship work. He could not move in with Alexa and break up with his girlfriend at the same time. He would be crucified.

With those gloomy thoughts, Marcus threw on his pyjama pants and headed to the bathroom.

"Aren't we feeling at home already," smiled Alexa, as she sat in her pyjamas, eating breakfast on the lounge.

Marcus flinched, startled by her presence, then noticed his half-naked state. His eyes flicked between his body and hers, horrified by his actions, though he noticed she did not look too disturbed as her eyes roved over his chest. "Sorry. I'll go put a shirt on," he replied hurriedly, backtracking towards his room.

"I was joking," coughed Alexa, trying to smile through her choking. "This is your place as well now. I'm not going to tell you what to wear. Just don't get too comfortable and start walking around naked."

Marcus smiled and headed towards the bathroom, feeling Alexa's appraising eyes on him. It was strange, though very pleasing, to think that she was checking him out. If they ever went down to the beach together, he would be afforded a similar luxury. Those thoughts made for a very pleasant shower, though he had to pull himself back from imagining things going too far, then wondered if that was wise. If he kept his fantasies, he might be better able to keep his hands to himself. Denying everything did not seem feasible.

Stepping out of the shower, Marcus thought he heard voices in the hallway. He wondered who Alexa had told about his moving in and what their reaction had been. No matter who it was, Marcus was sure that walking out in a towel was not an option so threw his pyjama pants back on.

"I was going to tell you, I just didn't —" Marcus heard Alexa say as he opened the door. From there, all Marcus knew was that someone had grabbed him and thrown him up against the hall wall. "Ben, please, I —"

"What the hell are you doing here?" growled Ben fearsomely.

Marcus felt his eyes grow wide as his heart began to hammer. He remembered Ben and would have put him at the bottom of the list of people he wanted to run into again, particularly like this.

"Ben, stop, please," Alexa cried, trying to pull Ben off him.

"I told you to stay the hell away from her!" spat Ben, his forearm pressing hard against Marcus's chest, pinning him against the wall.

"There's nothing going on. She just offered me a place to stay," gasped Marcus desperately. Apparently, it was not only his friends who were against them having any form of friendship.

"You should've said no. You have no right to be here," yelled Ben, pressing harder on Marcus's chest.

"I have the right to be her friend," said Marcus as firmly as Ben's forearm allowed, but his voice was barely more than a squeak.

"Is that what you're here for? I'm warning you now, if you lay as much as a finger on her."

"Ben, stop," cried Alexa, but Ben acted as if he could not hear her.

"I'd never hurt her," pleaded Marcus, but he got the feeling Ben could not be reasoned with.

"You'd never hurt her? You turned you back on her. You broke her heart. You don't deserve a thing," snarled Ben angrily.

"What about you?" retaliated Marcus angrily, hating having the actions he despised himself for thrown back at him. "Look how much she suffered when you turned your back on her."

An uneasy silence followed Marcus's stinging words, until a swift right hook sent him to the ground. Marcus opened and closed his mouth to disperse the pain in his jaw. He had never been hit before and he was surprised by how vulnerable it made him feel.

"Get out of my house," Alexa ordered in a calm voice as Marcus shook his head to try and focus his eyes. He wondered if she was speaking to him.

"Alexa," gasped Ben.

The fear in Ben's voice made Marcus realise something was not right. He was still trying to lift himself to his feet when he heard Alexa scream. "Get out!" she cried, her voice panicked and forceful.

Marcus stood unsteadily, then froze. Ben was backing away as Alexa moved slowly forward, a large kitchen knife held shakily in her right hand. Alexa's eyes were cold – a look Marcus knew well and perhaps Ben did too, because he was taking her very seriously.

"Alexa, wait. Ben, stay," said Marcus, finally finding his voice as he stepped hesitantly in between them. "We can sort this out. He's just worried about you. He doesn't want to see you hurt."

Alexa's hand shook violently. Two tears slipped lightly down her face when she closed her eyes. Approaching slowly, Marcus slipped his hands over Alexa's and carefully took the knife from her. Alexa's gaze did not meet his until she realised her hands were empty and he was what stood between her and the front door.

Marcus did not stop her as she fled the apartment in her pyjamas.

"What have I done?" gasped Ben, walking unsteadily towards the lounge before collapsing on it.

Marcus dropped the knife on the island bench, his hands shaking. "I honestly thought she was going to use it. She looked so serious," he said, sitting down on the other lounge, well away from Ben.

"She would have," muttered Ben. Perhaps that was true, and Marcus's heart ached for the fear Alexa must have felt. "She's never going to forgive me," gasped Ben, choking on a sob.

It was a statement Marcus was inclined to agree with, but did not say so. Alexa was amazing in so many ways, not least of all her ability to forgive, but he had never seen her in such a state before, and he was not even sure if their own friendship could remain unaltered by this.

Ben sat with his head in his hands, deep, heaving sighs shuddering his chest. Marcus felt for him. His head was still pounding from the impact of Ben's fist, but he also knew what a huge role Ben played in Alexa's life. It would be horrible for one incident to destroy all that.

"Alexa'll come around," said Marcus softly. "You said yourself things didn't end well when she was a child. She accepted you back into her life once. There's no reason to think she won't do it again."

"She doesn't remember me from back then. She has no memory of me before a year and a half ago," choked Ben. "And the only reason she let me back into her life was because I could help Bethany."

"Well she forgave me. I can guarantee she hasn't forgotten the hurt I caused her," continued Marcus, hoping to mend these bridges with Ben for Alexa's sake. It did not matter how upset, hurt or scared she was, Alexa loved and trusted Ben in a way she did few others. Alexa also deserved a parental figure in her life. His reappearance could not be the reason she lost those most important to her.

"Why are you here?" spat Ben, turning on him with fierce eyes, though Marcus could see he was so horrified by what had passed that he would not threaten him again.

"I'm back in Alexa's life because we ran into each other quite unexpectedly towards the end of last year and we both decided we wanted to be friends. I'm living here because I've suddenly found myself in a very difficult financial situation and Alexa is helping me out," explained Marcus in a very constrained voice.

"How exceptional that you should have these difficulties now," said Ben accusingly.

"You think I'm after her money? That payout does not even come close to compensating Alexa for what she suffered at that place. I'd never take a cent off her."

"Yet you would move in with her?"

"I'll be paying rent to the amount which Alexa asks," replied Marcus firmly. "But that's not what this is about, is it? What do you really want to know? Do I want to sleep with her? Date her?"

"That'll do to start with," replied Ben distrustfully.

"Of course I want those things. I want a lot of things, but more than anything I want Alexa to be happy and safe and successful. I can help her do that by being her friend. I risk jeopardising that by trying to be anything more. I'm not an idiot. I don't have amnesia. I remember that I was her teacher. I know she's only nineteen. I realise I'll be twenty-nine in a few weeks. I'm not deluded," said Marcus angrily, listing all the things he wished he had the power to change.

"Is this what you told her?" asked Ben sceptically.

Marcus wondered if Ben thought him talented enough to manipulate Alexa and everyone around her so he could be right where he was now. The truth was if he wanted, he could have been here months earlier. Chad had never been Alexa's shield the way Sam was – never as blindly protective – and could have been convinced to provide information, but Marcus had never wanted to find Alexa that way.

"We haven't spoken about it," Marcus answered truthfully. "We both have partners now. We've moved on," he explained in the least inflammatory way he could. "But you have to understand that we want to be friends and neither of us see any reason why we shouldn't be. You can try and stop it, but it mightn't work out in your favour."

Marcus knew it did no good to be so antagonistic. If there was one person he should be trying to win over it was Ben. However, it was not just the hurt Ben had caused Alexa preventing that. The ringing in his ear and the pain that accompanied movement of his jaw did not incline Marcus to think the best of Ben. It made Marcus determined that, irrespective of how angry he became in the future, he would never retaliate by raising his hand.

Alexa walked into her apartment hoping to find it empty. She could not believe she had threatened Ben with a knife, but feared she would want one if she ever saw him again. Of all the ways she imagined Ben leaving them, something like this had never crossed her mind. She never believed she would be so terrified of him that she would be prepared to harm him.

The sight of Marcus tending to Ben as he cried on the lounge took Alexa by surprise. It softened her heart – until Ben looked up. When their eyes met, she remembered why she never wanted to see him again. Ben stood and Alexa instantly backed away. She kept moving until she was in the kitchen, backed up against the bench. Ben held out his hand and opened his mouth, but nothing came out. Alexa felt behind her for the knife, but it was on the island bench between them. Eyeing it, she could not decide if it was safer to stay as far away from Ben as possible or to rush forward for the knife.

Ben held up his hands as if in surrender and walked towards the front door. As soon as it clicked closed, Alexa rushed to the balcony. She watched Ben stare mournfully up at her, watched him slouch over the steering wheel, and watched as he eventually drove off. When he disappeared, Alexa closed her eyes and waited for the tears, but they did not fall. She hated that Ben had betrayed them, but more than that, she hated that she had known it would happen sooner or later.

"He had your best interests at heart," said Marcus, joining her on the balcony. "He did apologise for hitting me. And I don't blame him, Alexa. We all want what's best for you."

"He didn't even talk to me. He just hit you," Alexa gasped, reliving that moment in her head. "Why does everyone think they know how to live my life better than me? Everyone thinks they know what's best for me, like if it was left up to me, I would ruin everything."

"No one thinks that. It's just that you've been through more than anyone could ever imagine and —"

"And I'm fine. I'm here. I'm not dead. Please, just let me be. Let me choose who my friends are. Let me choose how I live my life."

"I just want you to be happy."

Alexa turned to Marcus, desperate for his arms around her. She wondered if he wanted the same thing as he pushed his hands deeper into his pockets. "I don't know how to be happy," she confessed. "I have no family and now the one I've created is falling apart."

"We'll put it back together."

"I want Bethy," Alexa cried softly, her whole body aching with the pain of their continued separation.

"I know every day without her feels like forever, but time will pass. She'll come home to you," said Marcus, somehow expressing exactly how she felt. "Then you'll be able to start truly living that wonderful life that's ahead of you."

Alexa shook her head, knowing such a simple conclusion was not possible. Bethany would hate her for throwing Ben out of their lives. Marcus ushered Alexa inside and wrapped a blanket around her shoulders despite it being a warm day. He made them tea and sat on the other lounge, watching her surreptitiously, waiting for her to talk. When her silence continued, he made hot chocolate.

"You're only going to succeed in making me pee, not talk," Alexa said as Marcus smilingly handed her the mug.

"I disagree. Just made you talk then," he replied, very pleased with himself. Alexa could only shake her head. "So is there anyone else we need to tell about my living here?" he asked, clearly deciding she was talking now. "Anyone else we need to worry about? What about Sam?"

"Sam doesn't know," Alexa sighed, and she heard Marcus sigh as well. "My life," she retorted.

"My face," Marcus replied, pointing to his eye.

Alexa could not help but smile. She loved Marcus for that. "I can handle Sam. Bethy'll talk him round if need be. I'm not sure what I'm going to tell Damien."

Alexa heard Marcus sigh again and then cough before he spoke. She wanted to see the look on his face, but did not dare look up. "Does Damien know who I am? Where we met?" asked Marcus hesitantly, making Alexa wonder which part he was most afraid of.

"No, I've never mentioned you. That's the problem. I don't talk about my past – not to him, not to anyone if I can help it – and the lies I told when we met are starting to unravel. He hates finding things out. He went ape when he found out Sam and I used to date."

Alexa looked up to see Marcus smirking, though he tried to hide it when he saw her staring at him. "I can empathise slightly on that account," he smiled.

Alexa was surprised Marcus alluded to those things, but was glad he had. She did not want to forget the bond they shared. "You think Sam and I act like we're together?" she asked seriously.

"You've always been very close," Marcus replied, his words chosen carefully.

"You can tell me the truth."

"Sometimes, yeah, I used to think that. When you came back to school at the start of year twelve, you were holding his hand, yeah, I thought that. You two have a past – a long one. I guess sometimes that can be hard to escape."

"It's not like that any more," said Alexa. "Besides, me and Sam hardly ever see each other when Damien's around." Marcus just nodded and Alexa felt her stomach twist. "You know when I said we weren't together – that we'd moved on?" Marcus nodded again. "There was more to it than that."

"I guessed that," smiled Marcus.

"Just a week – when I came back from Europe. You were right. We did have a lot to work through. It made it better."

"Then that's good," said Marcus emphatically.

"We slept together," confessed Alexa, looking down at her hands.

Marcus jumped off the lounge and knelt in front of her. He lifted her chin with his hand and gently stroked her cheek with his thumb.

"Did he treat you well? Was it what you wanted?" Alexa nodded, feeling guilty. "And it helped? It felt good?" Alexa looked into Marcus's eyes as she nodded and was relieved to see there was no anger in them. "Before you were going out with Damien?"

"Before we met," smiled Alexa.

"Then why are you ashamed? You haven't done anything wrong. You can live your life the way you choose. Date who you want. Live with whoever you want," he added with a grin. "You can even make whatever mistakes you want – if any of those things turn out to be mistakes. You don't have to justify yourself to anyone."

"You think I should tell him?" Alexa asked, biting her lip, hoping the answer was no.

"Damien?" Marcus asked. Alexa nodded as he sat back up on the lounge. "No. No, I think that's the sort of stuff you keep to yourself."

"Really? I'm not being deceitful?"

"You realise people are allowed to have multiple partners, right? Lucy knows I was with Jackie, but I don't talk to her about it. We don't discuss our past and I certainly don't talk to Lucy about sex I used to have with Jackie."

"Why don't I know about any of these things?"

"Because you spent your teenage years in a repressive boarding school and when you did get out you spent your time doing lots of things that didn't involve TV," laughed Marcus. "Believe me, if you didn't learn these things from your friends, then you learnt them from TV. You just don't watch enough trash."

"So I'm not a freak?"

"Ha," Marcus laughed again. "Well, that all depends. Plenty of people would find your lack of interest in television freakish."

"I watch movies," said Alexa, feeling like she was making some progress socially. "Charlotte introduced me to them. I don't find them very informative."

Marcus laughed and Alexa smiled. It was surreal that just a couple of hours ago she had been fearing for her life, and yet now she was laughing and smiling on the lounge. Alexa had never known anyone who could moderate her moods quite like Marcus. It was as though he knew how to say just the right thing in just the right way. And it was not just Marcus's words that were perfect. It was his actions. When lunch time came, he got up without a word and made them something to eat. It was just a sandwich, but Alexa could not remember the last time someone had taken care of her in such a simple way. It was so nice for just a few moments not to have to think or decide.

When lunch was finished, they sat on the lounge and chatted. The conversation centred around the trivial. Marcus seemed to know what topics Alexa wanted to avoid, and somehow turned her whole day around from one of the worst to one of the best. When the intercom buzzed, Alexa was so relaxed that she just assumed it was Charlotte and let her straight up. Marcus was quietly questioning her security habits when Sam burst through the unlocked front door.

"So it's true! You're freaking kidding me," cried Sam, pushing past Alexa and towards Marcus.

"Sam, no!" screamed Alexa.

"Sam, just stop for a minute," said Marcus sternly, rising from the lounge.

"Don't you tell me what to do. You're not my teacher any more," snarled Sam.

"Sam, please," pleaded Alexa, grabbing the front of Sam's shirt, but he brushed her away and stepped in closer to Marcus.

Marcus grabbed Alexa's arm and pulled her behind him.

"You think she needs protection from me?" asked Sam viciously. "You're the one we've tried to keep her away from. You're the one who tore her heart out! What right do you have to walk back into her life like this – like nothing ever happened?"

"This is her choice," said Marcus firmly, as Alexa cowered behind him. "Alexa invited me to live here until I got myself sorted out financially. There's nothing else going on. It's her decision. Her life."

"You haven't been around this past year, so you've got no idea the trouble we've had getting her to face life. She's not in a position to be making these decisions. She doesn't know what's best for her. We do!"

"Sam, I'm begging you. Let this go," ordered Marcus. "You're the best friend Alexa has. Don't ruin it – not like this."

"You told us you wanted space – needed independence," said Sam, ignoring Marcus and talking directly to Alexa. "Yet you keep inviting people to live here – the wrong people – Charlotte, now him. If you're so desperate to live with someone why don't you live with Ben?"

"I asked Ben!" cried Alexa, feeling her heart tear out. "He rejected me. He never wanted me. He says all the right things to everyone else, but I'm not good enough for him – or you."

"Alexa, please, you don't know what you're talking about," argued Sam. "Me and Ben, we only want the best for you. And Damien. What about Damien?"

"Can you accept this, Sam?" Alexa asked.

"You're making a big mistake. You've pushed Ben away. You're pushing me away and for what? For him?"

"Sam, please," cried Alexa.

"It's a mistake, Lex, a big mistake," said Sam, shaking his head. Glowering at Marcus, he stormed out of the apartment, slamming the door behind him.

"Alexa, perhaps I should go. I never wanted to cause problems," said Marcus, as she continued to stare at the front door.

"Do you want to go?" she asked timidly, her glance never shifting from the door.

"No, I don't. These two days – I've never enjoyed living somewhere so much, but I have no right to come in and screw up your life."

"I invited you to stay. Leave whenever you want. Just leave your key on the kitchen bench," said Alexa, feeling her heart turn to stone as she walked into her bedroom and fell on to her bed.

All night, Alexa waited to hear the front door open and close, waited for the sound of a key being left behind, but if Marcus left, he did it quietly. When morning finally came, Alexa was not glad to see it. She did not even have that single blissful second where she could believe it had just been a horrid dream. The only consolation was the sight of Marcus walking topless out of the bathroom.

"You decided to stay?" she asked softly.

"I'm a sucker for punishment," Marcus smiled. Alexa could not return it. "If you don't want me to leave and I don't want to leave, then why would I? Our lives, right?" Alexa smiled slightly as she nodded. "I'm going to go tell me family today," said Marcus softly.

Alexa blanched. "At least they don't know where I live. I get to do it on my terms – then run away," he added happily.

That brief light-hearted moment did not last long. Damien called just as Alexa got out of the shower. She knew she needed to tell him straight away, but this was one encounter she would not have in her own home. Leaving immediately, Alexa wasted no time in telling Damien about Marcus moving in. She emphasised Marcus's financial crisis and the fact that they had only ever been friends. The age gap and a phoney story about Marcus being an old family friend were enough for Damien to accept there was no risk of anything going between them, but she could tell Damien was far from happy.

"If you're letting him stay, does that mean I get to stay over?" Damien asked with a hint of bitterness.

"You've stayed before," Alexa replied, before realising how that would sound. "I just want to keep my home separate from the world. I know you can't understand that and I can't explain, but I want to be able to decide who stays and who doesn't."

"That's fine. I just don't understand why I'm one of the people you need to lock out of your home."

Alexa was not sure why she kept Damien locked out either. With everything still tallying in his favour there was no reason to keep him at arm's length from her life. She just knew she had to.

The conversation did not improve much, and it was called to a thankful end when Alexa had to go and sit her driving test. Given the state of mind she was in, she fully expected to fail. She considered cancelling it, worried about the money she was wasting. She tried to focus, but nothing was going right. Five minutes into the test a pedestrian ran across the road in front of her, forcing her to brake hard. Then it took her twice as many attempts as it should have to reverse park the car. When the instructor had to ask her to back the car up at an intersection, she knew she had failed. It left her genuinely surprised when they handed her P-plates and a new licence.

"You sure?" she asked, double checking.

"Yes, you passed," replied the instructor. "Drive safely."

It was the first lucky break Alexa had had in a long time, so she decided not to argue and rushed home to get her car. Swapping the L-plates for P-plates, she drove straight to the detention centre. Bethany was practically dancing on the other side of the door, waiting for it to be opened. Alexa held up her licence, smiling happily, but Bethany did not seem to care about her newfound independence.

"Oh, Lex. Why didn't you tell them?" cried Bethany, pulling her down to sit at the table. "Why'd you let them find out like that?"

"I don't want to talk about them," replied Alexa in a cold voice. Her heart was aching to the point where she was in physical pain just thinking about them.

"Lex, —"

"You're with me on this, right?" Alexa asked, for the first time terrified the answer might not be yes.

"Yeah, I'm with you," replied Bethany, squeezing her hand.

Alexa nodded and closed her eyes, two tears slipping down her face. Bethany immediately wrapped her arms around her and held her tight. They did not speak again. They just sat in silence, holding hands, their heads resting against each other's. When Ben and Sam arrived, Alexa jumped from her seat and left with barely a hurried goodbye.

"Any better?" asked Marcus when Alexa arrived home. Alexa shook her head. "Well there's dinner if you want it. Just spaghetti bolognaise. I'll warn you now, that's my staple dish. You invited the wrong person to stay if you wanted variety in your cooking."

Alexa smiled weakly and laid herself down on the lounge. She could not describe just how happy she was to have Marcus around. It seemed so odd that they could be so comfortable living together given their history. When she did not mention Sam or Ben, she was grateful to Marcus for not asking.

The surprise was the arrival of Sam first thing the next morning. He promised peace as he stood waiting at the front door to be invited in, but Alexa was still unsure.

"Come on, I'm not here to cause trouble," said Sam earnestly.

Alexa opened the door and allowed Sam inside. "Coffee?" she asked, walking to the kitchen as Sam peered around furtively. Sam did not answer, but Alexa made them one anyway. Perhaps she would feel better if she had something hot to throw at him.

"Why didn't you tell us beforehand?" asked Sam.

"You would've tried to change my mind," Alexa answered truthfully, keeping herself on the far side of the kitchen.

"You know this is a bad idea. You know you need to just walk away from him. He was our teacher. Can't you see how wrong this is?"

"You didn't feel that way before."

"Yes I did. I always did," Sam cried, his face twisting bitterly. "I just never said anything. If he was what you needed to get you through then I'd go along with it, but he wasn't. He betrayed you. Ben, who's only ever protected you, doesn't deserve this."

"Sam, I don't justify our friendship to anyone – even when we're criticised for it," said Alexa simply, refusing to back down. "I won't justify my friendship with Marcus either."

At that moment, Marcus emerged from the bathroom with only a towel wrapped around his waist. Sam turned and glared angrily at the sight, while Alexa could only sigh. The emergence of Marcus from the bathroom in the morning was one of her favourite parts of the day. His body was more sculpted than she remembered and she liked that she could look at him innocently in his semi-naked state.

"Sam," nodded Marcus curtly.

"Sir," replied Sam with a sneer.

Marcus's face dropped before he quickly recomposed himself. It hurt Alexa to see him pained that way. "Marc," she called as he walked towards his bedroom, deliberately using his first name, though she had nothing much to say. "Um, there was plenty of hot water left, yeah?"

"Heaps," replied Marcus, an unsure smile creeping on to his face.

"Great," Alexa smiled in return.

"Marc?" sneered Sam when Marcus was gone.

"Have we finished? I need to go see Bethy," said Alexa, not trying to hide her annoyance. Sam shook his head in disgust and left.

Alexa pulled into the detention centre car park, her heart feeling lighter than it should. The situation with Ben and Sam was problematic, but with Marcus around and Bethany's parole hearing approaching, Alexa could only get more excited as she counted down the days. There were still many things that could go wrong, but she did not want to think about that. She did not want to think there were people in the world who could look at Bethany and not believe she was truly contrite for what had happened or that she was not ready to be released back into the world.

Bethany was tempering her own excitement, always pulling herself back when she started talking about life on the outside. Instead, Bethany turned all her energy on trying to heal the rift between Alexa and Ben. "I don't want you two to be fighting. He's too important to us," she said. "Have you tried talking to him?"

"I didn't do anything wrong. Why should I have to crawl to him?" retorted Alexa.

"Because he's too ashamed to crawl to you. He knows he stuffed up and, God, even Marcus forgave him. Why can't you?"

"Because he hit him. No, attacked him," clarified Alexa. "You weren't there. You didn't see it. He snapped."

Bethany squeezed Alexa's hands tight and it was then that Alexa realised her body was shaking.

"He just wanted to protect you," Bethany said softly.

"From what? I was never in any danger. Marcus wasn't hurting me. He wasn't even near me," cried Alexa. "Ben, he just lost it. What happens if I ever make him that mad? I tried to talk to him – to reason – but he didn't say anything, didn't even give Marcus a chance to defend himself. I don't want to be hit again – not by anyone."

"Ben would never hit you. You have to believe that," gasped Bethany, making Alexa wonder if she was trying to convince herself.

"If you can hit one person, then you're capable of hitting anyone," replied Alexa, her voice breaking. "Can't you see he's just like everyone else? We can't trust him."

"I trust him, Lex," said Bethany firmly, though Alexa could feel her hand shaking too. "I want him around in my life – in our lives. I know he hurt you, but I need him. Please don't send him away."

"Angel, it's my job to protect you – protect us. I won't let him hurt you."

"He won't. He treats us like his daughters and we think of him as our father," said Bethany, as though urging Alexa to believe that.

"He's not our father," Alexa sighed in agitated frustration.

"No, Lex, our father was – Ben's only human. He made a mistake and wants to make it up to you. Please just give him a chance."

"I don't know if I can. Look, I should go. I'll be back as soon as I can. You be okay? There anything you need?" asked Alexa, unable to stay and talk about these things.

"No. Ben and Peter are going to be here a lot this week. They're going to take care of everything and make sure I'm prepared," replied Bethany firmly.

That annoyed Alexa. If it was just Peter, she would not be kept out of Bethany's parole proceedings.

"I'll talk to Peter, make sure you get everything you need for the hearing," Alexa promised, knowing that with Peter she still had more sway than Bethany.

Bethany smiled slightly and Alexa knew she was thinking about the prospect of finally leaving the detention centre. For Alexa, that possibility was the one shining beacon in her life. It was like a warm ball that sat in her chest, glowing softly, just waiting for its chance to really shine. If she had not had so much experience with her life, she might have let it consume her and transform her into a giant, blazing ball of hope. But that would only leave more of her burned when the fire of hope was inevitably extinguished.

It was that mixture of gloom and optimism which accompanied Alexa home. It made her glad Marcus had a lot of experience with her moods. She could not imagine many people being able to live with such extremes. Smiling at the thought of an evening at home with Marcus, Alexa was surprised to find Maria sitting on the lounge talking happily to him, drinks and cake on the coffee table in front of them. Marcus smiled awkwardly at her, but Maria was completely at ease.

"What's going on?" asked Alexa.

"I was just meeting Marcus," replied Maria with a bright smile.

"Of course you were."

"Sam brought me over. Thought you might like the company."

"Sure he did," Alexa replied. "He brought you over to meet Marcus in the hope you'd find him as deviant as they do, to then recruit you in their plan of making me kick him out."

"Oh, don't be like that," replied Maria in a commanding sigh. "You know as well as I do that if Marcus was even close to the person you described to me when we first met I'd think of him the way you do."

"So you think he's nice too?" Alexa asked.

"Of course I do. He's a lovely young man," Maria smiled, patting Marcus's leg warmly, making him blush. "But what's this about you not talking to Ben?"

"See his black eye," said Alexa, raising her voice in spite of herself. She did not want to be angry with Maria. "That's what it's about. He attacked him, in my house, against my wishes. I tried to talk to him. I begged him and he just brushed me aside."

"I don't mean to make Marcus uncomfortable, but you forgave him – and I know he hurt you. I won't let you lie and pretend he didn't."

"That's different," Alexa answered, her body starting to tremble. "Marcus never threatened to hit me."

"And neither did Ben," retorted Maria quickly.

It was true, but Alexa could not explain why Ben's attack on Marcus felt like an attack on her or why it made her fear Ben as if it had been.

"Perhaps just try not to be so angry," said Marcus as the silence stretched into tension. "Ben made a mistake – one I'm sure he regrets – but he can't take it back. We can't change what happened or how it was handled. Maybe just let go of the anger and see if you can trust him again."

Alexa scowled at Marcus and went to the kitchen to make herself a coffee. She hated that he made so much sense, but it was not anger she had to let go of. It was fear. And that was not a matter of her letting go of it. It was a matter of it letting go of her. Yet day after day, wherever Alexa went, it felt like there was someone wanting to talk to her about Ben. It was relentless and there was only one escape.

Alexa had not been able to tell Damien about what happened with Ben. It was easier to have a refuge than to explain why Ben's violence frightened her so much, especially while Damien was still intent on being disgruntled about Marcus's presence. Alexa did whatever she could to assuage Damien. She went out with him more often and stayed at his place whenever he asked. She tried to manoeuvre all their outings to be closer to his place than hers so the logical option was to stay there and it worked for the most part. If Alexa did not always feel as though their whole relationship was like a game of chess she may have enjoyed herself more, but lately she was just waiting for some-thing to slip and for Damien to be annoyed with her once again. However, none of that was enough to convince her that she was not in love with Damien. She knew it was her putting the pressure on their relationship and that she would never be able to expect anything from a man but to be eternally frustrated by her deficiencies.

"I'm glad I didn't ruin everything over Christmas," said Damien, as they walked along the beach, his arm firmly around Alexa's waist.

"I'm glad I didn't ruin everything," Alexa replied with a relieved smile. "It's not like I make it easy for you. But Christmas is a shitty time of year, whether you realise or not. Too many expectations. I hate it. I'm glad it's over."

"What about me in your life? Have I moved up the rankings any?"

"You have to stop thinking about my life in terms of rankings," sighed Alexa, closing her eyes to try and contain her frustration. "I love you and spending time with you. Can't that be enough?"

"I'm sorry. I didn't mean to upset you. I'm glad we're seeing each other more. It's been really good. That reminds me, my mate Glen's having a birthday party on Friday night. You want to meet at mine?"

"I can't. I told you, not Fridays, they're for me and Charlotte to hang out."

"Can't you change the day?" snapped Damien.

"No, then it wouldn't be special."

"It's just one week."

"Then it'll just be every week. I made her this promise because you made her feel unwelcome when she was living with me. I'm not having that again," Alexa said determinedly, feeling like she was defending her own importance, not just Charlotte's. "I'm not having anyone make her feel unwanted."

"Yeah sure," muttered Damien, dropping her hand. "It's amazing how much effort you put into making everyone else feel welcome in your home, but just not your boyfriend." Alexa could not reply. "I'd better get going. I'll talk to you later."

"I'm sorry," Alexa sighed, hating that her life would never be good enough for Damien. "Maybe if we hadn't just started this whole Friday night thing, it'd be different. I don't want her to think I'm not serious. Why don't you come over on Saturday night and I'll make it up to you then?"

"Okay," smiled Damien, looking triumphant.

Alexa sighed as she walked home, thinking that she would have to warn Marcus about Damien coming over. She had told him and Sam the story she had woven for Damien about him, but preferred it was not tested too much. Sam planned on feigning ignorance, still disgruntled about the whole situation, but Marcus could hardly do that.

As Alexa considered the idea of Marcus meeting Damien, she started worrying about Bethany meeting Damien and Marcus. If all went well, Bethany would be released in just a few weeks. Alexa had not warned either of them and had nothing prepared. That approach was unlikely to make introducing Bethany to Damien an easy process. Alexa could only hope that Marcus, with so much more understanding of their situation, would not take offence to the way she was handling it. However, she worried that might be too much to ask, even of Marcus.

Deep in thought, Alexa was taken by surprise by the sight of Ben pacing her lounge room. She had not even noticed his car downstairs. "What are you doing here?" she asked coldly.

Ben stopped and looked at her, his mouth opening slowly though no words came out. Alexa's heart turned to ice as her legs shook. She did not even need Ben to speak the words that swirled around her brain.

"It's Bethany."

Chapter Twelve

"ALEXA, I ..."

Ben's voice broke and Alexa strained to lift her lead-filled feet towards him, all her anger forgotten in her absolute terror. Something had gone wrong. Her eyes focused in on Ben as he sat her down on the lounge, taking no notice of Marcus and Charlotte as they slipped quietly into the kitchen.

"What happened? Where is she? Please don't tell me," Alexa gasped, her heart straining.

"There was a riot today – at the detention centre," said Ben softly, choking slightly on his words.

Silent tears slipped slowly down Alexa's face as she shook it from side to side, her heart disintegrating with every passing second. She did not want to hear that Bethany was dead. Her life meant nothing without her, and she knew that none of the gains she had made in the past twelve months would be enough to make her stay and live on.

"It's okay. She's okay," said Ben, trying to comfort her. "Parole hearings have been cancelled as punishment – everyone's. There's no indication of when they'll be rescheduled, but it won't be soon."

Ben's words took many moments to sink in. So convinced that Bethany was dead, Alexa was relieved until reality set in. "She's not coming home?" she whispered, looking up at Ben.

"I'm sorry," he replied, shaking his head as he blinked back tears. "I know neither of you tried to get your hopes up, but that doesn't make this any easier."

Alexa's breath came in shuddering gasps as she tried to grasp yet another setback. Ben watched her warily, as if evaluating her reaction. It made Alexa nervous. Perhaps he knew her too well.

"Is she okay?" Alexa asked him firmly, never breaking eye contact.

"A few bumps and bruises, nothing major. I promise," Ben replied earnestly. "She's upset about the parole, but won't show it."

"I want to see her," Alexa commanded, refusing to let Ben keep them apart.

"You can't. They've cancelled all visiting hours. Punishment. You won't be able to see her until next weekend."

Alexa lunged into Ben's chest. He wrapped his arms around her, holding her tight. Another set of arms joined his, engulfing her from the other side. Alexa grabbed Charlotte's hand held it tight as she sobbed into Ben's chest. The arms held her as her tears slowed. That was when Alexa realised that one set of comforting arms was Ben's. Quickly recomposing herself, Alexa pushed away and wiped her eyes, sitting herself down on the lounge well away from him.

"I'm okay," Alexa said, refusing to look up.

Ben moved to the kitchen, where he swayed uncertainly between her and the door.

"He can't prove that he's sorry if you keep pushing him away," whispered Charlotte, sitting down next to Alexa. "He's real sorry for what he did. He just wants to be able to say it. You know you need him, just like Bethany does … and I kinda need him too." Alexa turned to see Charlotte's embarrassed face. "He'd been talking to me more before that happened. Seemed to be trying to get to know me. It was just for you, but – you're lucky. You have the nicest people in your life."

Charlotte looked away, as if ashamed by her statement, but Alexa could not dismiss it so easily. Speaking up was not one of Charlotte's strengths, not even with her.

"I'm going to go," said Ben, moving towards the door.

Alexa rose, turning between Ben and Charlotte. Charlotte nodded, helping to make up Alexa's mind. Ben had made one mistake – one that still terrified her – but if Charlotte and Bethany needed him, she could not be the one to deny them. She could not be responsible for tearing this makeshift family apart.

"Ben, you don't have to go," Alexa said softly, reaching him as he walked out the door.

"I don't expect your forgiveness, not after what I did," he replied sombrely, not meeting her eyes. "It's okay. I'll go."

"I want you to stay," Alexa replied, her whole body shaking, knowing it was both truth and lie she was speaking. "Please, don't go."

"You sure?"

Alexa breathed deeply, feeling the air stick in her chest. No, she was not sure. "I still don't like what you did and want you to promise never to hit anyone ever again, but, please, stay," she replied, her voice shaking with her body.

Ben scooped her up in his arms and held her tight to his chest as his tears fell slipped on to her silky hair. "I'm so sorry I put you through this," he said in a choking voice, and she knew he was truly contrite, but somehow it was still not enough to wipe away her fear. "It should never've happened. I don't want you to ever be scared of me. I'm going to take such good care of you."

"I don't need you to take care of me," Alexa replied automatically, pushing out of his arms.

Ben nodded in passive acceptance. Alexa tried to smile, but had to settle for an answering nod. Ben's arm slipped around her shoulders as he led them back into the lounge room.

Alexa was not sure how she felt about having Ben around again. Accepting him back in her life meant she would have to put what happened behind her, but feared it would be easier said than done. It made Alexa selfishly thankful that Charlotte started having problems with her family. If Alexa was not with Damien, then Charlotte would be at the apartment. Marcus never made Charlotte feel unwelcome, for which Alexa was truly grateful. However, as she and Marcus had spent very little time alone recently, Alexa was not sure what he really thought about Charlotte. Part of her did not even care. A very large part of Alexa was struggling to care about anything, unwilling to believe her faith would be rewarded.

"Cheer up," said Maria, placing a large plate of scones on the table. "Being down won't make the situation better.

"She'll be out as soon as they reschedule the parole hearings," said Sam, tucking into the food. "I know you're disappointed, but it'll work out for the best."

"I just feel like we're going to be kept apart forever," replied Alexa grimly, trying not to take Sam's comment literally, as though any good could come from extending Bethany's incarceration.

"You have us for now. I know it's not what you want, but she'll be out soon and then you'll forget all about being without her," said Charlotte softly.

Alexa was touched. It was clear something had happened to make Charlotte so sad, but after recent events Alexa was struggling to let anyone too close. It was not fair, so after a silent drive home Alexa forced her mind away from her own troubles. "Do you want to tell me what's wrong?" she asked Charlotte, when they walked inside.

"It's nothing. I'm fine," replied Charlotte softly, turning without meeting Alexa's eyes.

"You sure?" asked Alexa hesitantly, knowing it was a lie. "You've been pretty quiet and spending a lot more time here than you used to."

"Don't you want me here?"

Charlotte took a step back towards the door and Alexa had to grab her hand. Tears stung the sides of her eyes thinking about how much she needed Charlotte around, and she had to control them. The best thing for Charlotte was to make things better with her family.

"I didn't say that," Alexa said, releasing Charlotte's hand. "It's been great having you around. You've helped me a lot. I'm just worried it's come at the consequence of you. I don't want you to think I don't care."

"I'm fine, really," nodded Charlotte with a faint smile. "Why don't you have your shower? We can talk more while we're cooking dinner."

Alexa smiled and rubbed Charlotte's arm. It was remarkable how far they had come. Their relationship did genuinely feel more sisterly than friendly. Alexa was thankful that this time, unlike with Hayley and the Whites, it did not feel as though it was coming at the expense of Bethany. Alexa just had to be careful to make sure it did not come at the expense of Charlotte's family, because she knew, in the end, Charlotte would only end up hating her for that.

"What the hell are you doing?"

Marcus's cry startled Alexa. She immediately looked around the shower, trying to work out what she had been doing, before realising it must be Charlotte he was yelling at.

"It's none of your business. Get away from me!" cried Charlotte as Alexa tried to dry and dress as quickly as possible.

"This is my business," snapped back Marcus angrily. Alexa rushed out of the bathroom. Marcus turned on her with the angriest eyes she had ever seen. "Did you know? Did you teach her your little method of coping?"

Marcus had Charlotte by the wrist, her arm covered in blood and cuts, while his other hand waved Charlotte's razor in Alexa's face.

"Let her go!" Alexa cried, pulling Charlotte out of his grasp and behind her.

"You knew!" yelled Marcus.

"Of course I knew," Alexa sighed.

"And you let her do it!"

"I want her to stop," Alexa growled, hating having to explain to him. "But I don't think the best way is to scream at her. You can't just tell people to stop and expect them to listen. It doesn't work like that."

"Then what do you think the best way is?"

"The same way you stopped me, okay. With love." Marcus stopped dead, as did Alexa. Charlotte twisted out of her loose grip and rushed to the bathroom, locking the door behind her. "I don't want to force her to stop against her will," cried Alexa, pointing at the bathroom door. "It'll only push her away. I want to give her reasons to stop once and for all. I want her to be happy. She's not doing it because she's bored. I explained it to you. I thought you understood."

Marcus walked to the bin and disposed of the bloody razor. Alexa could see him breathing hard as he walked back out to confront her. "You believe that logic. I never said I did," he replied gravely. "I still don't think it's enough to sit back and hope she'll stop cutting her arm. Besides, I wasn't the reason you stopped and you know it. Peter was."

"Peter's my lawyer. He couldn't have told anyone anyway, but he did stop me having to face Clinton ever again. That's what he asked for in return. I could hardly deny him."

"That's my point," replied Marcus fiercely. "You were forced. It wasn't my ... love had nothing to do with it."

"You were the first one to ever make me feel like I didn't need to – even just for a bit. Didn't you know that?" cried Alexa, stunned that Marcus never realised the impact his affections had. "I don't think I could've kept my promise without you. You've no idea what love can do, especially for someone who doesn't feel it all that often."

Marcus walked out on to the balcony feeling sick. He had promised Alexa so much. Watching her now, he wished he could take it back. He had found ways to justify his feelings back then, as though in time it could somehow be right. He loved Alexa more than he could or would love anyone else, but also knew that would never be enough and he could never again offer her things he could not provide.

When Alexa had told him about the young girl who reminded her of herself, she had spoken of emotional similarities, but they went well beyond that. Charlotte looked like Alexa, spoke like her, and was as wilfully stubborn and defiant as her. Marcus would never know how much was coincidence and how much was Alexa's influence. It hardly mattered. What Marcus liked most about Charlotte was that, in spite of all her similarities to Alexa, he had no affection for her beyond that of a concerned adult – and it never threatened to be anything more. It gave him the courage to believe that his feelings for Alexa had not developed simply because she was a vulnerable child.

"I'm sorry I upset you," said Charlotte softly, breaking him away from his thoughts.

"You understand why I'm upset, don't you?" Marcus asked, feeling his voice slide automatically into teacher mode.

"Yeah, you remember what Alexa used to do."

"This isn't about Alexa. It's about you," groaned Marcus, frustrated by Charlotte's Alexa-like defiance.

"No it's not. The only reason you even talk to me is to make Alexa happy."

"That's not true."

"Look, I'm sorry. You won't see me do it again," replied Charlotte in an agitated manner.

"How about you won't do it again?"

It was too late. Charlotte was out the door before Marcus could finish his sentence.

"Hey, wait. Come back, you don't have to go," puffed Alexa, catching up to Charlotte at the lift.

"Nobody cares."

"What are you talking about? We all care," said Alexa sincerely, holding on to Charlotte's shoulders so she could not leave.

"Only because you have to," snapped Charlotte.

"What do you mean? Why do I have to care about you?" Alexa asked, genuinely confused by Charlotte's statement.

"To stop me cutting my arm. What happens when I stop? Who'll care then? People only talk to me because of you, and my family only talks to me because they think they have to. What happens when they all find out they don't have to care any more?"

"I'll always care about you," said Alexa imploringly. "I'd love you to stop feeling so sad you have to cut yourself to cope. The day you stop will be a happy day and I'll love you even more. Charlotte, you're like a sister to me. I want you around. I know we all want to give up on family sometimes, and we don't because they are family, but they'll always be family and you can't change that, even if you wanted to."

"I wish that were true," replied Charlotte sadly as she stepped into the lift.

Alexa was concerned when Charlotte did not return until Friday. The sight of Charlotte bounding happily into the apartment made it clear she was not interested in discussing her problems, so Alexa did not even ask how she had been.

It was a good day. They did not do anything in particular, just kept each other company and pretended their lives were not horrible. In the evening they watched television and jeered at the movie's unrealistic representation of life, while Marcus sat and smirked.

"I hope you're not planning on watching tomorrow night's movie, then," he laughed when the show finally ended.

"Probably not," Alexa sighed. "Damien's staying over. Are you going to be around?" she asked warily.

"I had no plans to be out of the house," Marcus replied, looking at her seriously. "Do you want me to make some?"

"No, I mean, you don't have to – it's just – I mean, I told you I didn't really have people over – except Charlotte."

"This is your place. I'm never going to tell you who you can have over and when. You reserve the right to tell me that," answered Marcus with a smile. "That said, I care a lot about you, and I'm very interested in meeting Damien. I want to make sure he's good enough for you."

"I really don't think that's the problem," Alexa muttered.

"You think he's too good for you?" asked Marcus seriously. Alexa nodded, her eyebrows raised as though that was a given. "Then I want to meet him even more. Must be a great guy."

Damien appeared just as eager to meet Marcus. As soon as they met in the city, Damien was asking whether Marcus would be at home that night. It took all Alexa's persuasive skills to keep them from going home that moment. She had never intended this night to be about Damien meeting Marcus. However, when the introduction became inevitable, they trekked nervously home.

Marcus was sitting casually on the lounge when they arrived. The television was on, but he was not really watching it, as he had a book in his hand and a pen and notepad next to him. Damien turned to Alexa. She opened her mouth to introduce them, but Damien had that covered.

"Hi, I'm Damien, Alexa's boyfriend," he added unnecessarily as he shook Marcus's hand. "You must be her new flatmate."

"Marc," nodded Marcus, making Alexa smile.

"I was going to cook dinner. You going to be around?" Alexa asked, hoping Marcus had changed his mind, but he seemed strangely happy to stay.

Marcus moved into the kitchen with her, casually helping her the way he often did, while Damien sat at the kitchen bench. Marcus questioned Damien about his degree and hobbies, clearly irritating Damien. That reaction only made Marcus smile. Not game enough to join in, Alexa cooked and watched the interaction between them. It was the first time she had ever thought of Damien as being young. A year older than her, he had always looked quite masculine, but next to Marcus he suddenly appeared very boyish.

"What's with the Spanish Inquisition?" asked Damien.

"Just want to know about the guy Alexa's dating. Make sure you're good enough for her," replied Marcus.

"Don't see how it's got anything to do with you," muttered Damien when Marcus walked out to set the table.

"I'm a close family friend. Alexa's welfare is very much my concern," retorted Marcus, his voice almost threatening.

"Yeah and which part of her family are you supposed to be friends with? She doesn't have any family," sneered Damien.

Alexa's heart pierced awfully. She turned away, focusing intently on dinner, unable to hear what Marcus said in response, but was glad that when he returned he said nothing about Damien. He just poured her a glass of water and started chatting meaninglessly.

Dinner was very quiet. It was hard for Alexa to make the effort required to keep things with Damien amiable and it was clear Marcus did not care for further conversation with him. When Marcus spoke to Alexa as though Damien was not there, she was able to be a little conversant, but that only annoyed Damien, making her silent again.

"Let's have an early night," said Damien as soon they finished eating.

"I need to clean up," answered Alexa.

"I can clean up," said Marcus, nodding.

"No, no, we'll do it," said Damien suddenly, smiling brightly.

It was odd. Damien never helped clean up, not even at his place, yet he happily trailed behind her into the kitchen. However, he did not actually do much cleaning. He stood behind Alexa as she washed the dishes, his hands running over her hips as his lips travelled down her neck. Marcus said nothing, but Alexa knew he was watching and it made her uncomfortable. She did not want to feel like she was being marked by Damien, but with the little she was able to give to the relationship, she had to allow him these concessions. For the fact that he wanted her enough to be jealous meant that she had to grant him nearly every concession he desired.

"Now, let's go to bed," said Damien as soon as the dishes were done, turning Alexa in his arms and kissing her passionately.

"Goodnight, Marc," said Alexa, walking through the lounge room.

"Goodnight, Alexa," Marcus smiled in reply, looking remarkably calm and relaxed; much more so than she thought she could be if the situation was reversed.

"You don't have to put up with him, you know," said Damien as Alexa closed her bedroom door.

"What do you mean?" she asked, surprised by the statement.

"Kick him out. Look at the mood he's put you in."

"No, it's not him. I was just nervous. I want you guys to get along."

"I don't care about getting along with him. I want to get along with you."

Damien did not give Alexa a chance to reply, pressing his lips to hers and pulling her to the bed. He was much more vocal than usual as they undressed, but Alexa had ways to ensure the spectacle was not long-lasting, and once Damien had what he wanted, he rolled over and fell asleep.

The next morning, Damien was more possessive of Alexa than ever. His hands were constantly on her body, holding and groping her. Marcus watched it all with pursed lips. It made Alexa grateful when Damien was called in to work.

"Don't say it," said Alexa as soon as she closed the front door.

Marcus was already standing by the kitchen bench, his arms folded. "Say what?" he asked casually.

"I'm trying, okay. I'm working really hard at this. You can't blame Damien for my deficiencies. I frustrate him. And my lies weren't well thought out. Of course I won't have any family friends!" Marcus pushed himself off the bench and turned away, his hand covering his mouth. "I swear, I'm trying," she said solemnly.

"You honestly think that's what I'm upset about?" asked Marcus, turning back around looking pained. "I can see you're trying. I can see how hard you're pushing yourself. What I want to know is why. Why are you even going out with that … boy?"

"He likes me."

"There'd better be more to it than that!"

"Like what? What else is there?" Alexa asked, not understanding what everyone expected of her.

"Hell, I don't know. Perhaps you liking him. Having things in common. Wanting to be with him," replied Marcus.

"I told you, I'm trying. What else can I do? Girls like me, they just can't —"

"No! Don't finish that sentence. Don't even finish that thought. I can't talk to you like this. I'm so furious I know I'll say something I'll regret, but don't think you've heard the last of this. Damn it, Alexa. Aarrggh!" Marcus grabbed his keys and stormed towards the door.

"You just don't like him," sighed Alexa, slumping down on the lounge.

"You're right, I don't like him," replied Marcus, turning back. Alexa did not look up at him. "I'll probably never like any guy you date, but when you're with the one who loves you the way you deserve, who you love just as much in return, I will respect him."

The door slammed shut and Alexa closed her eyes. For the first time since Marcus moved in, she was dreading his arrival home. The way he ignored the threatened conversation when he did return only made her more nervous.

"Can we just get this over with?" Alexa asked as they sat on the lounge on Tuesday afternoon.

One-way conversations with Bethany had done very little to ease the tension in Alexa's stomach over the previous two days. She had been off her food and found her mind swirling around dark thoughts.

"Can you let me talk? Listen to what I have to say without jumping in to defend yourself?" asked Marcus, switching off the television and moving to the same lounge as Alexa. They were facing each other now, but Alexa would not meet his eyes.

"This is going to be bad, isn't it?" she asked meekly.

"Yeah, but probably not for the reasons you think." Alexa looked up. Marcus was not smiling. "Just let me say what I have to, okay." Alexa nodded. Marcus sighed. "What I really want to do is question you and find out what the hell's going on, but unfortunately I think I know too many of the answers. I don't know why you're going out with Damien. You don't love him. I'm not even sure you like him." Alexa was about to argue, but Marcus put his hand up to stop her, a slight smile on his face. "You promised to let me speak."

"No, I didn't," Alexa replied with a petulant sneer that made Marcus smile.

"I can see you're trying. I've never seen anyone try so hard to like someone. My point is you shouldn't have to. You never had to try to like Sam. Hell, you guys had to try not to like each other. This isn't about Damien. It wouldn't matter if you were with a really nice guy who treated you well. If you didn't like him, we'd still be having this conversation."

"But I have to," gasped Alexa desperately. "I have to make it work. You don't understand."

"No, I don't," replied Marcus firmly.

"They'll think – if I don't – it was hard enough to convince them when you weren't around. Now you're here … it doesn't matter. I can't be expected to feel the same way about someone else as I did about Sam. Do you like Lucy the same way you liked your fiancée?"

"No, but I know what I'm getting myself into. The good and the bad. I know who – what I'm giving up."

"So do I!" cried Alexa. "You don't think I've weighed things up? I know all the fors and againsts. I could write it up for you. You want me to? Hell, we can compare lists if you've got it all figured out."

"I'm not perfect. Nor is my relationship," replied Marcus calmly. "I don't expect yours to be, but I'll have more in my for list than the fact that Lucy likes me. I'll have the fact that I like her. We have fun together. We have mutual friends. Want me to go on?" Alexa shook her head. "Then you tell me one other thing you have in that column."

Tears slipped down Alexa's cheeks as she shook her head. "Then tell me what I'm supposed to do? Everyone knows girls like me —"

"What kind of girls?" asked Marcus, his voice a growl before softening. "Pretty ones? Smart ones? Short? Blonde? Feisty? Stubborn?"

"Stop!"

"Snappy? Short-tempered? Generous? Kind? Beautiful? Amazing?"

"Tainted."

The smile slipped from Marcus's face as his hand gently lifted Alexa's chin, his thumb stroking her cheek. "You're not tainted," he said softly. "What those bastards did to you – you have nothing to be ashamed of."

"What about what I chose to do?" asked Alexa, refusing to meet Marcus's eyes.

"What part exactly is supposed to have tainted you? Having sex? We've all done that." Alexa shook her head. "Having sex with a stranger? Not alone there. Happens every Friday and Saturday night."

"But they aren't being paid for it."

"You think the guys are tainted for paying you for it?" questioned Marcus seriously. Alexa shook her head. "Just the woman? Either everyone's tainted or no one is."

"You're biased. And you didn't always feel that way," Alexa retorted, hating that it was true. "I remember the way to looked at me – what you thought about me."

"And that's why I know what I'm talking about. If someone can't look past those initial feelings of revulsion we're taught to have, then they don't deserve the privilege of loving you," replied Marcus, his voice firm yet tender. "You have control of your life now and one of the first things you did was hand it over to other people's opinions.

"You don't have to force yourself to go out with someone you don't like to make other people happy. That's not moving on. That's sacrificing your happiness for others, something you're far too skilled at doing. You know what you need to do? Look in the mirror and decide what you really want. If it's not what you're doing or working towards then stop what you're doing and start doing what you want. And if anyone – including me – doesn't like it, then you tell them to get stuffed. It's your life. You've spent too much of it being forced into things. You don't need to do it any more."

Alexa thought a lot about what Marcus said that night. Maybe she had done enough to prove that she was moving forward. Then she thought about Damien. Their relationship might be hard work at times, but she could not convince herself she did not at least like him. He was a nice guy and he had been so good to her. It seemed unfair to simply throw it all back at him because she had not been able to make herself feel the way she should about him. And yet every week, there was another source of tension between them or a boundary Damien insisted on pushing.

"No, Damien, I told you Friday nights were for me and Charlotte. I'm not coming out tonight," said Alexa in an agitated voice.

"Fine, will I ever get to see you then?" Damien asked petulantly.

"I've seen you most days this week. I spent all Wednesday with you and stayed over then. How much more do you want?"

"I miss you," said Damien, though he sounded more commanding than disappointed.

"I miss you too, but it's just one night. Can't you and your friends ever do things on Saturday nights?" asked Alexa.

"No," replied Damien firmly. "I understand you want a night with Charlotte, but why Friday? Why not change it when I want to see you?"

"Are we still going out tomorrow night?" asked Alexa calmly.

"Sure – unless someone above me on your priority list calls."

"I'll see you tomorrow," sighed Alexa.

"Dump him," said Charlotte boisterously from the kitchen, when Alexa hung up the phone. "He's not worth the grief. Do you even look forward to seeing him?"

"Yeah, I do. I mean, we get on when we're together. I just wish he'd accept my life the way it was rather than always fighting it."

"Still reckon you should dump him. Go out with Marcus. It's what you both want," said Charlotte.

"I don't know that it is," said Alexa indecisively. "Besides, you're forgetting he has a girlfriend."

"So? She's a skank."

"Don't say that," replied Alexa, trying not to smile. "You've never met her."

"She left him high and dry. You're the only reason he didn't end up bankrupt."

"Well, mind you keep those thoughts to yourself when he gets up. It's his birthday today and his girlfriend's taking him away for the weekend," said Alexa firmly. She would not have anyone ruining Marcus's birthday.

"You two aren't doing anything?" asked Charlotte with a slight smile.

"He's not my boyfriend," replied Alexa, grabbing Charlotte's hand and pulling her out the door.

It was already hot as they strolled down to the beach and the relief the cool water provided all but evaporated as they walked back to the apartment.

"So what else do you want to do today?" asked Alexa, preparing lunch while Charlotte collapsed on the lounge.

"Lay here. God, it's hot. Damn this global warming shit."

"We can go and get some DVDs if you like and a mountain of popcorn," replied Alexa. She had come to like the escapism of movies.

"What are you doing here? I thought you were going away."

Alexa turned to see Marcus looking startled in the lounge room, his eyes flicking between her, Charlotte and his bedroom door as though seeking an escape.

"Oh, um …"

"What's going on?" asked Alexa, concerned by his behaviour. She had not expected to see him today, purposely staying out of the house that morning to avoid a possible meeting with his girlfriend, even though he had promised she was not picking him up. "You not going away until later?"

"Not going at all," Marcus replied in a choked voice before stalking back to his room.

Alexa and Charlotte exchanged perplexed looks. This was not a conversation Alexa wanted to engage in, but if Marcus had been able to talk to her about Damien, then she owed it to him to be able to support him through his relationship.

"Hey, what happened?" Alexa asked, slipping into Marcus's room and sitting next to him on the bed. She had never seen him look so broken.

"Nothing, it's okay," he coughed, clearing his voice, though he kept his head in his hands.

"That's not going to wash with me. You wouldn't let me be upset without wanting to know what was wrong."

Marcus looked up and nodded. His eyes were watery, but he quickly recomposed himself, as if ashamed of his emotion.

"She went away – without me," said Marcus, not able to hide the hurt in his voice. "I only found out today. Some work trip she couldn't get out of."

"Oh, shit. I'm sorry. I would've planned something if I'd known," said Alexa, feeling horribly guilty, though she knew this situation was beyond her control.

"Thanks, but I think I might skip this birthday. Maybe I'll join you and stop celebrating them all together."

"We're going to avoid the heat with some DVDs, then maybe go back down to the beach in the afternoon. You're always welcome to join us. We can do something nice for dinner. It won't be as good as what you'd planned, but it won't totally suck," Alexa offered, hoping she would be able to organise something better than that.

"No thanks," smiled Marcus. "I might go out myself."

"And drink til you're refused service?"

"Something like that."

"Right, so Charlotte and me should go get our razors out when we're feeling down?"

Alexa rushed out before Marcus could answer. He wondered if it was a ploy or if she really did not want to face that conversation. Either way, it had the desired effect. Jumping up and looking in the mirror, he wiped his eyes and tried to make himself presentable. No matter what he was going through, he would not give Alexa an excuse to take another razor to her body.

"All right, so what are we watching?" asked Marcus, emerging from his room five minutes later, a smile fixed on his face.

"Nothing," smiled Charlotte, looking very pleased with herself.

"Oh, I thought, um —"

"We're taking you out," Charlotte announced proudly. "It's my day with Alexa so you have to put up with me as well."

"Look, we don't have —"

"This isn't negotiable," said Alexa, smiling softly. "We're taking you out. It's your birthday and you don't get a choice. You're going to have fun and smile, even if we have to fill your face with Botox so you can't possibly frown."

"Fine, we can go out," Marcus sighed, realising he was not going to win this battle.

"We weren't giving you a choice," retorted Alexa, as Charlotte took his hand and led him to the door.

Sitting in Alexa's car, Marcus watched her, believing she had to be most considerate person he knew. Between Bethany's imprisonment, her relationship with Damien and taking care of Charlotte, he was surprised she found time to think about him. It made it easy to imagine a life with Alexa by his side, wishing for more than was possible, but it was his birthday, and after another knock back from Lucy he would grant himself this one luxury. Yet reality was hard to keep at bay. Marcus knew he would never attempt to be more than Alexa's friend. It did not matter that Damien was not good enough for her. He would not go as far as breaking them up. He would be there for Alexa and give her the confidence to demand better for herself.

"Not my preferred option," Alexa said with a shrug as she pulled into a city parking station, making Marcus feel guilty for not noticing it as something odd. "But it'll let us fit more in."

Marcus smiled, not knowing or caring what Alexa had planned as long as they were together. However, it turned out that their activities for the day were actually Charlotte's gift to him. Her idea of birthday fun was two hours spinning and twirling over the harbour at Luna Park. It made Marcus grateful he had not eaten lunch. Alexa only laughed at him as he staggered after Charlotte from ride to ride, rarely joining them.

The ferry ride back to the city was thankfully very tame, but the adventure was not over as Charlotte pulled him towards a speed boat ride. "You'd better be coming with us," called Marcus, trying to grab Alexa's hand, but she just smiled and pointed to her phone, saying something about things to organise. Charlotte did not give him a chance to find out more.

It was fun, but Marcus got a bigger thrill from Charlotte's excitement. He thought Alexa did too from the way she smiled as Charlotte bounded along the wharf towards her.

"Please tell me that is the end of all the adventure rides today," gasped Marcus.

"Yep, it's food time now," said Charlotte, taking Marcus by the hand and pulling him next to Alexa before moving to the other side of her. The gesture made Alexa blush. It was a beautiful sight and made Marcus's heart ache, but he loved her enough to not grasp her hand and threaten to never let her go.

A lavish afternoon tea filled both the hours and their stomach as they sat watching the boats move in and out of the harbour. Charlotte smiled constantly, watching the interactions between him and Alexa, sometimes interjecting in an attempt to bring them closer together. It was very sweet, and when Marcus saw Alexa smiling wondrously at Charlotte, he properly understood their connection. Charlotte was the girl Alexa could have been.

"I'm afraid to ask, but is there any more to this day?" asked Marcus. He did not want to think about the girl Alexa could have been or the life she should have had.

"Actually, there is," smiled Alexa, and Marcus could not help but smile back. "I've arranged for us to go out to dinner tonight. So we'd better get home and find you both something to wear, because what you've got on really won't cut it."

Alexa did not let them dally. As soon as they pulled up in front of the apartment, she ushered them out of the car and pushed Charlotte straight under the shower.

"You have no idea what this day's meant to me," said Marcus, following Alexa out on to the balcony and resting against the banister. Alexa moved next to him and looked out towards the ocean.

"Yeah, I think I do," she nodded solemnly. "I've known my share of disappointment too."

Alexa turned and looked deep into his eyes. He wished the smile that sat lightly on her lips could also brighten her beautiful blue eyes, but knew it was too much to expect that this day of distraction could do anything to wipe away the pain of her life.

"Um, I'm finished in the shower," said Charlotte in a soft voice, a slight grin playing on her lips.

"You go," said Marcus, directing Alexa inside. "I know how long you girls take to get ready."

Alexa smiled and headed off to the shower, but she and Charlotte were ready to go long before he was. Marcus had somehow forgotten how different Alexa was to other girls, and felt like a preening peacock as he tried to get ready with her and Charlotte heckling him from the lounge room.

"Are you making your suit?" laughed Alexa, as Charlotte giggled.

"Okay, I'm ready," Marcus called, forgoing the rest of his usual preparations. He twirled as he entered the lounge room to the whistles of Charlotte. Alexa just smiled at him. The way her eyes roved over his body was magical. Marcus liked that they could be this close without anyone being able to tell them it was not allowed. But what he wanted was still forbidden, so he tried not to let his eyes run over Alexa's body as she walked in front of him, leading them to the restaurant. It was a near-impossible task. The blue dress she was wearing made her eyes sparkle when she smiled and showed off her body in the most flattering way.

"HAPPY BIRTHDAY!"

The cry almost knocked Marcus off his feet. He had been so caught up in his thoughts that he had barely registered walking into the restaurant or the small private room upstairs. Marcus looked around and saw the room full of people he would not have expected to share his birthday with. Ben, Maria, Sam and his grandparents were all there, along with a few of his own mates.

"I'm sorry I didn't get more of your friends here. I didn't know who you'd want to invite and most thought you were away so had other plans," said Alexa shyly, as though she was actually ashamed that she had not done more.

"This is the best day of my life and you're the most amazing person in the world. Don't ever forget that," Marcus whispered as they were descended on.

"Happy birthday, Marc. Sorry we're late," said Chad, slapping him on the back as he, Nick and Alan walked in behind them.

"Hey, guys. I didn't know you'd be here," said Marcus warmly.

"You didn't know you'd be here," laughed Chad.

"We weren't going to miss your big birthday bash after all you've done for us," said Nick with a smile and a shake of Marcus's hand.

"I just did my job."

"You stuck up for us. That's more than anyone else ever did. We don't forget that," said Alan.

"Plus, there's free food here. How could we pass that up?" grinned Chad, moving over to Alexa and placing a soft kiss on her cheek.

"I'll see you around," smiled Alexa, rolling her eyes as she walked away.

Marcus could not stop his eyes from trailing after her, but Nick and Alan quickly pulled him away and put a drink in his hand.

"Happy birthday, Marc," they said, charging their glasses.

Marcus smiled and drank merrily. He, Nick and Alan had been out a few times after the meetings about their court case. Chad joined them occasionally, though Sam never did and Marcus was a little concerned when he and Ben suddenly made their way over to them.

"Happy birthday, Sir," said Sam stiffly.

"We're not in school any more, Sammy. Let it go," said Nick.

"You hurt her and I'll kill you," replied Sam, pointing at Marcus.

"How's this?" said Chad, wrapping an arm around Sam's

shoulders. "If anyone hurts Alexa, we'll all hunt them down and kill them. You don't have a monopoly on her, mate. This group, more than you realise, cares for her. We've all seen what she's suffered and it's hurt us too. None of us would ever intentionally hurt her, so let's not turn on each other when we all want the same thing."

"C'mon, Sam, it's true. We love her too," said Alan. "You're not the only one who cares and Marcus isn't the only one who's made mistakes that've hurt Alexa."

"Well, I'm in," said Ben gruffly. "Happy birthday, Marcus," he said, holding out his hand. Marcus took it thankfully. He was not delusional enough to believe the gesture was anything more than a ceasefire, but he would take any break he could get. Sam reluctantly extended the same courtesy, but almost did not manage to grasp his hand as Alexa slammed into him, hugging him tight.

"You do realise that I was the one who orchestrated this truce, right?" said Chad, gently prodding Alexa until she disengaged from Sam. Alexa immediately hugged Chad, who spun her around to his side. "C'mon, show us where you're sitting. We're stealing the seats next to you so we can catch up," smiled Chad as he, Nick and Alan swept her away.

Through dinner, dessert and the mingling afterwards Marcus could not keep his eyes off Alexa. He had never seen her look so beautiful. No one else had done so much for him in just one day, and this was the second time she had come to his rescue in the space of a few weeks.

"You know you shouldn't be thinking that," said Marcus's best mate, Brandon, looking over at Alexa. "Go down that path and your life's over. Family, friends all disowning you, too ashamed to be associated with you."

"I'm not thinking anything," muttered Marcus angrily. If his family and friends took the time to get to know Alexa, rather than just the stories that surrounded her, they would understand his dilemma.

"Yeah, you are," contradicted Brandon. "You've somehow forgotten everything we said last year. She's trouble and you need to get away from her. Don't lose another great girl to her. You remember Jackie, right? The brilliant fiancée you gave up to be with this girl. The prostitute. Druggie. And God knows what else."

"I think you should go," growled Marcus.

"I'm your best mate. I'm not going to let you look at her through rose-coloured glasses. Continue with your fantasy for a while. Shacking up with your student who's ten years younger than you. It's sick. So just maybe she's a nice kid, but is that enough to ruin your life for? Your parents nearly had a heart attack when they found out you had feelings for her. So'd we. You did the right thing picking up with Lucy. Take that path, not the one that's going to lose you your friends and family. Not the one that gets you landed on a sex offenders register." Marcus turned on Brandon, incoherent with rage. Brandon just shook his head as he stepped backwards. "Happy Birthday, mate."

Chapter Thirteen

UNSEASONAL RAINS LASHED Alexa as she walked the hundred metres from her car to the detention centre entrance. It had been a late night, but despite her tiredness she was determined to be there the minute the gates finally reopened.

"No hangover then?" whispered Ben over her shoulder, as she sheltered inside, waiting to be allowed into the visiting room.

"What are you doing here?" asked Alexa.

"You're not the only one who's missed seeing her. You want me to come back in an hour to give you two time alone?"

"No, it's okay. I think she'll be happy to see us together," Alexa nodded, prepared to do anything to make Bethany feel even a little bit better.

"It was a good night, last night. Was very nice what you did for Marcus," said Ben supportively. "Did he enjoy himself?"

"Yeah, I think so, though he seemed a little put out towards the end of the night. That's when he started to drink a bit more."

"When you went home – he didn't, um …"

"Try anything?" Alexa asked pointedly, unimpressed by the question. "What kind of guy do you think he is? He'd never do that, no matter how much he drank."

Ben did not appear entirely convinced, but did not get a chance to argue as the doors to the meeting room opened. All thoughts of Marcus evaporated the second Alexa laid eyes on Bethany. It was the greatest and the saddest sight she had even seen – just like the first time she had visited Bethany in the detention centre – pure joy at seeing her and heartbreaking distress at her incarceration.

"Hey," said Bethany solemnly, giving Alexa a loving rub on the cheek, but not allowing her a hug.

"How're you feeling?" asked Alexa, unsure of what to say in the face of Bethany's sadness.

"Can we have some time alone?" asked Bethany, looking up at Ben.

Ben glanced between them before smiling and nodding. Alexa moved to sit next to Bethany and rested her head against Bethany's. There they sat in silence for over half an hour, just holding hands. Tears slowly trickled down Bethany's cheeks and Alexa collected every one.

"Sorry to interrupt," said Ben, laying his hands on their shoulders. "Peter's here. He wants to speak with Bethany for a while."

"Do you want me to stay?" asked Alexa.

"You're coming back tomorrow?" asked Bethany in a soft, sad voice.

"You bet. Wouldn't miss it for the world."

Bethany smiled just slightly and Alexa squeezed her hand tight before finding the strength to walk away.

Dressed casually in his jacket-less suit, Peter looked too carefree to be a true visitor at this place. He knew Alexa believed it was because he saw her and Bethany as little more than his clients, but she could not have been further from the truth. Bethany and Alexa had been lifelong cases, and he had known from the first time he met them that he would do anything for them, whenever they needed it.

It was rare for clients to touch him so deeply, but Alexa had captured his heart from the beginning. He had never met such a selfless and kind-hearted child who was so deeply disturbed. He could still not understand how Alexa managed to remain so caring and open when she had been through so much. She might be deeply distrustful in many regards, but she was also ridiculously trusting in many others.

That mixture of trust and fear was what kept Peter out of Alexa's childhood life. He could not have given her the home she needed, and being more involved would have only risked her finding reasons to distrust him. As her lawyer, the law gave her a reason to accept his assistance, and through that continuous contact, he had been able to help, if not protect, her the way he promised he always would.

Alexa insisted on paying him now she had the means, but Peter loathed accepting it. He had a successful law practice and did not need her money, but soon learned it was easier to invoice her for the most basic costs than to continue to refuse her. He would return it one day.

The moment Alexa reached him, the tears in her eyes began to overflow. Peter stepped forward and pulled her into a tight embrace as she sobbed quietly. "You have to get her out of here," she said desperately, looking up into his eyes. "Please. Do anything. I don't care. Bribe them if that'll help. You have to get her out of here."

"I'm doing everything I can, I promise," replied Peter solemnly, stepping backwards to release Alexa. He put his hands on her shoulders and squeezed them gently. "It won't be long. They'll have to reschedule the parole hearings, especially because those with hearings had very little to do with the riot. Bethany has a good case. I'll get her out of here. I promise."

Peter rubbed Alexa's shoulder before releasing her and making his way in to see Bethany. She was sitting with Ben. There were no tears in her eyes. He was surprised by Bethany's stoicism. She had always been the weaker one. However, her first words were much less surprising.

"When they reschedule the hearing, I don't want Lex to know. Just in case."

"This to protect you or her?" asked Peter.

"Both," replied Bethany in a broken voice, tears slipping down her cheeks as her brave façade suddenly broke. "I can't hold her hope and mine. I can't even hold mine any more. I just want – I don't want – I know it won't be for much longer, but every day I'm in here …"

Peter did not need to ask what Bethany no longer wanted to do. He had seen that look in her eyes before. He had seen in it Alexa's. When he left, he made sure Bethany was put on suicide watch. They may have been strong, determined girls, but everyone had their limits and Peter knew most people could not have suffered what they had.

As he walked across the carpark, Peter noticed Alexa sitting in her car and altered course towards her. His stomach gave a frightened lurch when he saw light reflecting off a razor she was twirling slowly between her fingers. She was staring intently at it as he strode quickly towards her. It was a relief to see her skin uncut when he approached her open window.

"I hope you haven't forgotten a little promise you made me," said Peter, startling Alexa.

She looked at the razor then up. He liked that she did not try to hide what she had been doing. "I haven't," she replied weakly.

"Good."

Peter was tempted to reach in and take the razor, but there were few people whose word he trusted more than Alexa's. He just placed his hand on her shoulder and squeezed it reassuringly before walking towards his car.

"You still on your uni break?" asked Peter, doubling back and startling Alexa again. She nodded, looking up at him with wondering eyes. "Call my secretary. We can have lunch."

"Do I get to pay?" asked Alexa with a smile, making Peter laugh. It was the first time he had suggested they meet without her questioning his motives.

"No. I get to write it off for tax purposes when I take my clients out for lunch."

"Just lunch, right? Nothing's wrong?" asked Alexa, concern etching her voice and eyes.

"No, nothing's wrong," smiled Peter.

***

The clouds parted, allowing the sun to peak in through the curtains, slowly nudging Alexa awake. She rolled over and almost jumped feeling Damien beside her. She had forgotten that she had let him stay, but quickly recovered and snuggled into him. It had been a lonely week. Charlotte had returned to school, Sam had been busy with things he refused to talk about and, since his birthday, Marcus had been spending fewer and fewer nights at home. Ben came by occasionally, but there was still a distance between them they had not managed to bridge. Despite not wanting to be, Alexa could not help but be scared of being alone with him. It made her avoid him and make sure someone else was around when they were together. Maria helped as often as she could and Alexa was grateful. She did not want to hurt Ben, and did want to see him, but needed help. That Maria never chastised her for how she felt made her more willing to continue to try.

"Good morning," yawned Damien, waking noisily as he turned to kiss her.

"Good morning," Alexa replied, hugging him tight.

"What've you got on today?"

"Nothing much, I don't think. I'll visit Bethy, but I don't have anything else planned."

"Maybe we can do this again tonight? God, you're good. Last night was great." Alexa smiled slightly. She was not one to talk about sex – unlike Damien. He was happy to whisper crude insinuations in her ear when they were out. He did not even mind sharing details with his mates when they were all together. She had learned it was easier to smile and laugh it off than complain.

When she did not reply, Damien rolled away to check the time. It must not have been time to leave, because he rolled back over and ran his finger softly down Alexa's neck. A sickening chill accompanied his touch, but Alexa forced herself to ignore it. Knowing what Damien was after, and that it was easier to just give it to him, she nimbly rolled on top of him, straddling him between her legs. Damien smiled. He was used to girls who lay beneath him stiff as a plank, something he had once described to her in far too much detail. She apparently paid attention to him and let him enjoy the moment. The reality was that she just wanted control. She had never allowed Damien on top of her, or in any dominant position, when they made love. There was no way she was leaving herself without a quick escape route.

Groaning, Damien kneaded Alexa's breasts as he ground his hips into hers. His hands did not move until he was ready to finish, when they tightened around her hips and moved her to his will. He never noticed that she did not obtain the same sense of pleasure as he did, he never had, and Alexa did not bother trying to pretend.

"I should probably get going," said Damien, kissing Alexa's lips as he slipped out from under her. "I don't want to be late. Mum's got a very long list of things for me to do today."

"Call me when you're done and I can meet you somewhere."

Alexa lay in bed until Damien left. She always avoided getting ready with him. The mechanical nature of their intercourse reminded her too much of her time in the city pleasuring men for money. Those memories made her shiver and wonder if Damien would enjoy the sex so much if he knew about her past. It was a question she had no intention of ever finding out the answer to. She had already decided that the ultimate test of their relationship would not be her past, but her near future. If Damien caused a fuss about Bethany, she would tell him it was over. What they had was not special enough to hold on to at the expense of Bethany, and she did not think anybody would fight her on that point. They all loved Bethany as well.

The trill of the telephone provided Alexa a welcome distraction from her thoughts. She looked at the clock. It was just after eleven. She really had been moving slowly that morning and would have to get ready soon to see Bethany.

"Lex! I mean Alexa," cried Sam jubilantly.

"Hey, Sam, what's up?"

He had not sounded so happy to speak to her since the start of the year and it made her realise just how much she had missed him.

"Are you free tonight?" asked Sam happily.

"I told Damien I'd meet up with him," answered Alexa, wondering if Sam would give her a good excuse to cancel.

"That's okay. Bring him along," Sam replied cheerfully.

"Where? What's going on?" Alexa asked curiously. This was not typical behaviour for Sam over the past month.

"My place. Seven-thirty. We have some celebrating to do."

"What for?"

"You'll find out when you get here."

"Is it about Bethy?" Alexa asked with cautious hope.

"No," said Sam sadly, the happiness fading from his voice. "I'm sorry. It's not. And I wouldn't do that to you. Please, will you come?"

"Yeah, I'll be there," Alexa replied, her enthusiasm for Sam's mystery instantly fading.

It made her trek to the detention centre particularly sombre. There was still no news about a new parole hearing date, and every visit now felt like an additional punishment designed to torture them. The best they could do was grab the sun-drenched table and stretch out their bodies, pretending they were sun-baking in freedom. Bethany was not privy to the reasons for Sam's gathering that night, and did not seem to care. Alexa could not be annoyed by her ambivalence. It was something she was too prone to feel. Now more than ever she found herself wishing there was a way she could stay with Bethany. It did not matter that she would be in prison, she would be living with Bethany.

"So you taking Damien tonight?" asked Bethany, trying hard to make conversation.

"Yeah, why? You sound like it's a bad idea," asked Alexa softly, not sure Bethany really wanted to talk about this. Damien had not been happy about the change of plans, but had thankfully decided it would be a good excuse to get out of more chores at his mum's house. Alexa was glad he found a bright side himself. She did not need another fight.

"I just wonder if he's really okay with you and Sam," answered Bethany flatly.

"Sam and I are just friends," sighed Alexa. "When's everyone going to get that? I thought you —"

"I know and I've seen you together. Things are so much better after you spent that week together. I wasn't sure it was a good idea, but it was. It's just that Damien's insecure and the friendship you and Sam have is still pretty powerful."

"What am I supposed to do?"

"Nothing, I'm sorry. It'll be fine. How are you and Damien?"

"Good, I think. Though I sometimes wonder if he just stays with me for the sex," grinned Alexa.

"Modesty, that's a good quality," smirked Bethany, a genuine smile crossing her face for the first time in weeks.

"Shut up," laughed Alexa.

Bethany's smile faded as she laid her head tenderly against Alexa's shoulder. "How bout for you though?" Bethany asked affectionately. "Has he gotten you off yet?"

"Bethy!" cried Alexa.

"What? He's your boyfriend. It's his job," replied Bethany, turning to Alexa with a mixture of seriousness and amusement on her face.

"I'm not going to talk about this. He's my boyfriend."

"So? What, you embarrassed? Everyone does it … well, except me, but it's not like I don't know what I'm talking about."

"No," replied Alexa firmly.

"No, I don't know what I'm talking about or no, he hasn't made you come yet?" asked Bethany with raised eyebrows.

"Both," smiled Alexa, feeling her cheeks blush.

"And you've been going out, what, seven months now? That's really bad, Lex. Does he know what he's doing?"

"It isn't important."

"Hell yeah, it is. It's not all about the boy, you know. You have the right to pleasure too."

"Who has the right to what pleasure?"

Alexa swung around to see Ben sitting down beside Bethany. Bethany stifled her giggles, while Alexa turned a bright shade of red.

"Sorry. Did I interrupt something?" asked Ben meekly.

"No, no," smiled Bethany. "We were just discussing the fact that Damien has never made Alexa orgasm."

Alexa was no longer the only red face as Ben blushed with embarrassment and Bethany looked close to bursting with laughter.

"Oh my God," gasped Alexa. "I'm going to go now. And I will kill you later."

Alexa wrapped her arm around Bethany's chest and ruffed up her hair, before hugging her tightly and kissing her lovingly on the forehead. Despite her embarrassment, Alexa decided to wait for Ben to finish his visit, sitting solemnly on a bench outside the entrance. It might not have been the best idea. With just her own thoughts and the view of the high walls and razor wire keeping her company, it was difficult to keep her composure.

"You still here?" asked Ben, sitting down beside her and wrapping a loving arm around her shoulder. "It won't be long. She'll be out before you know it."

"Yeah," replied Alexa absently, refusing to agree any further.

"Listen, about you and Damien. Beth's right —"

"Oh, no. I'm not having a sex talk from you as well," said Alexa, her mouth curled in exacerbation.

"Someone has to —"

"No, they don't. I'm nineteen. I'm not a virgin – far from it. I think we can safely assume I know what I'm doing."

"I'm sure you do, but does he? Love and sexual relationships are a two-way street. Has he really never noticed that you've never —?"

"I'm going unless we change the subject," said Alexa, stepping away.

"What time do you have to be at Sam's?" asked Ben, instantly complying.

"Are you coming?"

"No, I'm working. Come on, I'll take you for a coffee and I promise no more talk about sex."

***

A small drop of spit trickled down Alexa's chin as Damien greeted her overenthusiastically at the apartment door. His hands wrapped around her waist and down over her bottom, pulling her hard against him. "We don't have to go yet," he said lustfully. "We can have a bit of fun. I want to do something for you for a change."

Alexa had wanted to get to Sam's early to find out what was going on, but after the conversations of earlier that day, she thought it best to give Damien a chance to prove himself. She liked the idea of enjoying sex the way other girls seemed to.

Damien led Alexa to her bedroom and laid her down on her bed, his hands undressing her quickly. It was not at all what Alexa had expected. Within minutes they were naked and before she could move Damien was in top of her and between her legs.

He kissed her forcefully, as though he had not had sex in ten years, not just ten hours. His hands moved to her chest and her heart froze. When she looked up, his face was no longer defined, replaced instead by the dark shadow that for so many years had haunted her dreams. She felt herself kicking and screaming for him to stop, but she was not sure if she was even moving.

Damien continued his groping and thrusting, unaware of the turmoil below him. Alexa's mind was on fire, trying to reconcile the image before her with the knowledge that it was Damien she was with. Pain seared through her pelvis as her mind continued to scream and fight against the invasion. She could not tell whether the pain was real or in her mind. All she knew was that she wanted it to stop. Damien's body became more frantic, intensifying the pain. He held her down by the wrists, the fingers on his left hand entwining hers, making her wonder if she really was fighting him. His voice swirled around her, but it was muffled and Alexa could not make out the words. All she could hear was the menacing voice of the shadowy man from her dream cackling viciously at her pain.

When it was finally over, Damien rolled off Alexa, wrapping her tenderly in his arms as the shadow fled the room.

"Was that good for you?" asked Damien affectionately, kissing her forehead. Alexa wondered if she had just suffered an extreme delusion. She could not imagine how he could not have noticed her lack of involvement. "Can't have you always doing all the work," he smiled, kissing her again.

Alexa quickly gave her approval to all Damien did before rushing to the shower. Damien jumped in after her and she was glad he was not there to see her body shaking as she dressed. It was taking everything she had not to have a complete panic attack. The quivering finally subsided as they pulled up in front of Sam's place. Damien had been easily reassured there was nothing wrong. He had only noticed her quaking in the car and assumed she was coming down with something as she shivered against the warm air.

"Hey, hey. This is starting to get a bit familiar," said Nick happily as he opened Sam's front door.

"What are you doing here?" asked Alexa.

"What, not happy to see me?" asked Nick jokingly.

"No, I just didn't know you'd be here. I actually don't even know why I'm here," added Alexa. "Want to tell me?"

"All in good time," smiled Nick jubilantly. "But would you just come in and give me a hug?"

Alexa smiled and cocked her head slightly before giving Nick the hug he requested. Although they had known each other in school they had never been that close.

"Hello," smiled Alan, walking up behind Nick.

Alan did not ask for a hug, giving Alexa one himself, with a brief smile to Damien who stood perplexed at the door, again transported to a world he knew nothing about.

"Oh, sorry," smiled Alexa, turning in Alan's arm, which remained wrapped around her. "Damien, this is Nick and Al. We all went to school together with Sam."

From the look on Damien's face, Alexa could tell that her story about having gone to high school interstate had finally cracked. Unless she could convince Damien that all her friends had moved interstate with her to go to university, there would be a lot of explaining to do.

"Where's Sam?" asked Alexa, looking around.

"Oh, he's doing a drop off and pick up. His grandparents are going to dinner with someone called Maria," said Nick.

"Oh, Maria. That's great," replied Alexa happily.

"Yeah, and he's picking up Ezra and Lizzie from the train station," continued Alan. "And here's Chad."

Chad walked in the house, dumping two bags of ice at their feet so he could wrap Alexa up in his arms, squeezing her tight.

"You'd better tell me what's wrong before Sam gets here. He's so excited and if he sees your face he'll be very disappointed," whispered Chad. Alexa was startled by the comment, but let Chad pull her out into the backyard after fixing Damien a drink. "So what's wrong?"

"Nothing, I'm fine," said Alexa, even as her heart stammered.

"I may not be Sam and I'd never presume to know you like he does, but I know you better than you think and I know something's wrong," continued Chad in a tender but strangely commanding voice.

"He's right," said Alan, stepping out into the backyard with Nick, surprising Alexa with their interjection.

"Look, I know you think we were never really friends," said Nick. "But we all went through a lot together and despite what you may think, we've always cared. You can't discount six years of getting in trouble with each other," he added with a smile.

"Where's Damien?" asked Alexa, fear tingeing her voice.

"With Sam. He's back and he'll be out here soon looking for you, so you'd better let us cheer you up before he finds you," smiled Alan.

"Okay," nodded Alexa.

It was easier than she thought it, telling the trio about what had transpired just an hour before. Chad wrapped his arm around Alexa as soon as she got to the part about Damien climbing on top of her.

"And he didn't even notice?" asked Nick.

Alexa was glad they did not ask for an explanation. She did not want to be told it was nothing, or that she was crazy. That they just believed her was the greatest relief of all.

"No, I don't think so," said Alexa shaking her head. "He asked if it was good for me too," she added with a sad laugh.

"What a dick," spat Alan, as Chad and Nick coughed over their laughs. There was a bitterness to Alan's voice that Alexa could not place, but it was quickly brushed aside by Damien's appearance.

The trio each took their turn hugging her and kissing her gently on the cheek before walking back inside. "Sam won't notice. You look heaps better just from talking," whispered Alan.

Alexa smiled and squeezed his hand. For a place that had given her so much heartache and pain, Redgrove had produced some of the best friends she could have ever hoped for.

"What was that about?" asked Damien.

"Nothing, just catching up," Alexa replied, taking Damien's hand and walking them inside.

A joyful squeal filled the room as Alexa entered the house. She rushed forward to take part in the exchange of hugs. She had never thought the sight of so many school friends would give her so much joy. Lizzie introduced herself to Damien after being released from Alexa's arms, while Alexa greeted Ezra.

"Is Bianca coming?" asked Alexa curiously.

"I don't think so," replied Ezra.

"I couldn't bring myself to invite her," smiled Sam, wrapping his arms around Alexa as soon as Ezra released her. "Chad's my best mate and I wanted this to be a pleasant evening."

"Fair enough," replied Alexa.

They had been right, Sam did not notice her sadness, but over his shoulder Alexa caught sight of Marcus and in that brief meeting of eyes she knew that he knew something was wrong. With Sam insisting everyone had a drink before he made any announcements, Alexa moved over to Marcus. He shifted next to her, placing his glass next to hers.

"Unless you give me a very good reason why I shouldn't, I'm taking you home with me tonight and Damien is not staying over," Marcus said in an angry whisper.

"Did they tell you what happened?" asked Alexa frantically.

"No, but you will," Marcus replied in a controlled voice. Alexa found herself almost hyperventilating. "When you can," he added kindly, pouring her a drink. "Only when you can. But right now, you need to get ready to celebrate. It's going to be a good night."

Marcus put her drink in her hand. Sam immediately grabbed her other hand and pulled her into the circle that had formed in the centre of the lounge room. Marcus stayed in the corner. Alexa's eyes flicked worriedly back to him as Damien's arm wrapped possessively around her body, but Marcus only nodded and pointed towards Sam.

"Now, half of us know why we're here tonight," smiled Sam, moving into the centre of the circle. "But I'd like to inform the girls as to why we're having this little celebration."

Lizzie, Ezra and Alexa exchanged nervous smiles. They were not sure they liked being in the dark with the joyous grins that covered everyone else's face. Even Marcus was wearing a genuine smile, something Alexa had not seen for a while.

"Wait, wait," cried Chad, rushing over to the television and turning the sound up loud. "I have to hear this."

"Controversy over the million-dollar pay out to six former students of the notorious Redgrove College. The school says it cannot afford to pay and will be forced to close. This comes less than a year after the school reportedly paid out an even larger sum to another student, who was strangled and almost killed by a teacher she was having an affair with. Full report coming up next."

Alexa turned to Sam in shock, her face breaking into a smile larger than any in the room had seen for many years.

"What a crock of shit," said Damien, turning back to the circle, unaware of her excitement.

"What?" exclaimed the room in unison.

"That. That whole thing," cried Damien, throwing his hand out at the television. "Six upstarts sue the school just cos they got blamed for a few things they didn't do. When you cause so much trouble, you have to expect the school'll suspect you of other things."

"I think there was more to it than that," said Marcus firmly, as everyone else stared at Damien in shock.

"Yeah, but the school was forced to pay out to that slut last year," Damien retorted in a derisive tone.

"What!" cried Chad, Alan and Nick.

Marcus and Sam stood mute, while Lizzie and Ezra gasped softly.

"The girl was a slut. She fucked the teacher and then turns around and says he raped her just cos he'd dragged her out of a brothel," Damien snorted. "Didn't even want to go – wanted to be a hooker. You can't even rape chicks like that. I would've strangled her myself if I'd've found out that kind of shit about my girlfriend. Imagine meeting the dirty whore. You'd have to wash for the next century to get clean."

A deathly silence filled the room. Damien looked around, clearly expecting a wave of support that would never come. Sam looked mortified, giving Alexa some hope that Damien had never expressed these views in front of him before. She closed her eyes slowly, waiting for the rush of tears, but her cheeks remained dry. In an instant, all her feelings for Damien, whatever they had been, simply vanished.

"I think it's time you left, mate," said Marcus slowly, walking towards Damien to lead him out the door.

214

"Why?" Damien retorted, clearly thrown by the sudden mood change.

"Do you know we all went to Redgrove?" asked Lizzie, her shock evident in her voice.

"So you know those people and that girl?" murmured Damien, starting to catch on.

"We are those people," said Nick, looking around the room to Alan, Chad and Sam.

"And I am that girl," added Alexa in a cold, emotionless voice. Damien spun to look into her eyes, horrified. "So get out. I never want to see you again."

"Alexa, no. I wasn't talking about you. I didn't … how was I supposed to know?" Damien stuttered. "You never told me."

"I'm glad I didn't. I'd be dead if I had."

"I didn't mean that. I wouldn't hurt you."

"You said you would've strangled your girlfriend if you found out those things about her," said Alexa, throwing Damien's words back at him. "Well, I am your girlfriend and those things are about me."

"I didn't mean it. I was just talking shit. God, Alexa, I'm sorry. So that teacher was the one who raped you?"

"Get out of my life. If you come near me again, I'll call the police."

Taking their cue from Alexa, the boys walked towards Damien and dragged him out of the house, though he offered little resistance. Sam rushed back into the room and pulled Alexa into him, lifting her chin to force her eyes to meet his.

"Don't, Alexa. Don't shut down because of him," pleaded Sam. "He's not worth it."

Alexa did not answer, determined to deny the existence of her pain.

"Just leave her, Sam? Don't pressure her now," said Marcus in a pained voice.

"No," replied Sam frantically. "If I leave her now, by tomorrow she'll have built a wall around her heart so thick that even you won't be able to get through."

Alexa could feel herself being pulled along, but was barely aware that it was Sam holding her hand. He sat her down on his bed and knelt in front of her, her hands in his.

"Don't tell me you're not upset," said Sam urgently. "You should be screaming. He's a bastard and if it wasn't for Marcus we'd've beaten the crap out of him. Don't sit there like nothing's happened."

"It doesn't matter, Sam. It's over, okay," replied Alexa in a calm voice, though it was not as cold as it could be.

"No, it's not okay! He said, in front of everyone, that you deserved to be raped and killed. Your boyfriend."

"He didn't realise he was talking about me," said Alexa simply. She did not want to think about Damien ever again. She wanted to close off her mind and pretend he never existed.

"But he knew what he was saying and by him not knowing it was you, you got his true feelings, his real thoughts about you."

Alexa knew what Sam was doing and hated that he was getting through. She stayed silent, but tears were welling in her eyes as pain began to seep through her body. "What if I'd told him?" she gasped, as emotion suddenly overwhelmed her. "What if he'd found out and it was just us and I didn't have you guys around to protect me?"

"I know," replied Sam, jumping up on the bed and wrapping her tightly in his arms. "I'm sorry. I should never've pushed you into the relationship. I should've listened to you."

"I liked him, I did. He was nice and we got along, but I don't think I ever liked him the way everyone wanted me to," explained Alexa, hoping Sam might listen now. "I tried. For you and for Ben, I tried. You made me believe that I couldn't trust my own feelings."

"I know. We were so wrong. We were so busy trying to protect you that we hurt you," nodded Sam, holding her tighter. "I should never've kept you away from Marcus. I should've let you know, let him know. I should never've interfered. I won't any more. If you want Marcus, then me and Ben, we won't stop you. Trust your own judgement, not mine. I'm sorry, Lex. I'm so sorry."

"I told you not to call me Lex," said Alexa flatly. "And there's no reason to be sorry. Me and Marc are never going to happen."

"Why?"

"Because he was my teacher. Because he's ten years older than me. For all the reasons nothing happened at school, for all the reasons that make him a decent man and for all the reasons I love him."

Tears soaked into Sam's shirt as Alexa curled into his chest. She wanted desperately to shut down and not feel the pain tearing through her, but Sam's presence was enough to stop that. Photos of them at his grandparents' property caught her eye and she felt privileged to have had Sam in her life for so long. On his bedside table sat a picture of him and Bethany, taken inside the detention centre. It warmed her heart to know that Bethany had him to rely on as well.

"So you guys really took Redgrove to the cleaners?" Alexa asked.

"You betcha. Less than we wanted, but enough to cripple them and enough that I can take care of Gran and Pop."

"Then I guess we have some celebrating to do."

"You sure?" asked Sam tenderly.

"Can't let that bastard ruin your night, can we?"

"Our night. This is for all of us. That place ruined all our lives. The only reason I don't regret ever going there is you and the guys. But we can finally stand up and show it wasn't our fault – that it was all lies."

Silence swept across the lounge room as Alexa followed Sam into the room. Everyone smiled encouragingly and although Alexa smiled back, her insides were screaming and she wished for some way of quieting them. Marcus stood at the side of the room near the table full of food and drinks. He offered Alexa a look of deepest love and it warmed her as much as anything could. They may never be together, but she could get by on looks like that. Standing next to him, she took his glass of champagne from his hand and had it to her lips before he retrieved it. He placed the glass on the table and poured orange juice into another cup before sliding it into her hand.

"If you want something stronger, I can get you coke – ca cola," he added with a smile, causing Alexa's lips to twitch slightly. "Caffeine's the only thing I'm offering you."

Alexa did not want to be grateful, but was. She was glad Marcus cared enough to protect her from her destructive desires.

By the end of the night, Alexa was as cheerful as she thought she could be. Nick, Alan and Chad were all in very merry moods and were determined to lift everyone else up to their level. The laughter and the joking was contagious, particularly when Marcus joined in. The blush that met Lizzie's cheeks every time she spoke to Marcus was not missed by anyone and was soon the focus of jokes. Even Marcus joined in. It made Alexa nervous that they would turn on her, but no one said anything about her and Marcus. However, none of that could stop Damien's words and the viciousness of his opinions swirling within her. Her instinct was to try and block it out, shut down all her feelings, but she knew Sam was right. She just could not face this pain alone.

"Sam," she said, as she and Marcus were walking out the door. "I know you're busy and you have to clean up and all, but —"

"I'll be over in about half hour, forty minutes tops," Sam smiled.

Marcus stayed quiet as they drove home. Alexa could not help but reminisce as she slouched in the passenger seat. It was the same car he had while she was in high school. The same car that had taken her on that forbidden journey to the beach, ferried her between school and her foster parents' home and on many fateful trips from hospitals and to police stations.

"Are you going to be all right?" asked Marcus, as he opened the door to their apartment.

"Yeah, I'll be fine. Thanks. And thanks for not letting me drink."

"Anytime."

Alexa slumped on the lounge, curling herself into a ball. Marcus stepped tentatively forward before seating himself on the floor in front of her, his head just inches from hers. Alexa dared to drape her arm over his shoulder, her hand resting against his chest. Marcus's hand immediately grabbed hers, holding it close.

"Did he ever hurt you?" asked Marcus tentatively.

Alexa's hand scrunched into a fist, holding Marcus's shirt tight. His grip on her hand tightened, but he said nothing, waiting for her to speak. "It's not what you think," she said eventually. "It wasn't him – I mean not his fault. He's just not very observant."

"Just tell me," sighed Marcus.

Marcus had a bad feeling already. It took all of his self-control to stay silent as Alexa recounted the incident earlier that evening. When she finished, Marcus took a deep breath, cutting Alexa off when she again tried to blame herself.

"I'm not happy about how things ended with you and Damien, but at least it saved me from breaking you up myself. You have to know that I'd never have let him near you again. That – what he did – how he treated you – it's not acceptable, Alexa. It's not. Please don't tell me it was always like that with him."

"No, that was the first time."

"That he raped you?"

"He didn't," gasped Alexa, protesting such a concept. "I've been raped. I know the difference."

"What's the difference?" asked Marcus seriously, because he had heard Alexa recount being raped and could not tell the difference.

"I know it felt like – but he didn't – that wasn't what he – he didn't. He didn't."

Marcus grasped Alexa's hand tighter, holding her arm to his chest. What did it matter what he thought Damien had done to her? Damien was gone. He could not harm her again.

218

"I don't want to be with anyone again right now," said Alexa softly, her head nestling into Marcus's neck, her arm holding him tighter.

"You don't have to," Marcus replied earnestly, turning to face her. "You don't have to be with anyone. You shouldn't be, not unless you want to."

"But if I'm not … they'll think – I just want to be free."

Marcus turned away, his heart aching. Alexa returned her head to his neck, her arm now just resting against his chest. He held her hand tighter to him. "Alexa, you and me – we … I wish …"

"It's okay. I know," said Alexa softly, squeezing his hand.

"You'll always have my heart," Marcus said earnestly, turning to face her once more. This part she had to know was the truth. "That can never, ever change."

"Done deal," Alexa replied flatly, her eyes locked on his.

"Long ago."

Chapter Fourteen

THE BUZZ OF the intercom broke the tender silence. Marcus shifted on to his knees, keeping a hold of Alexa's hand. Placing it gently on the lounge, he planted a long, soft kiss on her forehead before letting Sam in and retreating to his bedroom.

Sam immediately took Alexa in his arms. His breathing was uneven and when Alexa looked up, she saw tears welling in his eyes. "It's not your fault, Sam," she said, turning away. She did not have the energy to cheer him up.

"I should've known. Al called. There's a page on Facebook ... I blocked Damien from my feed almost as soon as I friended him. He just puts so much shit up there. But I still should've seen it."

"Seen what?" asked Alexa, feeling ill.

"The shit he said about you – not knowing it was you," answered Sam hesitantly.

"Show me."

Sam was taken aback by Alexa's request and did not immediately comply. It was not until she got up and placed her laptop in his hands that he unwillingly logged in. Damien had been bugging her for months to join all manner of social media, but Alexa had never thought of the media as being particularly social. It was the one thing that knew too much about her and she did not want to be connected to the media more than she already was.

When Sam turned the computer to face her, Alexa at least had the ability to realise it could have been worse. They really did not know her identity. It was grotesque and hurtful, but it did not name her. Clicking on Damien's profile, she was disturbed by the kinds of things he had posted.

"How could you let me —? You saw what he said – the kind of stuff he wrote. Why'd you tell me to go out with him?"

Sam could not articulate an answer and Alexa did not bother to push for one. It no longer mattered.

Examining Damien's profile further, Alexa realised with a thrill of horror that she had not remained as anonymous as she wanted. Damien had listed her as his girlfriend. "What's this mean?" asked Alexa, pointing at her name on the screen. "Can he really put my name up there? But I didn't want to be on it, not even as his girlfriend."

Sam grabbed the laptop and clicked on her name. Alexa gasped seeing a profile page under her name. Pictures she had never seen – never even realised Damien had taken, including one of her sleeping naked – were all up on her fake page. The more Sam clicked, the worse it got. Her posts were graphic and far too complimentary of Damien, and she could only assume he had written them himself.

"How do I get rid of it?" asked Alexa, her voice shaking. "Can you get rid of it?" Sam shook his head and tried to explain, but Alexa did not care. All she knew was that Damien was the only one who could make it go away.

Sam stayed the night, holding Alexa the entire time, but she did not sleep. He tried to comfort her, but besides Damien, all Alexa could think about was Marcus's kiss and his promise. She wondered what he would say in the morning, and if his heart would still belong to her when he saw these things. But Alexa did not get the chance to worry about Marcus's reaction. He slipped out of his bedroom without her noticing as she sat at the table looking at her fake profile. "Who the fuck put that up?" he asked, grabbing the laptop from her.

Alexa was shocked by his language. She had never heard him swear before. "Damien," she sighed, glad that Marcus did not feel the need to look for very long. "It gets worse."

Alexa opened the page dedicated to the 'Redgrove Slut', thinking it was better Marcus knew the extent of her exposure. Marcus examined the page intently. "Doesn't name you?" he asked.

Alexa could only shake her head as he sighed long and low, his hand squeezing her shoulder.

"Makes you wish you let us beat the crap out of him last night, doesn't it?" said Sam bitterly, walking out of the bathroom.

"No, it doesn't, Sam," replied Marcus angrily, before storming back to his bedroom. Alexa could not smile, but was relieved. She did not want anyone beaten up, not even Damien. "You're seeing Peter at eleven," said Marcus forcefully as he returned to the lounge room.

"What?" asked Alexa, confused by the direction.

"He knows the basics and is looking into what legal action you can take. He won't let that stuff stay up there. There're better ways to make sure Damien doesn't get away with this," Marcus added to Sam. "Make sure Chad, Al and Nick understand that."

The look on Peter's face when he saw the fake profile page was as close to furious as Alexa had ever seen it.

"Ben's looking into the police side of it," said Peter in a controlled voice as he turned off his monitor. "It's not really my area of the law, but I've made some calls. You want to proceed?"

"What'll it entail?" asked Alexa nervously. "I don't want more trials."

"At the very least, I have drafted an order, advising Damien to remove the profile and close the other page about you. If he doesn't comply within forty-eight hours, we will begin legal proceedings to forcibly remove them. I don't advise you sweep this under the carpet. You can't let your name be dragged through the mud by other people telling lies."

"It's not all lies," muttered Alexa uncomfortably.

"It's not exactly the truth either. And that is not your profile. It was created without your permission." Alexa shrugged, feeling defeated. "To be honest, I don't think we'll get far with any charges, not without making a big deal out of it and going public."

"Why?" sighed Alexa.

"Because this is a new area of law. Old laws don't always fit new technologies. It would be an important case. Don't think that you're the only person who's suffered this kind of thing and unfortunately you won't be the last. People think they can get away with anything on the internet."

"So if I don't stand up to this then I'll be letting it happen to other people?" asked Alexa mournfully.

"No," replied Peter, surprising Alexa. "You want my opinion." Alexa nodded warily. "Let me and Ben handle it. We are going to find out where the law stands from both sides and we are going to hammer Damien with it. If he complies, pulls his head in and learns his lesson, then we'll leave him alone and not chase him. If he doesn't, then I'm sorry, but I won't have that sort of thing left up there."

"Do you think he'll comply?" asked Alexa, wanting to know how hopeful she should be.

"He'd be a fool not to. We can make his life very uncomfortable."

Alexa did not move for a while. Peter brought her a coffee and let her sit in front of his desk while he worked. It was strangely soothing watching him, not having to think and being unable to understand any of the legal words he spoke.

"You want some lunch?" asked Peter, standing up.

"Somewhere without people?" asked Alexa tentatively.

Peter laughed, promising as few people as possible as he walked her downstairs. They settled on a small café that was emptying out after the lunchtime rush. Alexa could only pick at her food as Peter watched her.

"I have to admit that I was a little surprised to receive the call from Marcus this morning," said Peter, sitting back from the table.

"You thought I'd finally stopped getting into so much trouble?"

"This is not your fault," said Peter firmly, sitting forward and grasping her hand, before smiling slightly. "No, I was talking about hearing from Marcus. I wasn't aware you were in contact with him."

"It's a long story," Alexa sighed, not up for another lecture.

Peter scowled and looked at his watch. "Can you tell it quickly?"

If Alexa had the energy to argue, she would not have complied. It was just easier to give a very brief overview of their meeting and Marcus's unfortunate financial situation.

"That's a very nice thing you did for him," nodded Peter. Alexa glared at him. "What? You don't think so?"

"It's just you're the first person not to yell at me and tell me I'm an idiot," she said meekly, before explaining Ben and Sam's reactions.

Peter listened in silence, his face passive. It made Alexa worry that she had just convinced him to change his opinion of the situation.

"Did you make Marcus sign a lease?" asked Peter curiously. Alexa shook her head. "Would he be opposed to such a thing?"

"I don't know. I don't think so. But I trust him."

"Alexa, can I talk truthfully for a moment?" asked Peter seriously, sitting forward again. "I've met Marcus. I spoke to him a couple of times after everything fell apart at the end of school."

"You don't like him either, do you?" asked Alexa fearfully. In many ways she valued Peter's opinion more than most.

"On the contrary, I think he's a decent man, and if not for the fact that was your teacher, I'm not sure I would have many concerns."

"He never touched me then. He wouldn't do anything now. He's not that kind of guy."

"I'm not saying he is, but I do get paranoid. I don't profess to know him as well as you do, but you are offering someone very good living conditions. He wouldn't be the first person to take advantage of that," said Peter matter-of-factly. "I am asking you to let me draft a lease agreement. Nothing out of the ordinary, just good practice."

"He's a good man," Alexa replied, avoiding the question.

"Even good people have to sign leases," smiled Peter. "It's not personal. I trust you. If you're letting Marcus live with you – of your own volition – then you must trust him. I'm actually more surprised by your relationship with Damien. He doesn't seem like your kind of boy."

"You don't have time for that story too," Alexa sighed.

"Hmm, probably not," sighed Peter, looking at his watch. "You going to head home now?"

It was not the question Alexa wanted to face. She did not want to go home. Even talking about these distressing events, it was peaceful in Peter's company. All she wanted was sit quietly in a corner of his office for a while and just let the day pass her by, and was surprised when Peter raised no objection to her request.

"Did you end up getting a job? You said you'd wanted to once you got settled," asked Peter when they reached his office.

"It was too much. Uni, visiting Bethy, being a good girlfriend."

"And it's not likely to get any quieter once Bethany's released," mused Peter. "I can't imagine you wanting to be at work when you could be at home with her."

Alexa could only shrug. It was true, but Peter was being too understanding. "Feel like I should be doing more," she confessed. "Like I'm always playing catch up. Know I'll regret it later, but a lot of the time, I just don't care. I don't even believe that normal, picture-perfect future can exist for someone like me."

"You want the good news?" asked Peter, and she nodded slowly. "Doesn't exist for anyone. But," he emphasised before she could speak. "That life you want – house, family, job – that's not out of your reach. You are behind everyone else. I can't lie to you about the terrible start you and Bethany had, and I won't pretend it won't be harder for you than most, but I'm not content to let you miss out either."

"What do you mean?" Alexa asked hesitantly.

"I could use someone from time to time. Doesn't have to be regular. It won't be spectacular and could often be quite boring, but it will give you some basic office skills and experience that will mean you won't feel so out of place once you start working."

"Why are you so nice to me, Peter?" asked Alexa, finally unable to hold back the question. "I don't understand? I'm trouble and you keep helping and you never ask for money unless I make you and you never get mad at me. Don't you have better things to do than be nice to me. I still don't know how I even ended up with a lawyer. It's not normal."

"I can explain all that, but it means talking about your past." Alexa nodded and Peter directed her to a seat. He sat down at his desk and started working, but kept talking. "We'll start easy," he said. "The reason I never ask you for money is because I took you and Bethany on as pro bono cases."

"Pro what?"

"Pro bono," smiled Peter as he typed. "It means free of charge. Every lawyer – not just me – does pro bono work. So that's never been as big a deal as you may have thought. It's just part of what we do."

"What about how you met us? Did we do something wrong?" asked Alexa tentatively, wondering how much wanted to know.

"No. I was actually initially your mother's lawyer. I was her legal aid lawyer – appointed by the courts – it was luck that I ever met you."

"Bad luck," Alexa muttered sadly, hating that was what she was.

"Luck. I don't think good luck comes without consequences or bad luck without opportunities. Life's never that simple. Your mother was trying to ensure your father had no further part in your lives."

"Did you agree with her? You think it's a good thing I don't know who my father is?" asked Alexa curiously. She had always assumed the worst, but never knew where those feelings had come from.

"Yes. I know you don't remember back then, and I'm not sure that's a bad thing either, but you can trust me when I say your father was not a good man and he hurt your family very badly."

"That was it? You just represented my mother that one time?"

"No. I remained her lawyer – free of charge – until her death. It was only then that I became your lawyer. Your mother was frequently in some sort of trouble – drugs, money. I tried to keep her out of gaol, keep her around for you and Beth. I knew you would go back into care when she went away. Thankfully, that didn't happen too often."

"You must have liked her to do so much for her."

Peter sighed heavily and pushed away from his desk. He looked thoughtfully at Alexa before standing up and moving to the window. "We've known each other a long time now," he said slowly. "Truth is, I never cared much for your mother. You and Beth, but particularly you, were my concern. I just don't want you to start distrusting my motives. Your situation was not fair and there was nothing I could do to change that. All I had to offer were my professional skills.

"When you and Beth came to meetings with your mother, I took you out – all of you – to eat, so your mother learned to bring you along. I got to check up on you and do something very small and insignificant to help you."

"It was never insignificant to me," replied Alexa, her eyes to the ground. Part of her was screaming to run now, terrified of anyone wanting to help her and what they would want in return, but she knew Peter was not like that. More than that, she knew his profession still bound him not to get too close or care too much.

"No, I guess not. How about we see if this work I've got for you is too insignificant."

"What if it is?" Alexa asked, smiling slightly.

"Then you do it and I see if I can find more significant work, but I won't let you out of doing the mundane. Trust me, once you know what you're doing it all gets a bit routine."

After a couple of hours, Alexa was sure Peter would be ready to throw her out of his office. Everything he asked her to do, she had to ask a hundred questions back about what he meant or where things went. Yet somehow he smiled through it all, explaining that she could not possibly know what she had not learned. It was not comforting, and when he finally gave up on giving her more jobs she could not do, she sat down in a corner of his office, placed her head on her knees and tried to pretend nothing existed for a while.

"It will blow over," said Peter, rising from his desk. It was getting dark outside and Alexa wondered how she could have possibly been sitting there for so long thinking about nothing in particular. "You want a lift home?" he asked when she did not respond.

"No, it's way out of your way," replied Alexa, coming to her senses and jumping to her feet.

"It's not, actually," Peter laughed. "You don't even know where I live. How could you possibly know what's out of my way?"

Alexa smiled and Peter insisted on taking her home. He packed up his things, placing a stack of folders in his briefcase, before leading her down to the car park. Alexa could not help but admire his car. Peter laughed when he saw her stroking its interior affectionately.

"You would never spend that much money on a car," Peter said with a smile. "But you can take it for a spin one day if you want to see how she handles."

"You'd let me drive your car? Seriously? What's wrong with you?" Alexa asked incredulously. She explained how Ben had basically banned her from driving his car and Peter laughed again. She had never seen Peter this way before and it felt strange. He was treating her like an adult, almost like an equal, and she truly liked him for it.

"Ah, here," said Peter when they arrived at her apartment block, pulling out papers from his bag. "If Marcus has any problems signing, you let me know."

Alexa looked at the lease. It was not very long, and she decided she would read it before she gave it to Marcus.

"Ben and I will handle Damien – make sure the problem goes

away," Peter reassured her, squeezing her shoulder gently. "I'll let you know what happens. Don't let it bother you, okay. You just start getting ready to have your sister home."

"They've rescheduled the parole hearing?" Alexa asked excitedly, suddenly not caring for anything else.

Peter's face twisted as he shook his head, simply repeating what Ben had been saying; that it had to happen sooner rather than later.

"Oh, and this doesn't get you out of lunch with me," Peter added out the window. "Today definitely doesn't count."

Walking into her apartment a little more depressed than she wanted to be, Alexa smelt food and felt her stomach grumble.

"There's dinner if you want some," said Marcus. Smiling, Alexa walked into the kitchen to see saucepans of spaghetti and bolognaise sauce on the stove. It really did seem like the only thing he knew how to cook. "I warned you," he called from the lounge, as if reading her mind. It made her smile as she dished up some food.

Sitting with her dinner on the lounge, Alexa was unsure of how Marcus would treat her after what had happened the night before. He immediately asked about her meeting with Peter and she told him everything relating to Damien. The rest, even the part about working for Peter, was something she wanted to keep to herself.

"They'll sort it out," said Marcus reassuringly. Alexa could only grimace. "What? You don't think so?"

"No. It's not that. It's just – Peter – because you called him – he wanted to know – he knows you're living here. He's not angry," she added quickly. "But he didn't like that I – he wants you to sign a lease."

"Hell, Alexa, you scared the crap out of me," replied Marcus with a relieved smile. "I thought it was going to be something bad. Of course. As soon as you have it, I'll sign it."

"He actually gave it to me today, but I haven't read it yet."

"Then let's go through it in the morning. I'll sign it and you can send it back to Peter. It's not an issue. If it was anyone else, I'd want you to have one as well."

Alexa nodded, but said nothing. She finished her meal in silence, her nerves swirling anxiously. "We're friends, right?" she asked Marcus, putting her empty plate on the coffee table.

"Of course we are," he answered immediately.

"So it'd be okay if I sat with you?" Marcus only nodded and Alexa immediately jumped off her lounge and on to the one he was sitting on. "Pick something mind-numbing to watch."

Marcus reached for the remote as Alexa curled up in a ball, her feet resting against his leg. Marcus immediately stood up, disappointing her until he returned with a throw rug, placing it over her feet and resting his arm on her leg.

They watched the television in silence, their fingers just touching. Alexa only realised she had fallen asleep when Marcus moved, tearing her fearfully from her slumber.

"I wish you wouldn't always jump like that," Marcus said softly. "It scares the hell out of me."

Alexa managed a faint smile and Marcus wished her goodnight, kissing the top of her head as he squeezed her hand.

***

The prospect of going back to university was made easier for Alexa by Damien quickly complying with the order and taking down her fake profile page and the page set up to ridicule the lying Redgrove slut. Peter had shown her the order he had Damien served with. It used lots of complicated legal jargon, which made it sound very scary. Damien had often spoken about a career in politics, which Peter had been happy about; it would give Damien more reasons to want to make this situation go away. However, Ben also made Alexa lodge an official complaint with the police, which resulted in a visit and a stern lecture from the officers. No charges were laid, but Ben assured her that it would be marked on his file in case he ever did something similar.

That was where Alexa thought it would end, but it seemed Damien had more to say on the issue. She tried to avoid finding out what it was, refusing to take calls from him or any number she did not recognise, and eventually the calls stopped. Then Damien started turning up at her apartment. The first time only Marcus was home. The second time, Damien waited downstairs, obviously hoping to catch her on her way in or out. Thankfully, Alexa saw him before he noticed her and quickly backtracked down the street.

"Sam, you still close by?" Alexa stammered into her phone as her body shook. She never thought she would be this scared to see Damien.

"Is he there?" asked Sam angrily.

"I think so. I ran away – didn't want him to see me. Sorry. I know I should handle it myself."

"No! No, Lex. I'll be there in ten, okay. Don't go near him."

Alexa was surprised when Sam met up with her rather than going straight to the apartment, but he insisted that she needed to tell Damien to his face that he was not to come around. Holding hands, they walked to her apartment. Damien was still waiting. He looked furious.

"Right, nothing going on," Damien spat, charging up to Sam and pushing him in the chest. "You should be begging me to put that profile back up," he snarled, turning to Alexa. "It's so much more complimentary than the truth. You play the sweet, innocent girl, but really you're just a filthy, cheating slut."

"Is that all you came to say?" asked Alexa flatly. She did not even care to defend herself. Damien just glared his reply. "Good. Now fuck off. Don't come here again. Don't call me again. Don't speak to me again. Got it?"

"I'm not doing a damn thing you say. Do you know how much my parents are hassling me because of that court order? I've had cops at my house. My parents think I'm some kind of fucking reject because the cops showed them the fucking page. Now I'm in fucking trouble – because you can't keep your legs fucking closed."

Alexa shrugged in an unaffected manner. "Not my problem."

"You fucking, little —"

Damien lunged at her, but Sam moved in between them as the little courtyard exploded into sound. Two police officers were suddenly beside them, pulling Damien off Sam and standing him a couple of metres away. That was when Alexa noticed another person standing between her and Damien. Marcus just stood there, his arms folded, like a giant bodyguard. Alexa could not help but notice how much bigger he looked when he stood like that. It was intimidating, but the threat was completely implied.

"Damien's my ex-boyfriend," said Alexa when the officers started asking about the situation. "I've asked him to leave, but he's refusing. I want him to go and not come back. Otherwise I'll take out an AVO."

Those three letters set Damien off in a way Alexa had never seen before. The officers tried to calm him as he swore angrily at her. Marcus immediately moved back towards Alexa, while Sam stepped forward towards Damien.

"You're fucking dead, do you get that?" spat Damien, struggling against the officers. "You'd better watch your back."

That was when the officers lost their patience and handcuffed Damien. He was still wrestling with them as they put him in the car. Sam insisted on going with Alexa to the police station to take out the apprehended violence order. She was not surprised when Ben turned up five minutes after them. It was a simple process, but one Alexa wished she did not have to go through. It was never her intention to hit Damien so hard; she just wanted him to leave her alone.

However, it was clear it would take more than a piece of paper to stop Damien from speaking his mind. He was waiting for her outside her first lecture on the first day of semester. He stood casually, as if he was there by chance, but Alexa knew it was intentional. "You didn't have to set your attack dogs on me," he growled as a greeting.

"You didn't have to fraudulently use my identity," Alexa retorted, almost glad the attack was not worse. "If I could've taken those pages down without having anything to do with you, I would've. Now fuck off before I call the police."

"You're lucky I don't expose you to everyone," Damien spat bitterly. "Who you are. What you are. Bet that teacher never raped you. Bet you were screaming for more the whole time."

Alexa was stung. Was this the kind of person Damien really was? It seemed impossible that she had never realised just how cruel and vindictive he was. But she had been so desperate to make things work that she had pushed aside everything negative thing about him and their relationship, just because he has liked her.

"Say whatever you want about me," Alexa responded coldly. "I don't give a shit, but my attack dogs are just waiting for a reason to nail you. So go ahead, just try it."

"Hey, Alexa, you coming for coffee?" asked Jessica, bouncing up to her with several of their friends from class.

"Don't speak to me. Don't call. Don't come by," warned Alexa as she turned away. "Or you'll have even more visits from the cops."

"So, ah, I guess you guys broke up," said Jessica when Damien stalked off. Alexa just nodded. "I thought that might've been why you took down your Facebook page. I mean, you were so ... I don't know – crazy for him."

"You saw that?" asked Alexa, turning to Jessica in horror.

"Of course. We all did," laughed Jack. "We were all your friends. What'd you think? It was a private journal page?"

"Oh my God," Alexa whispered. "This is so much worse than I thought. I've never been on Facebook. Never set up a profile."

"Then how?" asked Jessica, though a look of realisation crossed her face as she finished the question.

When Alexa explained the situation that had unfolded, the whole group howled in protest. She was surprised by their unequivocal support, unsure if what Damien had done would be considered wrong among her university peers.

"What a loser," laughed Jessica. "Imagine making up a page for your girlfriend and boasting about yourself."

Jack and the others all expressed similar sentiments. Alexa felt lighter than she had in a long time. These people did not know much about her and still believed the lies about her schooling and childhood – though she was scared they knew the truth and were just playing along – and yet they were sitting with her being nice and supportive. It was amazing.

"How'd you expect us to react?" asked Jessica when Alexa again thanked them for their support.

"Not believe me. Or think it was okay," Alexa answered meekly.

"You're really strange, you know that," laughed Jessica. "There's no way what Damien did was okay."

The group promised they would let her know if she ever popped back up on Facebook or if Damien posted any more pictures of her. Alexa wished she could have told them about the Redgrove page, but it was better the guys monitored that front. Now that she finally felt like she had made some real friends at university, she did not want to destroy it all by exposing her past. She had never thought she would ever find support from people outside her inner circle and could not help but fear that, after a good night's sleep and time to think, they would change their minds and blame her. They didn't. They were all as supportive the next day as they had been on the first – and all the days after that.

Her concerns were highly amusing to Jessica, and Alexa found them becoming close over that first week back. They hung out all the time and even discussed Bethany. Through Jessica and Jake, Alexa found herself quickly connected to a new set of acquaintances across not only her course, but the university. It cut into her study time, but the smaller start-of-year workload allowed Alexa to stay on top of her study.

It was also made much easier with Marcus around. Since he was often the first one home, he cooked many nights of the week. He shopped in a much more generous way than Alexa ever had, and he never kept any of the food for himself. Sometimes Alexa got the feeling Marcus enjoyed buying foods, particularly sweets, she had never eaten before. He introduced her to things without making her feel strange for having never encountered them before. He also negotiated her moods in a way no one else could. One night, when she had been particularly worked up, he had pulled her to the lounge and made her play snap. The card game was completely new to her, but the inadvertent physical contact it entailed as they both tried to slap their hands down on the matching cards was very enjoyable. Then, after half an hour of playing, Marcus ran out of cards.

"So is the game over?" she asked confusedly. "Or do I give you some of my cards?"

"No, game's over. You won," Marcus smiled.

"Really?" Alexa squealed excitedly. "But I've never won anything. Did you let me win?"

"Haha, if only I could claim to be so noble. No, it was all you – or beginner's luck. Want to try again to find out?"

It was as close to perfect as anything could be. And when they were alone, there was never any pressure on their friendship and what else it could or should be. It just happened that they did not often have time alone, with Charlotte over every afternoon and staying over on Fridays.

"You don't mind me coming here to do my homework, do you?" asked Charlotte as they sat down at the table. "I just find it easier to work here."

"I love having you here," replied Alexa truthfully, scared of saying more. "But are things going okay at home?"

"They're okay – getting better," shrugged Charlotte. "I realised that even though my parents aren't great, it'd be worse to be without them. So I thought I'd give them a go, try behaving at school, that sort of thing."

Charlotte's voice had a tinge of sadness to it, which worried Alexa. She was sure there was more going on, but held her tongue. There was no guarantee she could fix Charlotte's problems and it was not fair to expect her to divulge everything. She never would have.

"So what are you two up to tonight?" asked Marcus.

"We're going out to dinner, then hangin' out. Want to come?" asked Charlotte excitedly.

"No, thank you. I'm meeting Lucy. You two have fun."

Charlotte's face fell at the rejection. Alexa could only smile. She had still never met Lucy, and while she remained absent from her life, it was difficult to ever feel rejected by Marcus. In many ways, it was like Lucy did not exist, and when she and Marcus were alone, Lucy was never mentioned. It was only Charlotte who needed reminding. However, over the next week, Charlotte stopped caring about playing matchmaker as she practically moved back into the apartment. Instead of going home for dinner, she often did not leave until late or stayed the night. She kept trying to tell Alexa nothing was wrong, but Alexa was not convinced.

"You can't keep telling me nothing wrong," said Alexa seriously. "You're here nearly all the time – which I love – but I'm worried."

"Okay," replied Charlotte, grimacing as she set the table. "It's just that Mia's sick. It's real stressful at home so it's better I'm here."

"Sick? What do you mean? Sick how? Cold?"

"Leukaemia."

"Charlotte, you should be at home, not here," cried Alexa, almost dropping the saucepan she was holding.

"Please. I spend time with Mia – everyday. It's Carla. She's so stressed with Mia being sick and she's never liked me much. Dad just thought it best I didn't spend too much time at home."

"But —"

"No, it's okay. We talked about it. Dad's happy I'm trying and doing better at school and we're getting along better. He doesn't want Carla taking out her frustrations on me. She's gone a bit mental. She's yelling at the doctors and nurses – not just me. I promise I spend time with Mia and do nice things for her. I just don't want to create more problems while she's so sick."

"Okay, you can come over and stay whenever you want," nodded Alexa, finally believing Charlotte had the situation under control. "Just make sure Mia knows you're there for her."

Marcus was just as concerned by Charlotte's revelation, though his focus was much more on Charlotte's well-being and how she was coping with Mia's diagnosis.

"What do you mean?" asked Charlotte. "I don't have cancer."

"Yes, but it'd still be very upsetting," continued Marcus caringly. "Mia's your sister. And with your step-mother being so stressed and taking that out on you. It's a lot to cope with."

"She's always taken her frustrations out on me," waved Charlotte dismissively. "I feel for the hospital people. I mean, they're trying to save Mia's life and she's yelling at them like a lunatic. I think it's scared Dylan though. We ended up hanging a bit at the hospital. Kinda nice in a way."

"You're not understanding what I'm getting at," sighed Marcus. "It's well known that the impact on siblings in these situations can be profound. It's important to realise that you're allowed to be affected by all this."

"Seriously, Mia's the one who has cancer. I really don't have any right to complain about anything," replied Charlotte firmly.

Marcus turned to Alexa, but she could only agree with Charlotte. "You just do whatever you can to get the other person through. That's the important thing – helping them," said Alexa.

"But what about the cost to you?" asked Marcus seriously.

"Who cares about the cost to me. I'm not sick," retorted Alexa immediately. "If Bethy, or you, or Charlotte or anyone I cared about – I'd do anything to help them. Whatever I could."

"You two are like peas in a pod," sighed Marcus, as Charlotte nodded her agreement.

Grabbing the plates, Marcus washed up as Alexa and Charlotte pulled out their books. Alexa was surprised by how diligent Charlotte was with her studies. For someone who had initially protested so vehemently against the idea, she often worked longer than Alexa, and Alexa was convinced she worked much harder too. It was amazing the volume of work Charlotte could get through, but Alexa never pointed any of this out. Charlotte did not speak about school or how she was going, even when she was asked.

"At least it's Wednesday," sighed Alexa, pushing her books away. She had been trying to read the same page for five minutes, disturbed by the speed with which Charlotte was writing her history essay. "Just two more days to go. Who wants tea?"

"How about hot chocolate?" asked Charlotte.

"Are you going to make it? Cos you said the one I made sucked," smiled Alexa.

"That's not what I said," retorted Charlotte.

"It's what you meant."

Charlotte shrugged and shook her head, but followed Alexa to the kitchen and started making the hot chocolate. Where Alexa was happy to make it like tea, Charlotte boiled the milk in the saucepan and made up her own cocoa mix. Alexa got the mugs ready, but when she turned back around she noticed Charlotte hunched by the stove, as though buckling under an invisible weight. Alexa moved behind Charlotte and slowly wrapped her arms around her chest. They did not really hug each other, but when Charlotte pushed back into her, Alexa knew she needed it.

"I never would've wished for this to happen to Mia – even though I don't get on with them," said Charlotte softly.

"Of course not. No one would ever think that," replied Alexa, resisting the urge to find out who had suggested such a thing.

"Sometimes I wish it was me. Imagine it would've helped us get closer – that Carla would've been all stressed and yelling at my doctors, cos she cares so much if I live or die, but I don't think she does. I reckon she'd be mad at me for disrupting her perfect life. No one's going to sympathise with her if her reject step-daughter gets sick."

"Don't think about those things," replied Alexa quickly, squeezing Charlotte tighter. "Bad circumstances – people react so different to what you expect. And you don't know, this could be the thing that brings you all together. Show them how much you care about Mia – cos I know you do – show them how hard you're trying. It could still be the miracle you're looking for."

"Yeah, maybe."

Charlotte shifted forward and Alexa released her. It was hard to have these conversations with Charlotte. Although Alexa wanted that same miracle for Charlotte, part of her selfishly hoped that Charlotte needed to move back in permanently. She enjoyed Charlotte being around and liked having someone to share her room with; though she wondered if Charlotte was a substitute for Bethany, and if she would stop caring for Charlotte once Bethany returned. It was a cruel suggestion and Alexa desperately prayed for its impossibility.

"Alexa, can you come in here," called Ben.

Alexa shot Charlotte a quizzical look before moving into the lounge room. She had not even heard Ben come in.

"I didn't know you were coming over," said Alexa accusingly, before regretting her tone. She needed to remember to be excited when she saw Ben, but thankfully he did not seem offended by her less than enthusiastic greeting.

"I found something for you today and wanted to surprise you," said Ben with a barely concealed grin.

Alexa felt her body quiver. She hated surprises. Marcus must have understood, because he shook his head and shrugged. Charlotte looked equally confused, reassuring Alexa that she was not being ambushed, but she was still so uncertain that she remained rooted to the spot.

"It's all right," smiled Ben reassuringly. "Come sit on the lounge."

Alexa did not move until Charlotte's hand guided her to the lounge. As soon as she was seated, Ben's large hands wrapped themselves over her eyes. It was disconcerting, but Alexa did not want to tell Ben how scared his actions made her. Images of unknown origin swirled in her mind, though the emotions were much easier to place. She knew this fear that was sweeping her body. Every muscle tensed as she quivered uncontrollably. She could not even run away. That time had passed. She was paralysed. Nothing would stop what was about to happen. Around her she could hear whispered voices, and she knew they were planning what they were going to do next.

Then there was movement.

Someone was in front of Alexa. If it was Marcus, Alexa wondered if she would trust him enough to throw herself in his arms and believe he would shield her and not join those wanting to harm her. If it was Charlotte, Alexa knew she would have no choice but to protect her – another little sister she had led to her doom.

Fingers started to pull Ben's hands off her eyes. Their touch was so familiar, but it was not possible. Alexa's body quaked as the fingers worked faster to peel back Ben's hands.

"Lex, open your eyes. It's okay. Please, Lex, look at me."

Gasping for breath, Alexa finally opened her eyes, but she could only stare. It was not real. It could not be true.

"Lex, it's okay. I'm real, Lex. I'm real. I'm here. I'm free."

Chapter Fifteen

"ANGEL," ALEXA GASPED, lunging forward and hugging Bethany fiercely. Falling to the floor, Alexa continued to hold Bethany tight as she sobbed. This was not the way she intended to be reunited with Bethany, but right then she did not care. Bethany was home.

"I'm sorry. I couldn't tell you," said Bethany, her voice shaking as she continued to hug Alexa. "It was so hard last time. I didn't want to be disappointed again. I couldn't handle it. I know you don't have space for me, but can I stay with you?"

"Oh, Angel, of course," sobbed Alexa, releasing Bethany so she could wipe the tears from her eyes. "There's always room for you."

Bethany lunged forward and hugged Alexa. It was the sweetest embrace Alexa ever received. She could still not quite believe it was real. Bethany was free. They were together. Everything was as it should be.

So engrossed with Bethany's arrival, Alexa did not notice that the others had moved out on to the balcony. The only thing that mattered was Bethany – until Alexa saw Charlotte sneaking out the front door.

"Hey, where're you going?" asked Alexa, grabbing Charlotte's hand to stop her from leaving if the lift came.

"I'm going home. You have more important things to do now."

"Don't be like that. Please. I still really care about you, Charlotte. This hasn't changed that."

"It's okay," said Charlotte firmly. "I'm happy for you, I really am. You need to be with your sister tonight and I should go and see mine."

"Okay, but nothing's changed," nodded Alexa, unable to fight that logic, even if it was a lie. "You're still welcome here whenever and I expect to see you on Friday night at the very least. Friday's still our night. You're a part of my life now and that's not going to change."

"Yeah, okay," smiled Charlotte, hugging Alexa. "I'm real glad Bethany's home."

"Yeah, me too," smiled Alexa.

Happy did not quite describe it. Alexa felt like she was dancing on clouds as she skipped back into the apartment. Ben had moved inside and was sitting with Bethany on the lounge.

"So that's the project," smiled Bethany.

"Don't call her that," Alexa replied, though she could not do so without smiling as she sat down next to Bethany and hugged her. "Her name's Charlotte, and you know why she's so important to me. She's sticking around, so you'd better get used to it and learn to like her."

"I must be in the wrong house," smiled Bethany, looking around dramatically. "You can't be my sister. You're putting someone before me."

"No one'll ever be more important to me than you, Bethy," replied Alexa seriously, never able to joke about such a thing. "You're just not the only person in my life any more."

Bethany smiled broadly and hugged Alexa tight, before grabbing her hand and lifting her from the lounge. "Give me the tour."

Alexa did just that. It did not matter that from the lounge they could see practically everything, Alexa held Bethany's hand and led her around the whole place. They spent many minutes in each room. Starting in the laundry, they looked through every cupboard and into every nook and cranny.

"Lex, this place is amazing," said Bethany as they walked into the bathroom. The exclamations only became more impressed as they made their way through the apartment. "And it's ours, Lex. They can't take it away. Our very own place. I mean, your place, but —"

"Our place," replied Alexa emphatically. "Will always be our place. We're in this together, okay. Come, I'll show you our room." Alexa opened the door to her bedroom and pulled Bethany in, closing the door behind them. "Our place," Alexa said emphatically, hugging Bethany tight. "There's a trundle bed or we can share my bed."

"Can I stay with you?" asked Bethany timidly.

"I was hoping you'd say that. I've missed you so much."

"Makes you glad we have Marcus around to force us to share a room," added Bethany with a sly smile. "Are we going to have enough space for clothes and stuff?" she asked looking around the room.

"Yeah, the built-in's pretty big. And I've already put some clothes in your half."

"Lex, there're more clothes in my half than yours," cried Bethany, looking in the wardrobe. "Why've you been spending your money on clothes for me when you have hardly any of your own?"

"I wanted you to have some nice things when you came home," answered Alexa, her voice breaking. "You deserve nice things."

Bethany walked up and hugged Alexa tight, burying her head in Alexa's neck where her tears soaked into her top. Alexa reciprocated, holding Bethany to her.

"Can I see Marcus's room?" asked Bethany, stepping back and smiling brightly, all evidence of her tears gone.

Alexa grimaced. She had always intended to speak to Marcus before Bethany was released to make sure that he was okay about living with her. He had never been particularly fond of Bethany, and now she was being thrust on him without any warning.

"Hey, Marc, do you mind if I show Bethy your room?" asked Alexa, walking out to the kitchen where he was trying to revive the hot chocolate.

"Of course," replied Marcus instantly. "It's your apartment. You don't have to ask those things."

Alexa smiled and grabbed Bethany's hand, rushing towards his room. It was one of Alexa's favourite places. Every time she walked in she could smell Marcus in the air. Sitting on his bed was almost like being with him.

"It's a nice room," said Bethany, walking around.

"Yeah, but don't listen to what he said. You need to ask him if you want to come in here. He never comes into our room without asking."

"No problem," smiled Bethany. "Can I have something to eat?"

"Absolutely!"

Marcus sat down on the balcony with a sigh. This was more than he expected. It was not as though he expected Bethany would live anywhere but with Alexa, but he had never intended to stick around for her return – at least not for very long. He was not quite financially secure yet, but was close enough that he could leave if he had to. The problem was, even with Bethany around, he did not want to leave.

Watching Alexa with Bethany was truly beautiful. The way they loved each other was simply phenomenal. Alexa's face lit up whenever Bethany was near. He was truly thankful he had been able to witness their reunion and even found his opinions of Bethany softening.

It was clear Bethany loved Alexa as much as Alexa loved her, something Marcus had never been quite convinced of before. The effects of Bethany's incarceration were also quite marked, and it affected him more than he expected to hear Bethany ask for a drink of water and permission to use the bathroom. The way Alexa always responded by making out that Bethany's hesitancy was because she was new to the apartment was pure kindness.

Before tonight, Marcus was sure he could not love Alexa more than he already did, but now he was sure he had never really known her at all. What he knew of Alexa was only the tip of a very large iceberg –

mostly hidden in the dark waters below. Realising that only made him desirous to stay to discover the rest.

The sound of the balcony door sliding open made Marcus jump. He shifted back against the railing unsure where to go. Despite his more recent kind thoughts towards Bethany, the sight of her standing just a couple of metres away was unnerving. This was still the girl who held a gun to Alexa's head and threatened to pull the trigger – who accidentally shot a young girl in her drug-induced state. In the time he had known and loved Alexa, no one had caused her more pain than Bethany and face to face with her, he did not know what to do.

The problem was that Bethany was the one person Alexa needed in her life to be happy – to be alive – and Marcus knew that to be a part of Alexa's life he had to find a way to get along with Bethany. Before Marcus could decide what to say, Bethany's arms were around his neck. He just stood there, unsure how to react. They had barely been introduced. Then he saw Alexa standing at the balcony door, clearly concerned by the one-way nature of the hug.

"Please," Alexa mouthed, her eyes wide and desperate.

It was a plea Marcus would never be able to resist. Closing his eyes, he wrapped his arms around Bethany's body. Bethany started shaking as she held him tighter, grasping his shirt as tears soaked into it. He could not imagine Alexa displaying such vulnerability, but he found Bethany's openness endearing.

"I'm sorry," said Bethany, pushing out of his arms as tears continued to tumble slowly down her cheeks. They did not look alike, but Marcus still saw so much of Alexa in Bethany, even down to the same sad blue eyes. "I know you must hate me. You love Lex so much it'd be impossible not to. I just needed to say thank you."

"For what?" asked Marcus, his voice harsher than intended. He had never thought he existed to Bethany.

"You saved Lex's life," replied Bethany incredulously. "You're the reason she's still here to hug me. I wouldn't be alive if it wasn't for you."

"You would've killed yourself if Alexa died?" Marcus asked, his voice soft and shaky.

"Within hours. My life is nothing without her."

Marcus could see Bethany was not overstating the situation. He had seen the same desperation in Alexa's eyes and suddenly felt very sorry for Bethany. Alexa was right. Bethany had not deserved her life any more than she had. "I don't hate you, Bethany," said Marcus, placing a gentle hand on her shoulder. "I'm glad you survived, and I'm glad you're home where you belong."

***

The sun was bright as Alexa raced down the street, the scenery a blur, all her concentration on the precious cargo in her arms. She gripped a bloody knife tightly, her only protection, while her little five-year-old arms ached with the strain of Bethany's weight, but she would not put her down until they were out of danger. They came across a field full of large pipes. Alexa knew it was not a safe place to hide, but she was tired and there was nowhere else to go. Finding the most hidden pipe they could squeeze into, Alexa pushed Bethany inside and held her close, her eyes never straying from the end of the pipe.

"Caitlin, I'm hungry," said Bethany softly, trying hard not to whine.

"I'll get us food when it's dark, Bethy. I promise," replied Alexa, scooping the three-year-old Bethany into her lap and stroking her hair until she fell asleep.

"Alexa," called a young, round-faced policeman at the end of the pipe. "Come out now. It's okay. You're safe now."

Alexa remained rooted to the spot, her heart pounding, knowing what was coming. She held Bethany tight, but all Bethany wanted was to rush into Ben's waiting arms. Struggling, Alexa's grip on Bethany finally failed and Bethany scurried towards Ben, but before she reached him a shadow descended upon them. Alexa knew what was going to happen and wished she could stop it, but all she could do was curl her body up and shake with fear.

The shot reverberated through the pipe. Alexa turned her head to see Ben lying face down at the end of the pipe. Bethany sat silently sobbing between Alexa and Ben, his blood pooling around her feet. Alexa tried desperately to fight against her paralysis as the shadow moved closer.

"No, don't hurt her," cried Alexa, finally able to rush forwards, but the shadow grabbed Bethany and threw her out of the pipe.

"Caitlin, you've been a naughty girl. I thought I could trust you. You let me down, Caitlin," hissed the shadow's raspy voice.

All the air left Alexa's lungs as the shadowy hand reached out for her. When it grabbed her arm, she knew she was going to die.

"Wake up, Lex, wake up."

Alexa gasped. Someone had hold of her. She scurried away, her body falling. The arms grabbed her tight and pulled her back towards them.

"It's okay, Lex. It's just a dream," said Bethany in a shaky voice, restraining her against the bed. "Please, just wake up."

"He called me Caitlin again," gasped Alexa, her heart rate slowing as she realised what was happening. "You did too. You called me Caitlin. But he didn't go after you. He always goes after you, but this time he wanted me. It was the first time he's ever come after me."

"It's okay. It's just a nightmare. It's not real," reassured Bethany, stroking Alexa's face and hair. "I'm okay, you're okay and Ben's okay. We're all still here. It's just a dream."

Alexa sighed, finally allowing her body to relax. Bethany slid down in the bed next to her, and Alexa pulled her close. Her heart was still pounding and she knew Bethany could feel it by the way she kept soothing her. Holding Bethany close, Alexa tried hard to calm herself down to sleep, clearing her mind of everything.

It was just a dream and she would not let it rule her life.

"Good morning."

Alexa blinked stupidly, trying to wake herself up. She hated dreaming about Bethany. Groaning unhappily, Alexa turned over to go back to sleep.

"Come on, sleepyhead. Wake up! I want to get up."

"Bethy?"

Alexa spun around and embraced Bethany. It was real. Those flickering memories that had been swirling and torturing her mind were real. Bethany was home where she belonged.

"Can I breathe?" asked Bethany, though she was returning the embrace just as fiercely.

"I'm so glad you're here. I thought it was just a dream and I'd wake up and be alone."

"I'm not going anywhere," smiled Bethany, pulling back and stroking Alexa's face. "But talking about dreams, I think it's time you spoke to Ben. You can't keep having nightmares."

"That's the first one I've had in ages, almost a year," waved Alexa dismissively. "It's okay. Just a bad dream. I stopped them before and I'll do it again."

Bethany did not look convinced, but Alexa did not care. Now Bethany was home, she was not going to worry about anything.

"Can I go to the bathroom?" asked Bethany as they got out of bed.

"Yeah, of course. You go first," smiled Alexa, hating that Bethany was still asking permission to do things.

Marcus was already dressed and in the kitchen when Alexa

walked out. "How'd she go?" he asked softly.

"Good. I'm so glad she's home, Marc, but are you okay with this? It was never meant to be a surprise."

"I love living here, but you guys need your space. You can't want me to stay while you two share that room."

"No, please," cried Alexa softly. "We need to be together. I don't want us to have an excuse to be apart yet. Stay. Please."

"You twisted my arm," smiled Marcus.

It took a while for Bethany to emerge from the bathroom, by which time Alexa could only offer rushed instructions about breakfast before dashing into the bathroom. She tried to be as quick as she could, desperate to spend every second of this day with Bethany.

"Are you having nightmares again?" asked Ben as soon as she emerged.

Ben had stayed so late that Alexa had no choice but to offer him a spot on the lounge for the night. The eagerness with which he accepted showed how much he had wanted to stay. It should have made her happy, but she was still so uncomfortable around him that she wished he had gone home.

"Yes, I had a nightmare," Alexa replied mechanically.

"I thought you weren't having them any more," said Marcus, looking up as he was about to leave.

"Oh, for Christ's sake, I've had nightmares my whole life. Why's everyone so concerned today?" Alexa sighed.

"You have to let us help you," implored Bethany, her eyes full of concern. Alexa smiled softly, loving that she was around to worry about her. "We can make them stop."

"You don't know that telling me about my past will make them go away," replied Alexa firmly. "It could make them worse and I seriously can't risk that."

A knock at the door distracted Alexa from her growing frustration. That was her real fear – that knowing her past would make things harder to deal with and that once she opened the door to her past there would be no way of closing it again.

"I heard Bethany was free," smiled Sam, practically bouncing as he spoke. "I didn't want to come over last night – thought you guys would want time to catch up – but I had to come over this morning."

Alexa grabbed Sam's hand and dragged him inside. Sam rushed at Bethany, hugging her and swinging her around before placing her back on the ground and kissing her softly on the side of the head. Ben looked cautiously at Alexa, but she did not understand why. Sam released Bethany, though continued to stand next to her with his arm around her waist, and surveyed the room.

"What's going on? What's wrong?" Sam asked, taking a step back from Bethany.

"Nothing," said Alexa dismissively, moving forward and hugging Sam tight. "Thank you for being her friend."

"You're avoiding the question," said Sam, stepping out of the hug.

"I just had a nightmare, okay."

Sam looked around before turning to face Alexa. His eyes were full of concern and sorrow now too. "Bad?" he asked softly.

"Had worse. Just haven't had one for a while," Alexa shrugged. "They're just dreams, Sam."

"We want to tell her about her past," said Bethany, almost pleading for Sam's support. "It's the only way she's going to stop them."

Sam looked down back at Alexa, but she would not meet his eyes. She did not care whose side he was on, she was not going to let anyone tell her about the life she had long forgotten.

"If she doesn't want to know, it's her choice," said Sam, squeezing Alexa's hand. "You can't be sure it'll stop the nightmares. Let her do things her way."

The debate was over – for now. While Alexa was thankful for Sam's support, she was not sure it would last. Bethany had managed to get him on her side about most things while she had been in gaol, and Alexa could not imagine her influence waning now.

Ben and Sam stayed for breakfast. It helped to dilute Bethany's constant permission asking, but only Sam came right out and told her she did not have to ask permission to do things.

"Sorry," replied Bethany automatically.

"Don't apologise, Angel," said Alexa firmly. "You're just settling in. Ask anything. Permission. Directions. I don't care."

"I'd better get to work," coughed Ben, looking at his watch. "I'll call you tonight."

Alexa felt her stomach roll over. Ben rarely called her just to see how she was going.

"What time do you finish? You should come for dinner," smiled Bethany brightly. "Sam, you should come too! And Gran and Pop."

"Ah, why don't you keep it simple tonight," said Ben cautiously. "I think that's more than Alexa can organise in a day. She's supposed to go to university today."

"I'm not going to uni today," said Alexa emphatically. "But maybe we can do a celebratory lunch on Sunday – invite everyone."

"Yeah, let's do that, but can Ben still come to dinner tonight?"

"Of course. Anything you want," smiled Alexa.

Sam left with Ben, leaving Alexa and Bethany smiling stupidly at each other as they hugged and jumped together around the apartment.

"Okay, what do you want to do today?" asked Alexa. "I think we should get the basics – keys, mobile, bank account – and I can show you all the local places along the way. I'm sorry, but I have to go to uni tomorrow, but it won't be all day."

"Lex, this is perfect. All of it. It's more than I deserve."

"It's nothing close to what you deserve, but I'm going to make up for that. That money from the school, that's going to help look after us – help while you finish your apprenticeship. If I could've planned it, I think I would've agreed to go through all of that just to make sure I had the means to take care of you the way you deserve."

"Don't say that!" cried Bethany. "I don't ever want bad things to happen to you. Can't we just hope for only good things to happen to us from now on?"

"Absolutely!" smiled Alexa, leading Bethany happily out the door.

The day was perfect. It did not matter what they were doing, because they were together. Bethany was excited by everything. She spent ten minutes selecting a key ring for her new house keys. The purchase of a mobile phone had her in raptures. Even the trip to the supermarket had her bouncing down the aisles. She was like a kid in a candy store and Alexa loved watching her like this.

They had lunch down at the beach, though Bethany could not be convinced to go in the water. Up close, the waves suddenly appeared more threatening than inviting. Bethany was much more interested in shopping than swimming. And shopping was something Bethany had a natural aptitude for. Alexa said nothing as the number of items and cost rapidly increased. She had the means to grant Bethany this one extravagance and could not deny her after her liberty had been curtailed for so long.

When they arrived home, Alexa started dinner while Bethany examined her new belongings. There was so much it covered an entire lounge. "How's this one look?" asked Bethany, walking out to the lounge room in a new outfit just as Marcus walked into the apartment. "You like it, Marcus?"

"Um, what am I liking?" he asked, looking confusedly between Bethany and Alexa.

"Bethy's new clothes," smiled Alexa.

"Look what else I got."

Bethany grabbed Marcus's hand and dragged him to the lounge to show him everything she had bought. Alexa could not help but smile at his genuinely perplexed look. There was just no way for him to understand how much she had told Bethany about him and how well Bethany felt like she knew him.

"So you shopped today," smiled Marcus, walking into the kitchen.

"She had fun. I can't ask for more than that," Alexa replied, turning to see his concerned face. Bethany danced into the kitchen before he could reply, opening the cupboard and rummaging for food. "You should probably ask Marc if you can eat that," said Alexa when Bethany pulled out a packet of chocolate biscuits.

"I thought it was all your stuff," replied Bethany edgily, quickly putting the food back in the cupboard.

"If it's junk food, then it's Marc's," explained Alexa smilingly.

"I don't mind if you eat it," said Marcus. "Seriously, it's fine."

"No, no. I'll just wait for dinner."

Bethany rushed from the kitchen and gathered her new purchases before retreating to the bedroom.

"I really don't care if you guys eat the biscuits. It's probably better for me that I don't eat them all myself."

"It's my fault," sighed Alexa. "I just wanted to show her what she should ask permission for and what she can just go for. It's just that food – we learned long ago not to eat food that wasn't ours."

"So that's why you keep asking me permission to eat the food I buy?" Alexa was not sure if it was a question or a statement, but nodded all the same, eliciting a soft smile from Marcus. "I'm going to get a basket with my name on it – and one for you and Bethany. If I don't put something in there, then it's fair game. You don't have to live in fear, not with me."

Bethany's first few days were not a smooth transition into living in the outside world. Just one day alone, back on the free streets that had always provided her with the heroin she desired, saw her cravings return full force. It left Bethany in a very agitated mood when Alexa returned home with Charlotte on Friday. The afternoon was very strained. Bethany spent most of her time in her room and refused to talk to Charlotte. Charlotte was anxious to leave, but Alexa and Marcus convinced her to stay, something that was helped by Ben's arrival. He managed to lift Bethany out of her mood enough to have to dinner with everyone, but it was clear she was not keen on being around people.

"Why don't you come and stay at my place tonight," said Ben when Bethany again snapped at something Charlotte said.

"But where'll she sleep?" questioned Alexa, her heart hammering frantically.

"In the spare room," replied Ben as if it were obvious.

"I'll go pack my stuff," said Bethany, rushing from the table.

Alexa could not respond. Ben had never even invited her over for a meal and now he was asking Bethany to stay the night. It made the isolation she had felt around them in the detention centre multiply a thousand-fold.

"Maybe I should go too," said Charlotte as soon as Bethany and Ben left.

"No," cried Alexa, her voice cracking. She did not want to be rejected again tonight. "Not unless you want to."

Knowing Charlotte would not want to stay, Alexa slumped on the lounge, pulling her knees into her chest. Charlotte immediately sat next to her, wrapping an arm around her shoulders. "I want to stay."

Alexa could not help it. Tears started leaking from her eyes, tracking down her cheeks. She had never imagined she could feel this empty with Bethany living with her.

"So what Friday night shenanigans are we getting up to?" asked Marcus with a bright smile as he sat down on the lounge. That the look on his face did not change when he saw Alexa's was a blessing.

"Aren't you going out tonight?" asked Charlotte.

"Nope," he replied with a casual shake of his head. It was a lie. Alexa had heard him talking earlier in the week about his plans, but she was not going to argue.

They quickly settled on a movie to watch, but it did not start for another hour. Charlotte decided that was the perfect amount of time to bake a cake and scurried to the kitchen. When Alexa offered to help, Marcus followed. There was nothing for them to do, so they just leaned against the bench and watched Charlotte cook. Marcus stood close, his side right next to Alexa's and his arm holding on to the bench behind her back. The warm comfort Marcus provided was so welcome that when they all sat down on the lounge, Alexa pulled Charlotte with her on to the lounge Marcus was sitting on. He did not pull away as her body leaned against his.

It was a better night than Alexa ever would have predicted. The only problem was the guilt she felt the next day. "I'm sorry about last night," she said to Marcus when they were alone the next morning.

"For what?" he asked, slightly stunned.

"For forcing myself on you," she whispered.

Marcus's face turned very serious for a few moments before he smiled broadly. "That was just three friends hanging out," he replied softly. "Nothing to apologise for."

Alexa wished they could have spent every night like that, but when anyone but Charlotte was around Marcus kept his distance. At Bethany's celebratory lunch he was so distant he looked out of place. Charlotte came by in the morning to help cook, but insisted on leaving before lunch. Not even Marcus's pleading for her to stay made a difference.

"It's for Bethany and what she wants," smiled Charlotte as she gathered her things. "I just wanted to help Alexa."

"You need to talk to Bethany about her," said Marcus as soon as Charlotte left.

"Yeah I know, but not this week. Give her a chance to settle in. It's overwhelming. You have no idea," replied Alexa, feeling like she was defending herself as much as Bethany.

"Who has no idea?" asked Bethany, waltzing into the room.

"Me," answered Marcus.

"That's okay. I'm sure we can fill you in. You're always helping us with the stuff we have no idea about," replied Bethany casually. She was in a good mood. "Where's Charlotte?"

"Gone home," said Marcus before Alexa could speak. "Wanted to make sure you had the day you wanted."

"What's that mean?" asked Bethany, clearly confused. "I don't care if she's here or not. She's Lex's project."

"Bethy! I told you not to call her that," cried Alexa much more harshly than she intended.

"Just a joke. Chill, Lexie. You stress too much."

Thankfully everyone started to arrive, saving them from that discussion. Everyone was in good spirits, wanting to make this the best day possible for Bethany. Even Marcus tried to hide his displeasure, but he had never been as forgiving when it came to Bethany. However, when Bethany was up early the next morning for the first day of her apprenticeship, Marcus smiled a warm greeting and wished her luck when she left. The impact on her mood was dramatic, and she smiled happily as Alexa travelled with her to work.

"You can leave me here," said Bethany in a shaky voice, a block from her building. "I know where to go from here."

"You'll be great," smiled Alexa, hugging Bethany tight. "Want me to meet you this afternoon? I can wait here."

"No. I can do this. I'll text you when I finish, let you know when I'm on my way home. I want to come home feeling like I've achieved something – even if it is only catching and bus and train by myself."

"You'll do great. And I'll make a nice dinner to celebrate."

"Can Ben come?"

"Yeah, sure, I'll let him know," Alexa replied, holding in her sigh.

It was the start of a very good week. Bethany loved her job. She loved carpentry and did not care about being given the jobs many of the other apprentices viewed as beneath them. It meant Bethany was in a good mood most evenings – good enough that her snide remarks Charlotte's way were somewhat minimal. Despite Alexa talking to Bethany about Charlotte, Bethany had still made no effort to have a conversation with Charlotte, and on Friday night Bethany packed as soon as she came home to spend the night at Ben's. Alexa was not impressed by the decision, but Ben was so happy when he came over to pick Bethany up that she could not say anything.

The following week was much worse. Bethany's good mood was gone as the cravings became more frequent and powerful. They knew it was all psychological. Bethany's body had been free of heroin long enough for the physical addiction to have dissolved. What was left was Bethany's habits and memories of her former life, much of which involved heroin. For Alexa, Bethany's bad moods were almost a blessing; they told her Bethany was fighting the cravings, not giving in. However, she was still fearful of Bethany relapsing, making her overprotective, always watching the clock whenever Bethany was due home. Bethany always let her know when she was running late. They were good signs, but not everyone was able to appreciate them.

Marcus held his tongue, but the looks and the shakes of his head were enough for Alexa to know what he was thinking. He became protective of Charlotte, defending her when Bethany said something smart. It left the apartment in a very uneasy state most days and Alexa wished she could fix it. "She's trying, you know," she said, while Marcus was making breakfast. "It's not easy for us. We've never known what a normal life is."

Marcus's eyes flicked towards the bathroom where Bethany was showering. Bethany had been particularly dismissive of Charlotte the afternoon before and Marcus had not been able to keep his thoughts to himself. When Charlotte went home, he had gone out; a pattern that had been getting horribly familiar.

"You're good at making it look easier than it is," he shrugged.

"Bethany wears her emotions a bit more than me," said Alexa with a half-smile, glad Marcus realised she still found living terribly difficult too. "The problem is she doesn't always wear the ones she's feeling. Most of the time when she's angry, she's really just scared."

"I just want to give you guys space. You don't need me around making things more difficult, though I did last night, I know."

"But you leave when it's just us around. I want you to get to know her," said Alexa, trying to keep the desperation from her voice.

"I will. I promise," Marcus nodded solemnly. "Just don't push it. Let her find her feet. I'm not going anywhere."

Alexa wished she could have hugged Marcus. If she had been asked to, she could not have crafted a better answer. It made it that much easier to bear Bethany's silent exit and grumpy return home.

Yet still, in the middle of all her struggles, Bethany was not just a walking bad mood. There were moments of pure delight, nearly always associated with Bethany experiencing something new, and at night no craving or mood could keep Bethany and Alexa from curling up together. Those nights were what made everything else bearable. They were the one reassurance Alexa had that Bethany would not be taken away from her and would still be there when she woke in the morning. It made Bethany's continued decision to stay with Ben on Friday nights that much more distressing.

Charlotte's solution was not acceptable to Alexa. She refused to have people pushed out of her life. And with Charlotte remaining more akin to a part of herself than a friend, Alexa could not possibly conceive how she could ask her to leave. "It's the best solution for everyone," argued Charlotte as they washed the dishes.

"It's the best for no one. Besides, it has nothing to do with you," replied Alexa.

"But she's your sister. She shouldn't be forced out of here because of me."

"She isn't. She likes spending time with Ben. They have something special," Alexa said, her stomach twisting at the truth of the statement. "Believe me, she's got nothing against you. She's just trying to work out her own life. We both know how hard that can be."

"Okay, I'm out of here," said Bethany in a gruff voice.

"Hey, Bethy, wait a sec. I need to talk to you," said Alexa, pulling Bethany back into their bedroom. "Charlotte thinks you don't like her and that you stay at Ben's because you're not happy that she's here. Could you talk to her before you go and let her know it's not true?"

"Who gives a shit if she thinks I'm leaving because of her? She ain't that important I'd change my life for her," replied Bethany in a loud and annoyed voice. "She's your project, not mine. I don't give a shit how she feels. I've got enough trouble dealing with how I feel."

Alexa held Bethany's arms as she closed her eyes and took a deep breath. It did none of them any good to react to Bethany's moods. She knew Bethany could almost taste heroin as if it was something in the air and her psychological craving for it was almost as overwhelming as her body's need for oxygen. "Let me call Ben. He can come pick you up," Alexa said soothingly, rubbing Bethany's shoulder.

"I can get there myself. I don't need a fucking chaperone," spat Bethany, brushing Alexa aside and slamming the front door.

"See, I shouldn't be here. I'm not family," cried Charlotte, as she stood in between the kitchen and lounge room on the verge of tears.

The hurt and vulnerability in Charlotte's voice made Alexa wonder if Bethany was the only thing upsetting her. Charlotte had tolerated Bethany and her moods admirably up until now, often joking that Bethany's bad moods were better than Carla's dislike of her.

"Just let me give Ben a call and then we'll talk, okay," said Alexa.

As soon as she was off the phone, Alexa sat down with Charlotte on the balcony. However, that slight delay was all Charlotte needed to recompose herself and reassure Alexa, albeit unsuccessfully, there was nothing else wrong and she was just concerned about coming between her and Bethany. It was not a situation Alexa knew how to push further. When she had shut down conversations, half the time she had wanted the other person to force her to confess, but just as often she had wanted them to leave her alone.

Charlotte was saved further discussion by the tearful return of Bethany with Ben, but it was not the apology Alexa had been looking for. She wanted Bethany to make things up to Charlotte, not her. When it came to Bethany, Alexa did not need apologies, but she got them anyway. "I'm sorry," cried Bethany into her shoulder. "I just get so frustrated at everything. More so because you're so good to me. I don't deserve it."

"Yes, you do," replied Alexa emphatically. "There's nothing you don't deserve from me. We knew it wouldn't be easy, but you're doing so well and I'm so, so proud of you. I know I ask a lot. I just want you to experience all the good things I've got in my life."

Bethany nodded in her shoulder as Ben stepped forward and stroked Bethany's hair tenderly. "If only you'd had this much patience when I was teaching you how to drive," he laughed.

Marcus watched from the balcony as Alexa scoffingly rejected Ben's claim, but knew Alexa was more tolerant of Bethany than anyone could be. As much as he could understand the difficulties Bethany faced, her constant mood swings and attitude to Charlotte infuriated him. He rarely reacted for Alexa's sake, but wondered if it would not be better for Bethany if someone just gave it to her straight.

Charlotte crept out on to the balcony as Ben, Bethany and Alexa sat talking on the lounge. She sat in the corner, tucked out of sight as much as possible. Marcus acknowledged her with a look, but said nothing. It was nice knowing how to deal with Charlotte, feeling like he had finally learnt from all the mistakes he had made with Alexa.

"Charlotte? You out here?" asked Bethany. Marcus pointed her gaze in the right direction, but did not move. He was not going to let Bethany tear strips off Charlotte if she accidently said the wrong thing. "I'm sorry I've made you feel uncomfortable," said Bethany, her voice quiet and remorseful as she sat down next to Charlotte.

"It's your house. I'm the one that doesn't deserve to be here," said Charlotte, her eyes downcast. Charlotte got up to leave, but Bethany grabbed her by the arm and pulled her hastily back into her chair.

"It's not true. I'm glad you're here, I am," said Bethany solemnly. "I just – I have to worry about myself right now and can't take much interest in you. It's not personal. I'm being a pain in the arse, I know it, but I'm just trying to survive. It's not you."

"Does Alexa really think of me as a project?" asked Charlotte.

"No," answered Bethany with a smile. "She thinks of you as her sister. And you are. You're like this younger version of her. You guys are so similar it's kinda creepy. It's just I thought – in the beginning – she was neglecting her own life by concentrating on yours. It's not true. You've helped her face up to things and been there for her."

"Do you hate me being around?"

"No, I actually quite like you," smiled Bethany, and Marcus could see she was telling the truth. Her mixture of sweetness and selfishness was strangely endearing when she was being sweet. "I know I've been a bit mean to you, but it's hard not to be jealous sometimes. You guys are so similar and get along so well. I feel left out."

"But you're everything to Alexa," said Charlotte, clearly astounded by Bethany's claim. "No one could be closer to her than you. You're the reason for everything she does. I'm nothing to that."

"Yeah, maybe," replied Bethany, though Marcus could see that she was reassured by Charlotte's words and could not imagine why she ever needed to hear them. "I wish I could be close to you the way Lex is. I want to be. I know you and Lex think it's cos I've got something against you. I just have to be selfish for a while. I don't want to go back to using drugs. I don't want to let Lex down, but it's hard – harder than I thought."

"It's just that Alexa told me so much about you and I was really looking forward to getting to know you," said Charlotte in a fragile voice. "I hoped maybe you'd like me as much as she did and I could feel like I belonged, even if it was all pretend."

"What do you mean pretend?" asked Bethany.

"I know how she feels, you know, trying to make a family out of nothing. Most of the time it's okay, but when it's not your heart just breaks knowing it's not really real – that it never will be."

Bethany turned to Marcus at this comment, clearly hoping he understood, but he could make no sense of it either. He was sure Alexa would have known what Charlotte meant. It seemed like Alexa was the one person who understood them all.

***

The air became thick and hard to breathe. Alexa started from her sleep, gasping for breath, her heart pounding against her ribs. It took a moment for her to realise she was safe in bed. Since Bethany's return, her nightmares had become more frequent and much harder to stop. The only consolation was that Bethany had not woken this time. The frequency of her nightmares had become a major focus of discussion between them, as it became harder for Alexa to deny how often she was having them. Bethany was still convinced all she needed to stop them was the story of their childhood, but that was one thing Alexa would not be swayed on.

In the hours she spent working with Peter, which she had still told no one about, she had dared to ask a few more questions about their childhood interactions. He always answered her questions, but very carefully, warning her when they were reaching territory her mind had chosen to forget. That Peter also felt it was up to her what she found out only strengthen her resolve to not have the truth forced upon her. Nothing she had learned so far had made her want to know much more. It usually stopped her questioning in its tracks.

Turning to the clock, Alexa realised there was no point trying to get back to sleep. Bethany's alarm would be waking her soon enough, and if she got up now she might be able to fit in a swim at the beach and some study before uni.

"Can't sleep either?" asked Marcus from the kitchen, as she crept her way to the bathroom.

"Nope," Alexa sighed.

"Nightmare?"

"Uh huh. What's your excuse?"

"No excuse, just restless. You all right?" Marcus asked, as he sat down at the table with his breakfast.

"Yeah, just a dream. I can handle it," Alexa replied, sitting across the table so she could let her eyes rove innocently over his naked chest.

She made no secret of checking him out and liked that he let her. She was not prepared to return the favour, but did like the glint in his eyes when he saw the necklace he bought her sitting around her neck. It meant she constantly ensured it was visible, even when he was not around. It was the part of him she got to always keep with her, and she often wished she had an excuse to give him a similar gift.

"Listen, I have a few things I wanted to talk to you about," said Marcus, his slight smile turning into a grimace. "The first is that Lucy's going to stay over tonight. I hope you don't mind. Lucy wants to spend more nights together, but apparently her flatmate has taken issue with me staying there so often, so I need to share the load."

"I never said she couldn't stay," replied Alexa, feeling her stomach roll over. She had never said it, but she had hoped Marcus would see it that way, and up until now he had. He had never had a guest over.

"I know, but it's not fair on you to just bring people over without notice. I also thought I should tell you I was going to start looking for another place. I'm out of debt now and you and Bethany need your space. You can't keep sharing that room."

"But you said you'd stay."

"I know," smiled Marcus. "But I hate thinking I'm inconveniencing you. You've done so much for me. I've even managed to get some savings back – all because of you. Don't let me outstay my welcome."

"Don't worry about looking for another place," said Alexa, deciding against telling Marcus that he would never be unwelcome. "I haven't told Bethy about the money yet," said added in a low voice, not wanting her to find out by accident. "I mean, she knows about the settlement, but she thinks I have less than I do. I need her to settle in, find her place on the outside, but once she's ready we're going to start looking for a new place. I love this place, but it's really mine and we can't start our lives like that. We need to get something that's ours. You can come with us if you want. I'm sure Bethy will insist on a place big enough for all of us. She's always been like that. Or I don't mind if you want to keep living here. Same rent if you like."

Marcus smiled and nodded, unsure of which part of Alexa's offer he was agreeing to. Driving to work, he found himself imagining moving with her, forever following her just to stay close. Sometimes he could justify it as the perfect compromise. As long as they were not together, anything else was acceptable, but that was not true. Marcus was not sure about the depth of Alexa's feelings for him, but if they were even a fraction of what he felt for her then meeting Lucy would hurt her.

Introducing Lucy to Alexa was the very last thing Marcus wanted. He had never intended to inflict his love life on to her, but Lucy was loved by his family and friends and knew his weak points. When he continued to refuse Lucy's requests to see where he was now living, the fights had started. In the beginning, he had the advantage; Lucy was the reason he was living with Alexa, but he lost that advantage as Lucy discussed the situation with more and more people. If he had nothing to hide, then he would have no problem inviting Lucy over. That Marcus had managed to resist up until this point was likely the reason Lucy had continued to randomly cancel their dates at the last minute or not show up at all.

Had he been in any other circumstances, Marcus would have broken up with Lucy by now, but he truly understood Alexa's dilemma with Damien. Lucy's behaviour always came back to his actions in the eyes of his friends and family. If he broke up with Lucy, they would assume it was so he could be with Alexa, and perhaps it was. Without Lucy, there would be nothing to draw him away from Alexa. They could live together, be together and love each other, just as long as they were never intimate with each other. That thought was so alluring it took longer than it should have to see just how selfish it was.

Alexa deserved to be with someone. She deserved to fall in love, get married, have children. Marcus wished there was a way it could all be with him, but that was just fantasy. What he really needed was to find the strength to leave Alexa. It was the only way forward for both of them. With Alexa around, he found it difficult to truly commit himself to Lucy and love her the way he told her he did. He was not sure Alexa faced the same romantic struggles. Part of him hoped she did, but the rational part knew that was exactly why he had to leave her sooner rather than later.

Chapter Sixteen

THE APARTMENT WAS full of nervous tension. Although Alexa tried to convince herself she was calm, she could not sit still and found herself tidying every part of the apartment, just for something to do. In all the years she and Marcus had known each other, she had never seen him with another woman. He had been engaged while she was at high school, but from before she had found out he had feelings for her, she had known his relationship was in trouble.

Back then, knowing Marcus was with another woman had not worried Alexa. She had not wanted to be with her teacher. Their love existed only in the abstract, and she had convinced herself she could be happy for him with someone else, just as long as she never had to see it. Now she was going to have to witness it up close.

"It's going to be okay," said Charlotte comfortingly.

Bethany nodded in agreement, but she looked tenser than Alexa felt. Charlotte noticed it too and continued to eye Bethany warily. It was clear the truce between them was still a little shaky.

"Or we could just go out. Then you won't have to meet her," said Bethany, bouncing anxiously. "That might be better. Gotta be better than this."

"No, I have to face up to it eventually," said Alexa, walking into the kitchen. She wanted Marcus in her life and that would only ever be possible if she could tolerate seeing him with his partner.

"Um, maybe if Bethany's going to stay and not go to Ben's, then perhaps I should go home," said Charlotte, ringing her hands as she looked between Bethany and Alexa.

"You can't leave," cried Bethany, jumping from the lounge and grabbing Charlotte's arm.

"You don't need me. I'll just be in the way. You're her sister. You're the one who should be here, not me."

"Char, I realise I've not been that nice to you, but what are you thinking, leaving me here?" asked Bethany, almost hyperventilating as she worked herself up into a panic.

"What do you mean? You're all Alexa needs," replied Charlotte, clearly bewildered by Bethany's reaction.

"Are you kidding?" cried Bethany. "Haven't you noticed my erratic moods? You're Little Lex. You have that freakish calm aura thing going on. You can't leave me here to face Lucy. I hate her. I'll ruin everything and you know it."

Charlotte's eyes were wide with confusion. Alexa had to smile. The way Bethany saw them was in complete contrast to the way they saw themselves.

"I'll beg," said Bethany seriously.

"You know you and Alexa do the same thing," said Charlotte, her voice still full of confused disbelief. "You both panic before there's anything to panic about."

"Ah, Lucy's going to be here soon and you're threatening to leave us to deal with her ourselves. There's everything to panic about, Char," countered Bethany, this time sarcastically.

"Okay, well you guys just need to relax. I mean, it's still early and she's not even going to be here for hours anyway."

"I can make us do that," smiled Bethany, suddenly inspired as she rushed across the room to the stereo before dashing into the kitchen and pulling Alexa back to the lounge room. "You remember this, right?"

Alexa smiled as Bethany twirled her around the room out of time with the music.

"This is how you relax?" shouted Charlotte over the music.

"Hell yeah," smiled Alexa. "Best thing in the world."

It really was, and with Bethany's infectious enthusiasm, it was hard to worry about anything but dancing. Bethany soon had Charlotte up with them in a cleared away section of the lounge room. Bethany wanted to teach them how to dance, after her quick evaluation told her their skills were lacking. Bethany had natural rhythm and movement. It did not matter what the song was, she could move her body in a way that was almost hypnotising. Alexa could only watch in admiration. While Bethany's moves flowed, she and Charlotte danced like dysfunctional robots.

"This is your problem, Lex," smiled Bethany, moving behind her and gripping her hips. "You need to loosen your hips more. See, look at Char. You've got good prospects for future happiness, girl."

"You have a sick mind," laughed Alexa, turning to wrestle Bethany as Charlotte blushed.

"I have to," smirked Bethany, pulling out of Alexa's grasp and dodging recapture. "I have no one to share my sick body with!"

"I hope we're all relaxed now," said Charlotte, collapsing on the lounge. "I'm stuffed."

"No way!" cried Bethany. "I'm going to teach you girls a dance tonight even if it kills you. C'mon, I'll teach you the Macarena."

"The what?" asked Charlotte, looking at Alexa as she was pulled off the lounge, but Alexa was as perplexed as Charlotte.

"You poor, sheltered children."

Bethany changed the music and started playing some horribly annoying song. Then she started dancing. The moves were simple and repetitive, but when Bethany danced them there was something truly beautiful about the way she moved. It was very different when Alexa and Charlotte joined in. They struggled to fit in any dancing between their laughing, but Bethany was determined. It was not enough for them to simply learn the moves. Bethany wanted complete immersion, release of their minds and bodies. Alexa felt like she would never get the irritating music out of her head, but after over half an hour she had to admit that she felt her body loosening. They were all smiling in the most carefree way, without a thought in the world besides the swirl of their hips when they jumped around to face the front door – and a snickering Marcus.

"Don't laugh at us," said Charlotte, reddening as she rushed to turn the music down.

"I thought Lucy was coming over," said Alexa, her heart pounding nervously. Marcus had been watching her when they turned and she could not help but wonder if he had been looking at her hips.

"Not til later, but please don't let that stop the little dance troupe you have going," he said, still trying to suppress a laugh.

"Well what music do you have to offer?" asked Bethany, pulling Marcus roughly but wholly unmenacingly to the stereo.

"Certainly nothing you can dance like that to," he responded in a slightly unsteady voice.

"I'm sure you're a closet Spice Girls fan just waiting to get out. Come on, hand over the collection."

Bethany leaned over Marcus as he pulled out his music collection. Alexa could see he was not very comfortable with her proximity, but Bethany had always been a very physical creature. She needed to be held and feel close to those around her. She was affectionate in a way Alexa had never been, and Alexa supposed it was why most people preferred Bethany over her.

"Hey, Lex, look. Mum's favourite album. You remember?" asked Bethany with feverish excitement.

"Yeah, I remember," smiled Alexa, hoping Bethany would not see the strain in it. "Why don't you put it on while I make dinner?"

Bethany smilingly complied and began to sing along to the music as Charlotte and Marcus followed Alexa into the kitchen.

"You okay?" asked Marcus.

"Yeah, I'm fine," smiled Alexa, her focus determinedly on dinner.

"What's with the music? Why the face?"

Alexa rolled her eyes. Sometimes she hated Marcus's observant nature. "She loves her, you know," replied Alexa with a determinedly casual shrug of her shoulders. "Nothing that's happened can shake it. She loves our mother and I can't."

"Why not?" asked Charlotte, while she started on the salad.

"You have to understand. Bethy was our angel. She was the only thing me and my mother had in common. We loved her and doted on her. To her, my mother was a good woman. Hell, even I think she was a pretty good mother to her."

"She was a heroin addict who allowed Beth to become addicted. That's not love," said Marcus harshly.

Alexa turned and shushed him before returning to the dinner preparations. "Bethy was in lots of pain. It hurts to withdraw. It could be really hard to resist her screams, and it wasn't like our mum was injecting her. Bethy never learned to use needles until she'd been on the streets a while."

"Yeah, mother of the year stuff, that," muttered Marcus.

"You don't understand, and I get that," said Alexa, turning to him and Charlotte. "But Bethy was loved. Who am I to take that away from her just because my mother didn't love me?"

"Does the music irritate you?" asked Charlotte kindly.

"No," smiled Alexa. "I quite like this CD. It was Bethy's favourite too. We listened to it a lot when we were young. I just don't always like being reminded that it was our mother's favourite – not in such a loving way. I don't share that emotion, but I can't take it from her."

Bethany spent the next hour pawing through Marcus's music, while Charlotte and Alexa cooked dinner. Music had been instrumental in diverting their attention from their troubles when they were young and since being released Bethany had become obsessed. Their music collection had expanded rapidly in the weeks since her release.

"Guys," said Marcus softly, instantly gaining the girls' attention. "This is Lucy, Lucy Ashton."

The soft rustling of a minute before shattered into deafening silence. Alexa looked Lucy up and down quickly, feeling slightly, and a little arrogantly, relieved. Lucy was as tall as Marcus with long thin legs, an impressive chest and short, stylish, almost-black hair. Her dress was impeccable and oozed money, but she looked uncomfortable and intimidated by the stares of three young girls. More than that, the sight of Marcus and Lucy together reassured Alexa that Marcus did not love Lucy the way he loved her.

"Hi," said Charlotte, the first one to find her voice as she stepped forward and waved her hand. "I'm Charlotte."

"Hi," replied Lucy with a slight raise of her eyebrows.

"This is Alexa," said Marcus, quickly taking up the introductions. "And that's Bethany."

"Hi," replied Alexa and Bethany in unison.

"Um, we were just about to have dinner. Did you want to join us?" asked Alexa pleasantly, though her voice shook.

"Sure," smiled Lucy. "You need some help?"

Alexa quickly dismissed Lucy's offer and pulled Bethany into the kitchen as Charlotte grabbed the CD sitting on the top of the pile in front of the stereo. From the moment Marcus had introduced them, Bethany's face had turned from defiant confidence to outright disgust.

"Hey, Marcus," asked Charlotte shakily, looking uneasily between him and the kitchen. "Who are these guys? I've never heard of them."

"That's my favourite CD of all time," replied Marcus with an unsure smile as he glanced over at Alexa and Bethany. "They were big when I was starting high school."

"Was I even born then?"

"Don't ask things like that. You make me feel old," smiled Marcus, taking the CD from Charlotte and putting it in the stereo.

"You know the deal with me and Marcus," hissed Alexa, as she and Bethany set the table. "There's no point getting angry at her because we can't be together. Marc and I can date other people."

"That's not why I'm angry. I've seen her – Lex, what's wrong?"

Alexa could not answer. Her body was shaking from the inside out. She could feel herself losing control of everything. The crashing sound told her she had dropped the dish of lasagne. Rushing to the bathroom, Alexa tried to expel the fear consuming her as she retched violently, but it was not hiding in her empty stomach. Shaking all over, her mind slowly started piecing together coherent thoughts. If she could stop the music, she could stop the threat. Walking unsteadily out of the bathroom, Alexa gripped the doorframe, hoping to any god that existed she could prevent anything happening to her and Bethany.

"Turn it off," cried Alexa, her voice distant and unrecognisable. Bethany turned immediately towards the stereo, but no one else moved. "Turn it off!"

Everyone's inaction frustrated Alexa. Did that not realise what was about to happen? Pushing off the wall with the little strength she had, she dashed across the room, angrily pushing buttons to dispel the CD. She could feel hands wrestling with hers as she tried to tear it from the CD player.

"Stop," cried Marcus.

Suddenly, another pair of hands roughly tore the CD out of her grasp. Alexa looked up in time to see Bethany slam the CD down on to her knee, breaking it in two. She did it twice more until it was nothing more than fractured mess.

"What the hell was that?" cried Marcus. "That was my favourite CD! You destroyed it."

Alexa felt the trance-like state fall from her body. She turned from the shattered CD to Marcus and saw the hurt that filled his eyes. There was nothing else to do. She turned and ran from the apartment.

"If I replace it," said Bethany, handing Marcus the pieces of plastic. "Then don't you ever play it near Lex again."

"You want me to go after her?" asked Charlotte quietly.

Bethany nodded, sighing softly, knowing Charlotte was the best person to face Alexa now. She had never imagined there would ever be anyone Alexa needed but her, but knew how ashamed Alexa would feel and it was better that someone who had no real understanding of their past stay with her. If she were with Alexa, there was little chance she could stay quiet on what she thought Alexa was reliving.

"What the hell happened?" asked Marcus.

"I don't know," sighed Bethany unevenly. "I've never seen it, but she's told me about it. Happened once with the Whites. Same thing – music made her feel like something really bad was going to happen. Just had to make the music stop."

"What music? This song? What?" gasped Marcus, holding out the fractured disc as though it was contaminated.

"I don't know. She didn't know the name of the other song. I don't know if it's the same one."

Bethany wished she did. Alexa had spent her entire life protecting her. She wished there was some way she could protect Alexa from the demons that continued to chase her.

"What's she think's going to happen?" asked Marcus softly. He looked like he might be sick, and Bethany suspected he was assuming something close to the truth.

"I don't know," sighed Bethany, closing her eyes. "Even Lex doesn't know. She doesn't remember back then. She doesn't ..."

"What about you? Does it happen to you?"

"No," she replied, surprised by the tender way Marcus asked that question, as though he actually cared.

"You know what she's remembering, don't you? You know what she's forgotten."

"I know what Ben's told me about my childhood," replied Bethany firmly, hating that she wanted Marcus to know the truth about them – hoping he would still like them once he did. "I don't know what Alexa remembers. I don't know what she feels. I'm not going to try and pretend I do and I'm not going to tell you all the things about our life Lex doesn't want to know. It's her life, not yours."

Marcus nodded and ruffled his hair in an agitated manner. "I didn't mean it like that," he replied, his voice full of anxious agitation as he looked around the near-empty apartment.

"I know," Bethany nodded, squeezing his hand softly, before catching the snide look on Lucy's face. "Look, it's probably better if you guys go out. Lex's going to be pretty embarrassed."

Bethany did not wait for Marcus's response before clearing the table. She was not going to sit down to dinner with just Marcus and Lucy under any circumstances and wanted them to take the hint and leave. The last thing Alexa needed when she returned was to be tortured with Lucy's sneering face.

As she placed the lasagne on the stove top, Bethany could feel her arms shaking. It was not fair that their lives could still be torn to shreds by something as simple as music. Bethany wished she knew what Alexa was remembering. She wanted to talk about the terrifying visions that flickered across her mind, but were never clear enough to place as real. Half a lifetime of heroin abuse had stolen many childhood memories, leaving her with mostly feelings and emotions rather than events. Even now she struggled to remember everything she needed.

Alexa was different. Whatever Alexa did not block out, she could remember as clear as day. The only problem was that Alexa was skilled at forgetting unwanted memories, and with no one around who knew their past to prompt her into remembering, it was more than just the early childhood years she had lost. Even the more recent past was just as likely to be wiped from Alexa's mind. Bethany had watched Sam recount a story once when they had all been together at the detention centre. Alexa never denied it was true, but it was clear she had no recollection of it, no matter how much Sam prompted. Now it seemed that the only remaining links to some of those memory black holes
262

were Alexa's nightmares and music.

What Ben had told Bethany about their childhood gave some explanation for what Alexa felt and feared, but she could never be sure that was what Alexa was remembering. Ben had only explained Alexa's dream and his place in their early lives, but the other images that tortured Bethany's mind were just as frightening. Bethany was aware Ben knew more about what had happened to them, but he was not comfortable divulging it while Alexa remained so unaware. It hardly mattered, Ben's knowledge of their lives stopped so long ago, and he would not be able to shed light on the things she could not quite remember and Alexa was determined to forget.

"The girl's insane," cried Lucy incredulously from Marcus's room.

"Keep your voice down! And don't say that," hissed Marcus, closing his bedroom door.

Bethany crept across the lounge room and stood with her ear to the edge of the door. Lucy's opinion meant nothing. It was Marcus's she cared about. If he could not love Alexa through this then he would never be good enough for her.

"They smashed your CD because the girl's a fruit loop. Is she always like that? Why'd you want to live with that kind of insanity?"

"I didn't, remember? I wanted to live with you," spat Marcus angrily. "The reason I'm here is because you left me in the lurch."

"Well you're not exactly in the lurch any more."

"No, but I moved twice in two weeks because of you. I'm not looking to move again. I'm happy here."

"Happy with her? I couldn't believe it when I saw her. Why would you've risked your career and reputation for her? I expected something a lot more impressive, not some Plain Jane little girl. Or is that what you look for in a girl? That why you tell me not to bother getting dressed up and wear make-up?"

There was only silence in response to Lucy's jibing questions.

"Fine, I see she's still a sensitive topic. We won't discuss your preference for young girls," said Lucy in an unkind voice. "Why don't we discuss why you're so happy living with the drug-addict sister and the little lost girl from down the street."

"You're incredible. Like you're so perfect," snapped Marcus.

"I never said that. I just don't understand what you see in her or why you're still here when you're financially secure again."

"No, you wouldn't. Let's just get going, okay."

Bethany tried to move out of the way, but it was obvious she had been eavesdropping. Lucy sneered at her, but it was Marcus she was concerned about. She knew he disliked her, so was surprised when he spoke so tenderly. "You all right?" he asked, gently rubbing her arm.

"Yeah," replied Bethany.

Marcus nodded, smiling softly at her before marching out of the apartment, Lucy close behind. Bethany watched him leave, her heart twisting slightly. Although she had always felt a strong obligation to like Marcus, she had never interacted with him in a way that allowed her to form any attachment to him beyond that of Alexa's saviour. However, that second of affection, just a fraction of what he felt for Alexa, was enough to melt her heart and she could only wish a man would one day love her half as much.

Charlotte returned with Alexa an hour after Marcus and Lucy left. Alexa looked like a shattered shell. Bethany went to hug her, but Alexa held back, stroking her face as she shook her head. Alexa walked straight to their bedroom and closed the door.

"I should probably go," said Charlotte, standing awkwardly near the front door.

"Why?" asked Bethany.

"Alexa has gone to bed and …"

"I thought I already went through all this."

"But you just wanted me around for Alexa while Lucy was here. They're gone now, right?"

"But I thought you wanted to get to know me," replied Bethany with a smile, trying to hide her fears that Charlotte did not want to be friends with her.

"I did – I do, I just …"

"I want to get to know you too," said Bethany sincerely. "Thing is, if you're going to be Lex's sister, then you're going to be mine too. That's just how it works with us."

"But I thought you'd want to be with Alexa," said Charlotte, taking a tentative step forward.

"Lex wants to be by herself. She won't talk to anyone – not even me – tonight. We can be there for her in the morning. There's plenty of space for you. And I'm feeling pretty good tonight," Bethany added with a smile. "It's a rare thing at the moment so you shouldn't pass it up. I have more bad days than good."

Charlotte smiled and headed to the kitchen. She dished them up dinner and heated it in the microwave. Even though Charlotte was younger than Bethany, Bethany could not help but notice that she had the same caring nature as Alexa. Charlotte looked after her the same way Alexa did, but the similarities ran deeper than that, and Bethany found herself liking Charlotte's company. It made her smile at the resistance she had put up to Alexa's suggestions that she just needed to get to know Charlotte. And without the history and guilt that tainted her relationship with Alexa, in many ways Bethany found she could enjoy Charlotte's company more easily than Alexa's.

Laughter drifted into the bedroom where Alexa was curled up on the bed. It was ironic how the things she wished for could come back and strike painfully at her. All she had wanted was for Charlotte and Bethany to get along together, but she had never imagined she would be so excluded from that moment.

The pain wracking Alexa's body was beyond physical. It was so deep she was not sure any number of cuts to her skin could draw it out. She just wished it would go away. She did not want to deal with her past. She did not want to remember the things that tormented her childhood. She wanted to forget and never be linked to that girl again.

Alexa wrapped her arms around her body to keep her hands from more destructive actions. Part of her wanted to grab Bethany and fulfil their pact, but Bethany was doing so well that it would be unfair to tear her away from her future because of her weakness.

Counting the minutes, just to make sure they were passing, Alexa was hatefully unsurprised by the way the time dragged on. It felt like a day had passed by the time Bethany and Charlotte crept into the room just after eleven. Alexa closed her eyes and pretended to be asleep, but she did not fool them. Charlotte squeezed her hand before moving to the trundle bed, while Bethany slipped into the bed and curled up behind Alexa. Charlotte's breathing soon became soft and rhythmic. Bethany took longer to fall asleep as she continued to hold Alexa tight, but she too was soon in a state of peaceful slumber. Alexa continued to watch the clock, waiting for her own release.

The soft click of the front door not long before midnight signalled Marcus's return. Alexa hoped he was alone, but Lucy's snide voice streaked through the apartment. Marcus may have promised her his heart, but after tonight she was sure he was glad he never promised anything more. She was a wreck, a pathetic excuse for a person and in no lifetime or any universe was she good enough for a man like Marcus. With each painful second, Alexa felt her self-worth crumble. She tried to imagine how she would feel when she woke in the morning, before realising that she was awake and it was morning. This torturous night was not going to be made any better by lying in bed watching the minutes tick by.

"Can't sleep?" whispered a sad voice, making Alexa jump.

"You scared me," she said, sitting on the lounge to face Marcus.

"Sorry," he replied softly, reaching out and taking her hand.

"You can't sleep either?" asked Alexa. Marcus shook his head. "I'm sorry. I didn't mean to ruin your stuff."

"Shh, I don't care about that. You're the most important – I don't want to own anything that hurts you."

"I don't want to be like this any more," Alexa said, tears spilling from her eyes as her pain boiled over.

With his free hand, Marcus wiped the tears from her cheeks and pulled her head forward into the crook of his neck. The way he held her was so comforting. It felt so safe, knowing he would never take advantage of her.

"I'll make us some tea," said Alexa, composing herself as she pulled out of Marcus's hug.

She untwisted her legs to stand, but felt herself arrested by his hand suddenly squeezing hers. His thumb looped in under her palm as he grasped her hand lovingly. "Let's go for hot chocolate," he said in a sad, tender voice as he pulled her to her feet.

"But I don't make it nice – not like Charlotte."

"I like your way," he replied as they stood facing each other with barely a foot between them.

Marcus's hand slip from Alexa's as she walked to the kitchen. He followed silently, watching as she filled the kettle and prepared their mugs. Her body quickly filled again with heavy desperation. She was not sure she had the strength to keep doing this. Marcus moved forward, standing in front of her, his eyes full of concern, as though he knew exactly what she was thinking.

"Are you all right?" he asked, taking her cheek in his hand and tilting her face up to his.

"No," she breathed, tears burning in her eyes as she shook her head.

Marcus's fingers gripped her cheek, but he did not move. In his eyes, Alexa could see that his heart was still hers. It was a comforting revelation, yet though she wanted to throw herself into his arms, she remained glued to the spot. They stood there, like frozen sculptures, just staring into each other's sad eyes. The kettle clicked, but neither noticed. They could have stayed there forever, but —

"Marc?"

Marcus's hand fell limply from Alexa's face as his eyes closed slowly. He looked pained. "Yeah," he replied grimly.

"What are you doing?" asked Lucy, though Alexa was sure it was a rhetorical question.

"Couldn't sleep. We were just making hot chocolates."

"Are you coming back to bed?"

Marcus nodded, his eyes still shut. They did not open again until he turned away. Alexa re-boiled the kettle and made her hot chocolate, then curled herself up on the lounge, waiting for the night to pass.

The apartment quickly became a music-free zone, with no one wanting a repeat of Alexa's breakdown, especially since no one, least of all Alexa, knew what music would induce a panic attack. However, that horrid night had done more than just destroy Alexa's enjoyment of music. It also triggered something in her subconscious, turning her nightmares into a nightly occurrence, tearing her from her sleep as she gasped for air; the fearsome shadow continuing to pursue her, rather than Bethany as it always had in the past. Despite this, Alexa was determined not to let her nightmare control her, unwilling to lose more sleep to her past.

"More nightmares?" asked Marcus at breakfast. Alexa nodded as she closed her eyes. She was desperately tired after weeks of broken sleep. "Then I'm probably not going to make your day any better by telling you that Lucy was planning on staying here tonight."

Alexa let her head fall on to her arms on the table. She was sure if she was not so tired, she would not care so much, but Lucy was not making for domestic harmony.

"You want me to tell her she can't stay?" asked Marcus seriously.

"No," murmured Alexa, moving her mouth away from her arm. She did not want to give Marcus any reason to stay away. "She's not really a problem when she's sleeping," she smiled tiredly.

"Her and Beth, yeah, I know."

"She doesn't like any of us. She thinks she's soo much better. Only child? Cushy life?"

"All of the above," replied Marcus flatly. Alexa rolled her eyes. "I can tell her she can't come by any more."

"It's your home too. She can stay. We'll survive."

Marcus watched Alexa close her eyes as the smile slid from her face. If Lucy had not caught them in the kitchen they would not be in this situation. He had kept Lucy from Alexa's apartment for as long as he could with excuses that varied enough to be continuously reused.

That one night changed everything. Lucy told Brandon what she saw and somehow that news made its way back to his family. Now Marcus was under intense pressure to move out, even move in with his parents, but he was resisting. Alexa's apartment was perfectly situated for almost all aspects of his life. The low rent allowed him to replenish his long-neglected savings account, and it was where Alexa was. He found very few enticements to leave, despite the warnings that staying with Alexa was risking his career and reputation.

However, with Marcus intent on staying, Lucy was determined to spend as much time with him as possible. Within weeks of their first introduction, Lucy was suddenly staying at least three times a week. Often, she would turn up without invitation, surprising Marcus as much as everyone else. Initially, Bethany stayed when Lucy arrived, but they clashed terribly. The mere presence of Lucy seemed to be enough to work Bethany up into a rage and Alexa could not coax her into giving an explanation. It did not take long for Bethany to simply pack a bag at the suggestion of Lucy's arrival and head to Ben's. On the nights Ben was at work, Bethany would abscond to any house she could, rotating between Maria's and Sam's.

The only positive to come out of the situation was the complete dissolving of Bethany's dislike of Charlotte. Charlotte had a way with Bethany that even Alexa did not have, and Marcus suspected it had to do with Bethany not feeling an intense need to protect Charlotte the way she did Alexa. Seeing the nicer side of Bethany made her much more likable, and Bethany seemed intent on making him like her. Even on the days she was clearly struggling, Bethany tried to make a good impression with him. She was also very physically affectionate. He and Alexa had barely hugged, yet Bethany hugged him at least once a day. Sometimes it was out of her own excitement, sometimes because he had done something simple for her, but most of the time there was no obvious reason.

If Bethany could have extended even a fraction of that welcoming spirit to Lucy then things might never have become so confrontational, although Marcus had to admit it was not all Bethany's fault. Lucy was just as antagonistic. Nothing Marcus said made a difference. Lucy did not care if she caused problems. When he began ensuring they were out of the apartment for all but sleeping, Lucy started her surprise visits.

Looking back, Marcus was sure these surprise visits set Bethany off more than the planned ones, and were what had contributed to her fleeing the house. If it was just Bethany it affected, Marcus was not sure he would care, but the strain Bethany's absences put on Alexa was excruciating. Alexa was never truly settled when she and Bethany were apart. Although she tried to hide it, it was clear she still worried about the temptations the outside world provided. The palpable relief on Alexa's face every time Bethany returned home was as endearing as it was heartbreaking. However, Marcus also noticed that Alexa's stress levels varied depending on who Bethany was with. If Bethany went to Maria's, Alexa was almost thankful for the opportunity for them to bond. She was slightly concerned if Bethany went out with Sam, not quite trusting that he knew how to keep her out of trouble. It was when Bethany stayed with Ben that Alexa really started to worry.

Though they were always pleasant and courteous to each other, the gulf between Alexa and Ben was evident. Marcus could not help but blame Ben for much of it. Alexa might push people away out of fear, but he suspected she did that to weed out those who were not prepared to stick around. To date, Ben was not quite failing that test, but he was definitely not the father he professed he wanted to be. Ben's obvious preference for Bethany was painful to watch, worse because he had no idea of the hurt he was inflicting. Being around to support Alexa gave Marcus some justification for staying, despite also knowing he was the reason why the household was in so much turmoil. The problem was that while Alexa not only refused to ask him to leave, but continued to plead for him to stay, he did not have the strength to leave.

***

"Hi, Alexa. I'm very glad you were able to come in today. I have some important, but tedious work I need you to do," smiled Peter as Alexa walked into his office. "You keen on an early lunch first?"

Alexa looked out the window. It was pouring rain and not at all conducive to the sandwich in the park lunch that had become their tradition. "You know somewhere good inside?" she asked tentatively.

"I think I know just the place," smiled Peter.

"Will I make a scene when I see the prices?"

She had done that once. Peter had taken her to a restaurant so ridiculously priced that she felt sick with the idea of eating. In the end Peter had no choice but to leave without ordering. That was when they found the sandwich shop. It was still expensive by Alexa's standards, but the quality and quantity helped make up for that.

"I've learned that lesson well," smiled Peter. "Come on, trust me."

Peter did not disappoint, taking her to a small noodle house and introducing her to Vietnamese food. "So how's uni going?" asked Peter as they made their way back to the office.

"Good. Better than last year. Kinda know what's expected of me, so I can focus my study better. Got a good group of friends. It's nice."

"No problems with Damien?"

"Not since I took out the AVO," replied Alexa, shaking her head. "Wish it never to came to that though."

"And Beth?"

Alexa took a deep breath. Things were going well, but she had had a sick feeling in her stomach all day that she could not explain or shake. She did not tell Peter about that. It was not that she thought he would be dismissive, quite the opposite, but Bethany had not given her a single reason to distrust her and all her paranoia to date had been a complete waste of time and energy.

"I'm glad things are going so well," smiled Peter, moving her in front of several large stacks of paper. "But just remember, bad days, weeks or even months don't mean anything is failing. They're part of life, and even though you're not expecting things to be perfect, don't get too concerned when they go well below that and hit disastrous. Together, we can pull things back from anywhere, okay."

Alexa nodded, wondering if Peter was psychic or if she had given away her concerns in her answers. Thankfully he did not let her dwell too much on the answer, giving her instructions for what he needed her to do. Mountains of shredding. Followed by helping other staff move boxes. Then laying out afternoon tea for the office.

"You sticking around?" asked Peter, grabbing a coffee and a piece of cake and heading back to his office.

"Not unless you need me. Charlotte'll be over soon. I don't want to be too late. They'll ask questions otherwise," Alexa shrugged, liking that Peter did not mind that she kept her employment a secret.

"Talking about questions, you've stopped asking them," noted Peter casually. "Everything okay?"

"Nightmares are back," confessed Alexa, slouching into the chair in front of Peter's desk. "I've had about enough of my past. I'm just over it. I don't want to deal with it any more."

"Okay."

Alexa had the feeling there was more to Peter's question than plain curiosity. However, he said nothing else about it and let her go with a query about her availability for a few extra hours next week.

It was a relief to arrive home. Charlotte was already there, preparing dinner. Alexa had never taken the key off her after she had moved back in with her family, but Charlotte had been reluctant to use it until Damien had left the scene.

"Hey, Char, smells good. Is Bethy home yet?" Alexa called, as she dumped her bag in her bedroom.

"No, but she's sometimes late on Fridays – works drinks," replied Charlotte.

Alexa looked at her watch. It was not yet late, but she could still not shake the sick feeling in her stomach. She tried to ignore it by helping Charlotte with dinner, but that only made her more aware of the time passing and the fact that Bethany was still not home.

"Give her a call," said Charlotte. "Ask if she likes roast beetroot."

"What?"

"I'm cooking beetroot," answered Charlotte, holding up a leftover one. "We bought them last week, remember. Just call and ask if she'll eat them or if we should make some other vegetables for her."

Alexa hugged Charlotte before grabbing her phone. Bethany would see through it, but it was a legitimate question. The phone rang, and rang. Bethany did not answer. Alexa rang again, but the outcome did not change. And now it was late. If Bethany was coming straight from work she would have been home an hour ago.

"Marc, is Lucy coming over today?" Alexa called out, checking her watch again to make sure she was not reading it wrong.

"No," replied Marcus, walking out of his room, dressed to go out. "I'm going out with the boys tonight. Why?"

"Did Lucy hint that she'd be here tonight?" continued Alexa, sure Lucy was behind Bethany's absence.

"No," he answered before looking at the clock. "It's Friday. Beth's probably over at Ben's. Maybe she just decided to go straight there."

"No, he's working tonight." Alexa knew Marcus could not have known that, but hated that he would think she would get this worked up if Bethany was just at Ben's place.

"Then what about Sam or Maria? You know she's been spending a lot of time with them lately. Don't panic. Call around. I'm sure she's just running late."

Marcus offered to help make the calls, but Alexa dismissed him with an agitated wave. She tried Ben first. He was at work and had not heard from Bethany all day. Then she tried Sam and Maria, calling Bethany's mobile in between, but no one had heard from Bethany. No one was expecting her and none of them could get in touch with her.

"Want me to stay?" asked Marcus, as Alexa paced the lounge room like a caged lion.

"What can you do here?" asked Alexa bitterly.

"I can support you," Marcus replied earnestly.

Alexa shot him a scathing look, but managed to hold on to the unkind words swirling in her mouth. Marcus's calm face surprised her. He did not scold her or even roll his eyes. When he was about to leave, he stood behind her, his hands firmly on her shoulders as he spoke softly in her ear. "It'll be okay, even if the worst's happened. Remember, there's always more than one solution to any problem and I'll be here to help you find one if you don't have one."

Everyone told Alexa her patience with Bethany was beyond comprehension, but Alexa thought Marcus's support of her was much more incredible. The way he was always there for her no matter what she put him through made her sometimes wish for a world without Bethany – a world with no ties, one she could walk away from and be with Marcus without any repercussions. Alexa had to quickly shut down that fantasy. She could not leave Bethany. Her life was tied to Bethany. This was the life she would walk away from if she had to, and as the time ticked by, she tried to find the resolve to return to the life she hated so much.

Sam and Maria soon arrived. Maria and Charlotte laid dinner out on the table, but Alexa could not eat. Her stomach was already tied in knots, knowing what Bethany was doing and why she was not home. With everyone else distracted, Alexa decided she had to find Bethany herself.

"No, no, Alexa, you have to stay," breathed Sam in her ear as he restrained her at the front door. "Ben needs you to stay here in case she comes home. He's looking for her. He'll find her."

Alexa struggled against Sam, but his grip was too strong and she had no choice but to go with him back to the lounge room. He sat with her and watched her every move. It was infuriating. Their ignorance was astounding. Though they wished to live in fanciful hope, she knew there was no other reason for Bethany's absence than heroin.

"You have to let Ben get her out of that place. Don't let yourself be dragged back down into it," said Maria softly.

It was a nice sentiment, but that place was where she had come from, where Alexa hated to admit she belonged to. If anyone was going to follow Bethany there, it should be her and it made her determined to leave, but every time she tried Sam was waiting for her.

"You can't stop me," Alexa cried, pushing Sam off her.

"Ben wants you here when she comes home," puffed Sam, panting as he tried to restrain her.

"She's not coming home!" cried Alexa, wondering how Sam could be so naïve. "She's in a gutter somewhere high as a fucking kite. She's not coming home unless I bring her home."

"Ben will find her. You need to stay here."

"I will find her! Now let me go. Why are you even stopping me? What do you care?"

"You're not the only one who cares about Beth," cried Sam passionately, pushing Alexa towards the lounge room. "You're not the only one who's hurting. She's let us all down, but most of all herself, so don't dare tell me I don't care. I was at that prison almost as much as you."

"I just need to find her. I need her not to die," gasped Alexa, Sam's anger robbing her of her own. Sam pulled her into his chest and held her tight, constantly reassuring her it would work out, but she could not place her faith in ignorant naivety the way he could.

Realising her only chance to escape would be by stealth, Alexa sat herself quietly on the lounge, trying to look compliant. Charlotte had spent most of the night on the balcony and after half an hour, Alexa joined her. "You need a decoy?" asked Charlotte immediately. If the situation had not been so horrible, Alexa would have laughed at how well Charlotte understood her. "I'm not feeling very creative, but when you see your chance, I'll keep them off your tail for as long as I can."

"I won't need long," replied Alexa in a gravelly voice.

Charlotte nodded and walked inside. Alexa stayed for a moment, wishing she had spent time examining escape routes. She just never imagined being trapped in her own apartment.

There were few opportunities for escape. Although Charlotte tried, Sam was not interested in engaging with her. He would not turn his gaze from Alexa, and the more Charlotte attempted to interact with him, the more suspicious he became.

Then Marcus came home.

One look was all it took for him to know she wanted out. Alexa could see the resolution building in his eyes and knew it was useless. There was no way she could get past him and Sam.

"I'll go with you," said Marcus softly, sitting next to her as she waited uselessly on the balcony.

"What?"

"As soon as everyone turns their backs, you'll be gone. Nothing I say or do will stop you, but you don't have to do this alone. I'll come with you."

It should have been impossible for Alexa's heart to warm right then, but she could see Marcus meant what he said. He would walk the streets with her, searching for Bethany. She just could not let him. She already knew what happened to good people when they got mixed up in her world.

"No," Alexa replied, shaking her head. "You don't belong in that world."

"Either do you. Here – this world – this is where you belong."

"I belong with Bethany," replied Alexa flatly.

"Bethany belongs here with you. Here. This world."

Alexa could only shake her head. She did not want to fight with Marcus. She could not risk him convincing her she truly belonged in his world – with him – because that was what her heart yearned for. All she had ever wanted was for her and Bethany to live the boring, mundane life of the average person.

The night became darker as dawn approached. Marcus continued to sit out on the balcony with Alexa and Charlotte. Alexa tried not to appreciate his company. It would not make leaving easier, because she had decided she was leaving at dawn. She did not care who stood in front of her or what they said. Wherever Bethany was, she would find her, and no one was going to stop her joining her. Dead or alive. Her strengthening resolve must have shown on her face, because the next time she looked over at Marcus he was staring at her intently.

"You go, I go," he reiterated.

Alexa realised he was not kidding, and doubted she would be able to leave without him following. However, his determination gave her reason to believe she would be able to leave the apartment. If she was not alone, they would have to let her pass. After that, it would just be a matter of losing Marcus. She did not think it would be too hard. He was unlikely to physically restrain her.

When the first rays of light hit the horizon, Marcus turned to Alexa, his face full of sombre expectation. "We leaving?" he asked, somehow knowing her deadline for sitting and waiting.

Alexa nodded and he took her hand, pulling her to her feet. They just made it inside when the front door clicked. The sight of Ben was not unexpected. It seemed fated that she would face the maximum amount of resistance. Ben turned on the light and Alexa's legs weakened. Bethany was standing behind him, but it was not the sister Alexa loved. It was an imposter and she hated it. Yet under it, Alexa

274

knew Bethany was there cowering in fear and she was determined to tear Bethany away from the heroin that had hold of her.

"Oh, Angel, what've you done," cried Alexa, stroking Bethany's face and grabbing her hands.

"I got wasted. So? Like you're going to do anything," replied Bethany petulantly, throwing off Alexa's hands.

"No, we can do something. We can beat this. I'll help you. We'll do whatever we have to. I'm not giving up, Angel. I love you," gasped Alexa desperately, again grabbing Bethany's hands, but she continued to pull out of her grasp.

"See," Bethany spat at Ben. "Nothing I say changes her. She's completely irrational. Can't you get mad? Can't you just break?" cried Bethany, turning back to Alexa.

"I'm not mad at you. It's just a setback. We can get past this. I'm never giving up on you," replied Alexa calmly, determined Bethany would understand that.

"What will it take?" cried Bethany with such anger Alexa had to stop herself recoiling. "What do I have to do to you to get you to hate me?"

"I could never hate you," said Alexa sincerely, shaking her head, willing her tears to stay at bay. "Never, ever. You're my sister. I'll never stop loving you. I want to help you. I want to help you through this."

"Your love does nothing for me," snarled Bethany viciously, before her voice softened slightly. "After everything I've done to you, you should hate me. Why can't you ever just hate me? Stop pretending you're so goddamned perfect!"

Alexa felt her heart split apart. The very fabric of her existence was being shredded by Bethany's words, opening wounds she had tried to keep sealed.

"Is that why you did all those things?" asked Alexa, her voice shaking. "To get me to hate you? Is that what'll make you better? Will hating you keep you clean?"

"Well loving me certainly hasn't worked," spat Bethany savagely.

A burning stake ran through Alexa's heart. She wanted Bethany to be well more than anything in the world and if hating her was what had to be done to achieve that, she would find a way.

"Alexa, wait," cried Ben, as she rushed out the door.

"You selfish —!"

"Don't you dare talk to her like that!"

Marcus glared hatefully as Ben moved between him and Bethany.

He did not like to think that Bethany needed protection from him, but right then all he wanted to do was shake her until she finally saw sense. It had been a struggle to get along with her before and he had only ever done so for Alexa's sake. Now he was sure he would never feel anything less than disgust for Bethany.

"Who's going after Alexa?" asked Charlotte.

"She'll come back once she's calmed down," sighed Ben before looking around the room. "I'm going to take Beth back to my place til she's clean."

"Alexa's not coming back," said Charlotte as though pointing out the blatantly obvious. "She doesn't hate by nature and Bethany's just asked her to hate the one person her whole soul's devoted to loving. She'll destroy herself to give you what you asked, Beth."

Bethany's gaze did not alter and it was not clear if she even heard what was said, but Marcus knew it was true. He raced out of the apartment. It was only when he reached the street and heard Sam yelling at him to go to the right that he realised he was not alone. Marcus ran up the street, looking down every side street and every conceivable direction Alexa could have gone in. He searched every bus that passed. She was not on any of them. She was not anywhere.

Rushing back towards the apartment, hoping Sam had found her, Marcus was met by a lifeless car park. Sam returned alone minutes later, shaking his head. It did not matter that Alexa had only left five minutes before them and not taken anything with her. She was gone.

"Where would she go?" Marcus asked Charlotte as soon as they walked back into the apartment. Charlotte was standing with Maria near the kitchen, waiting to see if anyone was going to take up Maria's offer of breakfast, which he had ignored.

"I don't know," replied Charlotte, but Marcus was not sure he believed her.

"She'll be back," said Sam firmly, as he stood arms folded, glaring at Alexa's bedroom as Bethany emerged with Ben. "She always storms out when things get too much and she always comes back."

"Yeah, when she can do what she's been asked to," replied Charlotte, voicing her opinion in a much stronger manner than she ever had before. "Do you even know how much of herself she gives up for you guys?"

"I know how much some people ask her to give up," snarled Sam, looking over at Marcus.

Marcus wished he could deny that, but he knew this situation was as much his fault as Bethany's.

"Do you even realise why Alexa never meets up with you at uni?" cried Charlotte, turning all eyes her way. "She thinks the girl you like might go to uni with you and she's so scared she'll mess things up by being too friendly or appearing like more than just a friend that she stays away. Doesn't matter how much she wants to hang with you, if you're with friends, she won't be there. You matter more."

Sam looked at Bethany, then back at Charlotte, his face twisting into a grimace. It was so Alexa there was no way he could deny it.

"Need me to continue?" asked Charlotte, turning from Sam to Ben.

Ben shook his head. Marcus wished he hadn't. He thought Ben needed to hear the things Alexa was never going to say.

"I should probably go," muttered Charlotte, suddenly recovering her shy demeanour.

"I'll drive you," said Marcus. It was only a short walk, but Marcus could not stay. He needed to look for Alexa. He needed to find her before she ended up in more trouble. "You don't think she would – you know – she wouldn't try and kill herself, would she?" Marcus asked when they slipped into the car. His heart was pounding at the thought of Alexa's broken body under a train.

"They still have the pact. She'd have to take Bethany with her," replied Charlotte softly, her eyes on her hands. "But right now I think Beth would go if she asked."

Marcus hated that he loved Alexa so much, hated her suffering so much, that he almost accepted the idea of her and Bethany removing themselves from the world. He could imagine them in a world of calm nothingness. Sometimes he imagined that place with just him and Alexa.

"I just wouldn't be so sure she might not take things too far to stop the pain of trying to hate Beth," added Charlotte solemnly as she stepped from the car. "I don't know if she's even going to be able to do it, and if she can't, she might never come back."

Chapter Seventeen

MARCUS DID NOT go home. He drove straight to the city and started searching. This time he did not limit his mind as to which parts of the city Alexa would be in and started with the part he least wanted to associate with her. It just did not feel right. Alexa had worked in a brothel to save Bethany, not for her own satisfaction. Without Bethany, it just did not seem like the place she would go.

All day Marcus searched. Only when his body was so exhausted he could barely stand did he concede that he needed to sleep. It was a strange sensation opening the door to a dark and vacant apartment. He walked into Alexa's room, hoping she would be there now Bethany was gone. It was wishful thinking.

The complete emptiness of the apartment made it easy for Marcus to leave the next morning. He did not feel at home there any more, and realised he had only ever felt at home there because it was where Alexa was. He returned to the city to look for Alexa, but had to accept that it was useless. What did he know about where homeless people spent their days? Just as pointless were the hours he spent driving around the greater metropolitan area – just in case he spotted her. There was no reason for Alexa to be there. There was no reason for her to be anywhere in particular, but he could not stop trying.

Once again he went home disappointed. Lying sleepless in bed, Marcus realised he did not have the information he needed. Charlotte's words swirled in his mind. A way for Alexa to hate Bethany. He could not think of a single one. It seemed like an impossible concept. No matter what Bethany had done, he had never seen Alexa come close to hating her. Everything Bethany did, Alexa blamed herself for. What Marcus needed was someone who knew Alexa and Bethany, because Bethany was the key to finding Alexa. It made him wish he had made more of an effort with Bethany so he could approach her now, but he was not even sure what state she was in. There was Ben, but Marcus knew he would not tell him anything, and sometimes he was not sure Ben knew Alexa at all. Then Marcus realised there was someone else.

"What's wrong?" asked Peter anxiously as soon as he answered his phone. "Is Alexa okay?"

Marcus was surprised by the assumption. Peter had not even said hello. "She's missing," Marcus replied grimly.

"Since when?"

"Saturday morning."

"What time can you meet me tomorrow morning?"

"Um, I don't know. What time do you get in?"

"I don't care about that. I want to know what's the earliest time you can get to my office tomorrow morning."

"Seven – quarter to seven, probably."

"I'll be waiting. Don't be late."

Marcus was early, but Peter was already waiting, pacing the footpath in front of his building. As they walked up to Peter's office, Marcus gave him a quick summary of the situation. Peter did not speak. He just listened, his face impassive. The dark and lifeless offices reminded Marcus of the apartment. It was a blessing when Peter turned on a few lights. Peter directed him to a seat, but remained standing himself, pacing back and forth. It was so distracting Marcus had to rise from his seat.

"Where's Bethany?" asked Peter.

"With Ben," Marcus replied through gritted teeth.

Peter stormed towards the door before stopping, breathing deeply. "She's withdrawing?" asked Peter, turning back. Marcus nodded. "Then she needs to focus on that." Peter moved slowly back to his desk and sat down, sighing heavily. "Alexa knew something was wrong. All Friday – she was so distracted. It wasn't like her. I was worried things weren't going as well as she was making out. And I told her – I told her not to do anything rash."

"Friday? What? Has something happened with Damien? She in trouble?" Peter pursed his. "Sorry," said Marcus, holding up his hand to stop Peter from speaking. "Out of line, I understand. What'd she say? How'd she react?"

"She didn't. When it comes to Beth it's very hard to get Alexa to take on advice. I can't blame her. In many respects she's been the sole carer of Beth for a very long time and Beth survived. It's a feat that should not be underestimated."

Marcus considered that for a moment. He did not feel as though he had ever underestimated how amazing Alexa was, but when he put together what she and Bethany had each gone through in their lives – what he knew of what they had gone through – survival to this point did seem fairly miraculous.

"Damn Ben!" cried Peter angrily, jumping from his seat, startling Marcus with the vehemence of his exclamation. "This is his doing."

"What?" stammered Marcus. He blamed Ben for a lot, but not this.

"For months – over a year – he's been at Bethany, telling her she needs to do more to redeem herself – that what she put Alexa through was unforgivable."

"It was," replied Marcus harshly.

"Don't make that mistake," said Peter firmly. "If you care about Alexa, you need to see things from her point of view. To the rest of the world, sure, what Bethany has done is completely unforgivable – inconceivable – but not to Alexa. To Alexa, her actions were a natural consequence of their situation. That's why she blames herself, because she hasn't been able to change their situations.

"Do you honestly think Alexa hating Bethany will do anything to help her? You think Bethany can survive without Alexa's love and guidance?" asked Peter seriously. Marcus did not answer. The answers were obvious enough. "Of course she won't. It will cripple Bethany to the point of destruction, which will only take Alexa out with her. Ben should know better. You don't come between Alexa and Bethany, no matter how right you think you are."

"You've tried?"

"Of course I have," cried Peter in frustration. "But I had to stop. The lengths Alexa would go to just to be with Bethany. The few times they were split up – it just wasn't safe and I never tried again. Not until I found out about that damned pact. You don't think I've tried to talk them out of it – both of them – convince them that their lives are more than that?"

"Alexa wouldn't kill herself. She's not like Bethany. She wouldn't want Bethany to die because of her," said Marcus firmly, hating that Bethany would take Alexa down just to ease her own pain.

"Don't bet on that. Leave them alone with each other and you might find it's Alexa who's the more desperate to end things," replied Peter with firm conviction. "She's the only one of them who's actually tried to kill herself. Beth couldn't do it. That's why she went looking for Alexa. If she could have killed Alexa, she would have been free of her tether to life, but while Alexa lives, so does Beth. I don't think the reverse is actually true."

"So what do you think she'll do?" gasped Marcus, realising Peter was right. Bethany had a degree of enthusiasm and excitement about life that Alexa did not have.

"Exactly what Bethany asked her to," replied Peter grimly. "I just don't know how she'll do it. The only thing that came close to making

Alexa hate Beth was that incident with Hayley White."

"Leo," gagged Marcus, choking on the thoughts of what Alexa was put through in those days of captivity.

"Yes, but not what he did to her," said Peter, as if reading his mind. "Alexa never blamed Bethany for that. Leo's a vicious thug. Don't think for a minute Bethany did not suffer at his hands. The only reason she blames Bethany is because she thinks she told him to go after Hayley. If she wants to hate Bethany, that will be the way to it."

"Do you know where they are?" asked Marcus coyly, knowing this was again crossing a line.

"If she's gone to them, I can't promise I'll bring her home," said Peter as he slouched into his chair. "I won't even promise I'll tell you I've found her. I'm sick of seeing her in these situations."

Marcus imagined that – Alexa home with the Whites again. He saw her smile the Friday afternoon before that fateful weekend, full of child-like excitement, brimming with hope and possibility. "Whatever you have to do to," Marcus nodded. "I just want her to be happy. I'll do anything I have to – whatever she needs."

"Leave?" asked Peter pointedly.

Marcus swallowed hard. "Absolutely," he answered sincerely.

"Good. Just don't go yet. You might need to do the exact opposite," said Peter. Marcus raised his eyebrows. "She loves you. She's not a child and you're no longer in a position of authority over her. I might not agree, but that doesn't mean I disapprove either."

"Nothing's ever going to happen between us," said Marcus firmly. "It wouldn't be right."

"Doesn't make loving her any less special, does it?" Marcus shook his head, his heart burning. His life would mean very little if he could not love Alexa. "I'll let you know if I find her."

"Thank you," nodded Marcus, understanding the significance of Peter's promise.

Trudging to work and into the classroom with Alexa still missing brought forth a torrent of horrid memories for Marcus. He tried to reassure himself that she was not locked in the apartment of some sadistic rapist, but part of him could not be convinced. If anyone could attract trouble, it was Alexa. It left Marcus distracted and on edge all day. His classes were terrible and almost wholly unprepared. Instead of the usual lively classroom discussions, his students were copying out of textbooks, leaving his mind free to imagine the worst.

As soon as the bell rang for the end of the day, Marcus rushed home, hoping to see Alexa already there. He did not care about the mood she was bound to be in. He would take a lifetime of her bad moods just to know she was safe. The sight of Bethany sitting on the lounge was not the welcome he had been looking for. It was clear she was clean, but Marcus could see the shadow of heroin on her face, surprising him that he knew her well enough to notice the difference.

"She's still missing," said Bethany, not looking up from her knees that were tucked into her body.

Marcus did not trust himself to answer. He just went to his room and sent Peter a text message to keep him updated. When he returned to the lounge room, he was ready to go back out to look for Alexa.

"Can you be useful and give me an idea of where I might find her?" Marcus asked Bethany harshly.

"If she knew, don't you think we would've already checked it out?" answered Ben angrily.

"Where've you looked?" retorted Marcus spitefully.

"I have everyone looking for her," spat Ben, squaring off with Marcus. "Missing persons have been notified. We will find her."

"If you're looking so hard, why haven't I seen anything in the media? Why's there nothing on the news? It's been three days! You know as well as I do what could be happening to her."

"Yes and I also know it's not in her interest to have it advertised that she's on the streets alone. She hasn't touched her bank account. She left with nothing and she's vulnerable. Telling the world that will only attract unwanted attention."

"What attention?" asked Marcus, his heart skipping a beat as his chest constricted. "Who? Leo? I thought he was still in gaol."

"That's one concern," replied Ben, his voice much quieter and more controlled, and Marcus felt as though he was choosing his words carefully. "Leo did a deal to hand over his accomplices, but we're not sure it was all of them."

The way Bethany buried her head into her knees, hands over her ears made Marcus almost feel sorry for her. She looked so young and fragile, so lacking in the basic skills required to live in the world. If she had been the one he loved, he would have been sympathetic and he could see his own hypocrisy, but he found it difficult to empathise with anyone who hurt Alexa.

"Well I can't just sit around here hoping she'll come home," said Marcus, trying not to sneer. This situation was not bringing out the best in any of them.

"Just remember that her home is with us," said Ben, his voice somewhere between demanding and heartbroken.

It took all of Marcus's control to just nod and not throw back another bitter remark. He wanted to be better than this. He wanted to be the kind of person who was deserving of Alexa, even if he could never be with her.

Lucy called as he drove aimlessly. He had ignored her all weekend and was not looking forward to explaining why he did not want to see her now. He needed all his concentration to think about where he could find Alexa. The most tempting thought was that she had gone somewhere special to them, but there was really only one place.

It was getting dark as Marcus pulled up at the cliff top. Standing there, looking down at the bay, he knew this was not where Alexa would come. Even without their association to the place, it was far too soothing a spot to conjure any hate.

Hate. It was one thing Marcus found remarkably absent in Alexa. Even when she spoke of hating her mother there was no venom behind it. It was more of a status than an emotion.

Bethany. Hate. Leo. Hate. Hayley. Hate. Bethany.

The answer was so obvious Marcus could not understand why he had not thought of it sooner. Wherever the Whites were now, Alexa would not go there as he had previously assumed. She wanted to hate, not be loved, and she could only do that where she could remember the loss.

It took longer than Marcus remembered to get to the Whites' old place, and without Alexa's directions through the suburban streets he found himself driving in a lot of frustrated circles. Pulling up in front of their house, Marcus got out and wandered the street. Alexa would not have gone in, but she had to be somewhere nearby. He just needed to find a place she could hide. He walked up and down the street, searching for any spot Alexa could stay out of sight, but still see the house. It was fruitless, and when a neighbour walked out of their house and started watching him he knew it was time to go.

Slumping over the steering wheel, Marcus finally gave in to the tearing pain in his chest. Alexa was gone and he could do nothing to change it. That horrid reality seeped through his body like a heavy weight. It made the thought of driving home torturous. However, he knew he would find no comfort with Lucy tonight either.

The apartment was dark when Marcus arrived home. If Bethany was there, he knew Ben would be as well, but he did not turn on any lights to find out. The sight of Bethany the next morning, working painfully to get herself ready for work, did not invoke the feelings of sympathy it should have. Peter was right. Bethany could not survive without Alexa. Marcus was not even sure he could. Just getting through the day was a struggle. He even stayed back a few hours to try and structure classes that were somewhere close to acceptable. He was not entirely successful, and it only delayed his dilemma of whether to continue his useless search for Alexa, go back to the apartment that no longer felt like home or throw himself at Lucy's mercy. Lucy still felt like his last resort – where he would go when he lost all hope of Alexa ever returning. When he woke on Wednesday morning with no hint that Alexa would ever return, he ran his fingers over his phone, twitching over Lucy's number.

"Let me go!" cried Bethany angrily.

Marcus rushed out of his room to see her wrapped in Ben's arms while he restrained her.

"I only just managed to cover up your relapse and now, one day back at work, you want me to let you back out on the streets. No!" said Ben firmly, pushing Bethany away from the door. "We will find her."

"I can find her!" cried Bethany.

"Then just tell us where she'll be and we'll find her."

"No, it's not like that," Bethany sighed in frustration. She and Alexa were more similar than Marcus had ever given them credit for. "I can't give you a street name. It's just like she always managed to find me. I can find her. I know I can."

"Let her go," said Marcus flatly from the kitchen where he was making a coffee. Ben turned on him, too full of rage to articulate an answer, but Bethany looked grateful for his support, even if came without an ounce of concern for her welfare. "Getting in between Beth and Alexa has never ended well. Live or die, they're going to do it together. Keeping them apart isn't sparing them anything."

From the corner of his eyes, Marcus could see the confusion on Bethany's face. Peter had let him know he had gone to see her at work the day before. He had not been able to get through to Bethany as well as he had hoped and planned to go back again today. Marcus could not help but think it was a pointless exercise. Watching Bethany reluctantly follow Ben's instructions, it was clear she was just going through the motions. Her thoughts did not extend past Alexa's fate, and he would not be surprised to hear that she too went missing today. Maybe it was better they were together – wherever that was – than watch them slowly destruct in each other's absence.

The interconnectedness of Alexa and Bethany made Marcus's heart soften for Bethany in a way he did not appreciate. He did not want to feel any sympathy for Bethany, but as her words swirled in his mind, a new plan formed. If he could tolerate being near Bethany, then together they might have a better chance of finding Alexa. He did not think Bethany would object to him going with her, and thought she was much more likely than Alexa to actually accept his help – as long as the object was to find Alexa. All they needed was to get around Ben.

Marcus found himself almost buoyed as he drove home, hopeful he might finally have a chance of bringing Alexa home where she belonged. The first chance he got, he would speak to Bethany. He wondered if they had any laxatives he could slip into Ben's tea. He was sure the bathroom was as far away from Bethany as Ben was prepared to move.

"What have I done? What have I done?"

Marcus walked into the lounge room to see Bethany repeating herself over and over, rocking back and forth on the floor, as Ben sat near her on the lounge. The sight pierced Marcus's heart. The real Bethany was back. He could hear it in her voice and see it in her face. It was as if she really was two different people, and he could almost understand why Alexa always fought so hard for this Bethany. If they could just get around Ben, Marcus knew he would have no trouble convincing Bethany to come looking for Alexa with him.

Moving to the kitchen under the guise of making a coffee, Marcus was sure he saw Bethany's eyes flick his way and wondered if she wanted him to take her looking for Alexa as well. Ben's phone rang and Marcus shifted, waiting for any opportunity to approach Bethany. When Ben moved away from her, he took another step forward.

"I really can't leave Beth," said Ben, his hand on his head. "If anything's happened to Alexa, Beth'll be dead in hours. I can't lose both of them. I know I should be out looking for her, but I just can't leave."

Bethany shifted at these words, her eyes flicking to the balcony. Marcus saw her body tense, as if ready to leap. He moved forward again, not prepared to watch Bethany kill herself. Keeping one eye on Bethany, Marcus tried to hear what was being said to Ben, but he was too far away. Ben sighed deeply, his eyes closing as his body slumped. Marcus's chest filled involuntarily with hope. That was not a sigh of despair.

"Okay, I'll be in as soon as I've found someone to watch Beth," nodded Ben, his voice lighter, before he suddenly stopped. "Has she used?" he croaked after a long silence.

Marcus's heart skipped a beat. Used. Alexa had been on the streets after all, not with the Whites. It was not what he had expected. Alexa hated drugs. She hated what they had done to her family and now she had thrown herself into its arms.

"Can you watch Beth?" asked Ben, suddenly turning to Marcus.

Marcus turned to Bethany in disgust. She was curled back up in in a ball, but he did not pity her any more. Now that he knew Alexa was alive, the sympathy he had felt for Bethany evaporated and he hated her once more for the suffering Alexa had endured.

"Forget it," snapped Ben, pulling Bethany to her feet. He marched her out the door and slammed it behind him.

***

Alexa sat in the interview room with so much hatred brewing within her she barely felt alive. It was a horrible way to exist, but she did not intend on living this way for long. As soon as she was sure Bethany was safe and settled, she would end the life she almost wished she never had. Bethany would be financially secure. The rest would be up to Ben.

"How are you feeling?" asked Ben, standing against the wall on the other side of the room. He had stood in silence for over five minutes, waiting for her to talk, but Alexa no longer cared for conversation.

"I'm not," she replied in a cold voice.

It was true. Beneath the swirling hatred, there was nothing left. The life and soul had been drained from her body and she could not care about anything – except giving Bethany what she needed. However, part of her mind was rational enough to realise that she should not make an enemy of Ben. He was the one who would look after Bethany in her absence. He would be the one to tell her if her sacrifice had been worthwhile. It had been willingly made. There was still nothing Alexa would not do for Bethany, but this had been harder than anything else she had ever had to endure. Hating Bethany was so unnatural it had almost killed her to try, but she had done her part.

It had been difficult to ignore the justifications she had always made for Bethany and it still felt as if it was violating her very soul to continue hating her. In the end, there had been only one thing that had allowed Alexa to achieve this level of hatred and it was where she had spent her first night – camped outside the Whites' old home. They had offered her everything and she had only rejected the concept of becoming their daughter for fear of losing Bethany. In the end, Alexa lost that one chance at a family because of Bethany and she could hate her for that. She relived the fateful night of Leo's attack over and over, but even the brutal rapes she had suffered at his hands were not enough for Alexa to hate Bethany. Instead, she imagined what would have happened if she had not been able to keep Leo from Hayley. She could hate Bethany for that.

The longer Alexa sat in front of the house, the more her hatred grew, but it sat so uncomfortably with her. It may have been what she needed to do, but she did not want to hate Bethany. The pain had been so immense that she almost broke her greatest promise to herself – to never contact the Whites again. Their new address was burned into her mind and she knew every route to their house, but she would not risk their lives for her happiness, no matter how desperate she was for it. Instead, when Alexa left the White's old house, she had gone in search of another way to deaden her pain.

"Do you want to tell me what's going on?" asked Ben, pulling Alexa out of her memories. His face was a contortion of anger, fear and frustration and he looked so much older than he did when she left.

"Nothing. I did what I had to. She needs my hate to stay clean. Now she has it. She can live with you. I don't want to see her again," replied Alexa coldly, the image of Leo on top of Hayley fuelling her anger.

"So you'll sacrifice your life for hers, is that what you think?"

"I'll get her clean no matter what the cost to me!" Alexa cried.

"What about the drugs? If you die, so does Beth and you know it!" There was anger in Ben's voice, but Alexa did not care for it. She would not care for anyone ever again. "How much did you take?"

"I don't know."

"How many times?"

"I don't know."

"Did you inject it?" asked Ben forcefully.

"No," Alexa growled angrily. She may be stupid, but she would not die with a needle in her arm like her mother. "What the fuck does it even matter?"

"Do you even know why you started drinking after your mother died?" The question took Alexa by surprise. Ben sat opposite her and took her hands in his. "Beth wasn't the only one addicted to heroin," he said, his voice shaking. "No one realised you were addicted until you started to withdraw. You didn't understand that was what was happening so you drank to ease the pain."

"If you knew this —"

"I only found out after you went missing from the Whites. You can't pull people's files for interest's sake," Ben interrupted agitatedly. "And it was just suspicion – supposition – what the doctors concluded when you went off the rails. You never let them do any blood tests."

Alexa shook her head. It did not matter. All that mattered was that Bethany stayed clean. She had to find a way to hate Bethany, not share in her affliction. Her mind started twisting the information, trying to find a way to bend it to her need. Bethany was not special. She was not the only addict. It had been her choice to keep using, her choice to destroy their lives, and Alexa could hate her for that too.

When Alexa looked up, she could see the shock on Ben's face. She felt barely human and wondered if she now looked it too. She had complete control of her emotions and would not let go. She would save Bethany and die at peace.

***

Marcus hesitated. He was still surprised Ben had voluntarily involved him in this situation, so knew it had to be bad. He tried to control his emotions as he walked into the interview room. What Alexa needed was more important than what he felt, but when he saw her curled up in a corner of the room, just a broken shell of a human, he was not sure if her needs and his desires were misaligned at all.

"Hey, I'm here to bust you out," Marcus said with a cheeky half-smile. Alexa looked up at him with a blank expression. His heart sank, seeing the vibrant girl he loved all but destroyed. "Quick, they'll never notice," Marcus continued, fixing his smile to his face.

Alexa did not move. It was as if she was incapable of comprehending what he was saying, but when he took her hand and pulled her to her feet, she did not resist. He held her close to his side, as if he was truly sneaking her out, but resisted the urge to kiss the top of her head. This level of physical contact would hurt him later when he would have to resist her, but right now he would do anything to bring Alexa back to the world of the living.

It surprised Marcus how close Alexa clung to him. Her arms were wrapped around his waist as her head and body pressed against his chest. He wondered if it was him she was truly clinging to or just the offer of an escape. The thought of escaping with her was tantalising. No Bethany, no pain, just him and her. But that life was a fantasy. Alexa did not exist without Bethany. That much was patently obvious.

As Alexa slid into his car, Marcus could not help hearing Ben's desperate voice questioning if she had used. Just one look was all Marcus needed to know the answer and his heart ached for what Alexa had been through, but he had to make her see sense. He had to make her understand that she could not continue to be so reactive to Bethany's every move.

"She is sorry, you know," said Marcus, as he pulled out on to the road, trying not to grimace. He hated defending Bethany. "She regrets everything that's happened and wants your forgiveness."

"I don't care what she wants. What she needs is more important. I'll do anything to make sure she stays clean," replied Alexa forcefully.

"I know you will, but have you considered that this isn't the best thing for her? Did you really think hating Beth would help her?"

"But it's what she asked for."

Marcus could hear the strain in Alexa's voice as the certainty of her convictions began to wane ever so slightly. "I don't think Bethany has any idea what she needs," he said sincerely. "I think you do. I think you were doing a brilliant job – have always done a brilliant job – before this whole stupid thing. It was one setback, not the end of the world. When it comes to Beth, you've done a pretty damn good job up til now on your own judgement. I think you should've stuck to that rather than listening to Bethany while she's high. You're the one who always told me how she's not herself when she's on drugs. Why'd you listen to her?" Alexa turned away, and he could see in the reflection her eyes were turning colder with every passing silent second. "Listen, I'm sorry for my part in all this."

"What part?" asked Alexa immediately.

Marcus managed to keep the smile from his face. "Lucy. She's my girlfriend and the reason Beth was struggling so much. Beth didn't feel comfortable in her own home. That's my fault," he said, any hint of a smile dissolving with that confession. "I think the best thing will be for me to look for another place."

"Doesn't matter," replied Alexa glumly, sinking lower in her seat. "Stay forever. Bethy's not staying. She'll go and live with Ben."

"Now that's just the way I always imagined you'd ask me to spend the rest of my life with you," laughed Marcus.

When Alexa turned to face him, Marcus thought he saw the slightest hint of a smile. "Doesn't look like you've been propositioned with a better offer," she said in a flat voice that was much less cold than it had been.

Marcus could not help but smile at the truth of that statement. Spending the rest of his life with Alexa was the best offer he had ever received and he decided to tell her that. This time Alexa smiled.

"Don't we present a pathetic picture," she said in a heavily sarcastic voice. "My ex thinks I deserve to die for my sins and you get a place to live forever cos I finally gave up on my pathetic drug-addicted sister."

"This is giving up?" asked Marcus with a smile, determined not to let Alexa indulge her grief. "I never would've counted sacrificing yourself for Bethany as giving up."

Alexa turned away. Marcus said nothing as she stared silently out the window. She shifted every so often, showing a restlessness that had not been there before, so he continued to wait in silence.

"You never gave me an answer," Alexa said suddenly, turning with a calm, blank face.

"To what?" Marcus asked, confused.

"Whether you're staying forever."

"For as long as you want me," he smiled, taking Alexa's hand and squeezing it tight. The feel of her hand in his was sublime, but his heart was already aching, knowing he was going to have to let her go. Pulling her hand on to the gear stick, he held his hand over hers until they pulled up in front their apartment.

Alexa did not move her hand as Marcus parked the car and turned off the engine. If she could not have Bethany, she was determined to have Marcus. It did not matter how selfish, stupid or self-destructive she or anyone thought it was. If she had to live, then she was not going to be forced to give up everything. It was a decision Alexa thought would get her through the entry into her empty apartment. She took Marcus's hand as they walked, moving in closer so his arms wrapped around her body, but as they approached the entrance to the apartment block she noticed Ben's car sitting in the visitors' parking.

"She'd better not be here," said Alexa, looking between the door and the car. In that short drive, Marcus had managed to strip her of all her anger and hatred. It was impressive the way he could do that, but she could not afford to be impressed. She had to give Bethany what she needed.

"C'mon, let's get this over with," said Marcus, stepping in closer so his mouth was just above her ear. Alexa nodded and let him lead her upstairs, always staying recklessly close. Right then she felt sure she would let him lead her anywhere. "I'm here," said Marcus, as she hesitated at the door. Alexa nodded again and entered the apartment, surprised to see her lounge room so full. She had truly expected to come home to nothing.

"Oh, Lex, what have you done," gasped Bethany.

Bethany rushed forward and embraced Alexa fiercely. Alexa's arms remained locked by her side as she churned her anger, determined that Bethany would not die because of her weakness.

"Get out," Alexa hissed, pushing Bethany off her. "You wanted my hatred. Now you have it. So go, get clean. Live your life. I don't want you here anymore. I hate you."

"No, no, no, please," cried Bethany, tears falling down her cheeks as her legs weakened. "I'm sorry. I felt so guilty about all the love and support you've given me. I thought I needed you to hate me so I could forgive myself, but I can't live with you like this. I need you to love me. I need you to support me. I've stopped. Cold turkey, no clinics, no methadone, just me against my mind and I can't do it without you. I don't need your love. I want it. I want you. I want you to teach me to be as good a person as you. Please don't tell me I've lost you."

Alexa's anger began to falter with Bethany's pleas. All she wanted was for Bethany to get clean and would do whatever was necessary, but she had spent so much time and effort conjuring her anger that she could not just let it go. Suddenly, warmth spread through Alexa's body as Marcus moved behind her, his hand slipping over her waist to pull her into him. "Give it up," he whispered in her ear. "I'll be here. I'll see you through. Give up your anger. Love your sister. You know you want to."

Alexa knew if she agreed, it would be the end of her and Marcus – before it had ever truly begun. But she also knew there was no real choice and her heart ached terribly as she pulled out of Marcus's grasp and hugged Bethany.

The pain that speared through Alexa's body was so immense her legs collapsed as tears streamed mercilessly down her cheeks. Bethany held her tight as they slumped to the floor. Alexa could not stop herself from curling into Bethany's embrace. For ten minutes the scene remained unchanged, until Ben pulled Alexa and Bethany to their feet. Alexa's tears continued to slip down her cheeks every so often. Bethany's face was dry, but Alexa could see the deep and true remorse in her eyes and it made her believe all the pain may just be worth it.

"Now," said Ben firmly, guiding Alexa and Bethany into the arms of Sam, Maria and Charlotte. Marcus sat on the lounge just watching.

"This is going to stop. We're going to start again and our relationships are going to be based on openness and honesty. Beth, you should've come to us. We would've helped you through."

"I'm sorry," replied Bethany, her voice soft and sincere.

"We're going to get through this together. Beth's not the only one who needs to quit a bad habit. I'm giving up smoking and drinking. Cold turkey. There're no excuses and no quick fixes. We're going to have to fight these additions we have."

"Well I'm definitely giving up heroin and smoking and drinking," said Bethany, her voice meek, but confident.

"I'll give up the midnight snacks that are clogging my arteries and frustrating my doctors," said Maria with a sly smile.

"I'll give up drinking," said Sam.

"Me too," said Marcus, looking up from the lounge. "What about you, Charlotte?"

"Yeah, okay," agreed Charlotte reluctantly. "I'll give up my stuff."

"And you're going to give up too," said Bethany, turning to Alexa, her voice shaking. "Never again, okay. You have to promise. Nothing's worth that, believe me. I don't ever want to lose you. Promise me."

"I promise," replied Alexa flatly, though like Charlotte she did not want to articulate her actions.

Feeling the hands of her surrogate family on her, Alexa wondered how things had managed to get this out of control. No wonder no one trusted her to her own instincts. Only one person in that room had ever professed any trust in her ability to live her own life and he sat on the lounge with his head in his hands, looking as pained as she felt.

Marcus looked up, immediately catching Alexa's eye. He rubbed his fingers together and then pointed at Bethany. Alexa shook her head, but Marcus continued his insistent gestures before finally pointing between her and himself, then to the door. Alexa knew what he was getting at. He wanted her to test Bethany when she was at her weakest, because this would not be the last time she would fall so low. If all failed, he would offer himself.

"We need to talk," said Alexa flatly, pulling Bethany out into the cold night air sweeping the balcony. "There's more you have to know. I kept it from you, because I wanted to be sure you could stay clean, but now I need to know you can stay clean with this information."

"What information?" asked Bethany cautiously.

"We have money – lots of it." Bethany's eyes widened, making Alexa's heart stutter in fear. "In high school – before I lost Clinton's baby and you disappeared – I had a dream. It gave me the winning lottery numbers. We entered them in all these games and finally won," Alexa explained matter-of-factly.

"How much?" asked Bethany almost fearfully.

"Almost eight and a half million each. Plus the money from the school payout," answered Alexa calmly. "I've spent some of it overseas, here on the apartment, that kind of stuff. I live off the interest – part of it. I want to give some to you – supplement your income, save, whatever. But this isn't money so you can sit around living the good life. You'll finish your trade and work, and work hard. You're not to sit back and put your feet up. The money's security, nothing more – and it's not yours," added Alexa firmly, though in her mind it was half Bethany's. "It's in my name and I'll never give you a cent for drugs."

Bethany stood stunned. Eventually, she managed to nod slowly. Alexa let her take it all in. She was not capable of much else anyway.

"What're you going to do with it?" asked Bethany tentatively.

"I want to find us a home. This place is too small, but I didn't want to live in a big place by myself and I really wanted to buy something together – somewhere we both choose, something we'll both love. I don't care how much it costs, but we both have to want it."

"This is why you chose your finance course, isn't it? So you could take care of the money and us."

"I didn't know the first thing about money. We never had any," smiled Alexa, eliciting a small smile from Bethany. "We've been given a gift and I didn't want to waste it. So many things can go wrong and I always wanted enough to face anything."

Tears rolled softly down Bethany's cheeks. Alexa let them fall. She had never felt so distant from Bethany as she did in that moment. "I don't deserve you," sobbed Bethany, straining to control herself. "I thought that pushing you away – giving you the chance at life without me burdening you was best for both of us, but I don't want that and now I hate myself more for what I've done. Then, after everything, you sit here still hating me while telling me all the plans you have. You don't take them back, you don't despise me like you should. I don't know how you do it, but I'm so glad you can. I love you, Lex, and I'm going to prove I'm worth it. I'm not now, but I will be. Don't even tell me you believe me," added Bethany quickly when Alexa tried to speak. "Just wait and let me prove it."

Marcus kept out of the way as everyone continued to mill around the apartment. Charlotte looked as uncomfortable as he felt so when she suggested she should get home he immediately offered to take her. They did not speak as they drove.

"If Alexa asks, but I don't think she will, tell her I'll come back next Friday. I think they need time without me," said Charlotte softly.

"She might need you before then," replied Marcus.

"She needs Beth."

"To survive, yes, but you're the one who's been helping her live. And I think Beth might need you too."

Charlotte only nodded as she stepped from the car. When Marcus returned home, he was thankful to see it emptier than when he left. Ben was still there, but Bethany was urging him to leave as she made up a bed on the lounge.

"You can't sleep on the lounge," he heard Ben argue from his room. "Come home with me if Alexa's not going to let you stay in her room. You shouldn't even have to share a room."

"You care that Marcus lives here. Me and Lex don't. And me sleeping on the lounge is about the best outcome from all this. Lex should hate me for everything I've done," said Bethany, her voice breaking. "But she doesn't. She only hates me because I asked her to. We've been apart too long. I'm staying here."

"Then let me stay," said Ben.

"Not tonight, okay."

Marcus was not sure what Ben's response was. There were rustling sounds for the next fifteen minutes before the lights went out. Marcus waited another five before emerging and heading to the bathroom. He did not look Bethany's way. However, when he made his way back to his room, he noticed Bethany's silhouette on the balcony.

"I swear to God, Beth, if you ever hurt Alexa like that again —"

Bethany rushed at him as he stood at the balcony door and threw her arms around him, trying to hug him tight. Marcus pushed her off him much harder than he intended, causing her to stumble against a chair. He walked to the edge of the balcony, while Bethany stayed up against the wall.

"I know how much you must hate me," Bethany said quietly, stoking Marcus's fury.

"You have no idea. You could have no idea how I feel," he growled, trying to keep his temper in check. "I've watched you hold a gun to her head. I've watched you strip the very life and soul out of her. I've seen her after she was beaten and raped within an inch of her life. All because of you."

"You pulled her back from a train that would've killed her. You resuscitated her when Clinton strangled her. You've been our living force since you moved in here and you brought her back to me tonight even though I know it's the last thing in the world you wanted to do. I know what I've done and I know what you've done. I know how much you hate me."

Marcus hated that Bethany had the same sickening grip on reality Alexa had. He believed her ignorant and indulgent, because it was easier, but had to grudgingly admit that in some ways Bethany's life had probably been tougher than Alexa's. "I don't hate you, Beth," he sighed, closing his eyes.

"Then you're as saint-like as my sister," said Bethany, taking Marcus by surprise as she leant next to him against the railing and took his hand in hers. "And I may not've seen what you have, but I've seen Alexa suffer. I've seen her beaten by foster parents and siblings just for fun. I've seen her desperate face try to save me over and over and inside I'm screaming for her to succeed as my body desperately tries to make sure she fails. I don't want this life. So often I wish that when I close my eyes they'll never open again. Sometimes I want to go alone – free Lex from me and give her the life she deserves. Other times I want a world where it's just me and Lex – nothing else, no real life, no real anything – just us."

Marcus was surprised to find himself hugging Bethany. Her tears soaked his shirt as he held her gently to his chest, wondering why he could never hold Alexa so easily. "You and me share similar dreams," he said heavily. "But you're the one that tethers Alexa to life. You have to beat this, because the two of you will never be free from each other."

"And you truly think you and Lex can ever be free of each other?" asked Bethany, pushing out of his arms to look him in the eyes.

"Alexa would get over me," said Marcus firmly. "I'm happy about that too. I don't want to think that Alexa can't live without me when she can't have me."

"But she can! You two are the only ones holding yourselves back. Why can't you realise there's nothing wrong with you being together?"

"Because that's just fantasy, Beth. You want to hear it?" asked Marcus angrily. "I love her, okay. I love her so much it hurts, but we can never be together. She deserves so much more than me."

"She deserves a man that loves her. Every woman does."

"Love will never be enough to make this right. If that was all it took …" Marcus took a deep breath, unwilling to finish that sentence. "Sometimes I think I'm doing Alexa a great disservice by staying.

Torturing myself is one thing, but she's so young and needs to move on. She can live without me, but like this – I feel like I'm holding her back on a false promise. If something ever happened to me, she'd be free – she could move on knowing she wasn't betraying … something."

"You can't wish something like that. You can't," gasped Bethany.

"I don't wish it," smiled Marcus wryly. "I've stayed here much longer than I should've. I've forced you and Alexa to share a room for months. I've inflicted Lucy on you – all because I've stayed. I'm as selfish as it's possible to be. I brought Alexa back because she's not complete without you. I stay because I'm not complete without her."

"Then stay with her forever," pleaded Bethany, grasping his hands. "Be with her. It's not wrong. How could it possibly be wrong when you both want it so much?"

"Is that what you tell yourself when you're craving heroin?" Marcus asked spitefully. Bethany did not respond, her eyes lowering away from his glare. "I'm going to stay long enough to make sure you keep your promise, but after that, I need to go. I can't be selfish forever. I will set her free."

"I'm not going to break my promise," said Bethany, standing tall and resolute, her hands continuing to hold Marcus's.

"I don't care for your words, Beth. I don't believe a thing that comes out of your mouth," replied Marcus, pushing Bethany away, though much more gently this time. "Just understand that if you do anything like this again, I won't bring Alexa back. You can track her to the ends of the earth, I don't care. I don't trust you. I don't like you. I don't want anything to do with you."

Marcus stomped to his room. He did not sleep well and the sound of Alexa's violent retching woke him early the next morning. He dressed quickly, but was not surprised to find Bethany already with her. It was pleasing to see them huddled together on the lounge, despite Alexa's clearly shaking body. Marcus tried to keep his use of the bathroom as short as possible, but it was not enough. Alexa was vomiting in the kitchen sink when he emerged, Bethany still by her side. When he was dressed for work, they were back on the lounge, Bethany's eyes flicking up to the clock.

"Beth, if you can't take time off work, I'll stay with Alexa today," he said, watching Alexa's reaction carefully. There was a flicker of hope in them, and Marcus guessed she was not keen on sharing this experience with Bethany. However, he noticed Alexa did not loosen her grip on Bethany's arms.

"No, I want to stay," nodded Bethany, and Alexa moved in closer to her.

"I'll stay with her," said a firm voice from the door.

Marcus turned to see Ben and Sam walking into the lounge room. Ben quickly ushered Bethany up to get ready for work as Sam took her place on the lounge. Alexa curled into a ball away from him.

"You need to go to work, Beth. There's no choice in the matter," Ben said firmly, pushing Bethany towards the bathroom. "You'll stay with me until Alexa's better."

Bethany protested – at every step – but was argued over by Ben and glared at by Sam. Marcus did not like it. Sam was acting strangely possessive of Alexa, something Marcus had not seen since high school. Ben was worse. It was the first time he had seen him act police-like with Bethany or Alexa. The way Bethany submissively complied, her body shrinking a little every time she did, was horrible to watch. Tears stream down Bethany's cheeks as she moved around the kitchen, trying to gather food for work.

"I'll do it," Marcus said, moving her gently to the side. "You make me a coffee," he added with a half-smile.

Bethany nodded and quickly boiled the kettle. Marcus made them sandwiches and started wrapping them in cling film. Bethany's hand shook so much as she carried his coffee across the kitchen that half of it ended up on the floor. "I want to stay here," she cried softly, her voice barely above a whisper as he took the mug from her hand.

"I know," he replied just as quietly. "But maybe it's for the best." It was a lie, but Ben and Sam were not going to be talked out of their course of action. "Can we really stay without tearing ourselves apart with guilt for what we've done?"

"We?" asked Bethany, looking up with wide, astonished eyes.

"You going to be as amazing as your sister and not blame me for bringing Lucy into your lives?" asked Marcus seriously. Bethany did not respond. "Maybe it's better we come back on Sunday – start fresh."

"I don't want to leave her," Bethany whispered, her voice broken.

"Neither do I," replied Marcus truthfully. "But it'll pass. It won't be long and we'll be back here." Marcus put his hands on Bethany's shoulders and felt her stand straighter. She looked up into his eyes and nodded, but the sight did not comfort him. It was a look he had seen too many times in Alexa's eyes. "You want me to drive you to work?" he asked tenderly.

Bethany started to nod when Ben moved in and pulled her away, barking angrily that he would take her. Alexa curled into a tighter ball on the lounge as Sam threw him and Bethany a hateful glare. Marcus packed his bag quickly, just throwing clothes in, not caring if they were appropriate or not. Walking out, Marcus wished he would have the chance to said goodbye to Alexa, but Sam was standing guard as Bethany knelt in front of her, grasping her hands. Marcus was almost at the door when Bethany called his name. He backtracked slowly, unsure of how to face her, but when their eyes met hers flicked to Alexa. Alexa stared up at him, her eyes full of sorrow as she held Bethany's hand to her chest. He thought she mouthed the word sorry, but could not be sure as Ben started demanding Bethany get ready to go.

That sight haunted Marcus all day. He did not want Alexa to be sorry for choosing Bethany. They both knew it was only fantasy that they could run away together and he cursed himself for again offering her a world he could never deliver.

Alexa's existence did not extend much beyond her bed. The vomiting lasted all day, but her body ached so much she could only roll over and expel the poison into the bucket next to her bed. It was a long, torturous day, but the evening provided no release. The pain continued, hour after endless hour.

Sam stayed the entire time. He periodically emptied the bucket of vomit. Occasionally he spoke, but Alexa could not concentrate on his words enough to understand or answer. What else he did was beyond her comprehension. All that existed was her timelessly painful void.

There was a horrible familiarity to the pain that made Alexa wonder if Ben's claim was true, while the fevered visions that danced before her eyes tried to torture her with memories she did not possess. When her eyes finally opened, the dreams became confusing swirls in her subconscious, tainting her moods and haunting her mind, but never developing into solid images.

"How you feeling?" asked Sam, as she struggled to drag herself out of bed.

"How the fuck do you think I feel?" Alexa snapped back.

This was why she wanted Bethany or Marcus to stay with her. They knew not to ask stupid questions. Sam had a different tact. He seemed to want to question her into a good mood. It did not work and Alexa was sure that when she was not vomiting, the only other things coming out of her mouth were expletives. What surprised Alexa was that Sam withstood it all. They had not spent much time with each other this year. Things had been too strained with Marcus's reappearance in her life, and even when Sam had been around he had been helping Bethany settle in. It was sweet to think that despite all their recent fights Sam was still willing to sacrifice so much just to help her out.

It took Alexa a while to realise that her near-coherent musings about Sam were a sign she was starting to feel better. The vomiting had stopped and her sleep had started to become longer and less restless.

"What time is it?" she moaned, trying to piece together some kind of timeline.

"Four pm," replied Sam from somewhere in the room.

"What day?"

"Saturday."

Alexa nodded and, feeling fatigued from the conversation, fell back against her pillow. The next time she woke, she felt decidedly better and rolled out of bed. She could hear Sam snoring lightly and assumed he was on the trundle bed. It was dark, but Alexa did not bother with lights. The movement was refreshing, but her body still ached from the days of vomiting and shaking. Her stomach grumbled, propelling her into the kitchen, but the effort of cooking, even something as simple as toast, was too much. Noticing that it was too early to justifiably wake Sam, she slipped back into bed and fell instantly to sleep.

"Hey, how you feeling?" asked Sam as Alexa slowly lifted her head, feeling the sun on her eyes. Alexa blinked and rolled over. She could not believe she still felt fatigued after doing nothing but sleep for three days. An arm reached under her and to sit her up. "Want to try getting up today? Might make you feel better."

"Got up this morning. Didn't make me feel better," Alexa retorted.

"Well, you look – and smell – like crap, so if you want to feel better, you might want to try a shower. I'll strip the bed."

Sam did not let her reply, helping her from the bed and walking her to the bathroom.

"Sure you trust me enough to shower by myself or you need to join me," Alexa sneered.

"I have good memories of you and me in that shower," replied Sam calmly, a soft smile on his face. "I don't intend to replace them with you like this."

That shower was perhaps the longest Alexa ever had. It was like its own journey; the searing water slowly heating her back to life, but that was not without its consequences. As her mind cleared, Alexa started to realise what she had done. If she could believe her actions would safeguard Bethany's future, she would not regret a moment, but it was getting harder to convince herself things would work out. All the setbacks and horrible events that marked her and Bethany's lives only accumulated to tell her that this would not be the last time they fell this low. It was a depressing thought. Alexa was not sure how much of this she could withstand, and hated that Bethany seemed to be able to pull herself out of this situation better than she could.

The way Bethany had cared for her was so sweet and tender. Alexa hated that Sam and Ben had been so convinced Bethany was not strong enough to look after her, hated that Marcus had been forced to make up some lie just to allow Bethany to leave in peace. Perhaps Bethany would be better off without her, but the thought of leaving Bethany was still too much. It gave Alexa enough strength to consider facing her future and fight for something better – to dare to try and be more than what she was. Then the realisation that she would fail returned and her resolve faltered.

Stepping out of the shower, Alexa pulled out a small bag from the back of the cabinet and twirled a razor between her fingers. If she could not face her future, there was no point lingering in this torturous existence. Pressing the razor to her wrist, Alexa closed her eyes and willed a decision to be made.

"Alexa?" knocked Sam on the door. Alexa put the razor back and jumped to her feet. "Food?" asked Sam as soon as Alexa walked out of the bathroom, thankfully thinking nothing of her agitated state. "You'd better be hungry, cos I'm starving."

The negativity that had been swirling menacingly swamped Alexa. A conversation about food should not be this crippling. "I'm not up to cooking," she admitted reluctantly. "Can we just get fish and chips on the beach or something?"

"Fish and chips, huh? Fats and oil. No salad. You must be hung over," smiled Sam, still determined to talk her out of this mood. "You had me at fish. Now go get dressed. Not kidding – starving!"

The day was sunny and clear, but there was a cool breeze off the water. Alexa felt better having the wind rush through her. Sam held her hand loosely. When he moved in closer and put his arm around her, there was no part of her that longed for something else and she hoped he did not see this suddenly going somewhere.

"It's good, just being friends, not feeling guilty, isn't it?" said Sam.

"Are you psychic?" asked Alexa, bewildered by his comment.

"You do it to me more than you realise," he replied flatly.

It was selfish, but Alexa was glad Sam was no longer in a happy, shiny mood. It somehow made him easier to talk to.

"Whatever happened to your glimpse of love? You get anywhere with that?" Alexa asked, not wanting to focus on her mood for a while, but was concerned by the grimace that crossed Sam's face.

"I was thinking about that too." Sam shook his head and Alexa turned to face him, taking his hands in hers, making his eyes roll in a sarcastically annoyed fashion. "Fine. If you must know, it was going well. Slow, but really nice. It's complex, but it was getting to the point where I was going to talk to you about it. Then it just fell apart."

"What are you going to do?" asked Alexa.

"I don't know. I don't even know how I feel about her any more," Sam sighed, continuing their walk along the beach.

It was a concept Alexa understood well. Her whole world felt as though it was filled with conflicting emotions. That only intensified when they arrived back at the apartment to see Bethany and Ben there. It was an awkward reunion, made worse by Marcus's arrival. There were too many people – too many eyes. All Alexa wanted was time alone, but as dinner approached, the apartment only became fuller with Maria's arrival. At least Alexa could see Maria was unsure about the need for her presence. Alexa did not like that someone had called Maria over just to cook. It was rude, but her attempts to say so were dismissed, none more so than by Maria.

"Anything I can do for you and Bethany," Maria smiled, rubbing her arm tenderly.

Alexa said nothing else. She refused to get angry at Maria. If Maria had been the only guest, she would not have minded at all. It was really Ben and Sam's overbearing stares she did not like. She felt monitored.

Marcus did not stick around long. He helped Maria wash up then disappeared into his room. When Maria left, Alexa looked around the lounge room expecting to feel more at ease, but felt more claustrophobic than ever. Bethany was curled up on the lounge. Alexa tried to catch her eye, but Bethany looked as shell-like as she felt. Her heart ached at the sight, but not the way it used to. Previously, Alexa would not have cared who was around. Nothing would have stopped her from curling up with Bethany. It was different now. She did not have the strength to defy and battle everyone who did not understand them, but more than that she feared she did not have the strength to help Bethany through this – not when she was still so unsure she wanted to get through this.

Deciding she needed to escape, Alexa used her lingering fatigue as an excuse to go to bed, but even that attracted a comment about how quickly Bethany recovered from her withdrawal. Bethany responded, but her voice was so meek that Alexa could not make out what she said. With eyes turned away from her, Alexa dashed to her room. She leaned against the wall, thankful for the solitude, but she was not alone for long. "Do you want me to sleep on the lounge?" asked Bethany meekly, slipping into the room.

Alexa just shook her head. If she thought it would prevent the others from staying, she might have said yes. Alexa climbed into bed, sick of this day – her life – already. She just wanted it to end. Bethany did not join her. She sat on the bed, looking down at her.

"I'm sorry I brought you down to this level," said Bethany softly, tears filling her eyes. "I know how you're feeling and how bad it is. I hate what I've done to you."

"You think you did this?" scoffed Alexa, strangely unaffected by Bethany's tears. "You're incredible."

"What? It is my fault. I pushed you to this. Don't try and tell me it's somehow all your fault," cried Bethany, her tears falling down her cheeks as she fought for blame.

"Fine. It's not all my fault," huffed Alexa angrily. "But it's not all yours either. I don't blame you for this – and that's not me being some kind of fucking saint. It's just me in a bad mood – with everything brought to the surface. It's not new. It's not the drugs. It's not you. It's me. This is what I'm really like." Tears continued to stream down Bethany's face. Alexa wanted to comfort her the way she always had, but was simply too frustrated and defeated. "What now?" Alexa huffed, causing more tears to slip down Bethany's face.

"I just know I'm going to let you down. I don't want to, but I'm no good. Thought I was. Thought I had potential, but I don't. I want to be like you, but I'm just not that good."

"You think I'm something special?" Alexa spat, wondering how she could be so deluded. "What've I done, Bethy? Except survive?"

"You've done everything. You protected me, withstood so much."

"And you haven't? I spent days, weeks, maybe, on the streets. You spent years. I couldn't have survived that. You survived heroin. You survived Leo." Bethany's face blanched at the name, but Alexa did not care for her discomfort. "I know what kind of man he was. I know how old you were. Tell me he never hurt you. Tell me it was love. Come on, Bethy, lie to me." Bethany's eyes were wide as she slowly shook her head. "Tell me you enjoyed all those foster homes. Tell me you liked all the foster brothers and sisters. Tell me you enjoyed the beatings. Tell me you liked all the boyfriends. Tell me you liked it when the Christies lied – sent me away and kept you from me. Tell me, Bethy, just how great your life has been."

Bethany kept slowly shaking her head as the tears continued to fall.

"So what, then? You don't want to do this. I don't want to do this." Bethany did not answer. Alexa moved to the door and locked it. This time, she would not be interrupted. Walking to the bedside table, she grabbed two razors and joined Bethany on the bed. Bethany's eyes widened as Alexa put the razor in her hand. "Let's not do this any more," Alexa said, thankful for the imminent release.

"Lex, wait."

"For what? For things to get better? Let's face it, Angel, things are never going to get any better. We're never going to escape this. We're just playing pretend and I don't want to any more. Let's just do what we always planned."

Alexa pushed the razor into the middle of her left wrist.

"Lex, I'm not sure. Maybe we can …"

"I can't. I don't want to. Please, you promised. We go together."

Bethany nodded, her tears drying as she pushed the razor into her wrist. Alexa sighed, relieved Bethany was not backing away from their pact. Their pain would finally end.

"Together on three," Alexa instructed, stroking Bethany's cheek.

Bethany nodded again, their eyes locked.

"One. Two. Three."

Chapter Eighteen

PAIN SPEARED THROUGH Alexa's wrist. Bethany gasped, quickly letting go of her. Bethany's razor fell on to the bed, but Alexa's was still pressed into her wrist.

"Careful, careful," whispered Bethany, slowly pulling the razor out.

Blood poured down Alexa's arm. She did not try to stem the flow. The pain was liberating; a beautiful contrast to her mental anguish. This was something her body knew how to deal with. Bethany ripped a pillow out of its case and wrapped the case around Alexa's wrist.

"I choose not to go," said Bethany, speaking as firmly as she was grasping Alexa wrist. "You're right. I don't want to do this. I don't think I can, but I'd rather this than watch you die."

"You'd rather watch me suffer through life?" asked Alexa flatly, honestly disappointed she was still alive to have this conversation.

"Yes. We can do this," urged Bethany. "You used to believe that too. I don't think we're ever going to achieve anything except survival. I want more too. I want to forget where we came from and so much of myself. I always thought you had it figured, but you don't. You're just like me – scared of everything and most of all yourself."

Alexa felt her anger begin to slide from her body, as if carried away by the blood that was quickly turning the pillowcase red. It reminded her of how she had previous dealt with her emotions and wondered if she would have done better if she had not had the use of her razor taken from her.

Bethany pulled back the pillow case to inspect the wounds. They were still bleeding, but she was as reluctant as Alexa to seek further attention. Pulling another pillow case off its pillow, Bethany folded and wrapped it more precisely around Alexa's wrist. With nothing else in the room, Bethany secured it with a hairband.

"We can sort it out properly in the morning," said Bethany softly. "I really didn't mean to stab you. Was trying to save you."

"I wanted to save you too," said Alexa sadly, laying her head in Bethany's lap. "I just failed."

"Me too. Maybe we should leave lifesaving to the knights of this world," replied Bethany meaningfully. "You're nineteen. I'm seventeen. We have to be able to save ourselves."

"What's that mean?" asked Alexa, sitting up, her heart stuttering.

"It means I'm breaking the pact. If you die, Lex, I won't go with you." Bethany closed eyes as she spoke. "I choose to hope. I choose to believe something better lies ahead of us and I'll fight for it – even if you won't."

Bethany's statement left Alexa numb. She did not want to fight. She did not have the energy to fight. If she could live without every day being an endless struggle, then perhaps she could motivate herself to stay for that. All she knew was that unless she chose otherwise, tomorrow would come as surely as this day would end. Life would continue on no matter how desperately she needed it to stop for a while so she could get her bearings, and that even making it stop permanently would take more energy than she had.

Allowing Bethany to lay her down, they crawled under the covers and held each other close. Alexa closed her eyes, concentrating on the burning in her wrist. Bethany kept hold of it, but part of Alexa could only hope that she would simply bleed to death in the night.

"You going to uni today? Or should I get dressed in the dark?"

Alexa blinked and looked out the window. It really was morning. It felt like only a second since she had closed her eyes. "Uni," she replied flatly. "Already missed a week."

"You still going to be able to hand in that assignment that was due last week?"

Alexa was surprised Bethany remembered – it certainly wasn't what was on her mind. "Will go to the doctor today," Alexa sighed.

It was not a fun visit. Finding a doctor Alexa trusted had taken a while, but now she had one the consultations were open and honest. In many ways, it was easier to tell the truth, particularly when the information was protected by confidentiality.

The doctor took the story well. She did not even blanch when Alexa showed her the wounds on her wrist, which looked worse in the daylight. There were two cuts. The deep one was from her own razor. The long one was from Bethany's razor running along her wrist as she tried to stop her from taking her life.

"You're very lucky this isn't worse," said Dr Carter. "I'll glue it up and give you antibiotics. I don't want any problems from it being open so long. I will also give you a certificate to cover this last week. I trust I won't have to give you one under similar circumstances again."

"Does anyone ever actually make promises like that?" asked Alexa, determined not to do so herself.

"No, but taking illicit drugs is not a medical condition."

"Withdrawing from them is. Just cover me for that part," replied Alexa defiantly.

"I'm also going to give you a referral to a psychologist." Alexa sat stony faced. Dr Carter had pressed her on this issue before. She had even written a referral before, but Alexa had torn it up – just as she intended to do this time. "Just remember, Alexa. If I have concerns about the risk you pose to yourself, I can take more drastic action. I don't want to, but I will to save your life. Right now, your situation is that serious. Getting help does not make you weak."

Weakness was not what Alexa feared. She was terrified of releasing the images that had taunted her during her withdrawal – images she could not quite see, but could still feel. They made her hate herself, hate her very existence and feel as if she needed to grab Bethany and run forever. It was hard enough to deal with those things lurking in her subconscious. Alexa was not sure she was strong enough to drag them to the surface.

Walking into the university was a strange sensation. It felt like it belonged to a different world to that which Alexa inhabited. She was timid approaching her friends, unsure if they would somehow guess what had happened and where she had been – or if they had even noticed her absence.

"Oh my God, Alexa. Where've you been?" asked Jessica. "I tried calling."

"Sick," replied Alexa. "Was in bed most of last week."

"You sure you're okay to be here? No offence, but you don't look great. What'd you have?"

"Just some virus."

Jessica took a step back, a smile on her face as she joked that she was not prepared to catch whatever she had. Alexa quickly reassured her that she was no longer contagious and Jessica laughingly put her arm around Alexa's shoulders. Jessica even came with Alexa to ask for her extension, walking out much more amused than she went in.

"What?" snapped Alexa.

"Whoa, who picked up a temper? I'm laughing at you, you freak. Who argues with a lecturer to get a shorter extension? You get offered a week and fight for less. You know that's not normal, right?"

"I just want it done." And not just the assignment, Alexa thought miserably.

Her mood made her bad company and she was thankful for the excuse to rush home after her last lecture. Jessica tried to convince her to stay for coffee, but she just wanted peace and quiet. It was not what she found. Ben and Bethany were already at the apartment when Alexa arrived. The way Bethany told her that Ben had picked her up from work gave the impression it was not something Bethany had asked for. Normally, Bethany would have felt special, but all this extra attention felt much more authoritative and supervisory rather than supportive, and only set Alexa's temper further on edge.

When Sam arrived and promptly sat with Ben in front of the TV, Alexa was infuriated. Marcus joined her at the dining table to work, his hand suddenly next to hers, forcing her to face him.

"Ignore it. It's misguided, but they just want to help," whispered Marcus. "You gave us a fright. Give it a few days. They'll get over it."

Alexa wished his psychic powers were a little more accurate. By mid-week there was no sign anyone was prepared to leave the apartment. When Alexa dared to complain about all the take-out food being ordered while they looked after her and Bethany by refusing to let them cook, Maria was once again roped into the fiasco.

Unable to spend any time alone with Bethany unless they were sleeping, Alexa could not wait for Friday to see Charlotte, so insisted she come by earlier. Charlotte was a useful bridge between her and Bethany, though Charlotte's presence was not openly welcomed by Ben or Sam. Alexa was sure they only tolerated her because Bethany often pulled Charlotte on to the lounge and spoke softly to her, their arms and legs entwined. That was how Alexa knew Bethany was feeling as trapped as she was, despite the smiling reassurances she gave Ben and Sam. Ben always received them well, pulling Bethany close. Sam just nodded, intent on holding a grudge. It was ridiculous. Even Marcus did not treat Bethany as indifferently as Sam did, but any attempt to say anything was always dismissed.

"Charlotte and I are going to do our Friday night thing out tonight," said Alexa on Friday morning as she and Bethany dressed. "Where can we meet you? We'll do something fun. Movies, bowling. I don't care."

"But Ben was going to pick me up after work," sighed Bethany.

"Tell him we have plans. We're allowed to do things without him. I don't get it. Has he quit his job and moved in here – just to be your personal chauffeur?"

"That's mean, Lex. He's just trying to help and be close."

Alexa held her tongue. The sad, defeated tone in Bethany's voice was more than she could take, and she would not hurt her more by voicing her opinion about Ben. She would just have to confront Ben directly.

"No!" replied Ben emphatically when Alexa told him of their plans.

She had not asked for permission.

"What they hell do you mean 'no'? You can't tell us what we can and can't do. We're adults," snapped Alexa.

"Bethany's not an adult," replied Ben firmly.

"And you're not her father," retorted Alexa in a steely voice.

"No, but Bethany was released on parole into my care, not yours."

Alexa felt her heart fall through her body. Bethany looked at her apologetically, tears welling in her eyes. It was like Bethany was being torn away from her all over again. It was too much. Alexa grabbed her bag and stormed out of the apartment.

"Wait. Alexa, slow down."

"Did you know?" Alexa cried, turning on Marcus as he chased her down the street.

"No. I had no idea. I never thought about it. I always assumed she'd be released into your care," Marcus replied earnestly.

His sincerity and the knowledge that he was on her side was more than her heart could take and tears started tumbling down her face. "He took her away from me."

"Alexa, no," replied Marcus gently. "Nothing could take Bethany away from you. I'm sure it was just a technical thing. Bethany wanted her release to be secret and you weren't there to sign the papers."

"Peter," growled Alexa.

"What?"

"He knew! He knew and he never told me. All this time."

Alexa felt doubly betrayed. Pulling out her phone, Peter answered on the second ring and immediately agreed to meet her. He was waiting as calmly as he always did, but that only infuriated her more.

"How could you give her to him?" Alexa cried rushing at Peter. He stood quickly and grabbed her wrists before she could hit him. "She belongs with me. How could you do that? I'm losing her and it's your fault. I can't save her and she won't stay with me."

"Alexa, what happened?" asked Peter urgently.

"He told me. He told me he has custody of Bethy, not me!" spat Alexa. "He gets to decide what she does and where she lives. You let him steal her from me."

Alexa did not care for Peter's response as her legs collapsed beneath her. Peter slowly lowered her to the floor and leant her against the side of his desk as he knelt beside her.

"That was never my choice," said Peter, his voice firm and calm. "I would have preferred that you had custody of Bethany, but there was a chance the Parole Board would not have released her to you.

Ben was always going to be the back-up in that situation.

"When Bethany asked that you not be told about the rescheduled hearing that changed things. I'm sorry I could not tell you – and that I did not tell you later – but I was acting as Bethany's lawyer, not yours. The things we discuss – the things you tell me when I'm acting as your lawyer – I don't tell anyone that. Not even Bethany."

"He's keeping her from me. I'm losing her."

"He will never keep her from you. I swear. You won't lose her."

"But I am. She won't stay with me. She told me," cried Alexa softly.

"What happened, Alexa? Why won't she stay with you?" asked Peter, his voice suddenly cautious.

"She broke the pact. She won't go with me. I need her to. I need her with me."

"How much do you need to go?" Alexa looked up, hopeful Peter would understand how much she needed this life to end. Perhaps he could convince Bethany to stay with her forever. "Okay, shhh," he said quickly, stroking her hair. "Do you need to go to uni? Is it vital?"

"I missed too much last week. I was sick."

"What are you doing after uni? I'm in court soon, but if you need to you can come up here. I'll find some work for you to do."

"I'm meeting Charlotte. Bethy's not allowed to come."

"Alexa, I need you to promise —"

"No!" she snapped immediately, unprepared to make any more promises of the kind she knew Peter would want.

"Can you let me finish?" asked Peter politely, though he did not wait for an answer. "I have some new work for you next week. It's a bit more challenging. I need you to promise you'll give it a chance – give yourself a chance – before telling me you can't do it."

"That's not what you were going to ask," Alexa retorted.

"Prove it," smiled Peter. Alexa did not answer. "Okay then, I will see you next week."

"You really think that's all it'll take? If I promise to come to work next week I'll live to see that day?"

"No. I'm not that naïve," replied Peter solemnly. "Nothing I say will ever be able to stop you doing something when you want it enough. That's one of the most brilliant – and terrifying – things about you. I'm not a fool, Alexa, but that does not stop me hoping that when you leave my office it will not be the last time I see you."

***

Marcus tossed his body to the other side, but it was no use. Sleep was not going to come. Peter's words had been swirling in his head all night. Their conversations always agitated him. Client confidentiality kept Peter from speaking plainly, but Marcus had quickly learned to read between the lines.

Jumping out of bed, Marcus decided early would be the easiest time to catch Alexa. Time alone had become a foreign concept over the last week. There was never a morning where Ben or Sam – sometimes both of them – were not camped out in the lounge room. Their behaviour was excessive in the extreme, but nothing he or anyone else said would convince them they were not required to be around to take care of Bethany and Alexa. And now Peter was asking him to look out for them.

Ben was still asleep on the lounge when Marcus walked to the bathroom, and Sam had arrived by the time he emerged. Marcus gave them each a silent nod of greeting and went to the kitchen. While he his back was turned, Alexa snuck quietly to the bathroom. This was going to be harder than he thought. Moving to the dining table, Marcus kept a close eye on the bathroom door. At the first sound of movement, he stood next to it, acting as though his need for the room was urgent.

"Sorry, you should've knocked," said Alexa.

"I can wait," Marcus smiled. "I actually wanted to just steal two quiet seconds with you to say hello."

Alexa's smile was radiant, though he could see annoyance burning in her eyes. Reaching forward, Marcus tucked her hair behind her ear. Alexa's hand automatically mimicked the action, causing the sleeve of her top to slide down her forearm. The sight of her bandaged wrist was excruciating. Peter was right. Alexa was the most desperate to die. Marcus touched the bandage gently and silently raised his eyebrows. Alexa immediately dropped her hand and pulled her sleeve down. "Not as bad as it seems," she whispered, not quite meeting his eyes.

"That's good to hear," Marcus replied, trying to keep his voice light. Lecturing her was not going to help. He needed to pull her out of this state not condemn her for being in it.

"Bethy – she was trying to stop me. She just ended up pushing my razor deeper into my wrist and sliced hers across it."

Marcus could not help but smile as he shook his head, his heart twisting at how close he had come to losing Alexa. He decided not to ask all the obvious questions. He knew why they each had a razor and how they had been pushed to this point.

"While I'm glad Bethany managed to stop you – and I guess I owe her one for that – I can't say I'm a fan of her methods," Marcus said, just managing a half-smile at the end.

"What would you've done? Crash-tackled me?" asked Alexa in a fiery voice.

It was fascinating how defensive Alexa still became over Bethany.

"No, that would be the back-up if my way didn't work."

"Which is?"

Marcus leaned forward so that his mouth was near Alexa's ear. "Distraction. Would have no choice. If you were doing that in front of me, I'd be forced to kiss you. If it made no difference then at least I'd have one kiss with you before you died."

Alexa's breath hitched and Marcus panicked, wondering if he had taken this too far. "I thought you were trying to convince me not to do something like this again, not entice me," she whispered.

Marcus had just enough time to register her words when he saw Ben and Sam staring at them, their arms folded. His body must have shifted, because Alexa immediately flinched and turned to face them. She stalked to her room, slamming the door behind her.

"Just tying on a bit more rope so you can string her along from anywhere in the world?" snarled Sam.

The comment was too close to home – too close to Marcus's own concerns about his behaviour – to simply brush off. All he could do was leave the apartment before Alexa re-emerged, with few intentions of being around much for a while.

***

Alexa spent a lot of time thinking about Marcus's promised kiss. In those brief moments in the car dreaming of their life together, she had envisaged many happy moments and numerous intimate ones. The feelings they generated were proving harder than expected to switch off, and now she had to contend with the knowledge that he would kiss her to save her. She was just not convinced one kiss could save her, and she did not want their first – and possibly only – kiss to be right before she died.

Without noticing, Alexa's resolve started to rebuild. She wanted to find another way of having that kiss in a situation that would not be followed by her suicide. Various scenarios ran through her head, but the one she liked the most was of her in a graduation gown and Marcus celebrating with her. It was an event she knew he would be proud of her for and one he would never miss if she wanted him there. The only problem with these visions was that they never ended with one kiss. Perhaps it was why she never dared to move forward in their private moments together. All she knew was that she liked the idea of where things went, and had to continually remind herself it could never be. She and Marcus would never be together. They would not allow it. But if she managed to graduate and achieve something worthwhile in her life, perhaps she would allow herself that one moment of weakness.

The re-emergence of her desire to do well at university saw Alexa move her study from the dining room table to the university library. Charlotte even joined her. The only negative was Bethany's absence. Ben was still insisting on escorting Bethany to and from work. Alexa tried to talk him out of his stance, but while Bethany refused to speak up Ben was unmoved. Bethany had never been one to advocate on her own behalf.

"Don't you think it's a bit late to be arriving home?" asked Ben.

Alexa looked over at Bethany, but she just tucked her knees into her chest and stared into space.

"I was studying at the library. I told Bethy. I asked her to meet me. You told her she couldn't," replied Alexa with forced calmness.

"What's Beth going to do at the library? It's not a suitable place for her. If you want to be the person responsible for her, then don't you think you should be home in the afternoons? Don't you think you should be cooking her dinner rather than leaving it to someone else?"

Alexa opened her mouth, but managed to hold her tongue. If she responded it would end up in a huge fight, and she would say things she might regret. It was not as though she did not know the debt she and Bethany owed Ben. Even with his overbearing ways, she wanted him in their lives. It was a strange problem to have someone who cared too much about them. The only compromise Alexa could make was to escape to her room and to breathe away her fury. It was made easier by Bethany joining her ten minutes later and wrapping her in her arms. That hug reminded her of the dark years; the type of hug they shared when they knew they were going to be torn apart.

Hoping to defuse the situation, Alexa made sure she was home to cook dinner, but it was difficult to convince herself to go home any earlier than necessary. "This is not them caring, Charlotte," said Alexa with frustration as they sat at the beach, delaying their trip home. "This is them not trusting us. Don't you want our place back?"

"It's not my place," smiled Charlotte. "Remember?"

Alexa waved her hand in frustration, starting to realise just how much she considered Charlotte a part of her home. It was unbelievably selfish. Charlotte had her own family and was getting along much better with all of them, including her step-mother, and Alexa knew she had no right to claim more of her.

"Just ask them to leave, then," said Charlotte. "You want your house back, then take it."

Alexa was desperately avoiding that confrontation. Her temper was constantly getting the better of her these days. At uni, they treated it as a joke, claiming she had actually been struck down with distemper. Jessica thought it was hilarious. Alexa struggled to be as amused, but that only made the joke stick. It was a different story at home. Every time she snapped, Sam and Ben exchanged meaningful glances, as if she was proving how incapable she was.

On Friday night, everyone was at the apartment, as Alexa and Charlotte had decided they would not have another Friday away from Bethany. They were determined they would not have any afternoons away from her next week either – even if they had to pretend it was only the three of them in the apartment. Bethany was not convinced by their plan. The threat of conflict was already proving too much for her as she curled up on the lounge between Ben and Maria. When Maria stroked her arm gently, Bethany shuffled over and curled her body into Maria's. Alexa watched from the dining table. It was nice Bethany found comfort in Maria's company, but this was never the way she had envisaged it.

"Should we cook or order in?" asked Ben in an upbeat voice.

Bethany eyes flicked Alexa's way before she pressed even further into Maria, Maria's arm holding her close. Alexa and Charlotte said nothing, so Sam and Ben debated the merits of different take-away food, flicking through the mountain of menus they had accumulated over the last two weeks. Maria offered to cook, but Ben and Sam did not appear to hear her and she did not press the point.

Marcus walked out of his bedroom dressed to go out. Alexa liked the concern that filled his eyes when he saw Bethany. He and Bethany might not get along very well, but he did not hate her and she thought that if he and Bethany ever had the chance to spend time together, he might learn to love her as she did.

As Marcus left, he touched Alexa's hand, smiling sympathetically as she sat at the table with her head lying on her arms. She could not manage a smile in return. It was difficult not to throw herself into his arms and beg him to help her escape – just for a while – especially when that one smile from Marcus was enough to draw disapproving looks from Ben and Sam, halting their dinner discussions.

"I feel like pizza," said Bethany softly, turning the focus back to dinner.

"All you ever feel like is pizza," sighed Sam tersely.

Bethany did not reply or take any further part of the conversation. Charlotte shifted her position at the table so it mimicked Alexa's pose, reaching out one of her hands to take Alexa's. Alexa squeezed it tight, trying to find the strength to see the night through. She had no idea how they were going to survive next week.

Ben and Sam decided on Indian food, never realising that Bethany had little experience with spicy foods and still struggled to eat anything with too much chilli. They only chastised her for not trying new things, before laughing when she could not eat it.

"Here, drink some milk," said Maria, returning from the kitchen with glasses for Bethany and Charlotte, who was also struggling. "It'll help more than the water."

"Did you have to order all spicy dishes?" asked Alexa, refusing to eat more out of principle.

"You could've contributed to the decision," retorted Sam. "We're not just here for our own amusement, you know."

Alexa did not reply and started to clear the table, but Ben insisted the girls settle in on the lounge and pick a movie. Ben and Sam's idea of clearing did not sit well with Alexa. They dumped the dirty dishes in the sink, claiming they could be worried about in the morning, and threw all the containers – uneaten food and all – straight into the bin.

"You know what'd be nice," said Maria as they clambered on to the lounge together. "A girls' night – just the four of us."

"Next Friday?" suggested Bethany hopefully, her eyes lighting up. "Can we go to your place? Can we go out? Walk along the water?"

"Anything you want," smiled Maria, stroking Bethany's face.

"Anything who wants?" asked Ben, sitting on the other lounge.

"We're just organising a girls' night for next Friday," replied Maria, a serene smile on her face.

"I'm sorry, Maria, but I don't think that's very wise. I don't think you could handle the situation if it got out of hand."

Alexa jumped off the lounge, and felt a hand instantly restraining her. It was Maria's. Bethany had curled back into her ball.

"I have to respectfully disagree, Ben," replied Maria firmly. "These girls don't need handling. I trust them."

"I don't. I love them, but I don't trust two heroin addicts and —"

"And what?" asked Alexa dangerously, refusing to have Charlotte dragged into this.

"And a girl we barely know."

"That's where we differ," said Maria, letting go of Alexa's arm and putting her arms around Bethany's balled up body. "I know Charlotte quite well. I know Alexa and trust her implicitly – irrespective of the events of the last few weeks. I admit I don't know Bethany nearly as well, but likewise these events have not changed my opinion of her. Yes, she broke our trust, but she'll never be able to earn it back until she's given the chance – and that includes the chance to break it again."

"We'll have to see how they go next week before we decide," said Ben firmly, as if that settled it. "Now, what did we decide to watch?"

Alexa stalked to her room and slammed the door. A minute later the door creaked open and she was disappointed to see Charlotte slipping into the room.

"Is Beth going to be okay?" asked Charlotte, sitting on the bed. "She needs to be with you."

"I miss her, Char."

"I miss her too. Isn't that funny? She hates me for ages and now I miss her when she's still around. I even want her to yell at me again."

Alexa could not respond. Her mood kept wavering from desolation to agitation and frustration, and occasionally to outright fury. All she wanted was to smile.

"You guys coming out? Movie's about to start," said Sam, walking in and sitting on the bed. It was strange the way he could go from condemning them to friendly with seemingly no effort.

"No, thanks. We're just going to hang in here," replied Charlotte when Alexa did not respond.

"And do what?" asked Sam in a condescending voice.

"Whatever we like," snapped Alexa, hating that anything that did not have his or Ben's approval was suddenly unacceptable.

"You're going to have snap out of this, Lex."

"My name is Alexa."

"That's right, change the subject."

"You want to talk to me then the least you can do is call me by my name," snapped Alexa.

"Fine! Alexa, you're going to have to stop this," retorted Sam. "We're all here trying to help you. You can't keep hiding away from the world. When are you going to start living again?"

"When are you going to let me?" Alexa cried, frustrated to the point of tears.

"What the hell does that mean?"

"I mean, how am I supposed to get back to living a normal life when I have you all camped out in my house twenty-four–seven?"

"You're unbelievable," snapped Sam, storming out of the room.

"Alexa, don't," said Charlotte, grabbing her hand as she rose.

"You wanted this."

"Not like this."

Alexa shrugged and stalked after Sam, unsurprised to see him in the lounge room openly berating her attitude.

"I don't think it's like that," Alexa heard Bethany say meekly.

The way Bethany continued to speak her mind with so little conviction burned Alexa more than anything else. She would walk away from all of this if she had to, but Bethany never would, and Bethany would never stand up and demand better.

"I think it's time you all left," said Alexa as calmly as she could, hating that she was having to say this in front of Maria.

"Excuse me?" said Sam.

"I want you to go home," Alexa repeated, enunciating every word.

"So you can do what? Hide from the world? Pretend not to be hung up on a man you'll never have – who continues to string you along?"

"Sam's right," said Ben quickly, before Alexa could coherently gather her expletives. "You might not like his tone, but he's right. You can't keep sitting here pretending you and Marcus will one day be together. He's leading you on." Alexa crossed her arms and turned away, so angry her thoughts were completely disjointed. "You have to start getting your life back together."

"What do you think I've been trying to do?" Alexa cried.

"I don't know, but I'm glad we've been here to take care of you this last fortnight," said Ben.

"Take care of me? I don't need to be taken care of," growled Alexa.

"Then what do you think you need?" asked Ben, clearly trying to control his own frustrations.

"To be left alone! How can I do anything when every time I turn there's one of you hovering, just waiting for me to fail – jumping in to save me when I haven't even had the chance to make a mistake?"

"We're sick of where your mistakes take you," said Sam bitterly.

"I'm sick of where your mistakes take me too," snapped Alexa in return. "If you'd just trusted me – trusted that I knew how I felt about Damien, that I wasn't holding out for Marcus, but for someone better – then I never would've forced myself to be with a guy who was disgusted by the very thought of me."

Sam did not answer as his gaze fell to the ground.

"That's not really fair, Alexa," said Ben gravely.

"Really? What's not fair's that I used to trust you," Alexa cried, her voice trembling. "I never used to be scared of you. You were one of those rare people I held separate from the rest, but then you attacked Marcus in my house, in front of me, with no provocation."

"We only want the best for you and Bethany," said Maria in a kind voice, as Ben and Sam remained silent.

"I understand that," replied Alexa through gritted teeth, hating the idea of ever yelling at Maria. "But they don't understand that they need to learn to trust us. They need to stop hovering over us so sure we're going to fail. Stop telling us everything we think or feel is wrong. We already doubt ourselves and our worth more than enough. Why do they have to keep proving they don't believe in us either?"

"I think you're taking things the wrong way. We do believe in you – and Beth. Beth, you don't feel like this, do you? You need us here too, right?" asked Ben.

Bethany got up and stood next to Alexa. "No. I'm with Lex on this one," said Bethany, her voice just strong enough to sound like she meant it. "It was you and Sam always – always – telling me how much I owed Lex and how I needed to repay her. And I tried so hard, but it was never enough, because with everything she did the debt grew bigger and bigger. You never made me feel like I could pay it off and Lex was always so kind and supportive. I never did wrong in her eyes and, when I confessed that, you both told me it was my fault – told me I had to do more. But you never understood – you made me disbelieve that's just the way Lex is. She's perfect to me too and I'd forgive every mistake of hers. I always feel safe to fail with Lex, strive out, because if I fall she'll just pick me up and encourage me to go on. You guys just yell me for not doing better."

"I didn't realise you thought of us like that," said Ben, his voice choking as he stood to leave.

"Wait," cried Bethany, grabbing Ben's hand. "You do great too. Me and Lex'd be nowhere without you guys. It's just that … doing good doesn't mean never doing bad."

Bethany turned to Alexa, urging her to relay similar sentiments, but Alexa could not do it, not then. "I just want my place back," Alexa said, her eyes closed in a desperate attempt to control her frustration. "I love you all, I need you all and I want you around – just not all the time. Please, go home."

Sam grabbed his stuff and left immediately. Ben hugged Bethany tightly before giving Alexa a kiss on the top of her head. Maria pulled all of them into a large hug with an excited reminder about their girls' night next Friday and left with Ben.

"I should go too," said Charlotte meekly.

"No," cried Bethany, pulling her back. "It's Friday. It's our night together. Don't go, please."

Charlotte looked at Alexa, who just shrugged before collapsing on the lounge. "I want you to live here permanently," Alexa confessed. "The three of us, all in the same room, getting in each other's way – that's what I want."

"And Marcus hanging in the next room always ready with a smile," said Charlotte, collapsing on the lounge next to Alexa.

"Selfish and stupid, but yeah."

"Me too," said Bethany quietly, taking the seat next to Charlotte. "He hates me, but he feels like home."

***

Marcus sighed as he pressed the button for the lift. Going home had never been as tedious as it had been over the past fortnight. Perhaps it was Ben's way of getting him out of the apartment, because it was the one thing that had made him truly dislike living there. However, Marcus knew it would take more than that for him to leave Alexa.

Opening the front door, Marcus prepared himself to see one or more bodies cluttering the lounge room. It was the one time he wished he held some sway over Ben and Sam. Their actions were choking the life out of Bethany and Alexa. The change in Bethany was so dramatic Marcus could not help but feel sorry for her. The way Bethany curled up in a ball to hide from reality was such a contrast to Alexa's defiance. Part of Marcus wanted to believe it was because Alexa was strong and Bethany weak, but his little sister had always made him be her voice when confronting their parents. That had changed soon after Rhianna moved out of home.

Rhianna was now the confident one, prepared to take a defiant stand. Her last argument with their parents made Marcus glad for the reversal in temperaments. He and Rhianna had been talking more since he left Redgrove and the revelations that had followed. She had been the only one to support him, to not label him a paedophile for his feelings for Alexa, though she also encouraged him to move on and forget Alexa, but that had proved impossible. When Marcus had told Rhianna of his new living arrangements, she just laughed.

"Marc, just don't hurt her, okay. Screw around with other girls and screw over Lucy as much as you like. Just don't hurt her," Rhianna had said seriously.

It was a promise Marcus was still trying to keep. Rhianna asked every time she saw him. Her visit last weekend had been very well timed. With everything that had happened, he needed a confidant. He got more than that. He got a defender. When his parents had again pressed him to move out, calling his living arrangement indecent, he had said nothing. Thinking back, he had acted just like Bethany. It was Rhianna who stood up for him. Rhianna's blossoming from a shy child to a strong woman gave Marcus hope Bethany would similarly flourish when given the chance.

The sight of bodies on the lounge room floor made Marcus shake his head. He wanted to flick the light on, just to disturb them, but that seemed a little petty. However, as Marcus walked towards his room, he noticed a change in the configuration. Alexa, Bethany and Charlotte were all asleep, their limbs entwined. Bethany was in the middle, and even in her sleep he could see she had struggled to hug Alexa and Charlotte at the same time. What she had done was pull the blanket off Alexa and half off Charlotte and wrap it around herself. Grabbing another blanket, Marcus wished it was Bethany he had to put it over. Alexa was still so vulnerable in her sleep and he hated the fear that flickered in her eyes when she woke.

"Hey," Marcus smiled, when Alexa predictably startled herself awake. Alexa shifted so she was facing him and blinked sleepily, her hair tussled in an amazingly unattractive way. It made Marcus smile. Movies never depicted a person waking like this, and yet to his eyes she was the most beautiful girl in the world. "They finally left, huh?" he whispered, mastering the urge to reach out and stroke her face.

"Kicked them out," Alexa replied softly. "Wanted my house back."

"Need more room?" he asked, his heart twisting at the possible answer.

Alexa shook her head, smiling sleepily. Marcus always expected reason would one day kick in and she would see him the way the rest of the world seemed to. Part of him wished she would, so she might be spared the pain his presence would cause. Alexa's hand reached out and stroked his cheek, wiping a tear from the corner of his eye.

"My angel," Marcus said involuntarily, holding his hand over hers.

"I'm no angel," Alexa replied.

Marcus could feel her heaving breaths and wished he could hold her, but all he could do was grasp her hand tighter. "My angel," he repeated in a thick voice. "Always in my heart, never in my arms, always out of reach."

Alexa nodded, a tear slipping down her cheek. Marcus released her hand and wiped it away, while her hand continued to stroke the side of his face. It was tempting to lean down and kiss her, but he feared that with the way his heart was aching it would not end there. He did not want it to end anywhere, and knew the only way to prevent that was to stop it from starting. It was just not that easy to walk away from Alexa.

Bethany suddenly gasped and shuddered in her sleep, grabbing for Alexa as she rolled over. Alexa reciprocated soothing Bethany as she curled into her.

"She does this more than she realises," whispered Alexa, more tears slipping down her cheeks. "She doesn't have nightmares like me, but she doesn't sleep easy either."

"We all have our demons," Marcus said, rising to his feet.

"We all have our protectors too," Alexa replied, closing her eyes and pulling Bethany close. "Our knights," she whispered so softly Marcus was not sure he heard right.

Marcus rushed to his room and collapsed on the bed. He grabbed his pillow and held it to his chest, holding on to the desperate desires that were building in him.

"Nineteen, nineteen, nineteen," he repeated to himself, knowing the other arguments against them being together were losing their sway. Yet in the back of his mind, Marcus knew Alexa would not be nineteen forever. When she was twenty-five, their ten-year age gap would be much less significant. By that time, the fact that they met while she was his student would be much less important too. At twenty-five, few could claim she was not capable of making independent, rational decisions. If they had significant time apart prior to that, then there could be no claims that he groomed her to that point.

Twenty-five was like the new magic number, but even as Marcus thought that, he lamented how far away it was. Twenty-four, twenty-three – by that age Alexa would be finished university, have a job, a life direction. Twenty-two was too young. He would not justify any age below twenty-three.

As Marcus eyes closed, his mind swirled around his foolish fantasy. If he was to dare to consider ever asking Alexa out, he had to give her a real chance of finding love and moving on from him. Moving out would not be enough. The separation would have to be more complete. The best plan he had was to work overseas for a while. It would not be difficult. Teaching was an easy profession to travel with, and it did not matter where he went. Rhianna had suggested that from the start, but he had never been adventurous and by the time he convinced himself he could do it he and Lucy had started dating.

Lucy had broken up with her boyfriend three months earlier – a pilot she had been seeing for three years. The time apart had taken its toll, and she would not hear of Marcus leaving or them attempting a long-distance relationship. That one suggestion had even been used by Lucy as a reason why she had not moved in with him; she could not trust that he would stick around. Perhaps Lucy was right to distrust his loyalty, given he was mapping out his future around creating a slim chance to be with Alexa. What role Lucy played in his life until that moment was almost secondary, and as he finally fell asleep all his thoughts were of Alexa.

Marcus woke feeling much calmer, the future looking that little bit brighter. When he realised this was the first time in almost a month he and Alexa could steal a few quiet moments together, he jumped out of bed and threw on his pyjama pants.

"Charlotte's in the shower," said Alexa from the kitchen as soon as he walked out of his room.

Marcus walked into the kitchen, where Alexa was leaning against the bench. She looked relaxed, but did not look well. They had spent so little time together since her return that he had put everything down to her stress over Ben and Sam.

"Coffee?" Alexa asked. He nodded keenly. "Strong?"

"Hell, yeah," Marcus replied. Alexa smiled and dumped more coffee into the plunger. "How're you feeling? Body stopped aching?"

"Mostly," she shrugged, making Marcus guess that it was worse than she was letting on. "It's my temper that's been shot."

"Wow, you with a bad temper. That must be strange," replied Marcus, trying not to laugh.

Alexa threw a tea-towel behind her in his general direction. He caught it with a smile. The topic of conversation may not have been cheery, but it was nice to be chatting again.

"Worse than before. Can you believe that?" replied Alexa seriously. He shook his head, still smiling. "I wonder why I did it. I don't even know what I was trying to achieve."

"I know what you were trying to achieve," said Marcus solemnly. "You love her. You were trying to save her. It was misguided, but I understand what you were trying to do."

"Yeah, I know, but now it's done, I can't retrace my thoughts. I don't know why I thought doing *that* would help. All I remember is the image of Bethy dead and the feeling of desperation it created. I just had to stop it. I don't know how I pulled all that into a logical thought process, because I know – at the time – I thought I was doing the right thing by her."

"I know," nodded Marcus. "We all do stupid, painful things when we love someone. You hope it's the right thing, but sometimes it's just stupid and painful."

"Sometimes it's right and painful," replied Alexa, looking up with apologetic eyes.

"Morning," said Bethany, walking into the kitchen, forcing Marcus to swallow his reply. Bethany did not look at him as she proceeded to bear-hug Alexa. It made Marcus smile. When left to their own devices, they were such beautifully loving creatures. "You got more of that?" asked Bethany, looking down at Alexa's coffee.

Alexa nodded, but Bethany did not release her and Alexa was forced to make Bethany's coffee with Bethany hanging off her. Alexa did not appear to mind, and when she did not need her hands she was holding Bethany to her. They were completely different people to the ones he had seen the night before. It was impossible not to watch them.

"So we starting our house hunt today?" asked Bethany excitedly when Alexa handed her the coffee.

"Sure, if you still want to," replied Alexa hesitantly.

Marcus's heart skipped a beat, but he forced a supportive smile on his face as he nodded slightly.

"Hell yeah," replied Bethany, smiling brightly. "Big place – room enough for everyone to stay."

"We still really want that?" asked Alexa with a smile.

Bethany turned and headed to the lounge room, but stopped at the bench Marcus was leaning on. Putting her coffee down, Bethany threw her arms around his neck and hugged him warmly. "Big enough for everyone," she said again.

Marcus slid his arms around Bethany and returned her embrace, but it was awkward and he could see Alexa's amusement behind her hand. Bethany pushed out of his arms and grabbed her coffee, planting herself on the lounge with Alexa's laptop. Alexa moved to join Bethany, but Marcus shifted to her side, halting her exit.

"You know it's better I don't come with you, right?" he asked in a low voice.

"Better's a relative term," replied Alexa, glancing up at him.

Marcus wondered what Alexa was relating him to when she said that. If he had the courage to ask, he might not have rushed to the bathroom as soon as Charlotte emerged from it, but he had his plan and while Alexa was still just nineteen, there was no justification for him to position himself to be with her. He had to let her go and hope they would find their way back to each other.

Chapter Nineteen

IT TOOK A few weeks, but Alexa's life began to resemble something approaching normal again, although she was no longer sure what normal was. It did not seem normal to be in constant pain. If it had been physical, she was sure she could have dealt with it better. The mental anguish of her existence did lessen by the day, but only minimally. It was not helped by the near complete absence of Ben and Sam in the weeks following their confrontation.

Bethany had immediately tried to play peacemaker, something Alexa had never been very good at. It did not take much for Bethany to win back Ben, though he did not return to the apartment. Bethany assured Alexa he was not upset and understood how overprotective he had been, but Alexa only had her word for that. Ben never came and spoke to Alexa himself. He did not say anything about any of it, even when Bethany arranged for them all to have dinner at Maria's place.

"Don't be too hard on him," said Maria soothingly as she and Alexa tidied up in the kitchen.

Ben had asked Bethany if she wanted to stay the night at his place, and she had jumped at the chance. He never looked Alexa's way.

"Why's it always me who's in the wrong," cried Alexa, collapsing to the floor, her legs curled into her chest and she slouched against the kitchen cupboards. "Why doesn't anyone tell Ben to like me as much as Bethany? Why doesn't anyone tell him not to be too hard on me? I'm trying."

"Shhh. Of course you are," said Maria, kneeling down in front of Alexa and stroking her hair. "But you need to realise that Ben's trying too. He's not perfect. He makes mistakes as well and I know how much those mistakes have hurt him."

"He doesn't like me."

"Oh yes he does. He loves you so much he doesn't know what to do. I know from your side it looks like he loves Bethany more, but it's not true. Ben just doesn't know – he's so scared of losing you that he acts – I don't know why he can't show you how much he loves you. I don't understand why he finds it so much easier with Beth, but I do know how much he loves you. He's terrified of losing you. That's his

greatest fear. So maybe try not to push him away and it'll be easier for
him to step forward."

It was a good theory, one Alexa tried to put into practice, but it
never quite worked. She was so naturally defensive she would not
notice until later just how stand-offish her behaviour had been. If it
were not for Sam, Alexa would have thought it all her fault, but after
two weeks of stubborn silence, he came around and asked to be friends
again. If Ben had done the same thing, Alexa was sure she could have
hugged him the way she hugged Sam.

"I'm sorry, Sam," Alexa said softly into his chest as he held her
tight. "I love you. I never wanted to hurt you. I know I do stupid things
and I know you just want to help me. I'm sorry."

"It's all right," he chuckled, squeezing her tight. "You were right
about lots of things too."

It was nice the way Sam was able to forgive and forget. Alexa liked
having her best friend back. They did not always hang out at the
apartment though. Sam often found her at uni and either sat with her
friends or introduced her to his.

"Can you relax," he laughed when she kept looking cautiously
around his group of friends. "She's not here."

"What? What do you mean?" Alexa asked.

"Charlotte told me. So just relax. You can't ruin anything for me."

It was hard for Alexa to believe. She had a talent for ruining
things, but Sam was persistent – in a way Ben never.

"Didn't see you at uni today," Sam smiled, arriving unexpectedly
on Alexa's doorstep.

Charlotte was at home with her family and though Alexa had
more than enough study to see her through the night, it was not hard
to submit to Sam's suggestion of taking the afternoon off and hanging
out on the lounge. They laughed and Sam caught her up with all the
gossip among their high school friends.

"You're not going to tell them about what I did, are you?" Alexa
asked tentatively.

"I won't tell the girls," replied Sam, biting his lip. "Sorry, but I see
the guys every week – more if we can. You scared the hell out of us
disappearing like that. They know."

"Sam," Alexa sighed.

"Give us some credit. I know I got a bit crazy when you got back,
but we know the pressures you're under and how hard it is for you. I
get how scary it was for you to think you might lose Beth."

Sam pulled Alexa tight to her chest, his head in her neck as she sat in his lap. His breath shuddered and she remembered how rude she had been to him about his concerns for Bethany.

"I know you were worried about her too," Alexa said, rubbing his arm. "Shouldn't have questioned you reasons for caring."

"Yeah," he sighed.

There was deep sadness in Sam's voice and Alexa wondered if he really had forgiven her. The sound of the door opening stole her chance to ask. Sam suddenly shifted, his mood rousing as he pulled her closer.

"Oh, hello, Alexa. We didn't mean to interrupt. You should've told have told Marc you were having your boyfriend over. We would've given you some privacy."

Alexa rolled her eyes, gritting her teeth, but managed to recompose her face before Lucy and Marcus walked around in front of them.

"I'm just an old friend, actually," said Sam stiffly, before Marcus introduced him to Lucy.

"Another student of yours? How lovely," sneered Lucy.

Alexa could see from the look in Marcus's eyes the jibe wounded him deeply and wanted to ask why he would put up with Lucy, but she already knew.

"Beth not home?" asked Marcus, looking concerned. "It's late."

"She's out," replied Alexa happily, loving that Marcus cared.

"She's home, actually."

Everyone turned to see Bethany dumping her bag and keys on the kitchen bench. Bethany started at the sight of Sam, causing Sam to hold Alexa tighter. It made Alexa want to punch him. She did not need Sam holding a grudge against Bethany on her behalf.

"We'll be heading out for dinner soon. We'll probably be late home, so I'll catch you all later," said Marcus quickly, before pulling Lucy to his room.

Alexa turned to see Bethany shooting daggers at Marcus's door. She had hoped Bethany would be over her complete disgust of Lucy by now, but it was difficult. Lucy did not make herself very likeable.

"How was the thing?" asked Alexa, jumping up from the lounge and hugging Bethany tight before sliding into the kitchen. "You eat?"

"There was food, but I didn't know what most of it was. Didn't want to look like a weirdo spitting it out if I didn't like it, so didn't try most of it. Made me wish I was eating your cooking." Alexa smiled. Bethany was the one person whose praise she truly believed. "Would've been all right if I could've washed it down with a drink," shrugged Bethany, leaning over Alexa and nibbling the food she was preparing. "Couldn't say that though. It's strange how unacceptable it is to not drink. I wonder if claiming I'm an alcoholic would get people off my back. No worries that I don't want to eat, but go crazy when I say I don't want to drink."

"But you're only seventeen!" cried Alexa.

"Your innocence is kinda endearing," smiled Bethany, wrapping Alexa up in bear-hug.

"I know what you mean," said Sam, sitting himself on the other side of the kitchen bench. He looked warily at Bethany, as though he was not sure he wanted to be talking to her. "Since that pact – since we all decided to give up all the good stuff – I've never been more hassled in my life. You'd think I was refusing to love my child the way people treat you when you don't want a drink."

"I wish I was strong enough to just have one in my hand, but not drink it – or just drink it slow. Wouldn't be so hard if they all stopped offering me drinks," said Bethany, looking over at Sam, but his eyes flicked away.

Bethany released Alexa and began to morosely set the table. Sam watched her, looking equally distraught.

"Would you please just forgive her," whispered Alexa, moving over to Sam. "I don't know what part you're most angry about, but please. I mean, I'm the one who kicked you out and yelled at you and was mean and you're talking to me again. This isn't easy for her – and doing it without you ... please."

Sam shook his head and retreated to the bathroom. Alexa sighed, returning her concentration to dinner.

"Lex," said Bethany softly, slipping into the kitchen. Alexa waited for Bethany to continue, but she seemed undecided about whether to speak or not as her eyes flicked towards the bathroom. "There isn't something – I mean, you guys aren't ...."

"Not for me, Bethy," smiled Alexa, hugging Bethany tight. It was sweet that Bethany cared about her being hurt. "And I don't think for him either. We're just friends – trying to get back to friends."

Sam returned before Alexa could say more and Bethany walked away. Alexa focused solely on dinner, hoping if she ignored Sam he would talk to Bethany instead. By the time she had dinner cooking, Sam had stepped off his stool and was hovering between her and Bethany. Alexa stirred as she watched Sam shift awkwardly towards Bethany. She could not hear what Sam and Bethany were saying, but could see the tears slipping down Bethany's cheeks. Bethany quickly wiped them away and turned from Sam, fumbling with the plates. Sam grabbed her and pulled her into a tight embrace. When Bethany reciprocated, Alexa could not help but run out and hug them.

"Let's not do this any more," Alexa coughed, trying to hold back her own tears. "We need our best friend."

Sam choked out a laugh and opened his arms to pull her into their embrace. Alexa kissed them both before returning to the smoking food, while Sam and Bethany sat on the lounge in each other's arms.

It was strange the way things changed. From always being the strong one, Alexa felt impotent, left in awe by Bethany's progress. That had always been the amazing thing about Bethany. Under the right conditions, her determination could see her overcome anything. She liked reporting her doctors' surprise, and how much easier she was finding it to resist her cravings this time around.

"It's actually because of you," confessed Bethany when she and Alexa were alone. "Seeing what I did to you – what heroin did to you – when I get a craving, it always comes with that vision now. I don't want to hurt you. I know I've still got a lot to make up for – I'm sorry for what you suffered, but I think it did save me."

Alexa smiled grimly. Saving Bethany was all she had ever truly wanted from her life, and any sacrifices would be willingly made. However, seeing Bethany starting to actually live and enjoy her life only reminded Alexa of all her other failures.

Academically, Alexa was struggling to catch up. It was not made better by the Saturdays spent driving around the city inspecting houses. Bethany had taken to the house hunt with astounding vigour. Each week there was a list of no less than twenty houses on her list. Alexa's criteria ruled out a handful, while budget ruled out several more, but that still left them with more than they could see in a day.

It was hard to talk to Bethany about any of these issues without making her feel guilty. Alexa was able to confide in Charlotte about university, but not the house hunting. Most of the houses they were looking at were not near where they now lived and it seemed inevitable they would be moving away from Charlotte. It was something Alexa was still in denial about, and would not truly believe until it happened.

Alexa dared to talk to Sam, but he laughed off her money worries and dismissed her academic ones, telling her that she was expecting too much. It was not what she wanted to hear, but feared it was the truth. The person Alexa really wanted to talk to was Marcus. It might have been because he often gave the type of advice she was willing to accept, but more than anyone he knew her as a student and would know if she was setting her sights too high.

Marcus was around, but nearly always with Lucy, which did not make for free and easy conversation. Bethany decided she was not going to leave the apartment when Lucy was around unless she had prior plans. It made for a tense household. Alexa could see Bethany was genuinely trying – to be tolerant, at least – but she and Lucy still rubbed each other the wrong way. Lucy was polite enough to Alexa, but Alexa knew it was insincere so struggled to return the courtesy. Charlotte was the best at handling Lucy's sarcasm and snide remarks.

"She's like my step-mum," explained Charlotte with a casual shrug of her shoulders when Bethany questioned how she did it. "Actually, I think my step-mum's worse."

"She must be a real bitch then."

"Bethy!" cried Alexa, hitting her on the arm. "Don't say that."

Charlotte only laughed, agreeing with Bethany.

"See, Lex, you're way too nice," laughed Bethany. "Anyone else would've kicked Lucy out by now."

"I can't," breathed Alexa.

"He wouldn't leave," said Charlotte, understanding immediately.

"You don't know that," Alexa replied. "He can't put off his life forever for something I can never give him."

"You could just give it to him," smirked Bethany. "You know he'd have you."

"For how long?" questioned Alexa seriously. "Will he still want me when his career and reputation are ruined? What about after he realises how dysfunctional I am, or after a week of my nightmares?"

"I think he'd give up everything to be with you," said Charlotte earnestly.

"Yeah, but he shouldn't have to," said Alexa, her fist clenching. "I mean, he's getting stuck with me. He should get to keep everything and be given a thousand times more."

"Maybe it's better to have him, even it's for just a while, than to always wonder what could've been," said Charlotte tentatively.

"I know how to be with Marc while not being with him," smiled Alexa, before the grin slipped from her face. "I don't know how to live without him completely. I don't know how to lose him. I don't think I can do that. Don't think I can risk it."

"Okay, so loving from afar," said Bethany, squeezing Alexa's hand, and Alexa knew she truly understood. "Well from the next room," she added with a laugh. "We'll put up with Lucy – snide duck face and all."

Alexa knew she should not laugh, but could not help it. She loved the support Bethany and Charlotte gave her – and Lucy really did have a bit of a duck face.

"Good, well now you're in a better mood, can we look at the list of houses for this weekend?" asked Bethany cheerily.

Alexa looked warily Charlotte's way, but Charlotte was already scanning the list and giving her opinion. "It's fine," said Charlotte, smiling at Alexa. "I'll miss not having you guys so close, but it's not like I'll never see you again. Beth's already promised me the third-best room in the house," she added with a laugh.

Bethany smiled, hugging Charlotte roughly. It was amazing to see how well they got along now. All that early animosity had evaporated and at times Alexa felt Bethany was closer to Charlotte than she was.

"Angel, I love you, you know that, but I'm going to have to give the house hunting a miss for a while," said Alexa, ruffling Bethany's hair to try and sound less serious. "I've been given a tiny mercy with all my exams near the end of the exam period and I have to study."

"But, Lex, our dream house isn't going to wait for your exams to be over," cried Bethany with a mortified look on her face.

"Dream house? You've found our dream house?" asked Alexa with raised eyebrows.

"Okay, no," admitted Bethany with a little smile. "But I will."

"And I will look at it when you find it – but not twenty potential dream houses – not until my exams are over," said Alexa, standing her ground. "You have the list of things I need from a place. I need you give me those things. If after that you find something wonderful and perfect, then I'll look at it. I promise."

Bethany smiled happily at the compromise, but Alexa had the feeling Bethany's enthusiasm would get the better of her and the number of perfect houses Bethany just had to see would be many more than Alexa wanted to spend her time looking at.

"Where's your list?" asked Charlotte, nudging Alexa. "I can see you don't trust her. Give me your list and I'll be the wet rag."

"The wet what?" asked Bethany.

"You know, throw a wet rag over an idea – extinguish the flame," explained Charlotte. "You never heard it before?"

"Nope," replied Bethany. "But I know lots of different ways to tell someone to get lost and shut up," she added with a triumphant smile.

"Any of them polite enough to use at school?" asked Charlotte with a hopeful smile.

"No!" cried Alexa, covering Bethany's mouth before she could speak. "Definitely not," she laughed. "You'll never be allowed to stay with us if Bethany introduces you to her vocabulary list."

They all laughed and mucked around, Alexa accepting she would not get any study done tonight. It could be her last night of freedom before the hard slog of study, so spent it training Charlotte to moderate Bethany's housing fantasies. It was a great night and Alexa regretted there would be less of them in the future. Leaving Charlotte would be harder than leaving Marcus.

Life outside of university and study ceased the next morning. It was nice to have an excuse to ignore everything else. Up with Bethany each morning, Alexa managed to fit in several hours of study before classes and was back at the dining table the minute she arrived home. The only time she moved was for dinner, but that was soon overruled.

"We'll go back to eating at the table once your exams are over," said Marcus, directing Bethany to pull her to the lounge where her dinner was waiting. "It's fine. We'll eat real neat and not make a mess."

Almost on cue, Bethany tilted her plate a little too far, sending peas tumbling across the floor.

"Yeah, okay," sighed Alexa, as Bethany picked up the peas. "Better to have a couple of carpet stains than make me move my books."

Marcus chuckled, but said nothing. He did not have to. His actions spoke so much louder. Through her last week of classes and into study week, he did everything he could to make life at home simple for her. He shopped, cooked and cleaned, helped Charlotte with her homework and chatted to Bethany – just so Alexa could hear.

"You're going to make me fat," said Alexa, not raising her head as Marcus placed a small bowl of chocolate and a cup of tea in front of her. "I haven't been outside in two days and you keep force-feeding me junk food."

"Then you should take a break. Go for a run. It'll do you good," countered Marcus.

"I don't have time."

"Yes, you do. Besides, exercise will get blood to your brain – make you more productive." Alexa could not fight the logic, but as she mapped out the rest of her day, she could not justify the time away from her study. "You're making excuses," said Marcus, moving behind and leaning over her, his hands resting on the table on either side of her body. It brought his lips right near her ear and made her heart dance double time. "Go in the morning – ten, fifteen minutes, if that's all you can do – come back, jump in the shower and get straight into it. Isn't that better than yawning over your books for an hour as you wake up in the morning?"

"Maybe," replied Alexa, resisting the urge to agree with everything Marcus said. He was standing so close she could feel his body heat warming her. She could even smell him; a mixture of cologne and something that was distinctly him. It was intoxicating.

"Give it a try tomorrow. If it doesn't work, stick to sitting at the table all day."

"Fine, I'll give it a go," Alexa sighed dramatically. Marcus laughed as he stepped away, making her shiver with the sudden cold. Grabbing her tea to warm herself, she pushed away the chocolate and pulled her books forward.

"Don't feel the need to become one of those people who worries so much about their weight they can't eat without over-thinking the situation," said Marcus from his bedroom door.

"I don't worry about my weight," replied Alexa truthfully. "That's everyone else's issue. I worry about my health. I didn't go through all this to have a heart attack at twenty-five."

"Fair point," nodded Marcus thoughtfully.

He cooked a lot more vegetables in their dinner that night.

The next morning Alexa took Marcus's advice. She decided not to set her alarm any earlier, determined to test his theory that she would be more alert. From the smile that graced his face when she was sitting down studying solidly half an hour earlier than normal, she would have almost preferred him to be wrong.

"Yeah, yeah, all right, say it. You were right," she sighed, waving her hand at him.

Marcus laughed and sat down at the corner of table Alexa always left free out of courtesy to the rest of the household.

"I'll miss our mornings when you move," Marcus smiled.

"You could move with us," Alexa suggested as casually as possible.

"That's a very tempting suggestion, but you know as well as I do that this was only ever supposed to be a temporary arrangement. You and Beth, you guys need your space. We don't need to live together to be friends."

"No, I guess not," Alexa replied, her mouth pressed into a line. "But I never said anything about a timeframe. Nothing in your lease either. It's only temporary if you want it to be."

Marcus did not answer. He just threw down the rest of his coffee and left with best wishes for her study. Alexa needed them. Despite studying for two weeks straight, she felt completely unprepared.

"How'd you go?" asked Bethany as soon as Alexa walked into the apartment after her first exam.

"Not great," replied Alexa. That was an understatement. She was struggling not to cry. The exam had been harder than she expected and she had struggled to make up answers for some of the questions.

"I've got something to help take your mind off it," said Bethany tentatively, biting her lip to try and contain her smile.

"A house inspection in the middle of my exams isn't going to cheer me up, Angel," retorted Alexa, though there was lightness in her voice. Bethany had not pestered her for over a fortnight, something she had visibly struggled with. Alexa could not help but be amused by Bethany's excitement, but could not afford to get wrapped up in it. "I can't be bothered cooking. You have one hour while we go eat to tell me about it. After that, I'm back to exclusion mode. I can't afford to fail all my other exams too."

It was clear Bethany had anticipated Alexa's reaction and came well prepared. There were photos of the property, descriptions and floor plans. Then there was the assessment, matching the property to both Alexa's and Bethany's desires.

"Yeah, Charlotte did that," said Bethany, pointing to the assessment sheet. "But it's good, huh?"

"Just let me read it first," smiled Alexa.

Bethany's desires for their home were somewhat more abstract than Alexa's. It had made house-hunting with her highly amusing. There was the feel and the look, things that could never be properly judged until they were there. More than once they had gone to see a property and Bethany had turned away before they even reached the front gate. Bethany apologised the first time, but Alexa would not let her apologise again. She knew what it was like to have her body react adversely to things for no apparent reason and would not buy a house they could not be completely comfortable in.

When Alexa looked at her criteria, she was surprised by Charlotte's level of detail. It was truly impressive and included many things Alexa had not considered. Even so, it was still only a fifty-fifty split on what she really wanted.

"So?" asked Bethany, practically shaking with excitement.

"It's not perfect for me," sighed Alexa. Bethany's face turned heart-broken in an instant. "But it's close enough that I'll look at it if you're serious about it. If it's a maybe for you, then I want to pass."

"I want to check it out," replied Bethany earnestly, containing her newly re-formed excitement.

"And what about this – room for a workshop?" asked Alexa.

"And a pool," smiled Bethany, shifting her chair next to Alexa's and pointing at Charlotte's assessment.

"Yeah, I saw that. You've never mentioned a workshop before. Want to tell me about it?"

"I think I might be able to make furniture," answered Bethany, her eyes downcast and her voice no longer so confident. "Did a bit inside. I don't mind the carpentry I do now, but I really like making furniture."

"Okay, well I can't promise you this place, but if that's a criteria, we'll make sure any place we do buy can have a workshop. We'll start with the basics and as you get more serious, we can get more serious about what we put in it. Deal?"

Bethany's squeal was as close to a yes as Alexa was going to get. It was uplifting to see Bethany so excited that she practically bounced home, and made Alexa much more willing to consider the property. Bethany was going to Ben's to give Alexa space to study, but made sure she left the property information on the table.

"I won't forget, Angel," smiled Alexa, not looking up from her books as Bethany walked towards the door.

"You're the best in the world, Lex," Bethany replied, bouncing back and bear-hugging her before dancing out the door.

Marcus arrived home a couple of minutes, a bemused look on his face. "Bethany seems happy," he said. "Practically jumped on me as I got out of the lift.

"Yeah. Beth-hug. Much bigger than a bear-hug," Alexa replied with a smile, though did not look up from her books. She could not afford the distraction. "She found a place she likes," she explained when Marcus did not ask the obvious question.

"Oh." Marcus did not speak again straight away and when he did his voice was slightly muffled. "You – do you like it?"

"I'm withholding judgement. It's not ideal for me, but if Bethy loves it as much in practice as she does in theory then we'll probably go for it. Just hope we don't miss out. I think that'd really break her heart."

"You can't always have what you want," replied Marcus softly.

Alexa knew he was not being overly critical – that he might not have been referring to Bethany at all – but it still stung. "No, but Bethy hasn't exactly spent her life having all of her wishes fulfilled."

"But what about you? When do you get your perfect place?" asked Marcus tenderly.

Alexa flinched, startled by Marcus's sudden presence right behind her. This time she turned to face him. "I already have it," she replied truthfully, looking deep into his chocolate eyes. "Right here – with you and Bethy and Charlotte. This is my perfect place."

Marcus held her gaze for a moment before suddenly stepping back and shaking his head slightly. "Don't stay up too late, okay," he said in a gravelly voice, before turning and walking to his bedroom.

Alexa closed her eyes and sighed, letting the flood of emotions flow back out of her body. She was not going to pass anything by thinking about Marcus all night.

***

The drive to Bethany's dream house was a nice break from the books. Alexa found it difficult to be full of regret when Bethany was smiling so broadly. To Bethany's credit, she was more subdued than normal and Alexa wondered if she was preparing herself for disappointment.

As they got closer and the houses became bigger, Bethany's eyes lit up. This was the kind of place Bethany had always dreamed about living in. Once, in their younger years, they drove through a suburb like this on their way to yet another foster home. Bethany had been practically shaking at the possibility they were going to live with a nice family in a nice home. It was not to be. The house they pulled up in front of was pleasant enough, but small and run-down. The foster parents already had three other children in their care and looked as though they had taken them under threat. It was not one of their better life experiences.

They had run away that night and gone searching for the family they were truly meant to live with. Walking along the wide streets, looking into the huge mansion-like houses, they had imagined a better life – until someone had noticed them loitering and called the police.

Alexa had no idea where that place was. For all she knew they could be looking to buy one of the very houses they had stood in front of, dreaming of living in, all those years ago.

Pulling up in front of the house – though mansion was probably a more accurate description – Alexa could feel those dreams returning and found herself smiling as much as Bethany as they walked through the gates. The property was huge. The large front yard was dispersed around the semi-circular driveway and fountain. The backyard was three times as big as the front, though it was almost entirely garden and lawn with very little development. Then there was the house. Walking through it, Alexa felt her more practical side question their need for three floors, four bathrooms and up to ten bedrooms. There was only two of them. Their whole apartment would fit into the main living area. It was so much more than they needed, but they wanted it; Bethany desperately, Alexa more so because of Bethany, but of all the things their miracle money could buy, Bethany's dream home had to be one of them. It was all going to be a matter of affording it.

Speaking to the agent, Alexa was not disappointed to find they were keen to go to auction, which was still several weeks away. She would be able to finish her exams without risking the house being sold. However, she did register her interest with the agent and promised Bethany she would fill out the forms to be a registered bidder as soon as the agent sent them through. She would also send Peter a message begging him to help her with the purchase, and was confident that would finally be enough to set her up as his worst client ever.

Although Bethany was not completely satisfied with driving away from the house not guaranteed as its next owner, she was confident enough to let Alexa to return to her study when they arrived home. For Alexa, that had to be the end of it. She could not let her thoughts stray beyond her books and was thankful when Marcus asked when her last exam was and promised to make himself scarce until then. With Charlotte equally absent, catching up with Bethany outside of the apartment, Alexa dedicated herself solely to her study. It paid off. Although she could not guarantee she had aced it, she had not done as badly as in her first exam. Completing her exams so late in the exam period also meant that the wait for her marks would not be as long and torturous as it could have been.

"Geez, you don't seriously want you marks already, do you?" asked Jessica incredulously when they walked out of their final exam. "This is my favourite part of the year – can't stress because it's all done. It's weeks of joyous freedom. You need to enjoy them."

"I've got winter term classes," shrugged Alexa. "Need to make up for that semester I missed."

"You didn't miss it. You just started mid-year. Do you think the people who started a year after me need to catch up cos they missed it? You're seriously one strangely wired girl."

If Jessica had not said those things with the broadest smile and in the most endearing tone, Alexa was sure she would have been in tears, but Jessica seemed to genuinely enjoy her strangeness.

"Of course I do," laughed Jessica, wrapping her arm around Alexa's shoulders. "You makes life so much more enjoyable. It's scary how straight-laced some people are. You make me feel normal. I love it."

Alexa smiled, thankful for Jessica's friendship. She just wished she had someone who made her feel normal. The only person who did was Bethany, but she knew that was not a good thing. Bethany's life had not been normal and she would never want it to be considered so.

It was a relaxing afternoon having lunch with her friends as they celebrated the end of their exams. Alexa stayed quiet through most of the conversation. She would reveal her oddities to Jessica, but did not think everyone needed to know so much about her. Everyone else's plans for the holidays were just so different to hers. None of them were trying to buy a mansion and she did not want to tell them for fear they would think that typical of her life. For as much as she did not want to be known for her past experiences, she also did not want to be known for her present wealth.

Alexa's phone vibrated in her pocket. She pulled it out, her heart skipping a beat to see Bethany's name on the screen. No matter how many times they communicated, she could not help but fear the worst – even for a second – when she received a call or a text. This message was not so much alarming as confusing. Bethany was insisting she not arrive home before seven.

"Huh, well I guess I'm going to have to find something to do this afternoon," Alexa sighed, smiling at Jessica.

"Let's go shopping!" squealed Jessica. "I haven't let myself near a shop since before study week."

"Yeah, okay. I should probably get some new swimmers."

Shopping had never become a favoured pastime for Alexa, which meant that though she had enough clothes to see her from week to week, they were worn to the point falling apart. Her swimmers were so old that they were now testing the point of decency.

"They're not the swimmers you're buying, are they?" asked Jessica incredulously when Alexa pulled out a plain, black one-piece.

"Why? What's wrong with it? Is it torn?" Alexa asked, turning it over and inspecting it.

"No, it's boring."

"It's practical. I swim – actually swim. I don't need bits of swimmer flying off the bits of me they're supposed to be covering."

Jessica laughed, granting her that concession, but still would not let her leave the store without looking at the bikinis.

"Come summer time, when the focus is a little less on swimming and a little more on picking up, you'll want something more like this," said Jessica, holding up a yellow bikini.

"It's tiny!"

"So are you!" laughed Jessica. "Come on, try them on."

Alexa was not allowed to say no. Jessica pulled her to the change rooms and forced her to try on about ten different bikinis to figure out which style suited her best. It was more confronting than Alexa was prepared for. She had never been this exposed in front of another girl before that was not Bethany. Jessica chuckled, reassuring her there was nothing she needed to be ashamed of.

"Shy, actually," said Alexa. "Never done this sort of thing before."

"You've had a pretty strange life, haven't you?" asked Jessica seriously. Alexa nodded, feeling tears sting her eyes. "That's okay. I'm not going to bag you for it. And you don't have to tell me stuff you don't want to, just don't be scared to, okay."

Alexa smiled and turned to look in the mirror. "I think I like this one the best," she said, tilting her head and turning her body.

"Got someone in mind to show it off to?" asked Jessica with a grin. "You met anyone since Damien?"

"No. I'm not really in the market."

"Why not? You're not seriously going to let that arsehole put you off, are you? How he treated you was so wrong. Most guys aren't like that," Jessica reassured her.

"I know," replied Alexa, getting dressed. "I just – it's complex."

"That means you've met someone! Oh my God. Who? When?" asked Jessica. Alexa grimaced. "What? This one of the strange things?"

Alexa looked at her watch. There was still plenty of time until she was allowed home so let Jessica to drag her to the nearest coffee shop.

"Okay, spill," said Jessica when they sat down. "What's wrong with him that you're worried about telling anyone?"

"There's nothing wrong with him. He's great. Perfect, even," sighed Alexa. "We just can never be together."

"Why not?"

"Few reasons. First, he's with someone else."

"May not be forever," reasoned Jessica.

"Yeah, maybe," smiled Alexa. "He's also much older than me," she added when Jessica kept prompting her to continue. "Ten years."

"Yeah, that's a big, but it's not really bad. Twenty years would be getting a bit creepy. So he's at uni?"

"No, he's my flatmate," smiled Alexa. "It's very awkward at times."

"Oh man, so this guy moves in and you fall in love with him. That's bad luck. Maybe you could move."

"No, I knew him before – was in love with him before I asked him to move in. That's part of the problem. We met when I was sixteen.

The age gap was much more inappropriate then. It kinda taints things now – even when people tell me that, technically, there's no reason we can't be together."

"Is this an unrequited thing?" asked Jessica tentatively. Alexa shook her head. That was her only comfort in this whole situation. "Wow. That's tough, but I think you're making it harder on yourself. If you can't be together and neither of you are going to try to be, then you need to get over him. You need to put yourself out there to meet other guys."

"You ever had to do that?" asked Alexa.

"Doing it now – sort of – differently. The girl I have the hugest crush on – since about the day I met her – is definitely not into me. Not that way, anyway. And you're the first person I've told. My boyfriend definitely doesn't know."

Alexa could not help but smile broadly as she threw her arms around Jessica. "We can be losers in love together," she said brightly, drawing more amusement from Jessica.

They spent the next hour talking about their lives. Jessica opened up about her family and Alexa gave her the basic overview of her situation, though that really just opened the floodgates for questions she had always tried to avoid.

"So you really do specialise in the complex," said Jessica with an understanding smile. Alexa nodded emphatically. "Well Jack and Amy are going to be peeved that you finally spilled your guts. You're like the ultimate mystery in the group. I won't tell them anything!" Jessica cried when Alexa opened her mouth. "Seriously, don't freak out. Amy won't care either – though it might blow her innocent little brain a bit. So you're not allowed to tell her stuff without me around."

By the time Alexa arrived home, her final exam was just a faint memory. It seemed impossible that so much had happened since then. Part of her wanted to fear what she had said and done, but mostly she was giddy with the thrill of having a close female friend. Ezra had always been a good friend, but their lives were so different and Alexa had never felt truly free to confide in her.

"Congratulations!" cried Bethany as soon as Alexa walked in the door, startling her from her thoughts. "Must've gone pretty well. You look happy." Alexa hugged Bethany, but Bethany quickly released her and dragged her to the dining table. "To celebrate," smiled Bethany happily, waving her hand over the elaborately laid out dinner.

"Celebrate what? We don't even know if I passed yet," replied Alexa, all her doubts from that morning creeping back.

"That's okay. We can celebrate you finishing your exams, then celebrate you passing when we get your results."

Alexa looked up to see Marcus shrug, a bright smile on his face. She wondered if he had tried to temper Bethany's enthusiasm or found it was easier to go along.

"So how'd you go?" asked Marcus as they all sat down.

"Nah ah," replied Alexa, shaking her head. "If we want this to be a happy night, we're not talking about that. Let's just be thankful it's over. I think I can manage that."

"We can talk about the house," offered Bethany happily. "We should go see it this weekend. We can all go. Maybe the owners have changed their mind about the auction and we can just buy it."

"I'll come," smiled Charlotte. "If I don't have some family thing. Have to bags the third-best room before someone else gets it," she added, looking slyly Marcus's way.

Marcus pretended not to notice, but could not ignore Bethany's direct invitation. It gave Alexa the impression this was not the first time Bethany had approached him on the issue.

"Thank you, Beth, but Lucy and I have been talking about moving in together," said Marcus, not quite looking at any of them. "I think it's better we do that on our own. I doubt the house is big enough to pull off harmonious living with all of us."

Alexa was surprised by the wide smile that graced Bethany's face and the knowing look she shared with Charlotte. "That's okay. I'll choose your room and get it set up in preparation," replied Bethany, trying to sound nonchalant.

"In preparation for what?" asked Marcus warily.

"For Lucy leaving you in the lurch again."

Marcus was saved the task of replying by Alexa gasping while simultaneously trying to swallow. Bethany smiled for half a second until she realised Alexa really was choking. That was when Bethany started to panic. Alexa tried to calm her as she coughed violently, trying to dislodge the food. Marcus pulled Alexa up from her chair and hit her back forcefully until the offending bit of food flew across the table.

Marcus's arm under her body kept Alexa's from collapsing on the table as she tried to catch her breath. "You okay," he asked in a husky voice, pulling Alexa up to a standing position against his body. Alexa nodded gingerly, not seeking an opportunity to push out of his arms. "Don't scare us like that."

Alexa did not have the chance to find out how much that small episode scared him as Bethany lunged at them, hugging them both as tears streamed down her face. Her whole body was shaking.

"It's okay, Bethy. Shh, I'm okay. Was never going to die. Just went down the wrong way," said Alexa, but Bethany was not listening.

"You saved her. You saved her," cried Bethany hysterically, as she frantically hugged Marcus, squishing Alexa between them.

"Beth, calm down," said Marcus firmly, struggling to dislodge himself and Alexa from her grasp, but as soon as he did Bethany threw her arms around him once more. "Beth, it's okay. Listen to me." Marcus had to grab Bethany's face and hold it still so her eyes met his. Alexa could only imagine the effect of that. If he looked at her that way she was sure she would do anything he asked. "It's okay. Alexa's okay. I just patted her on the back. It's what you do if someone's choking. She wasn't in real danger. She just needed help. If it happens again, you can help her. Promise me you'll do that." Bethany nodded slowly. "Good. I need you to promise you'll take care of her – look out for her. She won't let anyone else do that. I need to know she'll be okay."

Bethany nodded again and threw her arms back around Marcus's neck. This time he returned the embrace, holding Bethany tenderly. It strained Alexa's heart to watch, knowing how he felt about Bethany.

"Thank you," said Alexa later, when Charlotte and Bethany were preparing dessert. "I know you don't – I know you still find it hard."

"I'm not blind. I see the Bethany you love. I know everything she does is guided by her desire to do best for you. It's stupidly misguided at times – I saw what that week did to her. When you're here and safe it's easy to be forgiving."

"Your unforgiving's still kinder than most people we've met – nicer than most people who were supposed to like us – who said they loved us. She knows that. You being here – lets you keep racking up the number of times you've saved my life," Alexa added jokingly.

"I'm going to miss this too," Marcus smiled.

"Dessert!" cried Bethany, dancing towards them with two bowls. She gave Marcus's his first, smiling broadly at him before jumping on to the lounge behind Alexa and placing the second bowl in her lap while simultaneously hugging her.

"Where's yours?" asked Alexa, leaning into Bethany's embrace.

"Charlotte's bringing it."

Almost on cue Charlotte came out with two more bowls, handing Bethany hers, but Bethany refused to disentangle herself from Alexa.

"This is really good, Charlotte," said Marcus.

"It's just mud cake and ice cream," replied Charlotte dismissively. "And the ice cream's bought."

Marcus shook his head and sighed, muttering words that sounded very much like stubborn and frustrating, but his compliment had not been totally disregarded. Charlotte's eyes roved the bowls intently, lighting up when they were enthusiastically emptied. When Bethany and Marcus both voiced their desire for seconds, Charlotte speedily complied, also bringing back small second serves for herself and Alexa.

It was the best night Alexa had had for a very long time. The four of them hung out together laughing and chatting, a movie on in the background. Bethany and Charlotte were up and down on the lounge like yo-yos, continually shuffling places until, by the end of the night, Alexa found herself nestled next to Marcus.

"You need to go home tonight, Charlotte?" asked Marcus, shifting so his body pressed innocently against Alexa's.

"Urgh, yeah, I'd better. I don't have books for some of my classes tomorrow and the stupid teachers keep getting in a fizz. Like it really matters what piece of paper I scrawl their dribble on," Charlotte sighed, pushing off the lounge.

Alexa stifled her giggles as Marcus twitched awkwardly. It took a little longer for Bethany to catch on, though Charlotte was the one who realised last what she had said.

"He's not my teacher, it doesn't count," said Charlotte.

"It's okay, Charlotte. I know better than anyone how flawed teachers are," said Marcus, rising from the lounge. His voice was light, but there was sad resignation there too.

When the front door clicked closed behind Marcus and Charlotte, Alexa found herself suddenly in tears.

"Lex, what's wrong?" asked Bethany in a panicked voice, wrapping her arms around Alexa.

"I don't want to leave this. It's the only place I've felt at home. You, me, Charlotte, Marc. I like it. I don't want it to end."

Bethany hugged Alexa tighter. "It's my first real home too," said Bethany quietly. "But we won't lose them. Char, she's going to come live with us. You know things'll get bad again. If we have space, she can stay forever. No one can tell us she can't. And Marcus, he won't stay away. He loves you." Alexa did not want to tell Bethany how wrong she was, so just nodded. "We can stay if you want."

"No," replied Alexa in a thick voice. Bethany's concession was enough to steel her resolve. "I want it too. I'm just going to miss this."

"Me too," confessed Bethany, further entangling her limbs with Alexa's.

***

Alexa sat down in front of the computer feeling recklessly hopeful. It had been such a good week that she could dare to believe things would continue that way. Completely free from study, she had been able to catch up with Maria and work extra hours with Peter. She even had lunch with Ben. It was the first time she and Ben had really been alone together since Marcus moved in. The conversation was stilted and awkward, but Ben did not rush off as soon as they had finished eating. He even came to Maria's with her for afternoon tea. Maria was always good at facilitating conversation, and when Ben left for work, Alexa felt hopeful that their relationship might be on the mend. He even joined them on their most recent trip to the dream house.

Bethany insisted they attend every open house – just in case. Alexa thought it was overkill, but was prepared to do whatever Bethany needed to feel secure that the house would not be sold as soon as they turned their backs. The auction was set down for the weekend. Alexa was not looking forward to it. She did not know how to battle for a house. Peter had offered to bid for her, to help take the passion out of event, and she was leaning towards that option. It had been hard enough convincing Bethany not to be there. If Bethany found out neither of them were going to be, she would panic. Ben offered Bethany his services, but until he made that offer to Alexa himself, Alexa would not accept it. Bethany wanted her to forgive Ben, but Alexa was standing firm on this point. If Ben wanted to be a part of her life, he had to stop trying to do it through Bethany.

That myriad of thoughts came to a stuttering halt as Alexa's end of semester results flashed up on the screen. The rational part of her brain was telling her it was okay, but that did not gel with the part pushing tears down her cheeks. It was such a contrast to last semester when she had jumped around the room ecstatically.

"Lex, what's wrong?" asked Bethany, rushing to hug her. Bethany looked at the screen then back at Alexa, holding her tighter. "It's okay, Lex. You'll do better next time."

"Aw, shit, did you fail?" asked Sam, sitting down at the table.

"What? No!" cried Alexa, horrified by the suggestion.

"Then what's the issue?" asked Sam, grabbing the laptop. "Seriously? You're disappointed? What did you expect?"

"Better!" Alexa cried. "I worked my arse off. It's not like you'd be happy with marks like that."

"Don't you think that's a somewhat unrealistic comparison?" asked Sam. "It's not like you were always topping the grade with me and the guys. I think you need to adjust your expectations."

"Why should she?" asked Marcus. Everyone looked up. It was clear from the scowl on Marcus's face that he had been standing there a while.

"You think she should be disappointed with these marks?" asked Sam, pointing at the screen, as if daring him to disagree.

Marcus moved forward, but did not look until Alexa nodded her consent. "What'd you get last semester?" he asked, pushing the computer back towards Alexa.

"Two credits, two distinctions," she replied in a small voice.

"See, she can do better. She has every right to expect as much, if not more, from herself – and she reserves the right to be disappointed if she doesn't achieve it."

"After all she's suffered? Don't you think it'd be a little wiser for her to be a bit more realistic?" suggested Sam forcefully.

"No. No one's ever achieved anything without believing they could," replied Marcus firmly. "She's capable and intelligent – when she's not being ridiculously stupid. She has every right to expect more. Setting her sights low will only guarantee she achieves nothing more than the bare minimum."

"Alexa," said Sam firmly, turning from Marcus and grasping her shoulders. "Four credits is nothing to be ashamed of."

"But I wanted to do better!" she cried, wishing she could believe what Marcus said. "And I just scrapped credits – barely above a pass!"

"What'd you honestly expect? You can't just want something and expect it to be given to you. It doesn't work like that," said Sam. Alexa assumed he was trying to be kind, but he sounded condescending. "I get better marks because I work really hard. I focus on my life and don't go investing all my energy into everyone but myself. Start doing that and maybe you can start expecting more. But, you know what? Some people are just never going to get high marks, no matter what they do. Stop comparing yourself to people right at the top. Compete with people on your own scale."

"Yeah, I guess you're right," nodded Alexa as Bethany hugged her tighter.

There was silence for a moment before Marcus stalked to his room, the door closing louder than usual.

"Me and Sam were going to go out for a bit – go down the beach – maybe get some dinner. Want to come?" asked Bethany softly.

Alexa shook her head. She was not sure she could take more of Sam's home truths today. Bethany went to the bedroom to change, but Alexa could not be alone in the same room as Sam right then, so headed to the balcony and looked out to the pounding ocean.

"I won't be home late," said Bethany softly from the balcony door. Alexa nodded, but did not turn to let Bethany see the tears in her eyes. She knew anyway, crouching beside her and wiping them away. "I know you're disappointed, but I'm real proud of you."

"Thank you," Alexa gasped, hugging Bethany fiercely. Maybe they would never be better than mediocre, but if they could be truly proud of each other, then that could be enough.

"Go have fun," smiled Alexa, pushing Bethany gently towards the door. Bethany kept hold of her hand, not letting go until distance pulled them apart.

"You're going to freeze if you keep sitting out here."

"I'm fine," replied Alexa, not turning her gaze.

"Why'd I know you'd say that," Marcus sighed, throwing a blanket over her shoulders before sitting down on the other side of the table. "I hope you're not taking what Sam said to heart. He doesn't know what he's talking about."

"Maybe he does. Maybe that's always been my problem – expecting more than I deserve," muttered Alexa unhappily.

"If anything, the opposite's true. You don't expect enough from yourself or life. You deserve so much more than you've been given."

"Look at where I am – what I have – you," added Alexa in a whisper. "I have so much – no, this is more than someone like me —"

"Don't. Don't finish that sentence. It'll make me very mad. You don't want that," Marcus added with a smile.

"But even you think I did really bad."

"No. I never said that. I said you had the right to be disappointed."

"What the hell's the difference?" cried Alexa.

"Alexa, I'm surprised you did that well. I know you worked hard and how much effort you put in. Work that hard next semester and you'll do better. You'll do really well as soon as you remember a week-long heroin binge isn't the path to academic success."

"You've never asked me about that week," said Alexa, looking up. "Where I went. What I did."

"I didn't think you wanted me to," replied Marcus flatly.

"You ever wonder? Think about it?" Alexa asked. Marcus nodded.

"Then why haven't you asked. Everyone else has."

"Answered any of them?" asked Marcus with a knowing smile. Alexa shook her head. "I've guessed some things, wondered others, and tried to deny the possibility of lots more. I guess a large part of me wants to stay in ignorance. Will it make you feel better if I knew?"

"Don't know," answered Alexa honestly. "You always find a way to forgive me. Sometimes I think – but then I get worried this'll be the one thing you can never forgive. I keep wondering what I'll do to make you go away."

"We're friends. I don't have to agree with everything you do," said Marcus earnestly. "When I don't, I might tell you, but I'm never going to stop being your friend because of it. That's the good thing about friendship. I'm not perfect either and you're my friend."

"You're perfect to me – close," Alexa nodded.

"You're pretty perfect in my eyes too. And I believe in you. I believe you'll do better next semester and you're going to get a great job and be successful. You're going to meet someone wonderful and start a family. You're going to have an amazing life. A few credits won't prevent that. I promise. They're pretty much all I got at university."

A noise in the kitchen alerted Alexa to Charlotte's presence. She had not even heard her come in.

"She's cooking dinner," said Marcus, looking towards the kitchen. "I think she likes cooking. She's good. I asked her if she ever thought about being a chef, but she never answered."

"Probably doesn't know yet. Doubt she's had a chance to think about it. I know she says things are better at home, but the more Bethy talks about us moving the better things get at home. I'm not looking forward to leaving her," confessed Alexa, feeling tears sting her eyes.

"You can't think like that," said Marcus tenderly. "Because of you, Charlotte's a much more confident and happy young girl. She's a lot like you, but because of you she hasn't had to suffer the way you did. You should be proud of your friendship with her and everything you've done for her. Makes it hard to believe it won't continue just because you move a bit further away."

"You're going to stay here, right? In the apartment. I want you to," Alexa said earnestly, daring to reach out and squeeze Marcus's hand.

"It'll feel a bit empty without the three of you, but if you're happy for me to stay, that'd be really good. It's a great apartment. Best place I've ever lived," added Marcus with a crooked smile.

"I'd feel better if there was someone I know living here – someone Charlotte knows. You'll keep an eye on her, right? You won't ignore her and not let her come by?"

"No, of course not. I'll be here if ever she needs me. She knows that. Wouldn't matter if I wasn't staying here. She's a good kid," smiled Marcus, grasping Alexa's hand tighter. "But if I'm going to do that, we might need to catch up every so often – chat about how's she's doing."

Alexa could not help but smile. "I am pretty worried about her. We'll have to meet up at least once a week for me to feel okay," she said, her heart fluttering, hoping Marcus would take the bait.

"At least," he nodded, smiling broadly.

Chapter Twenty

IT WAS ALREADY light when Alexa woke with a start. The urge to vomit subsided the more she focused on the very real surroundings of her room, forcing the visions of her nightmare from her mind. It felt like a bad omen.

The auction on Saturday had not gone the way Alexa expected. She decided on the day to attend, though Peter agreed to bid for her. They determined they would go to her pre-set limit without question, then to her emergency limit if the battle was between her and just one other bidder. What happened after that was something Alexa had tried not to think about.

There had been very few bidders, perhaps due to the cold and dreary weather. Peter played it very cool, not placing their first bid until the auctioneer looked ready to wrap it up – at a much lower price than Alexa had been prepared to pay. It led to a short bidding contest, but Peter's speed with upping the bids and the competitor's hesitancy was a clear sign they were reaching their limit. Then, when the hammer came down in Alexa's favour, the words the auctioneer spoke were not the ones she expected.

"What's going on?" asked Alexa when the auctioneer disappeared to talk to the owners. "Why didn't he say sold?"

"Our bid is below the reserve," said Peter, smiling softly as he placed a hand on her shoulder and started leading her towards the door the auctioneer went through. It was only then that she realised that were being summoned.

"Where're we going?"

"Relax," said Peter, hearing the panic in her voice. "As the highest bidder we get first option on negotiation. This is a good thing. We just need to speak to the owners to see if we can agree on a sale price."

Alexa was glad Peter was with her. She would not have known where to start the negotiations, though finishing them would have been easier. The reserve was still within her emergency limit, though what the owners really wanted was well beyond it. Peter played it very casual, leaving the owners with a value below her preferred limit, but above the auction price. Her bargaining chip was the fact that she had the money ready and the owners were desperate for a sale. With Alexa's desire for a short settlement period and the absence of higher bids, Peter was confident that when they went back into negotiations today the house would be hers. With the remnants of her nightmare lurking under her skin, Alexa struggled to be so assured.

"You okay?" asked Bethany as soon as she walked out of the bedroom. Alexa smiled grimly and nodded. "Bad one?"

"Yeah. Did I scream?" Alexa asked, looking over at Marcus's door.

"Not today," replied Bethany matter-of-factly. "The negotiations still set for tomorrow?"

"Yeah," Alexa lied, feeling her stomach twist. She did not want to let Bethany down. "Peter's going to meet me in the morning. He'll do the talking."

Bethany beamed, jumping over and hugging Alexa. "They'll let us have it. They will," said Bethany, as though she was willing it into reality. "No nightmare can stop that."

Alexa could not help but squeeze Bethany tighter. It was so easy to think Bethany ignorant with the way acted, but Alexa knew from the shaking fear in Bethany's body that she was ignorant of very little.

"I'll see you tonight," said Alexa, pulling out of the embrace to stroke Bethany's face. Looking into Bethany's eyes, Alexa decided she did not care how much money it took, she would buy the house for Bethany today. Tonight would be the best night of their lives.

Marcus emerged from his room just as Bethany was leaving, but she saw him in time to rush back and hug him before dancing out the door. Marcus smiled and shook his head before joining Alexa in the kitchen. "You have a bad night?" he asked.

"Did Bethy speak to you?" Alexa asked.

"No," laughed Marcus, pointing to the door. "It's your eyes. You're not as defensive at home – don't shut off the emotion – makes you easier to read." Alexa was not sure she liked that, but it did explain how much more perceptive Marcus had become since moving in with her. "What are you up to today?" asked Marcus, smirking at her scowl.

"Meeting Peter in an hour," Alexa replied. Marcus's eyes widened with concern. "He's helping with the house stuff."

"So it's really happening? I mean, I knew it was."

"I don't think I'll believe it until I leave either," said Alexa, her heart heavy. "What'll you do? You and Lucy going to live together?"

Alexa was not sure why she was initiating the conversation. It would be a painful revelation if Marcus said yes, but supposed forewarning was better than surprise.

"I'm not sure. We haven't spoken about it. Until you go – I'll always consider this your place."

Alexa felt the corner of her mouth curl up. These mini moments of triumph made being apart from Marcus that much more bearable.

"Oh, sorry, I should've mentioned, Lucy was going to stay tonight," said Marcus apologetically.

"Was?" asked Alexa.

"Is," clarified Marcus. Alexa sighed. This was destined to be a bad day. "I know. I've spoken to her – many times. She's promised not to get into anything with Beth and to stop using names to describe her and Charlotte."

"What?" cried Alexa furiously. "What names?"

Marcus blanched. He obviously thought she knew, because it was clear he did not want to discuss it, but she held her glare until he answered. "On occasion, she may've called Charlotte a stray and Beth a junkie loud enough for them to hear," said Marcus hesitantly. Alexa's mouth fell open. "I think Beth can take it, but I know it hurt Charlotte. I spoke to her, but you know what she's like. She takes things to heart."

Alexa felt like her insides had been torn open. "That's not on, Marc," she gasped, more upset with him than she could remember being for a long time. "This is my home." Marcus stepped forward, but she instantly retreated, her hands raised. "I want you here, I do, but if that means Lucy insulting Bethy and Charlotte, then I'll ask you to leave. I won't have it. I won't."

"I know, I understand. I'm sorry," said Marcus, moving backwards. "I don't agree with her and I've said so. She's just being unreasonable."

"Why does she come here when she obviously hates us so much?"

"That's complex," replied Marcus hesitantly, before shaking his head. "Well, not so complex. She doesn't trust me."

"She doesn't trust you or me?" asked Alexa spitefully.

"Both, probably."

Alexa threw her coffee – mug and all – into the sink, forcing Marcus to jump out of the way.

"I won't make things hard for you," said Marcus as she stormed out of the kitchen. "You want me to leave, I will. Just say the word. I'll never fight it. I don't want to hurt you."

Alexa held her tongue as she fled the apartment. She was angry enough that she might say something she regretted. Marcus was not responsible for Lucy's actions and Lucy's jealousy was not all his fault. If she was in Lucy's position she would be jealous too.

***

"What's wrong? What happened?" asked Peter, striding towards Alexa. "Is it Bethany?"

Alexa rearranged her features, wondering when she suddenly become so transparent. "It's fine," she replied grumpily. "Let's just go buy this stupid house."

"Alexa, I find it very hard to be a good lawyer for my clients when they refuse to confide in me. I have your previous instructions when it comes to buying this property, but with the mood you're in I'm not confident they still hold. I'm asking you to let me do my job."

"Fine," snapped Alexa, throwing her hands up in the air as she detailed the whole disastrous morning.

"Okay," sighed Peter, squeezing her shoulder and leading her towards his car. "Well at least I know where things stand with the house. Why don't we go get that sorted and you can feel like you've redeemed something from this day."

"That's it?" asked Alexa sceptically.

"What else do you want there to be?" asked Peter seriously. "I'm your lawyer, not your parent or psychologist. You're paying me – yes, I give in – to represent you and protect your interest. Do you want to pay me extra to give you personal advice?"

"I'd have to pay people to keep their advice to themselves," Alexa muttered darkly.

"Ha, well you're not alone in that frustration, but this is one job where you learn to keep your opinions to yourself. How about I give you one opinion," suggested Peter. Alexa scowled and crossed her arms. "Bad days happen. They suck and they drag you down right when you think things are going well. You're allowed to get annoyed. Just don't make snap judgements on days like today."

"So you think buying this house is a snap judgement?" huffed Alexa.

"No, your decisions about the house are about as you as anything can be, and it will be my absolute pleasure to help you and Bethany secure it. Let's just focus on that today. Let one thing go right and you might find everything else falls into place as well."

Alexa did not respond and Peter did not talk again. He turned the stereo up loud, filling the car with rock music. It pulsed through her so hard she would have bet her heart had started beating in time with it. It was so enveloping, her mind began focusing on the physical rather than emotional.

"Ready?" asked Peter, pulling up in front of the house.

Alexa's stomach squiggled at the idea that the next time she saw this house she might be its owner. Imagining Bethany's reaction – Bethany opening the front door, knowing it was theirs – was all the motivation Alexa needed. "Yep. Let's go spend a ludicrous amount of money," she smiled.

As they walked towards the house, Alexa readied herself for a long negotiation, but time had done much to mellow the expectations of the owners. When Peter made one last offer, they accepted, grateful for any increase in the sale price. Within half an hour of arriving, the contracts were signed.

"Congratulations," smiled Peter as they walked back to the car. "You now own a mansion."

"I can't believe how easy that was. It just – they just accepted," Alexa stuttered, feeling strangely light.

"Sometimes things just come together. Now, I think we should go celebrate."

"Thank you, Peter," said Alexa sincerely.

"Alexa, working for you is an absolute pleasure. You're not just my favourite client, you're one of my favourite people."

"You're one of my favourite people too," she smiled back, loving that when he squeezed her shoulder it still felt more professional than personal.

A strange feeling of contentment washed over Alexa as she drove to Maria's place. Peter had a way normalising her moods that no one else seemed able to achieve. She liked to think it was because of his professional detachment rather than because he had known her so long she was practically transparent. However, she was aware Peter was not always as detached as he appeared. He cared and that thought no longer terrified her the way it once would have. It was nice to feel like she had people on her side.

Their lunch together had been a nice retreat from the torrential rain that had struck soon after arriving at the restaurant. Peter argued that her insistence on being charged as a client negated any issues with him buying her lunch. Alexa realised she was only ever going to win one battle at a time with Peter, but she did not mind. He spoke to her as an equal, though there was a paternal quality about his actions. It made Alexa think of Ben. It had been so long since she and Ben had really spoken that she could not remember the man she had once considered him to be. When she dared to mention that to Peter, his response was so even-handed, acknowledging her frustrations while stating his belief in the depths of Ben's affections for her, that she could not understand how he could possibly argue for a living.

Pulling up in front on Maria's apartment, Alexa sat for a while, wondering if it was worth trying to wait out the downpour. It had been on and off all day, but as the minutes ticked by she realised she would have to run for it. She was soaked through before she made it across the road. The wind was blowing so hard the rain seemed to be coming at her from every direction.

"You swim here?" asked Maria with a smile, pulling Alexa inside.

"Just across the road," laughed Alexa, stripping off her jumper.

Maria ushered her to the bathroom, handing her dry clothes and demanding she have a hot shower and change. Alexa tried to be indignant, but could not manage it. No one had ever cared that she got wet before.

When Alexa emerged from the bathroom, she could hear the dryer churning as Maria laid out afternoon tea. The hot tea was amazingly welcome and Alexa could not stop herself from collapsing into the lounge with a satisfied smile.

"So?" asked Maria, sitting down next to Alexa. "How'd it go?"

"Yeah, I'm now the owner of a very big house. Just have to wait for settlement and it's ours. I can't wait to tell Bethy. She's going to be so excited."

Alexa was genuinely thrilled about telling Bethany, but Charlotte would be over tonight and she did not want to tell Bethany while Charlotte was around. They needed to be conscious of alienating her. It was not that Bethany did not appreciate that, she was just a very excitable creature who liked everyone to share in her joy. With Lucy also looming, Alexa decided she would have to wait. If Charlotte was not able to stay over, Alexa would drag Bethany out of the house in the middle of the night and tell her then. It would be torture waiting any longer to make Bethany happy.

"How much did it cost you in the end?" asked Maria. "Did you manage to keep to your limit?"

Alexa scrunched up her face. This was the part she really hated. "Just under the limit," she grimaced. "Peter did really well. I couldn't have negotiated so calmly. But, urgh, it's so much money. Real estate guy said I was getting a bargain and I suppose we are. It's much less than they wanted." Alexa hesitated, struggling to say the number out loud. "One-point-four-seven."

Maria smiled as Alexa shivered. It was expensive, but for what they were getting it was genuinely reasonable, though for Alexa, who had spent much of her life stealing just so she could eat, it was still incomprehensible. Knowing there was money left after all she had done was the most incredible part of all.

Most of her high school friends laughed at her frugality, though there was also constant astonishment that she could achieve such a state of living. Bianca had already burned through a large chunk of her money and showed no signs of stopping. Ezra was more conservative with her spending, but had made a large number of investments. Alexa knew she should consider such things, but while she was able to command a reasonable interest rate and her money was making money with no threat of losing money, she could not justify the risk. Alexa was determined that once she left university she would live off her own earnings. In the meantime, she would spend as little as possible to ensure the principle was not depleted further.

"I supposed I'd better start learning to navigate my way west," said Maria with an exaggerated sigh.

"No, no, we'll still come to you. You know we'd never make you wait on us. You do too much for us already," replied Alexa.

"I don't think I've given you anything you haven't repaid in equal measure," said Maria feelingly. "I have children and grandchildren, but I see little of them compared to you, Beth and Charlotte. I feel very blessed that you came into the lift and trampled my groceries."

Alexa felt her heart warm. This really had been a very good day. It was a level of contentment she had never felt – not without disaster striking soon after. It was an ominous thought she tried to ignore, but she could not help but wonder what would shatter her life this time. She thought about Ben being shot, anything happening to Bethany, Charlotte being hit by a car, Marcus suddenly seeing her the way most men did.

"Now, now, I know that look," said Maria, nudging Alexa. "Don't go looking into the future. You never imagine it right anyway. Just because something goes right doesn't mean something else has to go wrong."

"You don't know my life very well," said Alexa, trying to be joking.

Maria refused to listen and dragged her and into the kitchen to cook – just for something to do. They talked constantly, never allowing Alexa's mind to wander, and at the end of it Maria put the cake on a plate and handed it to Alexa. "Make the others remember how much they miss me," smiled Maria. "And make Bethany celebrate – even if she doesn't know why."

Tears filled Alexa's eyes as she suddenly feared what her world could do to Maria. It was selfish to pull Maria so close, to drag her into that place. Alexa should have run from there and never come back, she should have warned Maria what happened to people who got too close, but when she tried Maria just dismissed her fears as paranoia.

"Nothing's going to happen to me. I'm not going anywhere and you're going to promise that you, Beth and Charlotte are going to come and see me very soon. You're going to take me out to your new home and teach me all the ways to get there and I'm going to turn up unexpectedly with cake so you'd better be able to provide good coffee."

"I promise," said Alexa, lunging forward and hugging Maria tight.

***

Marcus pinched the bridge of his nose, praying for strength. This had not been the worst day of his life, but it was probably the worst he had felt about himself for a very long time. Over the years he had known Alexa, he had come to accept she would one day be taken from him. It seemed naïve to believe her life would not end suddenly, tragically and far too prematurely. It was an outcome he had prepared himself for. What he had never considered inevitable – or acceptable – was that while she lived, he would be responsible for bringing hurt into her life.

Alexa's reaction this morning should not have surprised him, except perhaps by the mildness of it. Marcus knew Lucy's actions had been deliberate and designed to hurt, but he had somehow convinced himself that disagreeing with her was enough to absolve him of any responsibility. The shock on Alexa's face was probably the worst part. She had trusted him to be better.

Walking up to the apartment, Marcus hoped Alexa's dislike of Lucy might take her and Bethany out of the apartment tonight. It was hardly fair, but with their move imminent, they would not have to put up with Lucy much longer. Marcus almost laughed at his selfishness. He would have if he were not so disgusted in himself. The sound of laughter in the apartment made Marcus sick. He would have to get Lucy out again quickly and not come back until late.

"Hi, Marc. Hi, Lucy," greeted Charlotte cheerfully from the kitchen.

"How you doing?" asked Bethany in a pleasant yet detached voice, and Marcus noticed she did not look directly at either of them. "We're cooking a layery-type thing for dinner. You guys want to stay?"

"Lasagne?" queried Marcus.

"Mexican lasagne," clarified Charlotte. "Mexican mince instead of bolognaise, tortilla instead of pasta, sour cream, salsa."

"Sounds good," smiled Marcus.

Charlotte smiled broadly and nudged Bethany.

"Great," said Bethany with forced enthusiasm. "Lex won't be home for a bit, so we're making some nibbles and non-alcoholic sangria. You guys just relax and we'll bring some out to you."

Marcus turned to see Lucy sneering. He grabbed her hand and dragged her into his bedroom. "What's your problem?" he growled, moving to the other side of the room to put some distance between them. "They're trying very hard to be nice to you."

"Oh, please. The stray offering to serve up some hash being passed off as food is hardly being nice," said Lucy derisively. "How do you know it's not laced with some homemade drug the junkie cooked up?"

Marcus felt his hand ball up, forcing him to take another step back. "You are un-fucking-believable," he hissed. "Don't you dare ever use those names again. Not in front of them. Not in front of me. Not even in front of God. You get that?"

"And if I do? Come on, Marc, what are you going to do if I do?" sneered Lucy, smiling viciously.

Marcus had no answer. It was why Lucy had been able to get away with everything she had said and done. He was hamstrung. Being single around Alexa was simply not an option. It was not as though he could not control himself, but there would come a moment where, without that added barrier, he would be tempted to test the waters.

"Why don't we just hide away in here?" asked Lucy in a seductive voice, walking towards him. "I'll teach you some new moves."

Lucy trailed her fingers down Marcus's chest. When he was open to her advances, she was able to seduce him with ease, but this was not one of those moments.

"We are going back out there and you're going to be civil. I realise pleasant might be too much to ask, but maybe just try to pretend you're a decent person for a couple of hours," snapped Marcus in a spiteful voice, pushing Lucy's hand off him.

Charlotte smiled as they emerged. There were corn chips and dips on the coffee table along with glasses. Lucy scoffed at the offering, but Marcus could not help but smile. It was not sophisticated or fancy, but it was so reflective of Charlotte and Bethany. Watching them in the kitchen together, it was easy to see them as the children they really were. Marcus could even imagine Alexa with them. He just wished it was as easy to see her true age.

Shaking his head to pull him from those thoughts, Marcus was surprised to see Charlotte in front of him, causing him to bump her as she was pouring Lucy a glass of sangria. Lucy's cry was indignant as she jumped off the lounge, sangria dripping down her top and skirt.

"What the hell 's wrong with you?" Lucy cried.

It took Marcus a moment to realise Lucy was not yelling at him. She was standing over Charlotte, pushing her back with a pointed finger.

"Oi!" yelled Bethany, diving in between them. Bethany's protective stance was very Alexa-like, though she was much more aggressive than her sister. "Don't you dare touch her," she snarled angrily.

Marcus wanted to intervene, but he felt Lucy deserved whatever Bethany gave her and was much more concerned about Charlotte, who was shaking in the kitchen. "I'm so sorry, Charlotte," he said, pulling her into his arms. It was the first time he had ever hugged her and was thankful he felt no desirous emotions swirl within him.

"What the hell's going on?"

Marcus had just enough time to register Alexa's voice before Charlotte was pulled out of his arms. When he turned, he saw Alexa not just hugging Charlotte, but actively shielding her from him.

"Char, what happened," asked Alexa softly, but Charlotte just shook her head, burying it in Alexa's shoulder.

Alexa turned on Marcus, her look accusatory. He had forgotten how fierce she could be.

"It was an accident, you stupid cow," shouted Bethany. Her height and forcefulness made her very intimidating, and Marcus could see Lucy trying to keep the confident sneer on her face.

"It's really not that hard to bring someone a drink," retorted Lucy. "Just a basic skill."

"Then why were you so incapable of doing it yourself?" snapped Bethany. "Besides, Marcus bumped her. Why don't you yell at him? Or don't you have the basic skill of eyesight?"

"Can you break them up, please," sighed Alexa.

Marcus knew from Alexa's tone she wanted him to pull Lucy into line. He moved in between Lucy and Bethany, keeping his back to Lucy. Bethany's eyes flared, assuming he was protecting Lucy from her, until he placed a gentle hand on her shoulder. "Alexa's home," he said softly, tilting his head towards the kitchen.

Bethany nodded and walked away. Marcus bowed his head and dragged Lucy to his room. He opened a drawer full of her clothes and threw a pair of jeans and top at her. When she complained she would be cold he went to his wardrobe and threw one of his jackets on the bed. He did not speak or look at her. He was far too angry for that.

"We might need rain jackets if you're insisting on staying for dinner," quipped Lucy bitterly.

"After that display, do you honestly think I'm prepared to let you stay here?" asked Marcus incredulously. "We're going out to dinner and then back to your place. You're never coming back here."

"And what happens when your girlfriend moves out? Are you moving with her now? Or you going to stay here and make it your secret love nest?"

"If you're so sure I'm having an affair with Alexa, why are you with me?" asked Marcus. "You didn't want to move in with me, but think you have the right to control where I live."

"Maybe I just didn't want to live where you wanted to," replied Lucy. "Maybe I wanted to have some say in it."

"You would've if you turned up occasionally."

"You try loving someone who doesn't love you as much as you love them," said Lucy, her voice wavering. "You try loving someone who's hung up on someone else. Then you see how you act."

Lucy turned away as she wiped her eyes. Marcus felt sick. She was right. It surprised him Alexa was even capable of liking him given how he treated her and Lucy. Perhaps he would treat Alexa this poorly as well.

"I'm sorry," Marcus said sincerely, turning Lucy into his arms and kissing her forehead. "You're right. It isn't fair on you. Let's get dinner and we'll figure something out. We'll be together. I love you too."

Lucy nodded into his chest. Lifting her head, her lips met his and pressed hard. It felt wrong, but Marcus closed off his heart, shutting Alexa out completely. When guided only by the physical, he had no problems being with Lucy. It was really all he had left to give.

The look of smug satisfaction on Lucy's face as they dressed was disheartening. Marcus needed to get Lucy away from Alexa and keep them apart forever. It would mean cutting most of his ties to Alexa, at least for the next few years, but he would have time to set things straight between them and make Alexa understand how much he loved her and that everything he did was to spare her pain.

Alexa, Bethany and Charlotte were in the kitchen when they exited his bedroom. Charlotte's face was in her hands and Alexa and Bethany were on either side of her, their arms wrapped around her.

"We're getting out of here," said Marcus softly, creeping into the kitchen. "I'm really sorry about all this. It won't happen again."

"Marc," called Alexa softly as he turned to leave. He turned back to see Bethany's eyes urging her on. "Are you happy with Lucy? Do you love her?"

Bethany shook her head. It made Marcus wonder what she had wanted Alexa to ask. "Yes," he replied. This was one lie he was very good at telling.

Alexa smiled softly, nodding, but it did not extend to her eyes. They were cold and detached, making them hard to read. When she turned back to Bethany, she stroked Bethany's hair and shook her head. Bethany's only response was to pull her into a hug. Marcus wanted to figure out what was going on, but knew he had to leave.

"Where's my wallet?" asked Lucy suddenly, rummaging through her bag as they walked towards the front door.

Marcus sighed as he followed Lucy back to the lounge room, where she searched the floor and under the lounge. He turned to the kitchen. Alexa was facing them, a hand on Bethany and Charlotte's cheeks, keeping their heads turned towards her.

"Where'd you leave it?" asked Marcus.

"Here, out here on the coffee table. I put it down when I came in."

Marcus did not remember that, but that hardly made it untrue.

Lucy was becoming more frantic, but no one else seemed to care. "It has to be around here somewhere. Have any of you seen Lucy's wallet?" asked Marcus, looking towards the kitchen.

No one responded for a while, then Alexa's eyes flicked from Bethany to Charlotte. She looked up at him and shook her head. Her face was blank and her eyes completely unemotional. He had forgotten how different she looked when she shut herself off.

"Maybe you left it in the bedroom. I'll check there," Marcus said.

"It was never in the bedroom," said Lucy angrily. "It was out here and if it's not here now then someone must've taken it."

"What!" exclaimed Alexa, storming out of the kitchen.

"It makes sense, doesn't it?" said Lucy viciously, walking towards Alexa. "Wallets don't just get up and walk off."

"No, but people can easily misplace them," hissed Alexa.

Marcus knew he needed to step in, but he was frozen. He would never accuse any of them of taking Lucy's wallet, but knew how much Bethany hated Lucy and would not put it past her or Charlotte.

"I did not misplace it. It was here on the coffee table and now it's gone and there are two people who had the opportunity to swipe it."

"You've got to be kidding," sighed Bethany from the kitchen.

"My bets are on the drug addict," said Lucy in an acidic voice.

Marcus was surprised by how passive Bethany's response was. She just looked benignly back at Lucy. Then he caught the movement in the corner of his eyes. His arm reached out just in time to grab Alexa around the waist. She pushed against him, trying to get to Lucy, but when she realised he was holding her, she pulled back.

"Get out of my house right now," said Alexa in a dangerous voice.

Marcus moved to stand in front of Alexa, his heart thumping. He did not want to have this conversation. "Just wait a minute," he said, trying to stay objective. "You have to consider the possibility."

Alexa glared hatefully at him. He held her stare until she finally turned away with a huff, beckoning Bethany and Charlotte forward. "Look at me, both of you," she commanded. Bethany immediately obeyed, staring into Alexa's eyes. Charlotte stared fearfully at the floor. When Alexa asked again, Charlotte complied.

"What is this shit?" questioned Lucy scornfully.

"Get out of my house," said Alexa, turning back to Lucy. "Neither of them took your wallet."

"You didn't even ask them!" cried Lucy indignantly.

"I don't have to," replied Alexa simply. "I know they didn't do it."

"She's a heroin addict," said Lucy, throwing her hand out at Bethany. "She probably steals out of sheer habit."

Marcus grabbed Lucy and moved her towards the front door. "Let's go," he whispered anxiously in her ear. "We'll sort it out later."

"She stole my wallet," repeated Lucy, standing her ground.

"Fine," he conceded. "But I'll deal with it later."

"Neither of them stole that wallet!" cried Alexa angrily.

"Alexa, we don't know that. You didn't even ask them," Marcus replied. This was exactly the conversation he had wanted to avoid.

"Fine," snapped Alexa, turning back to Bethany and Charlotte. "Did either of you steal Lucy's wallet?"

"No," they replied in unison.

"See?" retorted Alexa, as though that settled the situation.

"Alexa …" Marcus was lost for words.

"You've been here for months and you don't trust their word? When have they ever lied to you?" Alexa asked.

They could debate this for hours. Anything he accused Bethany of, Alexa would defend her against, or blame herself for. Bethany had a look of calm confidence. Against Lucy's victorious sneer, Marcus could not tell who had the most to gain from manufacturing this situation, but he could not deny that he suspected Bethany too. "I know what Bethany's capable of," Marcus replied. "No, I don't trust her word."

"What about mine?" asked Alexa softly, her steely façade cracking for an instant.

"You've been wrong about her before," Marcus answered, wishing he did not have to.

"So you believe her over me?" asked Alexa, pointing at Lucy.

Marcus pressed his lips together. He needed to lie, but the words would not form. Alexa's eyes widened in disbelief. She turned to Bethany and Charlotte and closed her eyes.

"There weren't any problems here til she came," said Alexa, turning back to Marcus, her eyes cold as ice. "Bethy and Charlotte never took that wallet. I won't have anyone blaming them without proof. Either she withdraws her accusation or she never steps foot in here again." Marcus turned to look at Lucy, who folder her arms and stood firm. "So?" asked Alexa pointedly. "It's up to you. Her or me? Your choice."

Marcus opened his mouth, but the words would not come out. He wanted to tell Alexa that it was her, that it would always be her, but he could not – would not. The silence dragged on. Alexa's eyes became harder as she stood her ground. "It's my place. I won't put up with it. I won't put up with her," said Alexa in a measured voice. "So you need to decide what you're going to do. It's a simple choice. Me or her."

It was a simple choice, but it was the hardest Marcus ever had to make. Taking a deep breath, he felt courage rise in his chest. He would do the right thing. It did not matter if Alexa hated him. It was probably better she did. His selfishness had brought them to this point. His conscience would finally bring it to an end.

"I choose Lucy."

Marcus could imagine Lucy's sneering smile as he took in the flash of horror in Alexa's eyes, but it was only momentary. Seconds later Alexa's face was emotionless and her eyes cold once more.

"Get out," said Alexa firmly. Marcus did not move. The sound of those words coming from her mouth was excruciating. "Get out," she repeated. "You made your choice. You don't live here any more."

"Lex, no, don't," cried Bethany, rushing between them, her hands outstretched.

"Get out," demanded Alexa, her words slow and deliberate.

Marcus nodded and took a step back. He reached behind him and grabbed Lucy's hand. With one last look into Alexa's cold, hard eyes, he turned and walked out of the apartment.

It took the sound of the door closing behind him for the reality of the situation to sink in. His breaths started to shorten as he realised he had lost Alexa, perhaps forever. Her reversion to the angry, defensive girl he had known at Redgrove demanded he give up his selfish plan to waltz back into her life in a few years.

"So much for her being such a lovely, generous girl," snarled Lucy. "Kicks you out because you question the honesty of a drug addict."

"Just stop, all right," snapped Marcus. "It's her apartment. She can do what she wants."

"Stop defending her."

"Alexa just did exactly what you wanted. So why don't you stop criticising her for it."

Lucy did not reply, but exuded a sense of smug satisfaction as she exited the lift. Marcus ignored it, focusing solely on keeping his feet moving forward and stopping his eyes from looking backwards.

"Marcus, wait!"

Marcus swung around, his heart leaping at the sound of her voice. The sight of Bethany running towards him caused him to groan audibly.

"We're not interested in what you have to say," said Lucy in a very superior voice.

"I have nothing to say to you," replied Bethany in a voice that demonstrated her disgust at Lucy talking to her.

Lucy raised herself to full height ready to retaliate. Marcus moved between them, not interested in another fight. "Just wait in the car," he said to Lucy. She glared at him for a few seconds before storming off. Bethany looked very relieved, but she did not speak. "What do you want, Beth?" Marcus asked in a dismissive voice.

"She's just being stubborn. You hurt her, not trusting her word," said Bethany in a tender voice, her hand reaching out for his. "You don't have to believe me. I've never given you reason to, but you're wrong. Lex can spot my lies a mile off."

"It doesn't matter," Marcus sighed.

"It does. We didn't steal her wallet. Don't leave – not like this."

Marcus choked out a bitter laugh. When he looked up, he could see Alexa standing on the balcony. His heart ached at the sight. He would gladly give his life for Alexa, and in a way he was.

"It's over, Beth. I'm going," he said sadly, determined to hold on to his resolve.

"No!" Bethany cried, grasping his hands tighter.

"What do you want from me?" Marcus cried, taking a step back and wrenching his hands from Bethany's.

"I want you to stay. Lex, she wants you to stay. She needs you."

"I'm the very last thing Alexa needs," laughed Marcus mirthlessly, looking back up at Alexa as she turned and walked inside. "She needs me to leave – more than she realises. I've hurt her – held her back. If you love her, let me go – and let her move on. Perhaps it's not the best way for this to happen, but at least it's not the worst."

"It doesn't have to happen at all," cried Bethany, making Marcus's heart ache for the possibilities she believed in, but happy endings were for fairy tales, not real life. "Don't throw Lex away. Not for her. You can't trust her. She isn't faithful to you."

"Stop, okay. Just stop," Marcus snarled. "Don't accuse Lucy of things just to get your own way. You've had it in for her since the day you met. You need to understand there never can and never will be anything between me and Alexa. Accept it. Let Alexa move on and be happy. Let me move on and be happy."

"Don't you understand Lex is your life?" asked Bethany sincerely. "You can't live without her. Lex can't live without you."

Marcus closed his eyes. He refused to believe that. It was true for him. He had long ago given up the fight against his heart's desire to love Alexa. No one would come close to her, but he refused to believe it would be the same for her.

"Goodbye, Beth," Marcus said forlornly, walking away. He was not strong enough to keep arguing.

Slumping behind the wheel of his car, Marcus took one last look up at the balcony. There was a heavy shadow against the wall. His heart reached out to Alexa, but he felt nothing but her cold, hard stare in return. With a deep breath, he started the ignition. Lucy's hand rubbed his leg comfortingly. He smiled at her, reminding himself of the amazing person she was when she was not jealous. Then he saw her handbag spread open at her feet. In the middle of it was her wallet. Closing his eyes, Marcus fought the compulsion to run back to Alexa and throw himself at her feet, begging for forgiveness, but it had never been about the wallet. The trigger was irrelevant. What mattered was doing what was right. He loved Alexa too much to stay.

Alexa was tough and resilient. She was beautiful, intelligent, generous and every other amazing adjective. Marcus knew it would not take long for the world to notice her. It would take Alexa longer to notice the world's admiration, but she would move on. She would be happy. If he could give her nothing else, he would give her this. He would abandon his plan of coming back into her life when she was twenty-three and resolved nothing in the future would send him back to her. They had done this too many times already. Their relationship was starting to feel like a bad soap opera. All the justifications for staying and pretending he and Alexa could just be friends without any consequences had finally evaporated. Alexa deserved so much more than that. She deserved the world. He could not give it to her, but he would imagine her with it.